Henry Jephson

**The real French revolutionist**

Henry Jephson

**The real French revolutionist**

ISBN/EAN: 9783337229832

Printed in Europe, USA, Canada, Australia, Japan

Cover: Foto ©Andreas Hilbeck / pixelio.de

More available books at **www.hansebooks.com**

# THE REAL
# FRENCH REVOLUTIONIST

BY

HENRY JEPHSON

AUTHOR OF "THE PLATFORM—ITS RISE AND PROGRESS"

London

MACMILLAN AND CO., LIMITED

NEW YORK: THE MACMILLAN COMPANY

1899

# PREFACE

In recent years there has been published in France a very large number of books and magazine articles which have given a great deal of new information about the French Revolution.

A set of able, conscientious, hard-working searchers for historical truth have devoted the best years of their lives to the examination of hitherto unattainable or unused material: the local archives—the records of local courts of justice—the registers of prisons—the minutes of proceedings of the local administrations.

Messieurs Taine, Berriat Saint Prix, and Wallon have done great service in this respect as regards France as a whole; but in the west of France, which was the scene of the Vendean struggle, Messieurs Ch-L. Chassin, Benjamin Fillon, A. Lallié, Charles Dugast-Matifeux, Camille Bourcier, and many others have been working on the same lines, and have brought to light a mass of documents of the utmost value. Startling facts have been discovered, details of events hitherto buried in obscurity have been unearthed, and the workings of the minds and the true characters of many revolutionists revealed and laid bare to the world.

The results of the toil of these labourers in the field

of history have from time to time been published, either
in reviews and magazines such as "La Révolution Française," "La Revue de Bretagne," "La Revue de la
Révolution," or as books such as M. Berriat Saint Prix's
*La Justice Révolutionnaire* or M. Chassin's series of
works on *La Vendée*.

Also in the older and contemporary books upon the
subject, of which there is such a splendid collection in
the British Museum, there is a mass of material which
has been but very partially drawn upon by historians or
brought within the reach of the general reader.

As the facts stated in these works must profoundly
modify the views generally held on the subject of that
Revolution, it is desirable that a wider public attention
should be directed to them than they have hitherto
received.

The information being derived almost exclusively
from revolutionary records, and the opinions being
mostly those of contemporary republicans—actors and
participators in the events described, whatever accounts
of revolutionary methods and proceedings are given can
scarcely be censured on account of anti-republican bias.

Notes on each page giving the exact chapter and verse
for verification of each statement are a constant interruption to a narrative. Instead thereof is given in an
Appendix to this work a list of the principal books
which have been utilised. The more recent ones are
easily obtainable. The earlier and rarer works are to be
found in the British Museum.

# CONTENTS

CONTENTS ix

CHAPTER XVI

# CHAPTER I

IN the mid-west of France, just south of where the Loire flows into the Atlantic, lies the Department which gave its name to the great civil war in that country in the latter part of the last century—La Vendée.

There, when French society was being shattered to its foundations by the fearful upheaval of the French Revolution, a prolonged and desperate conflict took place, which for splendid heroism on one side, and brutal ferocity on the other, finds scarcely a parallel in modern history.

That conflict, remarkable in itself in many ways, is now, however, mainly memorable for its connection with the infinitely greater event—the French Revolution, and for the illuminating light it throws upon aspects of that Revolution which are of the highest importance.

And the light is welcome; for that Revolution, with its violences, and horrors, and confused din of strife of voice and sword, remains one of the most momentous and inscrutable events in the world's history.

More than a century has passed since it took place, but interest in it has not flagged nor waned. Men are

B

still examining and discussing its principles, its incidents, and its effects,—in fact everything in connection with it, —in the hope of even yet discovering therein some clues to help in the unravelment of the tangled skein of human tendencies and passions, or of gaining inspiration for the solution of some of the great problems which so ceaselessly confront human society.

Is it, men still ask, in that direction that lies the amelioration, the regeneration of the social fabric ?

Or, is that Revolution, like the flashings of the lighthouse across the stormy waters of the deep, a warning to humanity from steering to shipwreck and destruction ?

In the true answer to those questions lies, so far as is permitted to us in this stage of the world's progress to discern, much of the future peace, happiness, and prosperity of civilised mankind.

It has been hitherto by far too generally the practice to judge the French Revolution by the events which occurred in Paris. Certainly there was a great temptation to do so; for their startling nature, their lurid horror, the thrilling incidents of the overthrow of the monarchy, the fierce struggle of Girondists and Jacobins, the courageous efforts to repel the onslaught of foreign foes, all these fascinate by their interest.

Important as those events were, however, they formed but a part of the Revolution of which France, and not only Paris, was the scene. And being but a part, they give a very dubious, indeed a misleading, light on the great issue of that terrible convulsion.

Paris was under the eyes of Europe: the incidents there in the great drama were reported daily in the Parisian press, and were discussed by many of the ablest writers and speakers of the time: actions had to some extent to be modified, because they had to be justified or accounted for ; certain semblances had to be kept up ; and reasons sometimes vouchsafed for particular lines of policy.

The Revolutionary Government in Paris was therefore somewhat hampered and restrained by opposition and by publicity : revolutionary principles did not have really free play : and the character of the revolutionist was not seen in its completeness.

But in France, as apart from Paris, the circumstances were different. The country and the country-towns were out of European ken ; and restraining or impeding influences there, of any and every sort, were non-existent. In them the revolutionist had a completely clear field for putting into action all his theories and principles, and free hands to do exactly as his feelings or ideas prompted him.

In them, therefore, his true character is unfolded to our eyes, and the actual workings of the Republican Government are presented undisturbed by any distorting medium.

And even still better and more clearly are these most instructive results displayed in the actions of the revolutionists in the Vendée : for there the Revolution was seen, not in its dealings with a tyrannical monarch or a worthless aristocracy, but in its dealings with the people —with the humblest, poorest, most hard-working classes of society—exactly those whom, theoretically, the Revolution was supposed to emancipate and benefit.

And the prolonged resistance made by the Vendeans to the Revolutionary Government brought into operation a whole phase of revolutionary activities and characteristics which showed themselves to only a limited extent in Paris.

Hence, the actions of the revolutionists in and around

the Vendée, and of the Revolutionary Government in combating the Vendeans, are of entirely exceptional value.

They throw, as it were, Röntgen rays on the nature and methods and character of the French revolutionist and republican, piercing through outward semblances and asseverations, and revealing to us the actualities, the innermost verities. The principles, policy, ideas, and the very nature of the revolutionist are shown to us, no longer as mere abstract theories, about which there might be any amount of debate, but in unimpeded operation, and being tested by actual experiment. The system and machinery of republican government is displayed actually at work in the country.

And the result is the most complete and realistic picture of the French revolutionist in his genuine character, and the most impressive illustration of French revolutionary principles in untrammelled operation.

Which things, as they help mankind in its onward march, are the only compensations, the only consolations, for a shuddering humanity, as it peers into the seething hell of human passions and brutalities presented to its affrighted gaze.

The scene of the sad, yet most instructive, drama was not an extensive one. Known generally as the Vendée, it was made up of parts of the old provinces of Poitou, Anjou, and Brittany. The majestic Loire swept along its northern portion, whilst its western side was caressed by the ebb and flow of the Atlantic tides, or fiercely battered by the tremendous waves of the great ocean as they rolled in on its shores.

South and east it had no precise boundaries; but a line drawn parallel to the Loire from Saumur to its estuary, and some sixty miles south, would approximately enclose the whole area.

More than once, however, the strife between Vendean and revolutionist flowed across the river on to the north side of the Loire; indeed Nantes, which might be regarded as practically the capital of the Vendée, and Angers also were throughout involved in and often the centres of revolutionary and Vendean operations.

This comparatively small extent of country was very varied in character. There was the Plain, an uninteresting, somewhat monotonous tract of rich agricultural land: the Marais, or marsh districts near the estuary of the Loire,—a half-reclaimed, half-submerged fen country, intersected in every direction by great ditches and canals. And there was the Bocage, a beautiful bewildering labyrinth of hills and valleys and woods.

The physical conformation of this Bocage had a great influence on the fortunes of the war waged on its soil. Successive ranges of low hills spread out in all directions over its surface; with successive series of valleys or ravines lying between them, each with its meandering stream or river flowing towards the Loire.

Clothing many of the hillsides were forests and woods and trees, with that deep richness of vegetation which is produced by the rain-laden breezes of the Atlantic. Down to the very last detail it was a Bocage, a leafy bower. Where the trees were not massed together, they grew in rows in the fences; and where the land was not under cultivation, or covered with trees, it was decked with great stretches of gorse and broom.

The greater part of this Bocage was impenetrable to all but those who lived in it, and who were familiar with its paths; and the Government had done but little

to make it accessible or to bring it into communication
with the outer world.

Few main roads intercepted it, and those were rough
in summer and often impassable in winter, fenced in
usually by high hedges or by the natural undergrowth
of the woods. The cross-roads could scarcely be called
roads: most of them being little better than the bed of
a stream many feet below the level of the land at their
sides, and beneath overarching trees through which the
light of the sun scarcely penetrated.

From off these roads branched narrow and tortuous
footpaths, known only to the inhabitants themselves,
and a source of confusion and perplexity to the traveller. It was in fact, as described by General Kleber, "a
dark and deep labyrinth, in which one can only march
by feeling or groping one's way."

Of towns actually in the Vendée there were none of
any size. On the very edge of it, separated from it only
by the Loire, was the great port and city of Nantes,
with some 80,000 inhabitants. And farther east, some
sixty miles or so, also on the north side of the river,
and some two or three miles away from it, was Angers,
another ancient town with a considerable population—
some 30,000, it was said. The towns on the south
side of the Loire were all small. Saumur, perched on a
height overlooking the river; and westward of Saumur,
Thouars, with its then almost impregnable castle on a
hill. Farther west again—and somewhat south—were
Bressuire and Fontenay; and, westernmost of all, the
small seaport of Sables-d'Olonne.

And there was a number of much smaller towns
called "bourgs," little more than big villages, such as
Cholet, Clisson, and Châtillon: most of them, and of
the not very numerous villages, being almost concealed

in the depths of the woods and in the rich masses of foliage.

Only a small portion of the Vendean people lived in the towns, or even in the villages; for there were no factories of importance or other industries to give them employment there. The greater number lived in detached farmhouses scattered over the country, ensconced in all sorts of out-of-the-way places. And there they carried on their farming operations, continuing in monotonous routine the old habits and practices and systems handed down to them by many generations; growing grain where grain would grow, the vine where it would thrive, and raising cattle and sheep; almost entirely self-supplying, self-supporting, and bartering their surplus produce in the towns and villages for such articles of clothing and other household goods as they could not themselves produce.

Taken as a whole, it was a most productive country. The extensive vineyards produced large quantities of wine and brandy; whilst its plains and fields produced immense quantities of grain of every kind. Over a million of cattle, it was estimated, and some two million of sheep were supported on the land, together with a large number of horses and mules, and the population was variously estimated at from 600,000 to 800,000 persons.

Of the Vendeans themselves—the people whose sad mission in history appears to have been to expose to mankind the true character of the revolutionist—there is a unanimity of description by those who knew them.

Hospitable, kind, simple in their tastes and manners, thrifty, sober, hard-working, robust in constitution, inured to fatigue; some fairly well off, but strangers to all sorts of luxury; others in hard circumstances, and but poorly fed.

Living in the midst of the hilly and wooded solitudes, far from the centres of life, without communication with towns, rarely having even the society of a village, they had little means of acquiring instruction—little to drag them out of the rut of monotony—or to incite them to progress. Indeed the lapse of a couple of centuries had scarcely altered their condition. Their ignorance was great. The State had done nothing for them : had left them for their education to their priests, who had brought them up in absolute submission to the Church, in absolute faith in the Roman Catholic religion, and who had won their deep devotion and unlimited confidence.

Living so much in contact with nature, and so solitarily, they were more or less superstitious, and extremely credulous ; but they were none the less passionately sincere in their religion.

By the republicans and revolutionists in subsequent years they were scorned and condemned as fanatics : but coming from that quarter the term carries no discredit with it.

And there was one other prominent trait in the Vendean's character, linked in a way with his intense religious belief—a magnificent, unquenchable courage,—a courage of which he was to give proof on hundreds of battlefields : and under the even greater trial—that of death by the most horrible and cruel forms which republican ingenuity could devise,—death in prison by the lingering torture of disease : or death on the scaffold, or by noyade, fusillade, or sabrade : death with the deep sense of bitter wrong and infamous injustice, which adds the last drops to the cup of human agony.

# CHAPTER II

## PART I

IT was this interesting and unfortunate country which was destined to become the prey of the French revolutionists, and these were the unfortunate people who first were driven and goaded into revolt, and then subjected to a tyranny infinitely greater and more cruel than anything from which the Revolution was delivering them.

It was a strange destiny; for the Vendeans were not antagonistic to the Revolution. They constituted a part of the French people who were making it, and in its earlier stages they took an active and sympathetic part. They had their deep wrongs and grievances, as the rest of France had; they suffered under the exorbitant privileges of the noblesse and upper ranks of the clergy, and under the countless tyrannies of the crown and the aristocracy; and they were weighed down by the merciless exactions and extortions of the tax-collector.

They belonged to the " third estate "— the people of France—which paid all the taxes, which bore all the expenses of the State, which by its labour fed and nourished the nation.

And now this third estate, unable longer to carry on life under the existing conditions, desired to end the tyrannies and injustices and inequalities it had long groaned under; to efface the badges of its servitude: and to make the other "estates" take their proper share of the national burdens.

In all these desires the Vendeans participated thoroughly, and the spirit of reform which possessed the people of France possessed them too. When the elections of deputies to the States-General took place in the early spring of 1789, and when the local assemblies were drawing up their *cahiers*, or petitions of grievances, the Vendeans joined in with no uncertain voice. They asked for the sovereignty of the law: for respect of property and personal liberty: for the suppression of the pecuniary privileges of the nobles and of the clergy: for the equalisation of taxation: for the abolition of the salt-tax: for the better administration of justice: for a popular system of local government: for the reform of the episcopacy, and payment of the clergy; and for grants of money for the construction of roads and the improvement of the means of communication. In fact, they asked for everything which the rest of their countrymen were asking for, and sent their representatives to the meeting of the States-General to help in the general efforts to obtain it.

The States-General assembled at Versailles on the 5th May 1789. But while it was talking instead of acting, a section of the people of Paris struck the first great blow against the existing order of things. On the 14th July they stormed the Bastille and captured it. The effects of this startling event were far-reaching.

Within almost a few days the greater part of the country, taking authority into its own hands, shook itself free of all the existing local powers and governments, and substituted therefor popular local committees, backed by the armed strength of the people.

Under so sharp a stimulus, the States-General (transformed into the Constituent or National Assembly) hurried on to actual work; and on the night of the 4th August, at one sitting, in an access of enthusiasm on the part of some of its members, and of desperation on the part of others, it effected such a wide-embracing mass of reforms that, so far as legislation went, the country passed through a revolution in that one night.

The Assembly abolished the privileges of rank, and exemptions from taxation; it wiped out tithes, seignorial dues, game laws, the salt-tax, and other burdens whose removal had been asked for. It swept away serfdom, and decreed the admission of all citizens, without distinction of birth, to public employment.

In this same month of August too, on the 26th, the Assembly, after much discussion, attained to a Declaration of the Rights of Man; it being deemed desirable to have in black and white a statement of the new order of things, and a record of the new position of man.

This celebrated measure, "made in the presence and under the auspices of the Supreme Being," declared as natural and imprescriptible rights of man—the right of liberty; security of property: the safety of his person; the right to resist oppression.

It flourished liberty of thought on high: according to each citizen freedom to speak, write, print, and publish his thoughts. It acclaimed freedom of religion and religious worship. It declared that every one should be presumed innocent until he was declared guilty. It

laid down a code of principles, many of which were
admirable in themselves, but every one of which was to
be most flagrantly set at naught by the revolutionists
in the course of the next few years.

And then the Assembly, impelled forwards by its
extremer sections, and by the incitements and terrorism
of the mob which packed its galleries, proceeded rapidly
in the career of reform. It established equality—at
least by law. Privileges of rank had been abolished;
now rank itself must go; and the noblesse, the peerage,
titles, hereditary distinctions, and orders, and all distinctions of birth, were abolished.

Still, however, events did not move rapidly enough
to please the wilder spirits of revolution; and early in
October the Paris mob once more took the bit in its
teeth, marched out to Versailles, captured the King and
Queen, and brought them back to Paris, practically as
prisoners. Thither also promptly followed the National
Assembly.

Seeing these events, and numerous other signs and
tokens of imminent ruin and peril to themselves, a great
body of the nobility fled from France; all to avoid a
pressing danger, some in the hope of obtaining foreign help
to enable them to re-establish the old order of things.

A large number of the Vendean noblesse followed the
example, whilst the few who remained sought retirement
in their country places. Fortunately for them, their
relations with the peasantry were friendly, and they
were not massacred or driven out of the country as the
noblesse in other parts of France were.

The National Assembly, now working at high speed
under constant pressure from within and without,
followed up its popular measures by a series of laws
which abolished the old and historic provinces and

provincial governments of France, and welded the country into one great whole—France.

And then it began constructing a new system of government.

For the purposes of local government, a wholly new division of the country was made—eighty-three Departments were formed, each with a government upon the basis of popular election.

All the ancient municipalities were abolished; and the new municipal authorities were also to be popularly elected.

And in addition to these great changes, the whole of the existing machinery for the administration of justice was abolished; royal jurisdictions, feudal jurisdictions, ecclesiastical jurisdictions—all were swept away, and a wholly new system substituted: each Department being given its own criminal and civil tribunal, and each district and commune its own court of justice.

The Assembly had further been giving its attention to the relationship of the Church to the State: and money being badly wanted by the new Government, and the Church having plenty, it decreed that all ecclesiastical property was to be at the disposition of the State, the State undertaking that adequate provision would be made for the clergy.[1]

In all these measures there was practically nothing which had not been petitioned for in the *cahiers*, and throughout the Vendée the reforms were received with approbation. When the elections for the new local government bodies took place in the earlier half of 1790, the Vendeans took a keen part in the proceedings, and when the ecclesiastical property was put up at public auction, they bought largely and freely.

[1] 2nd November 1789.

But the National Assembly, in entering upon a campaign against the Church, had taken the first step on a path of legislation which was to alienate the great mass of the Vendean people from the Revolutionary Government, and ultimately to drive them to appeal to arms in defence of that which they prized so highly, their religious faith.

The step which led to the great disaster of civil war was the decree of the Assembly made on the 12th July 1790, which enacted the civil constitution of the clergy.

This measure fundamentally altered the whole position and status of the Roman Catholic Church in France, and at one stroke transferred the authority in almost everything relating to the Church, except doctrine, from the Roman Catholic Hierarchy to the State.

By it almost all the ancient ecclesiastical institutions were swept away, and a plan of ecclesiastical government was formed on the same lines as that which had just been adopted for departmental government.

Ecclesiastical divisions were made to coincide with the new civil divisions of Departments; and each of the new eighty-three Departments was to have a bishop and a number of priests according to its size. The appointment of bishops and priests by the King was to cease, and in future all bishops and priests were to be elected to their offices.

But the most galling part of the enactment was that which imposed on both bishops and priests the necessity of taking an oath of allegiance to the new State. On a Sunday, in presence of the local authorities, and of the people, they were to take an oath " to be faithful to the nation, to the law, and to the King, and to maintain with all their strength the Constitution decreed by the

National Assembly and accepted by the King,"—a Constitution which was as yet in the air.

The clergy were in effect to be cut loose from their connection with Rome and the Pontiff, the spiritual and temporal head of the Church; their appointment was to be made by the people of each parish; and they were to become the servants of, and to be paid by, the State.

This new civil constitution of the clergy struck root and branch at the whole system of the Roman Catholic Church, both in temporal and spiritual spheres.

And it arrayed the great mass of the Catholic clergy — some 64,000 in number — in opposition to the Government.

" By the constitution of Jesus Christ," said the priests, " the supreme power of the Church rests with the bishops and the Pontiff; and it was to them that the government of the Church of God had been given. By your decrees, it is you who govern the Church and its ministers.

" What! Is it not enough to have made the sacrifice of all our property, of all our privileges, and of all the gold of the temple, but that one must abandon even the religion of which we are the ministers? . . .

" We warn you, that, since it is not a question of our fortunes, but of faith, and of the eternal salvation of the people, the time of complaisance is past. Our conscience forces us to tell you it is better to obey God than man.

" It is impossible, without apostasy, to accept this proposed constitution.

" Even the pretension to give to the Church this new constitution is an outrage, and a veritable blasphemy against the Author of our religion."

In terms such as these was the Government inveighed against, and a very small proportion of the clergy took the prescribed oath. The Government, however, was not to be trifled with, and after a few months' delay measures were adopted to enforce obedience to the new law.

On the 27th November 1790 the Assembly made a decree that all bishops and priests were to take the oath within eight days. A delay, however, occurred in its enforcement, owing to the King for some time withholding his sanction to it; but his sanction being at last obtained, the Assembly determined on itself beginning the enforcement of the law, and it fixed the 4th January 1791 as the day on which the oath was to be taken by the clergy who were members of the Assembly, some 300 in number.

The day came: two bishops and thirty or forty priests took the oath; but the great majority of them would not.

One by one they refused.

"I was born a Roman and Apostolic Catholic," said one; "I wish to die in that faith. I should not do so were I to take the oath you ask me to."

"Sirs," said another, the Bishop of Poitiers,—"Sirs, I am seventy years of age; for thirty-three of which I have been a bishop. I will not stain my white hairs by the oath of your decrees."

Furious with these replies, and this firm opposition, the Assembly shortened the scene. The President ordered all who had not yet taken the oath to come and take it collectively. No one came.

It was a question now of conscience, and there would be no flinching, even though the Assembly was at white heat, and outside a huge and excited mob, the sound of

whose voices reached the Chamber; and whose cries
were the now familiar "*À la lanterre!*" "*À la lanterne*
with the bishops and priests who will not take the
oath!"

Foiled for the moment in its object, the Assembly
ordered proceedings to be taken for the enforcement of
the penalties prescribed by the law; and decreed that
the King should order the election of other priests in
the place of those who refused to take the oath.

Here, in this anti-church legislation, lay the origin of
the Vendean war.

Republican writers, in their efforts to belaud the
Revolution, and to clear the revolutionary cause of the
infamy attached to it by the iniquities perpetrated
during the Vendean war, have done their utmost to lay
the blame on the royalists, on the Roman Catholic
clergy, on the fanaticism and ignorance of the peasantry,
on everybody except those upon whom it rightly
falls.

But their efforts are labour in vain, for the case is
so absolutely clear, the cause so very patent. The
whole and entire blame of the Vendean war rests unmistakably upon those who began and carried to the
bitter end a system of the most grievous religious
proscription and persecution.

There is no doubt that all sorts of vague and hopeless
schemes passed through the minds of the small number
of royalist noblesse left in the Vendée; and it is
perfectly true that efforts were made by some few of
the royalists in, and many out of, France, to organise in
the west of France a counter-revolutionary movement
which should lead to the restoration of the old régime;
but, from the very condition of things at the time, they
were feebly contrived, and had no practical effect.

Savary, who could speak with authority on the subject, wrote : " At this epoch all who pertained to the noblesse were closely watched by the local administrative bodies.   It would have been difficult to see each other, to consult together, to concert plans or put them in execution.   Living in isolation, all their thoughts were their own personal safety.   Thus, as was later avowed by d'Elbée, the noblesse did not organise the civil war. They were constrained to take part in it by circum-stances and by the wishes of the peasantry."

And the Catholic clergy used all their power to oppose a persecution which fell upon them with iron hand.   But not even they could have evoked a general movement if the Vendean people had not *en masse* been actually suffering and writhing under an unendurable state of affairs : and the efforts of the noblesse and the clergy were no more the original cause of the Vendean insurrection than Niagara is the cause of the Gulf Stream.   The first and main cause was the anti-church legislation, which, whilst striking at the Roman Catholic Church, fell with its full force on the Vendean people in the exercise of their religious creed.

With an intensely religious people religion goes infinitely deeper than loyalty to a particular Government, and in the belief of these Vendean people not merely their temporal but their eternal welfare was felt to be at stake in their religion, and though many of them may have been attached to their King, they cared for their religion infinitely more.   It has been said, indeed, and probably with truth, that they would have rebelled against him had he been responsible for the laws and the enforce-ment of those laws which finally broke down their patience and goaded them into insurrection.

The majority of republican writers on this period

have underrated the immense influence of religion upon the individual or upon a religious people. They have not realised that intense religious fervour before which every other consideration vanishes from view. Certainly they have underrated it in the case of the Vendean people. No royalist plots, no clerical intrigues, no "gold of Pitt," that nightmare of the French revolutionist, were required to account for resistance to a treatment which a religious people would naturally combat à l'outrance.

Indeed, neither the royalists, nor even the clergy, would have succeeded in so alienating the Vendean people from the Revolutionary Government as to have driven them en masse to appeal to arms.

It was the Revolutionary Government itself which first alienated them by enacting legislation which, though directed against the Church as an institution, yet was not in its effects limited to that Church or its priesthood, but fell with terrible effect upon the Vendean people. And it was the Revolutionary Government itself which drove them to arms by persevering in and savagely enforcing a policy so repugnant to them.

The stupidity of the legislation was that it was not possible to strike down the Roman Catholic Church in the manner attempted without at the same time hitting even harder the believers in the Roman Catholic faith. But the Assembly did not at first recognise this fact. As time went on it evinced its indifference to it, becoming more and more vindictive as it found itself met by a dogged and pertinacious opposition.

Thus, in their measures to compel obedience, the Assembly, setting at naught its solemn declarations of religious liberty, embarked on a career of violent and extreme religious persecution, and recklessly passed on from one measure of intolerance and violence to another.

Where the priest of a parish would not take the oath, he was deprived of his office, and another priest— one who was willing to take the oath—was foisted on the parish, after going through the form of election, to the indignation of the people. who designated him as an "intruder."—an *intrus*,—and who would have nothing to say to him.

The views and feelings of the Vendeans are easily to be understood by any one who has any knowledge of the Roman Catholic faith.

The Pope, by Bull of 13th April 1791, had denounced the civil constitution of the clergy as founded on heretical principles. A priest, therefore, who had taken the oath was regarded by them as a schismatic and a heretic. His offices, therefore, they felt, were of no avail, for he ceased to hold the divine authority of the Church, and his services therefore ceased to have any religious sanction or efficacy. The people accordingly would not attend his celebrations of the Mass. or listen to his instruction. or receive from him any sacrament. They would not confess to him, nor did they believe in the efficacy of his absolution.

These consequences in themselves were sufficient to have awakened the most bitter resentment. But they were by no means all : for the effects of the change of the law were not confined to the ministerial or religious offices of the priesthood. The *intrus*, or priest who, having taken the prescribed oath, was "intruded" into the parish as a successor to their own priest, became, by virtue of his office, the officer of State in the parish for matters concerning the civil state of the population. The position of the sworn priest carried with it the exclusive right of legally marrying people : with it also the legal registration of births and deaths. and the burial of the dead. And so the people could not be legally married except by a heretic; the birth of their children could not be legally registered except by a heretic; the last offices to their dead could not be performed except by a heretic.

The broad truth is, that the Vendean peasantry, a devoutly religious people, were, so far as the Revolutionary Government could make them so, practically excommunicated.

Their churches, they believed, were defiled by heretical priests officiating in them; and the rites of religion, rites in the exercise of which they believed their eternal welfare depended, were denied them. For their children to be born without baptism imperilled the salvation of their children; to die without confession and absolution meant, to them, eternal damnation. The sacrament of marriage, indeed its legitimacy, and therefore the legitimacy of the children, was denied them. In vain the Vendean peasant sought the Holy Sacrament to comfort and nourish his soul. The Revolutionary Government, with "religious liberty" as its motto, denied it to him. In vain the dying longed for the last consolations of religion, for confession, absolution, extreme unction, for the last rites of his faith which should secure him an entrance into the new world of happiness — the Revolutionary Government denied them to him.

The Revolutionary Government, with the assertion on its lips that it was "in the principles of the new constitution to respect liberty of conscience," denied the liberty it paraded, and excommunicated him from the Catholic Church almost as effectually as the Pope could do.

Nor were these mere grievances of the moment.

Day and night, and every hour of each, they pressed upon him. They were an ever-present, ever-constant, galling grief.

What more natural, then, that the Vendean people, thus injured in all the most sacred and cherished affairs of life, and the most deep-seated feelings of their nature, and thus practically excommunicated, should have become vehemently hostile to the Government which inflicted this cruel persecution upon them.

No other cause for the Vendean rebellion need be sought. It was all-sufficient in itself.

And the iron ate deep into their souls. The records of the time teem with poignant expressions of despair and unhappiness.

" Misery tortures us on every side. We have no consolation but in religion, and they wish to take that consolation from us. We are in absolute despair." But at the same time another spirit finds expression also. " We are determined to avenge ourselves. We must destroy those who are destroying religion. We must defend our religion with our lives. I write this with pen and ink ; but my blood will prove my words when the time is appropriate."

Patience and forbearance were not traits of the Revolutionary Government, and with but little delay, and regardless of warnings, the Government persevered in its punitive legislation against the priests who would not take the prescribed oath.

Measure after measure, each of increasing severity, was taken against them : the consequences of which were felt not alone by them, but also by the Vendeans, until at last, as time went on, the people were deprived of all the religious services rendered them by their priests, except such as they could obtain secretly and surreptitiously from those of their clergy who had fled from the tyranny of the Government, and who were in hiding in the woods or other remote places.

With the growing severity of legislation, actual opposition to the local authorities arose in many parishes, and there was rioting. In some cases even the National Guards had to be supported by the military.

And, as the feelings of the people became more deeply moved by this persecution, evidence of ever-growing religious excitement was revealed. Strange rumours were bruited abroad and whispered from one to the other—reports of apparitions of the Virgin, and miracles being performed by her.

An oak near St. Laurent, reputed to be sacred, was visited by thousands. At Bellefontaine, in a small chapel, an image of the Virgin, which had a great reputation as a worker of miracles, was worshipped by crowds. Nocturnal religious processions took place; nocturnal religious meetings were held. Late one night, from the crest of the highest hill in Anjou, where there was a celebrated sanctuary of a Madonna, a "patriot" patrol saw numerous lines of flickering lights; then, by the illuminated outlines made by blazing torches and lanterns and candles carried by processionists, they could trace the paths of processions coming from all sides; and then they could hear the subdued murmurs of voices, and borne upon the midnight air the solemn melodies of sacred ritual, the Salve Regina, and the litanies of the Virgin.

In places, too, the rising emotions and passions of the people showed themselves in hostility to the priests who had taken the oath—the *intrus*. At one village so serious were the disturbances that in the restoration of order five peasants were shot by the National Guards.

But the feelings and passions of the people were too deeply involved to be checked even by such severity. The removal of their favourite priests was more than they could quietly submit to. "Our priests are given us by God," said one ; "let them stay with us till their death. After that we will see. If you don't, there will be bloodshed. We will defend them till death."

But these incidents, instead of having any effect in warning the National Assembly of the danger of the path it was treading, and of inducing some moderation or modification of policy, only made it harden its heart.

Indeed, a revolutionary Assembly was not likely to be diverted from a revolutionary policy by any considerations of prudence, and the flight of the King from Paris in June did not improve the revolutionary temper generally, or incline the Assembly to a more lenient course.

Nor did the state of the Vendée improve. Rumours of royalist meetings and clerical plots, and equally reliable ones of mysterious ships hovering about the coast, added to the ferment.

But at last the National Assembly, somewhat puzzled and perplexed with the state of the Vendée, and feeling in need of enlightenment, sent down commissioners to make a thorough investigation and to report the result of their inquiries.

And then, for one moment, the dark masses of storm-cloud which had been covering the political sky broke : and a gleam of light—like a gleam of hope——came through.

The King accepted the new Constitution which had at length been produced by the Constituent Assembly, and swore fealty to it ; and on the 15th September 1791 the Assembly, in a transport of delight, declared that the object of the French Revolution was accomplished, and that here the Revolution was ended.

And as a sign and token of the new order of things, it proclaimed a general amnesty.

But, after a brief moment, the delusive gleam of light died out; the clouds closed in again darker and denser than ever. Some fearful destiny seemed to be impelling the country towards a catastrophe; and the stupendous folly of the Revolutionary Government drove the Vendeans to fearful and unescapable disaster.

# CHAPTER III

## PART II

In October (1791) the commissioners Gensonné and Gallois who had been sent into the Vendée reported to the new National Legislative Assembly—which had succeeded the National Constituent Assembly—the results of their investigations and inquiries.

The salient, decisive fact established by them in "their faithful picture of the political and religious situation of the Vendée at this time" was, that "the imposition on the clergy of the oath was the beginning of the troubles."

"Until then the people had enjoyed the most perfect tranquillity . . . they were disposed by their natural character to a love of peace, to the sentiment of order, and a respect of the law; they reaped the benefits of the Revolution without experiencing its storms . . . and they asked no favour beyond having priests in whom they would have confidence and trust."

And the commissioners also clearly showed that any excitement or disturbances there, any hostility to the Government, any clerical machinations, all had their

foundation in that cause, their starting-point from the
enforcement of that ill-omened decree.

The Assembly listened to the report of the commissioners, and the President, speaking in an oracular
way, declared that the Assembly would leave no stone
unturned to heal the evils described.    To re-establish
the public spirit was the first of its desires, as it was
the first of its duties.

But the Assembly set about this first of its desires,
this first of its duties, in a way directly the opposite of
that which would lead to quiet.

With the ink scarcely dry on the new Constitution
of France, and on as solemn a declaration of religious
liberty as any constituted body could possibly make, the
Assembly counted it no wrong to violate what had just
been laid down as the fundamental law of the country,
as the very basis of the Constitution, and to act in diametrically the opposite manner.

The truth was, the revolutionists had no intention
—Constitution or no Constitution—of being balked in
their attack on the Church and on religion.    And so
the Assembly not alone persevered in the course of
religious persecution commenced by its predecessor, the
Constituent Assembly, but became more violent in it.

On the 29th November 1791 it decreed that those
of the priests who had not taken the oath by the 7th
January next should be put under surveillance as suspects of revolt against the law ; and further, that if any
religious disturbances took place in the commune where
any refractory priests resided, they were to be held responsible, and were to be removed to and confined in
the chief town of the Department.

The King vetoed this decree ; but matters had gone
so far that his veto was contemptuously disregarded, and

the enthusiastic local patriots in the towns in or bordering on the Vendée enforced the decree as if it had been sanctioned by the King and had become law.

There was no one to call them to account for such violations of law, or for actions neither prescribed nor authorised by the Constitution.

And they were energetic in their persecution.

Thus, the Directory of the Department of Maine and Loire, intent on effectually preventing religious services being held, had a short time previously sent commissioners throughout the Department who despoiled several of the churches, carried away the sacred vessels and ornaments, overturned the altars, and pulled down the bells—proceedings which naturally caused the most intense indignation.

By some even these usurped powers were not held to be enough, for the mayor and people of Sables besought the National Assembly for still severer measures against the non-oath-taking priests.

"The Patrie," they said, "can no longer retain in her bosom these sanguinary monsters. . . She can no longer nourish children rebels to the law, and sworn against her. These perverse ministers must subscribe to the social pact, or be expelled. We call for the deportation and exile of these madmen. We demand that they be transported to the pestiferous marshes of Italy, there to be purged of the venom with which they poison us,—that they be sent thither to join the chief of their infernal cohort, Pope Pius VI."

All this, too, in spite of the Articles of the new Constitution, in spite of Article 10 of the great Declaration of the Rights of Man, the Charter of the Revolution, that " no one was to be interfered with (*inquiété*)" on account of his religious opinions—a declaration like so

many other laws and declarations of the French revolutionists and republicans, loud-sounding clap-trap, the
absolute antithesis to the actual intentions and actions
of its adherents.

The Vendeans, though excited and bitterly aggrieved
by the persecution of their priests, and though provoked
almost beyond endurance by the effects of that persecution, comported themselves during the early part of
1792 with great patience and self-possession. There
were mutterings and grumblings of deep, indeed threatening discontent, but there was little overt action. No
small part of the calm was due to the admirable tact
and effective military arrangements of General Dumouriez, who for some little time had been holding an
important military appointment in the Vendée, and
whose general line of conduct may be gathered from a
speech he made in the summer of 1791 at Sables.
" Let us remember," he said, " that the rebels, if we
come across any, are Frenchmen, dazed by fanaticism
and prejudice.  Let us be severe, as is the law which
orders us to act, but let us not be cruel or unjust; let
us not stain ourselves with the blood of unarmed individuals: let us not dishonour ourselves by pillaging;
let us not deliver to the flames houses which may one
day become the cradle of enlightened citizens.  We are
Frenchmen—that is to say, humane, generous.  Liberty
should add new virtues to those which Europe acknowledged we already possessed before our glorious Revolution."

The very things he said they ought not to do, were
the very things the true revolutionist wished to do,
and was about to do: and principles such as these laid
down by him were a long way below that revolutionary
height which was the hall-mark of the true sans-culotte.

Early in 1792 Dumouriez left the Vendée, and his skilful hand removed, the situation there became more strained.

The Assembly went on raining down blow upon blow upon the priesthood. On the 27th May it decreed that, at the request of twenty citizens of a canton, any non-juring priests might be sent to the chief town to be imprisoned, and in case of any further intriguing they might be sent over the frontier.

The decree was vetoed by the King, but as before, the local authorities, in their impatience to persecute, disregarded the veto, and acted on the decree.

And so, without any form of justice, and often for purely supposititious offences, the priests were arrested in hundreds, and hurried off to the chief town of the Department, there to be imprisoned, or thence sent over the frontier. For them there was not a glimmer of justice or consideration anywhere.

Apart from the anti-religious measures of the Revolutionary Government, other events necessitated measures which in their effects still further increased the irritation of the Vendeans.

Foreign affairs had assumed a very threatening aspect for France, and on the 12th July 1792 the National Assembly declared the country in danger, and called for 85,000 volunteers to defend the frontiers. Every man, too, was ordered to wear the tricoloured cockade as a mark of his loyalty to the new order of things, and the white cockade was declared to be a sign of rebellion punishable by death.

Very soon after, Prussia declared war against France, and the Duke of Brunswick issued his notorious manifesto, which evoked tremendous feeling against the King and the *émigré noblesse*, and rallied to the side of the Government many who disapproved of its actions.

The consequences were disastrous to the King.

On the 10th of August the Parisian mob, this time under orders from higher authorities, attacked and captured the Tuileries. The King took refuge with the Assembly, which there and then made a decree that he should be suspended from his functions, and that the French people should be invited to elect a National Convention to draw up a new constitution.

It was practically the end of the monarchy.

While Paris and France were thus in a state of the wildest excitement, the state of the Vendée grew more critical. The feeling among the Vendeans had become so exacerbated that the enrolment of volunteers for the army led to partial revolts. From the beginning of the year they had shown their disinclination to military service. Already in March there had been some slight disturbances on this account, and as time went on this aversion became stronger.

And now in August a gathering of the peasants took place in the neighbourhood of Châtillon, which they captured, and then they proceeded to make an attack on Bressuire, where after three days' fighting they were repulsed. Some thirty-five to fifty "patriots" were killed or wounded, while some three hundred to five hundred of the peasants were killed.

Here, in the first real engagement between the Vendeans and the republicans, the latter began their atrocities. Some hundreds of prisoners were massacred in cold blood; and it is a well-attested fact that after the fighting was over, some of the National Guards— like the Red Indians of America who carried the scalps of their enemies at their girdle—were seen carrying as

trophies on the points of their bayonets, noses, ears.
and strips of flesh of the Vendean peasants they had
defeated.

The defeat was a severe one, and checked for a time
any tendency to appeal to arms.

Even in the midst of the terrible days of August the
National Assembly found time, before its own dissolution.
to continue its system of religious persecution.   The law
as to taking the oath was extended to women who had
entered the cloisters.   And the decree was made that so
small a number as six citizens (instead of twenty as
heretofore) might demand the expulsion of an unsworn
priest from any district within eight days, and from
France itself within fifteen days.   If by that time the
priests had not cleared out, they were to be seized and
deported to French Guiana.   Priests of over sixty years
of age, or infirm, were excepted from this law. though.
indeed, as events turned out, the terrible sufferings
entailed by deportation would have been less poignant
than those which they had to undergo by remaining in
France.

Paris once more taking the lead, in the early days
of September, showed the real revolutionary way of
treating priests.   A large number of them were confined
in the Convent of the Carmelites.   The building was
attacked by a horde of Parisian sans-culottes. and they
were all butchered.   Dreadful massacres took place also
of prisoners in the Paris prisons.   And immediately
after these horrible events there was sent to the local
authorities throughout the country an address from the
Commune of Paris, containing a direct incitement to
similar brutalities.

"The Commune of Paris hastens to inform its
brothers in the Departments that a party of ferocious

conspirators detained in the prisons have been put to death by the people; an act of justice to deter, by terror, those traitors concealed within its walls at the moment that the people were marching to meet the enemy. And, without doubt, the entire nation, after the long series of treasons which have brought it to the edge of the abyss, will hasten to adopt this necessary means for the public safety, and all Frenchmen will cry, as did the Parisians, 'Let us march against the enemy, but let us not leave behind us these brigands to murder our children and our wives.' "

The legislative measures against the priests were rigorously enforced.

The priests who owing to age or infirmity remained in the Vendée were either interned in the chief towns of the Departments or put in prison. In Angers there were over 300 of them in custody, and the Chateau at Nantes was crammed with them. Others were leading a hunted life, concealing themselves in the Vendée as best they could, in secret hiding-places, or in the woods, where they were fed and cared for by the Vendeans.

In spite of this persecution, however, whenever the opportunity presented itself, open-air services were held. Neither distance, fatigue, nor danger deterred the peasants from attending, and they came armed with guns and scythes and pitchforks to defend their priests should any attempt be made to carry them off. But it was becoming ever more difficult for them to obtain the services of a priest, and the religious persecution was pressing more and more heavily upon them.

In only one matter did the National Assembly modify the previous laws, and that was as regarded the grievance connected with the registration of births and deaths, and the ceremony of marriage. On almost the very last day of its existence it decreed—not out of consideration for the Vendeans, but for other, with it more potent, reasons—that certain of the municipal officers should be charged with these duties, instead of the constitutional clergy. But the greater part of the Vendée had by this time reached such a state that this new law was inoperative, and it was powerless to affect the main point at issue between the Revolutionary Government and the Vendean people.

Even at this late hour, however, and far as things had already gone, the storm in the Vendée would have blown over had the Government given the Vendeans back the priests to whom they were so passionately attached, and had enabled them once more to enjoy the practice and consolations of their religion.

That was the centre of the whole matter.

The hope of such a thing was, however, utterly vain; and now more vain than ever; for with the accession to power of the National Convention, sterner hands were assuming the government of France, and the helm was being seized by men who hated not alone the Catholic religion, but all religion, and who would stop at no measure, however violent or extreme, to crush both, and to attain their own ideals.

On the 21st September (1792) the National Convention met, and, without discussion, decreed instantaneously and unanimously the abolition of royalty in France, and the establishment of the French Republic, one and indivisible.

The slender protection of the King's veto being gone, nothing stood between the objects of the Convention and their realisation. So far as religious matters were concerned, the aim of the revolutionary leaders became clearer. The abasement of Catholicism, even its total abolition, was the goal which they wished to attain. And in the Vendean country, the revolutionary local authorities, supported by the Convention, now in full accord with their sentiments, devoted the whole of the winter of 1792-93 to hunting down the non-juring priests and throwing difficulties in the way of any religious worship.

Early in the new year—on the 21st January 1793—the King was executed in Paris.

Had the Vendeans been as much under the influence of the royalists in the Vendée as republican writers endeavour to make out, they would have at once sprung to arms to avenge him; but no popular fury was caused by the event—the news only caused "great consternation."

Their own troubles and trials came far more home to them. For now, in addition to those in connection with their religion and their priests, other irritating measures were enforced by means of the district authorities. Perpetual domiciliary visits were made in search of arms, or non-juring priests, or *émigrés*, and their arms were seized and taken away, though in many cases they depended on them for their daily food. And their material interests were also suffering. The forced currency of paper money bore heavily on them; and over and above this was the "murderous scourge" of national taxation, the ruthless levy of which plunged the farmers into distress, and heavy local taxes imposed by the arbitrary decrees of local authorities, and fiercely executed.

As an instance, quite early in March, a fine of nearly £500 was imposed on a certain district to defray the costs of the forces employed to disperse an assembly of the Vendeans. There were protests; "but," wrote

Gallet, the republican official in command, "putting aside my natural sensitiveness, I pitilessly executed militarily on the spot all those who would not pay up. This method of getting money is, I can vouch for it, a good one."

All through February, too, the Vendeans were worried and harassed by the visits of commissioners to organise the National Guard as a weapon in the hands of the Revolutionary Government—and at several places there were assemblies and riots, and magistrates were insulted, and "patriots," as the revolutionists called themselves, were disarmed. The people were excited, too, by the rumours of the creation of new battalions of troops. Everything was in fact tending to a crisis.

"The fire was smouldering under the ashes," wrote Mercier. "I seemed to hear the noise of a volcano under my feet."

A measure of the Republican Government in Paris fanned the smouldering fire into instant flame. Foreign politics had become more than ever acute. War was declared against England on the 1st February.

On the 25th the Convention declared that a coalition of foreign despots menaced the Republic, and that liberty was threatened. And it was decreed that all French citizens from the ages of 18 to 40, unmarried, or widowers without children, were in a state of permanent requisition for military service until such period as the army was increased by the effective strength of 300,000 men.

Quite in the early part of March the news of the intended conscription reached the Vendée. Compulsory military or naval service had been a constant dread of the Vendeans. Even before the Revolution began, a petition had been addressed to the King setting forth that this cruel practice rendered families desolate, injured agriculture, and turned the fields into waste lands.

And now the feeling against it was infinitely stronger. At all times the Vendean had regarded his fields, his valleys, his streams, his home, his hearth, as his earthly Paradise: and was he to be forced to leave them? They were to him his life's blood—not to be parted from whilst life remained.   He did not believe that the country was in danger.   He simply saw that a Government which was pursuing him with a vindictive persecution, and which had become utterly detestable in his eyes, wished for its own advantage to seize on the manhood of the country and to send it to the frontiers to be killed.   The patience and forbearance of the Vendeans were at last strained to breaking-point.   For more than two years they had borne with the atrocious treatment meted out to them by the Revolutionary Government. They did not rise in revolt when their priests were torn from their parishes, as they still contrived to get some aid from them: they did not rebel as link after link was added to the chain of religious persecution; they were thoroughly alienated from the Government, but they abstained from opposing it by general armed resistance.   Now, however, the cup was filled to overflowing: and they were asked to support this detested Government with their lives and the lives of their sons.   That they would not do.   Be the consequences what they might, the limit of submission had been reached.

A thrill of intense excitement ensued—then mutterings and growlings.

And then the tocsin is set ringing from tower and steeple.   The sound of the bells clangs far and wide, and is taken up by church after church across the Vendée.

Borne on the breeze, or breaking in on the stillness of the night, it reaches the ears of all. And to the Vendean peasant it speaks in language of thrilling impressiveness. The voice of the bells, now summoning him to the trysting-place of the people, has bidden him through life to the temple of his faith, and to the worship in which his eternal hopes are founded; it has called him daily, in the midst of his labours, to offer to his Maker a tribute of prayer and praise: at their summons he has participated in the holy service and sacraments of his church, which have brought him nearer to his God; his best and purest and holiest associations are wrapped in those bells; and they are sacred to him.

But ringing thus at unusual time, with impetuous clamour, and the bells of neighbouring towers and steeples joining in distant chorus, the crisis must be of tre-mendous importance, requiring the presence and aid of the manhood of the country: and so, abandoning his work and his home, he seized whatever arms he possessed and hastened to meet his fellows.

It was, indeed, for all of them, the great crisis of their lives. The Government which, by long persecu-tion, had made itself hateful to them, had put forward demands from which there was no escape except by successful resistance. Compulsory conscription; compul-sory deportation from their homes and families, which would be left unprotected, a prey to revolutionary brutalities; compulsory military service for a Government which had treated them as the bitterest of enemies instead of as fellow-countrymen. Should they resist or not? that was the question. And to that question the answer was "Yes!" "Yes!" though they might only have a few pitchforks, and scythes, and fowling-pieces to defend themselves with. For life lately had scarcely been bearable. They could not bear the idea of being torn from their homes, or of their sons or brothers or friends being torn from them. They could not live without the consolations of their religion, or without those ministerial offices on which they believed their eternal salvation to depend.

And so the turning of the way was taken; taken heroically, for the way led to danger and trial, to persecution and death, at the hands of their own countrymen and of a Government whose motto, audaciously flaunted before the world, was " Liberty, Equality, and Fraternity," but whose practice was " Tyranny, Inequality, and Fratricide."

# CHAPTER IV

## THE VENDEAN WAR

## PART I

THE decision to resist conscription having been taken, but little time elapsed before the occasions arose for giving effect to it.

There were assemblies and resistance to the local authorities, and violence, first here, then there, and in a few days insurrection generally throughout the Vendée.

The rapid spread of the insurrection has been claimed by republican writers as convincing proof of long preparation, of skilfully contrived organisation, and of the whole movement therefore being a royalist and clerical conspiracy.

Some of these writers have gone so far in the way of absurdity as to declare it to be the work of Pitt and the English. But any theory served their purpose if it helped them to conceal the real fact, that the responsibility for the insurrection lay altogether on the shoulders of the Revolutionary Government. Could they but shift the responsibility elsewhere, the actions of the revolutionists would require less need of justification.

That the disturbances were almost simultaneous was

due, not to any royalist order or signal, as they allege,
but solely to the circumstance that the fixtures made by
the various local authorities for the conscription fell
within a very limited number of days, namely, from the
10th to the 18th of March.    On these days the
Vendeans were called upon to come up for enrolment.
They came, and in large numbers : but they would not
enlist.    If death were to be the penalty of their refusal,
they would rather, they said, die at home than elsewhere—" they would rather be cut in pieces than march."

From words they passed to more vigorous forms of
protest.    Quickly the first blows were struck, the first
blood shed, and the people, scarce knowing the gravity
of their actions, were irrevocably committed to arms.
The insurrection, in fact, really began on the impulse of
the moment, without plan, without concert, and almost
without hope.

If any further proof were required of its not being
the result of long preparation and deep-laid contrivance,
it is to be found in the utter unpreparedness of the
Vendeans for any serious strife.    Practically they had no
arms : only a few old fowling-pieces, very little gunpowder, and absolutely no artillery ; the most formidable
weapons of the majority were pikes and scythes fixed on
the ends of poles, and in most cases their only weapons
were sticks.    How courageous in such circumstances was
their determination to resist the armed forces of the
Republican Government—how deeply must the sense of
the long-continued ill-treatment have entered their souls
for them to face such desperate odds.

Of organisation there was not a vestige : of the plan
of a campaign they were equally guileless : ulterior
object, such as the restoration of the old régime, they
had none—only the desire of the moment to escape con-

scription, to have their priests restored to them, and to
be able to enjoy once more in peace and quiet the observ-
ances of their religious faith.

Moreover, they had at the outset no leaders. No
royal prince rushed to take the command, and to lead
them to victory ; no *émigré noblesse* flew to their aid with
counsel and military experience. Even the Vendean
noblesse who had remained in their own country did not
at first help them. In their first gatherings they were
an unled crowd, eager to follow any one who had the
most rudimentary knowledge of military matters, or who
was of at all superior position to themselves.

There was, in fact, not the vestige of a prepared
organisation for a revolt. After a while, and under a
sort of compulsion, the Vendean noblesse consented to
lead them. But at no time were the whole of the Vendeans under one recognised and responsible leader, nor
were they ever welded together into one army.

Later, when it was seen how considerable the movement was, the royalists endeavoured to turn it to their
own account; but, with the incapacity which distinguished all their efforts, they failed to do so: whilst that
contemptible creature the Count d'Artois, unwilling to
sacrifice his own ease and pleasure, and afraid to risk his
person in an effort to restore his own fortunes and those
of his family, fought shy of the leadership which he of
all others might with good prospects of success have
assumed.

The details of the first collisions of the Vendeans
with the republican authorities are not of any special
interest, with the exception of that at Machecoul, a
small town in the west of the Vendée. Here, on the
morning of the 11th March, a crowd of some 5000 to 6000
peasants arrived    men, women, and children; armed,

some few with guns, most with only scythes or sticks.
The republican commanding officer of the town endeavoured to resist; shots were fired; the Vendeans replied;
some republicans were killed; the National Guards fled,
and the town was taken possession of by the Vendeans.
A committee of government was promptly formed, and a
man named Souchu was placed, or placed himself, at its
head.    He declared for royalty, and raised the white
standard of the Bourbons, thus formally declaring war
against the Republic, and thus committing the Vendeans
generally to the adoption of that standard as their battle
flag, and to their being regarded henceforth as royalists.

But what stamps the war as in reality a religious and
not a royalist war is the fact that the Vendeans perpetu-
ally reiterated the assertion that the first, if not the
only, reason of their taking arms was to sustain the
religion of their fathers.    The restoration of royal
authority was always a secondary consideration.

The name of Machecoul has been brought into pro-
minence by the republicans on account of the severities
committed there by the Vendeans.    Many of the
" patriots " or republicans residing in the place were
seized, tried before an improvised court, sentenced to
death, and shot.    Exaggerated estimates say that 500
persons met their death thus in the course of a month;
more reliable ones say that about 100 suffered.

In explanation of the Vendean conduct, however,
much is to be said.    Long ill-treatment and strong provocation had embittered them.    The massacre in cold
blood of prisoners at Bressuire in the preceding August
by National Guards, when many of the Vendeans " had
been cut in strips," still rankled.    Furthermore, the
overtures they made to the republicans at Nantes for an
exchange of prisoners were not only scorned, but met by

the instant execution of one of those prisoners: and
fresh cause of exasperation was given them by the
massacre, on the night of the 23rd March, of some
hundreds of their companions at Pornic, a small coast
town a little distance off, which had been in possession
of the Vendeans, but from which they were driven by
the republicans, with a loss of over 200 men, and 300
prisoners, whom the republicans " in their fury put to
death."

The republican authorities turned up their eyes with
horror at the depravity and ferocity of the Vendeans at
Machecoul, and with rage at any one except themselves
adopting such a method of getting rid of opponents:
and republican writers, ignoring Pornic, have ever since
made the most of the severities in Machecoul, appealing
to them as a justification of all the subsequent republican
severities against the Vendeans.

Undoubtedly there were numerous cases of cruelty
and pillage on the first outburst of the Vendeans: nor
is it at all to be wondered at, having regard to the fearful state of anarchy in which France had been for some
years, and to the prolonged carnival of violence and
bloodshed in which such numbers of the people indulged.
But, certainly, it does not lie in the mouth of the
revolutionists to complain of harsh or unjust treatment:
for their own history was already stained by every
imaginable iniquity.    And it was ludicrous for those
to complain who had set precedents of wholesale slaughter
in the massacres in Paris, in the countless revolutionary
atrocities throughout France, and whose great solicitude
appeared to be to reserve for themselves the monopoly of
massacre.

Rather is it a matter of surprise that the outrages by
the Vendeans were so few.    And once they got leaders,

men of superior education, such violences ceased. Thenceforward the prisoners taken were treated with great humanity, and an example of mercy set, which, had it been followed by the republicans, would have been well for their reputation.

A few days after the capture of Machecoul, a much greater success was gained : the town of Cholet, the key of the Vendée, being taken by another Vendean gathering.

And here an incident showed the peculiarly religious character of the Vendeans. In pursuing the republicans they came to a calvary. Even the excitement of the fight did not make them pass it without acknowledgment : at it they paused, and falling on their knees, with bared head and folded hands, said a brief prayer. Then they resumed the struggle and their pursuit of the flying republicans.

The victory was an important one. The Vendeans captured several pieces of artillery, some powder, and a considerable number of muskets : but the capture of so important a place, and the victory over so large a force as some 700 republican troops, made a tremendous impression, not merely on the inhabitants of the Vendée, but upon the Republican Government in Paris.

The revolt was soon in full swing, both in the Upper and in the Lower Vendée : and the Vendeans did not let the grass grow under their feet, but pushed on from one success to another, driving out of the country all the National Guards or republican troops or authorities they came across, and arming themselves with the weapons taken from their adversaries. And as their numbers grew, and various assemblies met together, they gradually became a large army. They had succeeded, too, in providing themselves with leaders. At

St. Florent. Cathelineau had assumed the leadership. Stofflet—a gamekeeper—had gathered a force together, and assumed the command of it. In the west, Charette, a man of good family, had undertaken to lead them. They also induced or "constrained"—as d'Elbée later expressed it—the resident Vendean noblesse to join them: de Bonchamps, d'Elbée, de Lescure, Henry de la Rochejaquelein, men whose names are inscribed in the Vendean temple of fame for their valour and for their devotion to the Vendean cause.

And now, with leaders and with increasing numbers of fighting men, more important movements were attempted.

There was something strangely weird and awe-inspiring in the Vendean mode of warfare. Behind the impervious screen of wood which, in every direction, met the republicans in their efforts to thread the Vendean labyrinths, all was mystery. No sight, no sound, betrayed the existence, the presence, of an enemy. No scouts, no outposts, no barricades, no obstructions even on the rough and narrow road along which toiled the republican troops, encumbered with artillery, and caissons of ammunition, and waggons of food.

But the night before, the tocsin had been ringing, gathering the peasants together "for the service of God and King," and they had come, and got their instructions, and melted away again. And the bells again hung silent in the belfries. And then, just as the republican troops are in the roughest bit of the road, or in the narrowest part of a defile, just as they are least anticipating attack, an army springs apparently out of the ground, a murderous volley is poured into them, and another, and another, from behind the thick quickset hedges, or from out the woods: and fearful cries are heard—cries that appal the stoutest heart; and wild-looking men are seen running along behind the hedges to get fresh opportunities for a shot; and the cries grow louder and louder, now on one flank, then on the other, down the whole line, even to the very rear; until the republican troops feel trapped and ensnared, and surrounded by their enemy. And bearing down here and there on their extended line dash masses of men, ill-armed, it is true, but strong in the invincible reck-lessness of religious passion, and with loud shouts close in on their opponents. The republicans, surprised and staggered by the suddenness of the attack, confused by the terrible noise, feeling helpless from their inability to get at their foes, make a brief stand, then panic seizes them, those that have not fallen throw down their arms and fly, anywhither so that they get away from their foes, fortunate if they escape with their lives. And the Vendeans, having collected the spoils of victory, having distributed amongst the unarmed the muskets and am-munition which they have captured, having on their knees thanked God, who had given them the victory, vanish into the mysterious depths of the woods, to reassemble and repeat their victory on the first suitable opportunity.

Upon the republicans the effect of this species of warfare was terrifying. How terrifying may be gathered from the description of a contemporary writer. " The ' patriot ' marches with fear and trembling through the defiles of the Vendée—he shivers with dread—it seems to him as if he were on a soil which might at any moment suddenly explode, or as if the mountains might suddenly fall upon him."

It was not, however, only their method of warfare which made the Vendeans to be feared by the republicans, it was the spirit which animated them. Republicans and revolutionists called it "fanaticism," and were always gibing at it, as if it were something so utterly abominable as to remove the Vendeans from the category of human beings, and to justify any treatment of them.

There is no word in the dictionary of French revolutionary cant oftener used in the way of contemptuous condemnation than this one. But this so-called "fanaticism" was but the expression of the religious faith of these Vendean peasants, and it was the secret of their power and of their success. Death had no terrors for them, for were they not fighting for their God, — what mattered it, then, if they perished in the strife ?

Strong in this faith, "they threw themselves on the cannon and caissons of the republicans with the ferocity of a tiger which pursues and carries off its prey."

And so, time after time, prodigies of valour were performed by them. Where others would have been discouraged, they persevered ; where others would have succumbed in despair, they presented a bold front even against the most tremendous odds ; where others would have been cowed, they rose to the emergency and triumphed.

Just at the precise moment that the Vendean civil war was beginning, the National Convention in Paris had adopted two measures which were destined very materially to affect the vicissitudes of the Vendean strife.

The first was the establishment of the Revolutionary Tribunal in Paris, which was created to punish all attacks against the Republic, and which afforded a precedent and pattern for numerous similar tribunals in the country.

The second was the adoption, or more accurately the

extension, of a system of government which stamps the
revolutionary government of France as absolutely
despotic in form.

The Convention, finding itself unable to carry out a
vigorous and detailed execution of the system of revolutionary government throughout the country, and irritated by the resistance it met with, did not scruple to
call to its aid the resources of despotism.

The Constitution of 1791 had reduced the power of
the central executive almost to nothing: for the "administrations" in the Departments were popularly elected
bodies, and independent of the central power. The
defects of this organisation revealed themselves to the
Convention once that body had seized the executive
power of the State; and to govern the country with
effect, it felt the necessity of reassuming the lost power,
and of concentrating administration in its own hands.

Accordingly it divided France into forty-one sections
—two Departments in each—and eighty-two commissioners or "Representatives of the people," chosen from
the Convention itself, were sent in twos into each of the
sections to take the most vigorous and thorough measures
for suppressing all opposition, and to work the people in
them up to the proper pitch of revolutionary enthusiasm.
It gave these Representatives unlimited powers, and left
them free from all control except that of the Convention itself. In some few matters they could only act
provisionally, reporting to the Convention for its final
approval; but in almost everything their wish was to be
law, their word was to be law.

No authority, local, military, or judicial, could over-
rule them or set their actions aside. They could enforce
the most abject obedience. They could order the
military forces about as they wished. They could impose

on districts what penalties they thought fit. They could suspend or dissolve any local bodies that opposed them. They could suspend or cancel any process of law. They were absolute despots, worse even than previous royal despots, being more in number, more ubiquitous, more pettily omniscient, and without any of the restraints which surround a real sovereign, however despotic. Once they arrived in their districts every vestige of protection for life or property was gone, and every form of justice set aside, except what they considered justice.

It is really hard to realise that a Revolution which was to destroy tyranny should have set up a new and worse form of tyranny. But one of the most striking and interesting facts in connection with the Revolution is this—that the revolutionists were always repeating in a more aggravated form the evils which they proclaimed they intended to destroy, and were always belying the principles which they blazoned forth as the exclusive property of the revolutionary creed.

Nor were these tremendous powers given to the Representatives by the Convention with the intention that they were not to be used; for that the Convention might know that they were using them, they were to report every week direct to it, and every day to the Committee of Public Safety.

Here, then, the true nature of French revolutionary government discloses itself. As events develop themselves, one will see it in ever clearer colours; and not only that, but the true character of French revolutionary "justice," and the true nature of the French revolutionist—the "good sans-culotte," the "brave republican," so much belauded by his fellows and himself.

The fact is, that as a sort of government gradually developed out of the chaos and anarchy and violence

which for some years had prevailed in France, everything
that was worst and most violent in that anarchy, instead
of being eliminated, crystallised into the new system.

The tide of Vendean success swept on. By the end
of March almost the whole of the Vendée was in the
power of the Vendeans.

The insurrection had taken the Government by surprise. In that part of the country there were scarcely
any regular troops, nearly every available man of them
having been sent to the frontiers to defend France
against foreign enemies. A cry of alarm went up from
the towns in the neighbourhood of the insurrection,
Nantes, Angers, and Saumur all feeling menaced and un-
comfortable. The peril was great, they thought, and
prompt measures were required on the part of the Revolutionary Government to meet the danger.

The Convention was not slow in acting. On the
17th March it received tidings of the disturbances, and
on the 19th it passed the fearful, inexorable law which
was the doom of tens of thousands of Vendeans, the
charter, so to speak, of the revolutionists, the warrant,
or excuse, for all their inhumanities.

"It does not suffice," said Lanjuinais, in discussing
the measure in the Convention, "to threaten with the
Revolutionary Tribunal men who are evidently paid by
the English Government, and roused into revolt by the
nobles and priests, especially when this tribunal is eighty
leagues away from the scene of the insurrection. I
demand that chiefs and soldiers—all those who are
captured with arms in their hands, who oppose themselves to the recruiting, or who wear the white cockade,
shall be treated according to the laws against the *émigrés*
(that is to say, to the penalty of death within twenty-

four hours after trial by court-martial). I demand further that the property of all those who are killed in the insurrection shall be confiscated."

Against the enormity of this proposal several members even of the Mountain protested. Even Marat declared it to be " the maddest, and most unworthy of a thinking being " (*la plus insensée, la plus indigne d'un être pensant*, " for it is not against the misled men that severe measures should be taken, but against the chiefs."

The decree nevertheless was made. Furthermore, the Convention ordered the executive to take instantaneously the most vigorous measures for the suppression of the insurrection.

Great efforts were accordingly put forth to make a stand against the Vendeans. France had already nine armies on the frontiers. The Government decided on organising two new ones for service in the west.

A proclamation was made to the rebels calling on them to dissolve their gatherings, and lay down their arms; and announcing that those who did so within twenty-four hours should not be punished (*inquiétés*), nor those who surrendered the chiefs or instigators of the revolt.

" This decree of proscription and death," wrote Savary, " tended more to strengthen than to terminate the revolt. Chiefs, priests, and all felt that there remained no hope for them, and the necessity was impressed on them of firmer union, and of attaching to themselves the masses of the population."

The local republican authorities at Angers and Saumur did their utmost to get a force together to withstand the Vendeans, and crowds of men arrived, peasants without arms, or badly armed, conducted by officers of their own choosing, without experience, and without discipline, a motley lot "who knew neither how to command nor to obey."

These, and the National Guards, and some few regular troops, were all the Government had at first to oppose the Vendeans, and the generals who were sent to command them drew dismal pictures of them.

The local authorities appear to have had a very shrewd idea of their proclivities, for they issued a proclamation to them.

"Citizens,—You are commanded by the law. You march in the name of the law. You should behave according to the law. You are going to fight men whose greatest crime is to have listened to the perfidious counsels of those who deceived them. They are guilty, without doubt. They have forced you to take arms against them. If they are victors, they would perhaps not spare you; but you who are animated by the love of your country—you whose noble ambition should be to conquer and to know how to pardon—would you, in imitating your enemies, assassinate those whom the fortune of war places in your power? Consider that the man who is conquered and unarmed is under the protection of the law. In abusing your victory, in wasting the plains, in devastating property, you would be violating the law, which every citizen should respect, and you would render yourself culpable in his eyes."

This proclamation—interesting as an illustration of what the ideal revolutionist, as distinguished from the real one, should be—is noteworthy as being almost the last glimmer of fair dealing with or moderation towards the Vendeans. Henceforward, almost in vain does one seek for one sign of, not mercy, because that was never shown, but of fairness or justice. The mere mention of the word mercy was displeasing to "popular hearts."

Death, destruction, extermination, even these scarcely satisfied the overbearing spirit of the revolutionist, scarcely gratified his lust for bloodshed, and for the annihilation of all opposed to him. Conciliation and compromise were not thought of, or if mentioned were stigmatised as counter-revolutionary and worthy of death. Force was the only remedy, and nothing but force would meet the necessities of the case. No severity could be too great, no punishment too heavy, in dealing with the cursed Vendeans. No subterfuge but was justifiable to get hold of them. Treachery, lies, deceit were all pressed into service with this object, and all held to be commendable when so employed.

# CHAPTER V

## THE VENDEAN WAR

## PART II

THE so-called troops of the Republican Government in the Vendée were not much to boast of. For the first period of the war Representatives, commissioners, and generals were unanimous in condemnation of them.

There were, first, some few regular troops of the line : then there were the National Guards, or " Blues " as they were called, from their wearing a blue coat, a name which in Vendean parlance had already come to include all the Government forces : and then there were the newly enrolled volunteers, who constituted the bulk of the forces.

These new levies were in some ways the least useful. No sooner had they arrived at their quarters for military service, than they wanted to go away again, and they deserted by companies, sometimes by battalions, flying by every road as fast as their legs would take them (*à qui mieux mieux*). The " fathers of families " appear to have been usually the ringleaders, being anxious to get back to their families and their farms.

When a sufficient number of these levies could be kept together they were of little or no use, and were utterly unfitted for war in the Vendée.

" In these hastily formed assemblies, without discipline, experienced chiefs, or knowledge of arms, they were but feeble beings, frightened at the least sight of danger, and always ready to cry out that they were betrayed."

Enthusiasm did not make good these deficiencies—not even the enthusiasm of patriotism, for it was neither their own will nor the desire of defending their religion or their chief that had enlisted the soldiers of the Republic. "Requisitions and measures of terror had filled the ranks."

The National Guards, though having a little more discipline and training than these men, were not much better. "They have given proofs of the most signal cowardice," wrote Choudieu, a fiery Representative.

Whilst, as for the regulars, whatever little superiority they possessed in some ways was more than counter-balanced by their failings in other directions; for if they did not take the lead in running away, they took it in the perpetration of every enormity and atrocity that troops could be capable of.

The armies, or what were called by that name, were in fact composed for the greater part of ignorant and badly armed peasants—"poltroons to a degree of which one can form no idea," men who were saturated with " *la désastreuse habitude de fuir*." Often on the discharge of the first musket, even of one of their own muskets, they took to their heels and fled for miles, sometimes even for leagues. On the least excuse panic seized them, they broke their ranks, and, flinging down their arms, rushed back on their comrades, throwing all into disorder and causing a general *sauve qui peut*.

The generals complained bitterly of the material they were supposed to work with, and declared it impossible to carry on regular operations with such men.

"It is very hard upon an old military man," wrote General Berruyer, "to have to command cowards" (*de commander à des lâches*).

Insubordination was rampant among them: every one wanted to do exactly as he liked; even the self-styled officers would not obey orders.

At times the insubordination reached absolute mutiny, and on one occasion they pillaged their own cash-box.

From the very outset the republican troops gave themselves over to all sorts of excesses, which were more in their line than fighting.

Representatives belonging to the party in the Convention known as the Mountain can scarcely be regarded as hostile witnesses, yet two of them have drawn a damning picture of these, their own troops. In a proclamation addressed to the troops at Angers on 12th April, they wrote :—

"Houses have been pillaged, properties devastated, everywhere brigandage presents itself to our eyes. Women, children, old people, patriots even, are massacred without pity; and it is at the moment they waited for you as their deliverers, that they received death at the hand even of their brothers. . . .

"The troops are more dangerous to patriots than to the counter-revolutionists."

With troops of such character, and in such a state of indiscipline, the generals in command could not do much.

Nor, indeed, had the generals much chance otherwise, for they had not an atom of independence.

At their very elbows, and always among them, was a whole bevy of commissioners of every sort and kind, with which the country had been overrun. Commissioners of the Convention, or, as they are better known, "Representatives"; commissioners of the executive power: commissioners of the Departments, and of the district authorities; commissioners of the Commune of Paris, and of the sections: of the Minister of War: of the Committee of Public Safety: and commissioners of the popular societies.

Many of these commissioners had a colleague and sub-agents: and they all came and went among the troops just as they pleased, each of them giving orders, often contradictory, overriding the military authority: interfering in all the operations, and creating strife and confusion which paralysed the efforts of the army.

The ignorance, depravity, and incapacity of some, the fanaticism and malice of others, the conceited rivalry of all, disorganised the services and threw the administration of the army into the most frightful anarchy. Knowledge of strategy they naturally had none, but this did not prevent them criticising with the greatest freedom and assurance the plans of campaign adopted by the generals, and overruling them when and as they wished.

Woe to the general who did not listen to their advice, or who refused to obey their orders. He was immediately denounced, and he was lucky if his denunciation were not, as it often was, the first step to the scaffold.

Things were carried to such a pass in this respect that it was almost impossible for a general to keep his command for even a few weeks without being incriminated. Rightly or wrongly, justly or unjustly, mattered not.

Thus, General Marcé, who was one of the first generals to come into actual contact with the Vendeans, was obliged on the very field of battle and at the most

critical moment to act on the orders of Niou, one of
the commissioners from the Convention, and having,
in consequence, been defeated, Niou denounced him, and
he was sent to prison, and ultimately to the scaffold,
instead of Niou, who was really the culprit. But that
was only the usual style of revolutionary procedure.

And most of the earlier appointed generals, who
were military men, and had some military experience,
were not long left in command; for they were not of
the cruel, bloodthirsty, unprincipled, scoundrel type
which found most favour with the Revolutionary
Government.

At the back of all these Representatives and commissioners and their colleagues and agents was the
Minister of War, and again above him the Committee
of Public Safety and the National Convention.

In the end of April the important post of War
Minister was held by Bouchotte. On his taking office,
he fell in with Danton's politic suggestion to join
clemency to force; and on the 11th May the Convention was persuaded to moderate its decree of 19th
March, and to declare that only the chiefs and instigators of the rebels should be subjected to the death
penalty, whilst the ordinary rebels, if they laid down
their arms and surrendered, should be pardoned. But
this decree was never anything more than a dead letter.
It was neither obeyed nor followed, and it was soon
after superseded by others as ferocious as the one it
modified.

The momentary phase of moderation over, Bouchotte
inaugurated the reign of the "Mountain," or extreme
revolutionary party, in the war department.

He determined to republicanise the army. The
Vendean war was "counter-revolutionary." Necessarily,

therefore, it was to be opposed by revolutionary principles, by revolutionary troops, and revolutionary generals. What revolutionary troops were, and what revolutionary generals were, became more and more evident as time went on.

While the Revolutionary Government was making what military preparations it could to meet the Vendean revolt, the courage, dash, energy, and "fanaticism" of the Vendeans, and their numerous victories over the "Blues," were rapidly providing them with arms and ammunition at the expense of their enemies.

Emboldened by success they pressed on, and the republicans gave way.

On the 13th April the Vendeans drove Quetineau and some 5000 republicans out of Aubiers, and captured two guns and some ammunition; and at Beaupreau, on the 22nd, they captured five guns.

Appearing at all sorts of unexpected places, at unexpected times, and in unexpected numbers, they carried terror into the hearts of the republicans.

Indeed, except in the opener country of the maritime Vendée, none of their attacks could be foreseen, for the region where the rebellion was remained hermetically sealed.

Early in May (5th), the important town of Thouars, situated in an almost impregnable position, fell before their brilliant attack, led by Lescure and Henri de la Rochejaquelein. 2000 prisoners were captured, including General Quetineau: 12 cannon, several thousand muskets, pistols, sabres: 100 barrels of gunpowder, and other stores. No excesses were committed by the Vendeans beyond cutting down the "tree of liberty" which scarcely can be considered an excess and burning the papers of the revolutionary administration.

Not wishing to treat the prisoners they had taken
*à la République*—that is to say, to put them all to
death—the Vendeans released even the general, on his
taking an oath not to appear in arms again against the
Catholic army or the King of France. The men were
treated with similar leniency, except that they had half
their heads shaved, so that they might be identified
again.

An oath had little sanctity in the eyes of a revolutionist, and, soon after, these men were forced by the republican authorities to retract the oath they had taken,
and the Representatives declared that if they refused
to serve their country they would be treated as "suspects."

"For could there exist," said these Representatives,
"a binding agreement between revolted brigands and
free men, between the contemptible instruments of
fanaticism and royalty and the defenders of the first
Republic of the world?"

As for General Quetineau, a little later he again fell
into the hands of the Vendeans, they having captured
a town to which he had retired, but as he was not
fighting he was again released. He was then arrested
by the republicans and sent to Paris on a charge of
treason, and of having sold his army. Some months
later he was tried, sentenced to death, and executed;
and, with that extraordinary French revolutionary
brutality to women which is so appalling a feature in
this awful period, his wife was executed also for having
been heard to say "Vive le Roi."

In the farthest western extremity of the Vendée the
Vendeans had been foiled in an attack on the small
seaport of Sables, which they were anxious to acquire so
as to enable them to get help and supplies from England

or Spain, or from the *émigrés*. But on the 25th of May they captured Fontenay—the chief town of the Department—and with it 40 cannon, 7000 muskets, 4000 prisoners, and a large quantity of military stores.

The *débris* of the republicans fled to Niort, where Biron, *ci-devant* Duke and Count de Lauzun, who had been induced to take the appointment of commander-in-chief, had just arrived.

There, according to Biron's description, the confusion of chaos reigned.

At first sight he found it was not an army which he had under him, but a collection of men. He was in want of everything. There was no equipment for victualling or for hospitals, and there was no artillery. He had not a single officer of artillery or engineers, and other officers of all ranks were wanting. There were some 18,000 to 20,000 men in the town, but only some 2000 answered to the call of "assembly." It was the same here as on the eastern boundaries of the Vendée. Entire battalions of National Guards deserted at night, not leaving even a single man behind.

The commanding officers of the different detachments called their own detachment their "army," and called themselves generals. Their vanity and egotism were boundless. Each kept himself independent of all the others for fear of losing status, held no communication with them, gave no account of his proceedings to any one. "They did not, in fact, appear to belong to the same power."

Had the Vendeans pressed on from Fontenay, Niort must have fallen. But if not energetic here, farther east they were carrying everything before them. From Thouars they had advanced to Doué, which on the 8th

June they captured, and whence they threatened Saumur, a small but important town of great strategic value, having a bridge across the Loire.

Saumur had been made the eastern headquarters of the republicans, and here, about the middle of May, a central commission of sixteen commissioners and Representatives sat. There was also an army of 10,000 men here, but it remained in absolute inaction.

"One would have difficulty in believing it," wrote two of the Representatives. "One day when the generals were assembled with the Representatives, we have seen the chief of a corps come and declare that he and his comrades would not march against 4000 brigands unless they themselves were 6000." The chief referred to was Rossignol, who had been sent by his "brave comrades" to make this statement.

A contemporary republican has left a vivid description of towns in occupation of republican headquarters. Of Saumur he says: "The streets were crowded with aides-de-camp, who trailed long sabres after them and wore long moustachios; and with swindling or blackleg generals (*escrocs*) and others of that sort; with commissioners of the executive power, who preached anarchy, murder, and assassination. It appeared as if all the *roués* of Paris had made a meeting-place in these unhappy countries to stir up civil war and to despoil the inhabitants. This spectacle afflicted me, but I had only seen as yet a corner of this hideous picture. . . .

"I had perceived more than once at Paris, and Tours, and elsewhere, that extreme divisions existed between the Representatives. I had been a witness of a quarrel between two of them, about the appointment of an apothecary to the army, in which they abused each other in strong language (such as 'une vielle machine détraquée'). I knew that the Representatives described each other under the name of 'scélérat,' and that without much ceremony."

Of Tours he writes: " Here the number of debauchees (*hommes corrompus*), of these *suppôts de mauvais lieux*, was much greater; and it increased every day as the battalions from Paris arrived. I saw actors, jugglers, and mountebanks transformed into generals, with the most disgusting harlots in their train, occupying positions of rank in the army, or places of employment in the commissariat and forage departments, or in the military train, and these *insectes corrupteurs* had the insolence to call themselves republicans.

" I saw light cavalry, composed of cowardly Prussian and Austrian deserters, ' the Germanic legion ' which had been formed with the object of giving to the friends of Equality and Liberty in France the opportunity of developing their military talents for the service of France and in favour of the entire humanity. It was with brigands of this type that one wished to extinguish the civil war.

" ' It is thus,' I said sadly to myself, ' that one surrounds the statue of Liberty. One wishes to defend the Republic with men of the sort Catiline picked up for the destruction of his country.' "

The battalions which arrived from Paris were composed of, as Barère called them, "courageous patriots."

The Commune of Paris had cried out for severe measures against the Vendeans: " No pardon, no quarter to the rebels,"— and passed a decree (1st May) for the enlistment of 12,000 men to go and suppress them.

But though a "patriotic" appeal was made to the Parisians to enlist, their patriotism did not rise to that height, and a money inducement had to be added; as much as 500 livres to each man enrolled, and the promise of a pension on his return.

These pseudo-volunteers were everything which was vilest in Paris—convicts, lunatics, criminals of the deepest dye, men steeped in debauch and crime, and they quickly made themselves famous in the Vendée under the sarcastic epithet, "the 500-livres heroes."

Some of the republicans later, somewhat ashamed of the actions of these heroes, repudiated their *protégés*, and asserted that they were the leavings of the royalists.

They were, however, enlisted with the sanction and approval of the Republican Government by the Commune of Paris, were paid by it, and constituted part of the armed forces of the Republic.

This revolutionary crew had not even the redeeming trait of courage.

On the 9th of June the Vendeans attacked Saumur, and swept them out of it: the republican troops once more distinguishing themselves by their cowardice; the newly-arrived Parisians taking the lead in a rapid movement to the rear; the cry, "Sauve qui peut," "We are betrayed," having been started, they said, by disguised royalists, as republican troops would not, of course, do such a thing.

The victory was a brilliant one, and placed at the disposal of the Vendeans large quantities of artillery (46 guns were taken), 15,000 muskets, ammunition, and other military stores and supplies; in fact, the war material of a small arsenal. Some 2500 republicans, it is said, were killed or wounded, and some 8000 prisoners were taken.

Here once again the prisoners, amounting now to about 11,000 in all, instead of being slaughtered, were let go, on taking the oath not to bear arms again against religion or the King, and on some of their hair being shaved off as a mark of identification.

Prisoners were a constant difficulty with the Vendeans. They had no regular prisons, and no satisfactory means of keeping or feeding such large numbers as they captured.

The republicans would never exchange prisoners; that they would not condescend to—no matter what became of their own friends who had been captured.

The Vendeans had practically little choice—either to release them on the useless terms they did, or to put them to death, as the republicans put the Vendean prisoners to death under the law of the 19th March.

Though it must quickly have become apparent to them that in releasing prisoners they were but adding to the forces arrayed against them, as even an oath was not regarded as binding by their implacable foes, yet were they too magnanimous to follow the republican precedent; they, at any rate, had not sunk, could not sink, to the level of republican fraternity and humanity.

The contrast of conduct is magnificent testimony to the superiority of the Vendeans over their merciless foes and it was all the more splendid that, even under the most desperate aggravation, they persevered in a course which tended much towards their own undoing and defeat.

The Convention dealt with this matter of the republicans taking such an oath in a characteristically republican way.

On the 22nd June it decreed that any republican soldier taking such an oath, or receiving a passport from the Vendeans, should be deprived of the rights of citizenship for ten years; and he was further threatened with the penalty of being sent before the extraordinary tribunal on a charge of communicating with the rebels—an offence punishable with death.

With Saumur in their hands, and the republicans panic-struck, the way to all appearance was open to Paris; but the Vendean army, valiant and almost irresistible in its own country, was not equal to undertaking so formidable a task, so great a military adventure. They moved on to and occupied Angers, which in a panic had been abandoned by the republicans—though there was a force of several thousand troops there, and over twenty pieces of artillery.

But the high-water mark of Vendean success was here reached. For the first time, differences of opinion divided the Vendean Council. Some, whom success had made ambitious, wanted to go on, even to Paris; others to adhere to the line of action which so far had made them successful. Ultimately they agreed on the middle course of an attack on Nantes.

Thither, therefore, the army directed its way.

Nantes, with its 80,000 inhabitants, was plunged into great alarm when it became known that the Vendean army was advancing to attack it.

On the 19th June the Representatives declared the town to be in a state of siege, the civil authorities were superseded by military authorities, and military law was enforced.

Canclaux was the general commanding, and he had about 9000 to 10,000 men, of whom several thousand were troops of the line.

In the early hours of the morning of the 29th the attack was begun, and the battle raged for the whole day. It was a well-fought contest, and the Vendeans had almost triumphed; but the fate of the day appears to have been decided by the loss by the Vendeans of their beloved leader, Cathelineau, who had succeeded in forcing his way into the city, but who, in the moment of triumph, had there been mortally wounded.

Completely discouraged by this heavy blow, the Vendeans fell back, and their attack was repelled. Obliged to renounce the idea of carrying on war on the north side of the Loire, they retreated to their own side of the river, and there the army dissolved.

This heavy reverse was decisive of the ultimate fate of the Vendean war, so far as the probability of overthrowing the Republican Government was concerned; for it proved that Nantes could be held against the Vendeans, and that the power of the Vendeans was limited.

There was one great inherent weakness in the Vendean cause. The Vendeans could never be kept together for more than a few days at a time. They would assemble and fight, but, whether victorious or defeated, they returned to their homes after a few days, vanishing into the woods by the countless paths unknown to all but themselves. Even had they been successful in their attack on Nantes, it is doubtful whether they would or could have kept possession of it long. Saumur they had evacuated; Angers also; Fontenay too. It seemed impossible for them to hold a town for any length of time, and this limitation of aggressiveness practically foredoomed the Vendean struggle. Any extended sustained success, such as the more ambitious royalists coveted, was, under these circumstances, impossible. On their own ground, and in their own woods, they were able to hold their own against all the forces the Republic could bring against them; that practically was all they really wanted. Some of their leaders aspired to effecting a counter-revolution, and re-establishing the monarchy, though getting little encouragement from the quarter from which aid should have come; but the ambition of the Vendean peasants never soared so high. The restoration of their religion was for them the one object of their desires.

# CHAPTER VI

If the revolutionary authorities were unable to make
headway against the Vendeans in the field, with the
solitary exception of defeating the attacks on Nantes
and Sables, they gave the fullest vent to their wrath in
places where they had the upper hand.

Beaten on the field of battle, they were determined
to take their revenge in every other way they could on
the people and on the prisoners who were in their
power; and here in the civil as distinguished from
military government, horror rapidly accumulates on
horror, until the whole ghastly paraphernalia of revolutionary tyranny is complete and is displayed to human
sight.

From the time of the Vendean outbreak the Convention had fulminated one terrible law after another against
the Vendeans, against rebels, priests, *émigrés*, against
all who by any stretch of revolutionary imagination
could be construed into being counter-revolutionists;
crushing out liberty in any and every form, except
liberty for themselves; devising new offences; narrow-
ing the meshes of the revolutionary net so that no one
opposed to them should escape.

And the Representatives, endowed with despotic powers by the Convention, were carrying out on the scene, or in the immediate neighbourhood of the strife, its policy and its decrees in the most thorough fashion, improving even on its directions where any opportunity of improving on them presented itself.

The various local revolutionary authorities, acting under the influence of the local revolutionary clubs or popular societies, not alone kept in line with the Convention, but often went, illegally, in advance of it, making laws for themselves as requirements arose; and the Representatives, and the horde of restless and self-important commissioners sent by other public bodies, instead of condemning this excessive zeal, spurred them on to more vigorous efforts, and incited them to loftier heights of revolutionary fury. The suppressive laws were to be put into the fullest operation, and the extremest penalties were to be enforced. The refractory priests were to be hunted down; the rebels were to be annihilated; the *émigrés* were to be given short shrift when they could be caught; their relatives even were declared suspects; and everybody counter-revolutionary, or who did not actively support the authorities, was to be made feel the heavy weight of the revolutionary hand.

Very rapidly a system of revolutionary justice was built up by the Convention and filled in by the Representatives—a system which infinitely exceeded in injustice and tyranny that which the Revolution had overthrown—with execrations.

When the new Constitution was given to France by the National Assembly, a criminal tribunal was established in each Department to deal with the criminal business of the Department. At the outset, it was this tribunal which dealt with counter-revolutionary cases.

But its procedure was too sedate and slow, and fair to the prisoners, to satisfy the revolutionists; and as revolutionary momentum increased, and the number of persons to be dealt with grew larger, special tribunals on the model of the Revolutionary Tribunal in Paris were formed to administer justice revolutionarily.

To adjudicate in these new courts men of extremer views and reputation were appointed, and punishment was meted out more expeditiously and with less regard to innocence.

But once war began, and there were rebels to deal with, even these courts could not deal punishment out summarily and rapidly enough. Their forms of procedure were too slow, and too much in favour of the prisoner, to satisfy the impatient spirit of the "patriot"; and so the Convention, at the same time that it passed the terrible law of the 19th March, gave a great and general extension to those monstrous inventions of despotism, the Military Commissions.

It is said in defence of the policy which instituted these commissions that they were on the model of the Prévôtal Courts of the *Ancien Régime;* but if so, this only shows that the revolutionists, whose whole rationale was the abolition of tyranny and injustice and the remedy of abuses, were treading in the very steps of the system they abolished, and adopting its very instruments, and the argument is a most damaging admission on the part of the applauders of the Revolution.

The institution of Military Commissions was in existence since the previous autumn.

In October a severe law had been passed against the *émigrés,* according to which all *émigrés* captured with arms in their hands were to be handed over to "the executioner of high justice" within twenty-four hours, and put to death, after it had been declared by a Military Commission, composed of five persons nominated by the Headquarters Staff (*État-major de l'armée*), that they were *émigrés*, or that they had served against France.

This precedent was followed in the law of the 19th March, which began by declaring generally as *hors la loi* [1] all those suspected of taking part in the revolt, and those who wore the white cockade or other sign of rebellion. Such persons, therefore, could not avail themselves of the provisions of the laws concerning criminal procedure and of the institution of juries.

It enacted that those taken with arms in their hands should within twenty-four hours be delivered to the executioner of criminal judgments, and put to death after the fact had been certified (*reconnu et déclaré constant*) by a Military Commission of five members, formed by the officers of each division employed against the rebels.

Those who had carried arms, or who unarmed had taken part in the revolt or *attroupements*, should be sent to the prison of the criminal tribunal of the Department, to be tried by the judges of that tribunal.

Priests, former nobles, *émigrés*, and servants of all these persons were to be sentenced to death.

There was no appeal, no respite, no reprieve. Within twenty-four hours all was to be over—trial, sentence, execution.

How keen the republicans were to have recourse to extreme measures without any legal authority is well illustrated by the fact that the local republican authorities at Nantes adopted the machinery of Military Commissions before the law of the 19th March had even been proposed.

On the 13th March the "three administrative

---

[1] Outside the law, or outlaws.

bodies" of Nantes, when organising the first military
expedition to attack the Vendeans, directed that "a
court-martial should accompany each detachment of the
armed forces, and should judge on the spot and forthwith the rebels taken with arms in their hands, according to the rules and forms prescribed by the law relating
to *émigrés.*"

In principle the Military Commissions only dealt
with *révoltés* and *émigrés* taken with arms in their
hands.

Soon, however, these courts gave wide extension to
their own powers, and took cognisance of almost any
counter-revolutionary offences.

Though there are instances of the generals appointing
such commissions, the Representatives, with their unlimited powers, appear to have taken the appointment of
them into their own hands, and appointed them wherever
and whenever they thought they would be useful.

Each Commission or court consisted of five members,
but it was not necessary for the five members to act
together, and from the very outset these courts were
simply instruments in the hands of the Representative
in his task of "purging the country," of "purifying the
air of liberty," and of raising the country to the full
heights of revolutionary grandeur.

And so the Representatives, with these and other
objects before them, soon began dotting the Departments
over with Revolutionary Tribunals and Military Commissions.

The latter were the most convenient and simple
means of sending to death those whom the Representative wished to doom to death, and as they were there for
that purpose, instructions from him as to the treatment
of prisoners were in reality unnecessary.

These Military Commissions were the veriest mockery of a judicial tribunal. As was truly said of them, "they clad murder with the mantle of the law." Men were appointed to preside in them whose principal qualifications were, not knowledge, not integrity, not fair-mindedness, but vehement revolutionary views and true sans-culotte fervour, with the necessary callousness to give effect thereto. In most cases the members of them were the very scum of blackguardism, cruel, bloodthirsty men, often not even military men, ignorant of the commonest principles of law, swayed solely by their passions, prejudices, and desires.

And a procedure was adopted in these courts which deprived the prisoner of any opportunity, any possibility of defence. At first one *procès-verbal*, supported by the deposition of one witness, or the oral and uniform deposition of two witnesses,[1] were required for the establishment of the guilt of a prisoner, and as sufficient for his being sentenced to death. But, as time wore on, even this formality fell into abeyance, and procedure was reduced to a mere request for the prisoner's name, and then the sentence of death.

"One trembles," wrote a republican commissioner who witnessed their handiwork, "when one thinks of the horrors perpetrated by these tribunals of blood."

As for the nature of the justice administered by the various Revolutionary Tribunals, it was in flagrant violation of all the most elementary principles of justice in civilised countries. It is doubtful whether the extremest despotism has ever shown such a complete negation of justice, such a callous disregard of even the forms of fairness.

---

[1] "Le fait demeurera constant soit par un procès-verbal revêtu d'une seule signature confirmé par la déposition d'un temoin, soit par la déposition orale et uniforme de deux temoins."

It is this complete disregard of justice which is the most striking feature in the system of the Revolutionary Government, in every phase and aspect of its actions, in every grade of its organisation.

Running through all its acts, woven into its very tissue, was an absolute hostility to, a defiance of, justice.

Splendid speeches might be delivered in the Convention upon the beauties of justice, particularly of French justice; courts might laud the impartiality of the justice they administered, and the fairness of their proceedings; but the grim horrors of these years contrast facts with theories, contrast deeds with professions, tell, in fact, how justice was assassinated even by the highest officials of the State, and by every court in it, from the Revolutionary Tribunal in Paris to the worst of the roving Military Commissions in the country.

These desperate engines of tyranny, and the dreadful provisions of the law of 19th March,—"the Law of Death," as it was called,—were not long allowed to lie unused.

From Angers, General Berruyer wrote on the 5th April: "I have given orders to disarm and arrest all suspects." (This, be it remarked, was more than four months before the celebrated *Loi des Suspects* was passed.) "The Military Commissions are in vigour, and have already executed a large number of persons who have been taken with arms in their hands."

At Sables, the seaport of the Vendée, on the 1st April, the military officers elected a Military Commission which promptly proceeded to try prisoners charged with having joined the rebels, and having worn a white cockade.

A guillotine was erected on the highest of the sand-hills in the neighbourhood, so that all men might see it and its work, and in the course of the month some sixty-five to seventy executions took place there, all of persons in the humblest callings of life—took place in batches, those whose turn came last being forced to stand by and see their companions in misery being executed—until their own turn came. Many of these unfortunates had avowed themselves guilty, in complete ignorance of the fate awaiting them, but no mercy was shown them.

In the earlier days of the Military Commissions, when the members had not yet become quite inured to the work, and some hazy sense of responsibility existed, some discrimination was exercised as to the guilt of the prisoners, and there were acquittals.

Here at Sables many acquittals took place. In many cases the accused had been arrested without any legal formality, and sent for trial without a *procès-verbal* or written charge, without even a single declaration. Indeed, the form of the acquittals—"There exists against them no proof of rebellion. They have been arrested without arms, without a white cockade, and on their own hearths"—shows how unjustifiable the majority of arrests had been.

This Commission at Sables was so far conscientious as to acknowledge that it felt itself "cruelly embarrassed" by the terms of the law. As the military forces drew up no legal process against the persons arrested, how could the court declare what the crime of the prisoner was—or what proof was there even of the identity of the prisoner?

Subtleties such as these, however, were not of long duration. Convictions by the Military Commissions multiplied rapidly, and acquittals became rarer, until finally there were none.

Here and there in all this ghastly tragedy one comes across an idea so grim as almost to be humorous.

Thus the "patriot" authorities at Niort—the Directory there—did not think the new form of execution quite impressive enough, and having devoted some consideration to the subject, wrote to the Convention begging it, in order to show how much Frenchmen abhorred royalty, to decree that every man condemned to death as a counter-revolutionist should be led to the place of his execution with a crown on his head.

The execution once of the one King was evidently not sufficient. His execution over and over again—in living effigy—could not fail to impress the evil-disposed, whilst it would be a constant gratification to the multitude to witness the repetition of its triumph.

If the chances of escape were slender once a person came before the revolutionary courts, revolutionary justice displayed itself in as cruel and infamous a way in the stage preliminary to trial, namely the imprisonment—an imprisonment often if not usually equivalent to death.

It mattered little under what law action was taken, the people, on one charge or another, were torn from their homes in hundreds and thousands and sent to prison—many, if not most of them, innocent of any crime.

By the beginning of May the prisons in the towns which were not in the hands of the Vendeans were crammed with prisoners in a manner involving the gravest risk to life; but that was a trifling matter in the eyes of the revolutionist, if anything it was an advantage.

In the prisons of Fontenay and Sables alone more than 1250 prisoners were massed or heaped together, all of humble rank, there being no aristocrats, none of the noblesse—not even a single Vendean chief among them.

And in Nantes, from March onwards, National Guards had been arriving daily with numerous prisoners, women as well as men, all of whom were thrown pell-mell into one or other of the prisons in the city.

Here in the prisons the most appalling state of things existed.

One of the prisons was the grim old castle Le Bouffay, whose origin dated back to the tenth century, and whose walls under the régime of republican "liberty" were witnessing more suffering and misery in one day than in the darkest period of its existence it witnessed in a decade.

The report of some commissioners who visited it has come down to us.

There were three *cachots*, or cells, in it, dark, damp, and unhealthy, which only received light through a hole of three inches. Several other cells had no light when the door was shut. Everywhere there was want of air. Itch, scurvy, dysentery, and fever were habitual among the prisoners. There was no surgeon, and a doctor did not come once in three months to see the prisoners.

And in the prison of St. Claire things were not any better.

Ten or twelve were in each room. The air was pestiferous, and charged with mephitic miasmas.

The great majority were sick, and without even straw to lie on; they were devoured by vermin; and their state was so bad as to cause fears of a plague or epidemic, not only in the prison, but in the town.

The most horrible sufferings were undergone in these fearful pest-houses—these hells upon earth—and thousands of prisoners never came out alive; but at this date the state of the prisons was still far from being at its worst, and the climax of horrors was not reached until the government of "liberty and fraternity" was well settled in the seat of authority.

To complete the provisions for the extermination of the Vendeans and other counter-revolutionists, ample preparations were made by the revolutionary authorities for the final disposal of offenders. The newly-invented guillotine was adopted as the instrument of death. In 1792 a model guillotine, with minute instructions as to its use, had been sent to all the Departments, which forthwith provided themselves with the full-sized implement of revolutionary justice—the Department of Deux Sèvres, which was next to La Vendée, with an eye to the future, ordering a batch of five.

A little later—to facilitate and expedite matters—some of the Military Commissions carried their own guillotine about with them, as a part of their personal luggage. On one occasion some inconvenience was caused by the blade having been left behind in a cupboard at the last place where the Commission had been sitting.

The Revolutionary Government, in its dealings with the Vendeans, at this period of its existence, was like some mighty and horrible snake coiling itself round its victim, getting it ever more and more completely in its power before crushing the life out of it. With diabolical ingenuity, and without a shadow of relenting, or vestige of hesitation or remorse, the Revolutionary Government, and its agents and instruments, "brave republicans" all, took measure after measure to close

up any possible loophole of evasion or escape ; and then,
having got its victim powerless and harmless in its grasp,
deadening its ears to any appeals for mercy, dealt out to
it death in the most cruel and terrible forms—to guilty
and innocent alike, to man, woman, and child.

# CHAPTER VII

## THE VENDEAN WAR

## PART III

WHILST the central and local revolutionary governing bodies were thus getting everything into thorough working order for the reign of Liberty according to revolutionary ideas, a phase of moderation, real or assumed, suddenly passed over the Convention, but as suddenly vanished.

The Convention, on the 23rd May, stepped down off its high pedestal, and, in a " Proclamation to the citizens of the disturbed districts," condescended to argue with them.

"You desire to keep your religion. But who has endeavoured to take it from you, or to trouble your consciences? Has any one proposed to change anything in your belief, or in the ceremonies of your worship? No. You have been deprived of those whom you regard as the sole legitimate ministers. But have they not justified by their conduct these too necessary measures? These men who to-day preach murder and pillage, are they the true ministers of a God of peace, or the vile satellites of despots leagued against your country? . .

These priests who call themselves the only Catholics are paid by the gold of Protestant England."

The people were called on to abjure their errors.

" Show yourselves worthy of retaking the name of Frenchmen. You will find then none but brothers in the Republic, which arms itself with regret to punish you—which, ready to crush you with all its power, would weep over successes purchased at the price of your blood.

" If any scruples continue to agitate your consciences, remember that liberty of worship is one of the necessary conditions of a republican constitution."

Specious self-contradictory verbiage such as this was not likely to detach the Vendeans from their cause ; and they knew already too much of republican fraternity to trust the hazy promises hinted at rather than expressed.

But at the very same time this public proclamation was being made, with its painful alternative of submission, or of revolutionary tears and the employment of force, the Minister of War was answering certain questions which Biron, the newly appointed commander-in-chief in the Vendée, had asked him, and which were very much more to the point.

Biron wanted to know whether he could employ other means than those of arms to subdue the rebellious country. The evasive answer was given : " The Republic could but applaud the zeal which would suggest the best means of reclaiming the misguided Vendeans by circulating among them the instructions most likely to lead to this result."

To his other question, " Is it allowed to enter into negotiations with those of the chiefs who could be induced to abandon the counter-revolutionary army, and

who could bring with them considerable numbers?"
the reply was a very clear and distinct negative. "I
do not think that in any case it would be proper
to enter into negotiations with the chiefs of the
rebels."

So that was settled. The issue must be fought out.
And then, as it was plain to the Revolutionary Government that something was amiss with the army in the
west, its condition was seriously taken in hand.

The Minister of War sent one of his "colleagues,"
Ronsin, a Jacobin of Jacobins, to the Vendée with
extensive powers to "revolutionise" the army.

Ronsin began by appointing a lot of colleagues
*adjoints* : and as numerous other commissioners of all
sorts and kinds were already roving about, "a war
of reports arose, all more or less exaggerated, and
there were rivalries and denunciations — in a word,
complete anarchy."

Representatives, commissioners, and generals all
vied with each other in reports to the Minister of War
or to the Committee of Public Safety, filled with censure
of the proceedings of every one else, or insinuations
against their patriotism or their sense.

Some abused some, others abused others, a mutual
secret abuse society instead of a public admiration society,
though occasionally the proceedings of a *vrai sans-culotte*
were praised so as to be a foil to others who had the
taint of noblesse about them, or who were possessed of
any ability.

Even the Minister of War did not escape secret
adverse reports addressed to the Committee of Public
Safety.

Biron, by his conspicuous position, and his widely
known antecedents, attracted special hostility, and though

he struggled valiantly on, all his plans, military and political, were thwarted by an organised sans-culotte opposition.

To get what material of war and supplies he could, he went to Saumur, early in June, and thence on to Tours, where there was almost a rebellion among the troops, which he appeased.

Here he held a council of war, but he could get no detailed information from any one as to the number of troops.

Arms were wanted, but the Committee of Public Safety wrote : " We cannot possibly send you any. We have none available." These would be reasons for his inability to act against the Vendeans, but they were no excuse in the eyes of the *vrais sans-culottes*.

Already Bouchotte, " an excellent citizen but a very bad minister," was writing to him complaining of delay.

" The public desires to see an end put to the troubles in the Vendée. It bears them impatiently, and attributes them to *émigrés*. The general who wishes to preserve his reputation as a patriot cannot put too much activity into his movements."

And Biron wrote to the Minister of War exonerating himself, and complaining of " a multitude of disorganisers who preach indiscipline to the soldiers, pillage, defiance of the generals, contempt and hatred of the Convention, and of the Representatives delegated to this army. . . The agents of your agents preach everywhere insubordination and the division of property. They wish to meddle with everything. Some of them can scarcely read."

A specimen of this sort of " disorganiser " was one Félix, afterwards the notorious president of the Military Commission at Angers,—one of the most bloodthirsty and infamous wretches among the numerous herd of them at this period.

At Niort he publicly denounced the generals, and even the Representatives. He was a firebrand among revolutionists, if such a thing is imaginable: half-a-dozen times he was arrested for one reason or another, but he had a passport which described him as "the colleague of the colleague of the Minister of War, Ronsin," and he had to be released.

The system of denunciation and calumny which was carried on as regarded the army extended under the rule of the Representatives to all branches of administration ; it paralysed and disorganised all ; frightened the good citizens ; cooled the sincere ones ; and created enemies to the Republic among those even most favourably disposed to serve it.

But as the system met with the approval of the Revolutionary Government in Paris, and the actions of the Representatives were the result of the directions of the Government, there was no one to whom appeal could be made by those who were aggrieved.

The downfall of the Girondists left the extreme revolutionists freer than ever to govern on revolutionary principles, and to demonstrate for all time to the world at large the beauties and advantages of the republican form of government, and its superiority to all others.

The immediate effect of the Girondist defeat was a fresh impulse to the already despotic energies of the revolutionary authorities in the area of the Vendean strife. The way was made easier for the free working of revolutionary principles, and for the unchecked rule of the revolutionists ; and marvellous ingenuity was displayed in the elaboration of fresh instruments of tyranny.

The army was being seen to ; civil organisation must

also be rendered more effective; and so the grip of the revolutionist steadily tightened upon the towns.

Nantes, if not technically the capital of the Vendée, was at any rate one of the great centres of interest in the Vendean war.

From the outset, it had been strongly revolutionary, and had more or less kept pace with the Revolution in its progress.

Here, on the first outbreak of the Vendeans, the administrative bodies had established an extraordinary criminal tribunal to judge, without appeal, the brigands confined in the Chateau, though their authority to take any such measure appears questionable. To expedite its work, this tribunal was divided into two sections, and a number of capital sentences were pronounced.

And then, that means of punishment should be easily available, they directed that the guillotine should be immediately erected on the Place du Bouffay.

On the 20th March, still solicitous about that horrible instrument, they decreed that it should be painted red; and that under it sand a foot deep should be put, so that no traces of blood be left on the pavement. The executioner, too, was enjoined "to act promptly, and to keep the fatal instrument in good order."

Also the lighting it at night engaged attention; for there was a serious row one night owing to the execution of a man in the dark—no torches having been lighted— the populace being unable to see the sight, or, as they said, identify the victim, and fearing "a substitution or dangerous suppression."

In April a Revolutionary Tribunal, on the Paris model. was added to the different tribunals already in operation, and Phelippes de Tronjolly was made president of it.

Though for a considerable period Nantes was practically of one mind as regarded the Revolution, there had developed itself, as time went on, a difference of opinion as to the length to which the Revolution should be carried; the wealthier and more respectable classes supporting the opinions of the Girondists—Revolution without terror; while the more extreme men supported the desire of the Mountain for a radical Revolution, and adopted its view that terror was the only way of resisting foreign attacks and the internal efforts against the Republic.

The Club de la Halle was the principal club of those holding Girondist opinions; the Club St. Vincent that of those holding the extremer views.

When strife ran high in Paris between the Girondists and the Mountain, the local authorities at Nantes had pronounced in favour of the Girondists and against the Mountain, and on the 19th May, four of the Representatives came there, not as friends but as enemies, and Merlin de Douai accused them of inertia, egotism, and other transgressions. Baco, the Mayor, replied that the city had been declared "to have deserved well of the country,"—which in effect he said it had saved, during the terrible days of the 10th to 20th March,—and that since then, though daily menaced by the royalists, it had maintained a force of 5000 men and had held its own.

It again "deserved well of the country" by repelling the Vendean attack, but it did not give its adhesion to the Mountain, and by a decree of the Commune on the 5th July, recording its determination not to recognise the authority of the Convention, and to sustain the Girondists, it really placed itself in insurrection.

It was, however, but a flash in the pan. The more

extreme and energetic portion of the Club St. Vincent
vehemently opposed the step taken by the constituted
authorities; and many of the members of these bodies,
becoming afraid of what they had done, revoked their
action.    The decision of the 5th July was reversed, and
the authorities made their submission to the Convention.
The Representatives came then in triumph to Nantes :
the more active leaders in the recent movement were
removed from their posts; sounder and more genuine
revolutionists were appointed in their stead, and affairs
thus put in fair train at Nantes.

Angers was the other principal town within the scope
of the Vendean trouble, and its state may be gathered
from a document drawn up by the electors of Angers,
who met on the 30th of May and adopted an address to
the Convention.

It was a vehement complaint against the Representatives. "whose selection appeared to have been calculated
to degrade in the eyes of citizens the national represent-
ation, and to make them hate Liberty.

" To calumniate patriots of the highest integrity. and
the most devoted to the cause of Liberty ; to vilify and
menace the constituted authorities who are firmest at
their post and the most attached to their duties; to
chain the liberty of the Press: to throw the brand of
discord among the citizens: to commit arbitrary deeds
which even royal despotism would scarcely have dared
to allow itself: to endeavour to stifle the public voice
by the trenchant and dictatorial fiat of their individual
opinion,—it is thus they accomplish their mission.

" Hasten to recall these dangerous proconsuls."

It is evident the people of Angers were realising the
first - fruits of "liberty, equality, and fraternity," as
understood by the true republican.    But their request

betrayed their misapprehension of the true state of affairs.

The more moderate and respectable republicans in both Angers and Nantes were soon to find out that they themselves were at the beginning of their troubles; and that the despotic Representatives thus inveighed against were only, so to speak, getting settled in the saddle for their labours in the revolutionary cause.

And at Angers, in July, after the retirement of the Vendeans, and its reoccupation by the republicans, a fresh engine of terror and tyranny was created there—a Revolutionary Committee and also a Military Commission. That, for the time being, settled Angers.

At Saumur, which had " made so many sacrifices in the cause of the Revolution," but which like Angers had suffered the disgrace of being in the hands of the enemy for some time, a Revolutionary Committee was also appointed (on 1st July 1793) " to throw light on the conduct of the bad citizens, to discover any communication with the rebels, or acts of incivism, and to arrest those suspected of same."

A Military Commission of its own was not requisite, for that of Angers officiated here when required; but the first labours of that commission were cut short by the fact of the Vendean prisoners having typhus, and so the summary method was had recourse to of dragging these unfortunate beings out to a plain and there shooting them.

Thus all around the Vendée, north, south, east, and west, wherever the Revolutionary Government had authority, measures of ever-increasing severity were being taken to consolidate its power, and vengeance was being exercised on all who in any way opposed or were suspected of opposing it.

The revolutionists were already showing what, as their reign went on, was ever more and more clearly demonstrated, that the new régime of "liberty, fraternity, and equality," which was not only to do such wonders for France, but to usher in a new era for humanity, was the greatest sham and imposture ever presented to the human intelligence; that they themselves were impostors of the worst and rankest kind, tyrants aping liberty, despots aping equality, fratricides aping fraternity.

Here is a contemporary description of the actual state of affairs under the new régime, in Touraine, which was contiguous to the scene of the Vendean struggle.

"Every one here is in terror and despair. . . There is no other law than the will and caprice of the Representatives. The populations which believed themselves enfranchised by the Revolution of 1789 are reduced to a veritable slavery. Nevertheless the word 'Liberty' meets one everywhere. One sees it written in gigantic characters on all the monuments: it displays itself at the head of all the public documents. The men of government, from the executioner to the minister, have it always in their mouths: everything is done and ordered in the name of Liberty. But it is nothing but an abominable piece of jugglery; nothing but an infamous mockery.

"Never, in effect, at any epoch of humanity has personal liberty, liberty of worship, liberty of thought, liberty of conscience, the liberty of the Press, liberty of commerce been more ignored. Never has the contempt of the rights of man been pushed further, nor those rights been scouted at more insolently. Never, in fact, has power shown itself more despotic, more intolerant,

more cowardly malignant, more vile in its means of
action, and more eager to shed innocent blood than the
existing Government. Better a hundred times that we
were back in the feudal times. . . .

"Misery is everywhere. . . . There is no more commerce; the law of maximum has killed it. We are
crushed with imposts, with forced loans, and revolutionary
taxes, the amount of which is arbitrarily fixed by our
tyrants. They take away from agriculture the arms
which are essential for its work. Our horses are requi-
sitioned, and we are paid with dirty bits of paper of no
value. The feudal corvées which had been abolished in
the memorable night of the 4th August have been re-
established. . . . And if any one dares to make an
observation or to complain, he is shown the scaffold, in
permanence on the public place, and often . . . the
person is conducted to it."

Every word of this crushing indictment of the Revolutionary Government applied equally to life in those
parts of the Vendée where that Government reigned.
But the Vendeans had in addition to bear the sufferings
inflicted by the operations of a cruel and degraded
soldiery and all the horrors of actual war.

It has been argued by republican writers that the
unparalleled severity of the Revolutionary Government
was accounted for, and indeed justified, by the fact that
the Vendeans had put themselves in the same category
as the _émigrés_, namely that of traitors to France, by
appealing to England for help.

The details of the Vendean communications with
England fall into a later period than this. Suffice it
here to remark, that war with England was only declared in February 1793; that, until then, England,
though holding out the hand of charity and an asylum

to French *émigrés*, lay and cleric alike, had maintained
a strict neutrality; that the Vendean outbreak only took
place on the 10th or 11th March; that the fearful
law of 19th March—the warrant for the extermination
of the Vendeans — had been adopted by the Government, and the whole machinery of revolutionary
tyranny, Representatives, Military Commissions, etc.,
started, and got into working order, long before any
communication could have been made by the Vendean
leaders.   It is difficult, therefore, to see what value such
an argument has.

The real fact is, the career of merciless severity
towards the Vendeans had been decided on, and the first
momentum had been given to the various republican
authorities, to carry out the exterminating policy of the
Government, long before the element of an appeal by
them to England for help entered into the matter; and
it was the dogged resistance of the Vendeans, and the
crushing defeats and humiliations inflicted on the republican cause by them, that drove the revolutionists
to fury and to the excesses begotten of fury, and not
indignation at an appeal for foreign help which had not
yet been made.

# CHAPTER VIII

## THE VENDEAN WAR

## PART IV

AFTER their defeat at Nantes, which was a severe blow to them, the Vendeans re-entered the Vendée.

Here, during their absence on the north side of the Loire, the republican general Westermann, a thief and swindler, "an *escroc* of the Palais - Royal, a leader in the attack of the Tuileries, but of incredible courage," had appeared conspicuously on the scene, and had given the first demonstration of the revolutionary system of carrying on the war. He announced to all that he would burn and deliver over to pillage all the communes which should furnish recruits to the rebels, or give them any other assistance. "That will make the peasant tremble," he wrote; "this terrible example is necessary to stop the torrent which will destroy the Republic."

And he promptly proceeded to put his threats into execution.

On the 1st July he attacked the village of Amaillou, and as a reprisal for some Vendean pillage at Parthenay he delivered it up to pillage. But that was not all: he set fire to it and burned it to the ground; also the castle of Clisson, belonging to M. de Lescure.

"Here," wrote Savary, the most reliable historian of the war—a republican—"began the atrocities which were called reprisals."

Soon after this, he inflicted a severe defeat on the Vendeans at Châtillon, having signalised his march thither by "robbery, assassination, incendiary fire, pillage, and devastation."

His actions drew from the Vendean chiefs a strong protest in an address to the republican troops.

". . . You bathe inhumanly in the blood of our soldiers whom the fate of battle delivers into your hands. You penetrate into the retreats where our Vendean wounded still dispute with death over the languishing remains of a mutilated body. You plunge into their bosom the murderous steel. . . . You set fire to the dwellings and the crops of those whom you have not been able to conquer.

"O Frenchmen, is this then the boasted humanity? Are these the bitter fruits of the chimera of Liberty of which the phantom deceives and seduces you?"

Protests or appeals such as these had little weight, and the Vendeans, stung by his treatment, attacked him on the 5th near Châtillon, and almost annihilated his army. One republican battalion alone was reduced from 469 men to 17.

Westermann was forthwith denounced by his fellow-republicans as a traitor, and summoned to appear before the Convention. Under ordinary circumstances he would have been guillotined, but, being a creature of Ronsin's, things were made easy for him, and he was sent back to his command.

Any charge against a general was always listened to

if he had any leaven of the old régime about him whilst complaints made about the more advanced revolutionary generals were quietly ignored. The true sans-culotte could, in the eyes of the Revolutionary Government, do no wrong.

The explanation was that the "true republican" held that "liberty and equality could never be maintained by those against whom the Revolution had been made"; and that "the true means of saving the army and the country was summarily to get rid of all generals or officers who had any taint of *la noblesse* about them," and to compose it of generals "really sans-culottes in manners and principles."

"It is a great truth, and one on which our future success depends—republican commanders and we shall beat our enemies."

Biron, not being a sans-culotte, but one of the old régime, was denounced secretly by Rossignol about the middle of July, on an absolutely false charge, and was summoned to Paris—the first step to the scaffold: and Rossignol, one of "the conquerors of the Bastille,"—who had presided at the massacres of La Force,—who was an avowed assassin,—who had been currying favour with the troops by meeting them as they returned from forays and giving them glasses of brandy, and who now was at the bottom of most of the lies and intrigues against the generals, was made commander-in-chief. Ronsin became his chief of the staff and practically directed everything.

The rapidity with which revolutionary favourites were pushed on was remarkable. Even under the monarchy no parallel could be found for it. Military experience or knowledge was not required—only revolutionary principles and fervour—and men were given high military appointments who had no military knowledge, and who had not even mounted guard. Thus Grammont, a comic actor in Paris, was made " adjutant-general." Thus Ronsin became on the 1st July a captain of cavalry: on 2nd July he was given the command of a squadron; on the 3rd he was made chief of a brigade: and on the 4th, a general of brigade: and at the end of the month, chief of the staff—under Rossignol.

Rossignol's promotion was nearly as rapid. From a colonelcy on 3rd July he was promoted to be commander-in-chief before the end of the month.

The example of ferocity and destruction set by Westermann was quickly followed by other republicans, and soon became the common republican practice. It had been decided to strengthen the military forces at Nantes: a force of some 14,000 men started from Tours. Their own generals, Berthier and Dutruy, thus described the march: " During this march, in a country where the greater part of the inhabitants are devoted to the Republic, a great part of the troops gave themselves up to the most frightful pillage and violence— patriots were no more spared than suspected rebels: all were pillaged: and the small amount of discipline which had been previously established was in a moment lost. The battalions of Paris made daily requisitions of silver and other effects, contrary to the regulations, and they threatened not to march if their demands were not complied with. Many of them sold their boots and their arms, and when arrested replied that these things belonged to them, inasmuch their sections in Paris had given them to them. Santerre even had his life threatened."

Reports from other places also confirm this complete demoralisation of the republican troops.

In the force assembled at Saumur, after its abandonment by the Vendeans, it was impossible to establish discipline, or prevent pillage and drunkenness.

Hazard, one of the National Commissioners, wrote July 1st :—

"The decree which excludes women from the battalions is entirely evaded. One sees in the following of our armies a prodigious multitude of women dressed as men. The camps are infested with them. You know the unfortunate results of such an abuse. I will not disguise from you that these women have such an influence on the *esprit* of the battalions that they direct at their caprice the discontent, the insubordination, and the indiscipline of the soldiers and the officers. . . Many generals even participate in it."

And a commissioner of the Commune of Paris who was with the army wrote to a member of that Commune (July 28th) :—

"I cannot report to you all the violations, thefts, and assassinations which the men of 500 livres commit in the army. I will cite some which will make you tremble (*frémir*). They violated in the arms of her mother the daughter of the Mayor of Saumur, aged nineteen years. Two servants of the same house suffered the same fate. These women died of despair in the camp at Chinon."

All which is a most interesting picture of the revolutionary soldier in his own country, and particularly of such revolutionary *crème* as the Parisian volunteer.

Valiant pillagers, they were not much of fighters; for attacked by the Vendeans at Vihiers on the 18th July, they promptly ran away, leaving guns and stores in the hands of the victors; some flying so far that they did not stop till they got to Paris. "Our laurels are

turned into cypress, owing to the imbecility of Santerre,"
wrote Mercier.

And again on the 26th July they ran away at Ponts-
de-Cé, nearly 400, it was said, perishing in the river.
These are not the inventions of counter-revolutionists.
The Representatives themselves affirm the dreadful state
of the army.

"Every one knows that the cowardice of our troops
has caused all our misfortunes," wrote Choudieu, a red-
hot Montagnard.   And Momoro, another Representative,
wrote, "Our troops won't fight"; and he consoles himself
with the reflection, "It is easy for the rebels to conquer
men who don't want to resist them."

The Vendean victory of Vihiers had important consequences, as it drove the Convention into the adoption
of more severe measures.

At the end of July the general position of the
Republican Government was very critical.   Lyons, Mar-
seilles, Toulon, had withdrawn themselves from the
authority of the Convention : Mayence and Valenciennes
had capitulated to the Allies : the frontiers were invaded.
A fever of fear and rage took possession of the men in
power : and ideas of moderation of any sort were thrown
to the wind.

Now literally breathing fire and fury against the
Vendeans, the Convention, on the 1st August, decreed
that fire should be added to the sword.

Barère in addressing the Convention said : "In ex-
tirpating evil one is doing good.   Louvois was blamed
by history for having burned the Palatinate, and
Louvois ought to be blamed for it, for he worked for
tyrants.

"The Palatinate of the Republic is the Vendée.
Destroy it, and you save the Patrie. . . . The Committee

of Public Safety has prepared measures which tend to exterminate this rebel race of Vendeans, to destroy their haunts, to burn their forests, to cut down their crops."

The Minister of War was ordered to send down "combustibles" of every kind to burn the woods and copses in the Vendée.

The forests were to be hewn down: the haunts of the rebels were to be destroyed: the crops were to be cut and carried to the rear of the armies; and the cattle were to be seized.

The women, children, and sick were to be removed from it, and conducted into the interior of France, where provision would be made for their subsistence and safety, " with all due regard to humanity." All the property of the rebels was declared to belong to the Republic, and was to be used to indemnify those who had remained faithful.

A *levée en masse* of all male citizens between sixteen and sixty years of age in the surrounding localities was to be made for the purpose of crushing the rebels. And all the resources of revolutionary, indeed of scientific, ingenuity were ransacked for devices whereby to crush the Vendeans. Indeed "at this time there was no scheme, however wild, which the revolutionists were not disposed to try." "Mines, some powerful mines," suggested Santerre, "some soporific vapours, and then, fall upon them."

In due course five waggon-loads of sulphur were sent down from Paris—scarcely enough to do much burning with, but enough to prove that the decisions of the Convention were no idle threats.

It was a ferocious decree, passed too " with enthusiasm after one of the most lightning-laden reports of Barère." It was the deliberate avowal of the intention of the

Government to make a desert of the Vendée. Even the
presence of a large number of "patriots" or republicans
in the district to be destroyed—to whom the carrying
out of the decree would be complete ruin, and expatria-
tion—did not induce the Convention to hesitate. Innocent and guilty were alike involved in a common fate.
Revolutionary justice could not stay to discriminate.

But that the French revolutionist was dead to every
idea of policy except extermination and annihilation, the
thought might have occurred to him which was so
pathetically expressed by Biron in one of his reports:—

"Here, Frenchmen fall under the blows of Frenchmen. The villages which we ravage belong to us. The
harvests, the crops which we destroy are our property;
and all the blood which is shed is ours."

Sentiments such as these, however, were not "revolutionary." And the Convention bent all its energies towards the absolute wiping out of the Vendeans.

There was one phase of republican brutality which
was early noticeable in the Vendean strife, and which
as time went on became ever more and more conspicuous,
until it reached a height which stamped the French
revolutionist as a being of the most cowardly, debased,
and degraded type of humanity.

This was their treatment of women.

Cruel and fearful as was the treatment meted out to
men by the revolutionists, their treatment of women was
infinitely worse.

The defencelessness of women, their weakness, their
position of dependence on others, awoke no sense of pity
or consideration in the heart of the "brave republican":
their helplessness appealed in no way to the *vrai sans-
culotte* except as an encouragement to violence and
brutality.

The Committee of Public Safety and the Convention on some occasions meted out a less rigorous treatment to women than to men; but in most of their decrees, and those their most severe ones, no such discrimination was used.

And the local authorities and the Revolutionary Committees vigorously enforced those laws; and girls and women of all ages were swept into prison on any charge, and from there to the Revolutionary Tribunals or to the Military Commissions and thence to death; while by the military forces they were given but short shrift.

And the Representatives inspired and aided, abetted and encouraged this cowardly work.   Two of them, Garnier (de Saintes) and Mazade, wrote to the Convention in June: "It is the women and children and old people who do us the greatest harm, partly because they come among us and find out our plans and our strength. . . . It is necessary as our forces advance to carry off the women and children and place them in the interior of the Republic."

And they were effectually "carried off," by bullet or bayonet, and, in a very literal sense, "placed in the interior of the Republic."

A more formidable foe to the Vendeans than the five waggon-loads of sulphur was the large body of seasoned and experienced soldiers and capable generals which was sent with all possible speed to the Vendée about the end of August.

After the capture of Mayence and of Valenciennes by the Allies, the garrisons of those towns were allowed to return to France, on signing an engagement not to carry arms again within a year against the Allies, and the Committee of Public Safety ordered the troops so set free to proceed with all possible speed to the Vendée.

The 15,000 to 16,000 troops so sent were a formidable addition to the power of the Revolutionary Government in the Vendée. The men—"men of iron," as they were called—were well trained in the sharp school of experience; they knew what discipline was, and how to fight; their officers had acquired valuable knowledge of actual warfare, while several of them were brilliant generals.

Their arrival in the Vendée gave rise to fresh jealousies and divisions among the self-seeking worthless crew of sans-culotte Representatives and generals there, each of whom became anxious to get them placed under his command so as to reap the glory of their successes.

"The report alone of their arrival," wrote the Minister of War, "should make the rebels tremble."

But trembling was not a Vendean characteristic; and the Vendeans only braced themselves up still further to encounter the fresh and more formidable onslaught of the republicans.

The crisis of the struggle was now rapidly approaching. France was sore beset by foreign enemies, and revolutionary measures multiplied as danger increased.

By decree of the 23rd August the Convention put all Frenchmen in permanent requisition for military service.

On the 5th September it decreed the creation of a revolutionary army in Paris, and put the final seal and stamp to the policy of the Government by the celebrated resolution: "Plaçons la terreur à l'ordre du jour" ("Let terror be the order of the day"). As a matter of fact government by terror had already long been the order of the day.

The Vendeans were nevertheless quite undaunted. On the 5th September they lost a battle at Luçon, but the same day they won a great victory at Chantonay over Lecomte, against whom a plot had been made by the sans-culotte generals to secure the destruction of a man of too great promise. And on the 18th they won another at Coron over some 28,000 republicans, with Ronsin and Santerre at their head, and captured 12 guns and some 4000 prisoners.

On the 19th at Pont-Barré they won another battle, and the same day another at Torfou,[1] beating even the Mayençais troops under Kleber.

Two days later they beat the republicans at Montaigu, and the following day they were again victorious at St. Fulgent.

Thus five great battles were won in eight days.

Even the war-seasoned troops from Mayence had failed to check the victorious career of the Vendeans—animated as they still were by the deep religious enthusiasm which had carried them to victory in the earlier contests. "We fight for Jesus Christ," they said.

On one occasion a Vendean chief remonstrated against the men stopping to pray at a cross. "Let them pray," said Lescure, "they will fight the better for it."

On another occasion, where they were certain to be overwhelmed by numbers, they cried aloud, "Let us march to heaven," and they dashed at the battalions of the enemy, happy to rush on martyrdom.

---

[1] Strong grounds exist for the suspicion that the military plans which led up to the battle of Torfou were designed by Rossignol and Ronsin as a pitfall for the Mayençais troops, whom they hated, and who were likely to end the war quicker than suited the desires of these and other sans-culotte generals and officials (see Chassin, iii. 83, 87).

And they were fighting now with the added passion
of despair: for they knew by this time that their foes
were merciless, and that they were doomed to destruction
unless they could defend themselves.

They did not march upon the enemy, they hurled
themselves upon him, closed with him, and fought him
breast to breast, with obstinacy and fury.

And sometimes, when the battle was raging, and the
musketry and artillery were heard, "the women and
children, and all the inhabitants not engaged, repaired
to the churches, or prostrated themselves in the fields,
to pray for the success of the Vendean arms. And thus
through a whole country, and at one moment, there was
but one thought, one prayer! The fate of all hung
upon the same battle."

The losses on both sides were at times tremendous.
Thousands upon thousands fell in many a battle. The
accounts read as exaggerations—doubtless they were
often so,—indeed many of the revolutionary triumphs
were pure fictions of the sans-culotte generals. That
the losses were fearful, however, is acknowledged by
Barère, who ought to have known: and who gave expression to his exasperation against the generals for their
bad measures, which, he said, had already cost more than
200,000 republican lives.

And now to the religious fervour which had fired the
Vendeans with a heroic courage, and to the determination of despair, was added the fury of revenge.

With the exception of the Mayençais officers and
troops, the great bulk of revolutionary forces had carried
on the war in the most merciless fashion. From the
general down to the lowest rank, they had given free
rein to every vice. Villages and farms had been pillaged
and burned; every form of movable property had been

carried off: prisoners had been massacred in cold blood, and non-combatants had been seized and slaughtered.

"We execute your decree (of 1st August) to the letter," wrote the Representatives to the Convention, early in September,—that terrible decree ordering the burning and destruction of the Vendée.

"This great act of national severity strikes salutary terror into the hearts of the rebels. Great heaps of ashes, and famine, and death present themselves on every side to their eyes."

Of the barbarities committed during these autumn months a captain of the republican army, "an eye-witness and actor in the cruel war," has given an account in a letter to Robespierre.

"As soon as our army had entered the Vendée each soldier from that moment put to death whom he pleased, and pillaged whom he pleased, on the pretext that he whom he killed or pillaged was a rebel or a favourer of rebels, or thought as a royalist. No punishment has been inflicted, no precaution taken to repress or moderate the ardour for blood and pillage. Judge, then, to what excess the fury of the scoundrel has been carried, freed from the restraint of the law. Judge how many innocents have fallen victims to brigandage.

"I see among us men who do not cease to incite to carnage : who breathe only blood (*qui ne respirent que le sang*), who take a pleasure in butchering an unfortunate and defenceless wretch who has fallen into their hands,—and who fly at the first shot."

The exasperation caused by the cruel butchery of relatives found expression at times, and not unnaturally, in reprisals : and prisoners sometimes received but short shrift from some of the Vendeans : but considering the desperate provocation they had received, the instances

bore but an infinitesimal proportion to the wholesale
infamies of the revolutionists.

The *levée en masse* called together " by the tocsin of
Liberty " did not help the revolutionists.    It brought
together masses of men—50,000 it was said,—Barère
said 400,000,—" a fabulous army," in the double sense.
Unarmed and undisciplined and ill-disposed to fight, they
were an embarrassment to the republicans instead of a
help.

Against the Vendeans they were worse than useless.
Some fled at the first contact with the Vendeans; others
disappeared without even having seen the enemy ; some
were sent home because they had learned to pillage and
violate.    The *levée en masse* melted away.

# CHAPTER IX

## THE VENDEAN WAR

## PART V

THE successive victories of the Vendeans once more made the Revolutionary Government in Paris wild with fury, and it bent itself with greater energy to the task of crushing the Vendeans.

On the 1st October, Barère made a long report to the Convention:—

"The inexplicable Vendée exists still . . . and the efforts of the republicans up to this have been powerless against the brigandage, and the plots of the royalists concealed there. The Vendée threatens to become a dangerous volcano. . . . To the *levée en masse* of the Vendeans we opposed the *levée en masse* of the entire country, . . . but a panic of terror struck all, frightened all, dissipated all like a vapour."

And then, apparently with the object of exciting feeling against even women and children, and of justifying both the past and the future treatment of them which is so appalling a feature of the revolutionary despotism, he said :

"The brigands from the age of ten to sixty are in

requisition by the proclamation of the Vendean chiefs.
The women act as scouts or vedettes. The entire
population of the revolted country is in rebellion, and
in arms."

And, as the crowning incitement to exasperation
against the Vendeans, he declared that the Representatives at Nantes had proofs of the communication of the
Vendeans with the English.

Some of the defeats he attributed to the cowardice—
not of French republicans, for that would have been
too much for him to admit—but of some battalions
composed of foreigners, Neapolitans, Germans, and
Genoese, picked up in the streets of Paris by the
aristocrats, who had made this present to them—also
to some *émigrés* who had enrolled themselves among
the republican troops.

But he admitted that the Vendeans had made progress owing to the insatiable avarice of the administrators
of the army, who made a trade of war; who speculated
on battles being lost; who made their profits on the
disasters of their country; who increased their wealth
by the duration of the war; who opposed the military
plans of campaign so as to prolong the period of their
profits; and who enriched themselves by the piles of
dead.

But instead of his turning the wrath of the Convention on these sans-culottes, he impassionedly rang out
the changes on the phrase " Destroy the Vendée!"
" Destroy the Vendée!"

This was the revolutionary remedy for everything
that ran counter to the Revolution—destruction and
annihilation. Revolutionary intelligence appeared unable
to rise above this very primitive and barbaric policy.

If the term " administrator" included generals, his

description was not alone not exaggerated, but fell far short of the truth; for it was the sans-culotte generals and officers, as well as the administrators, who were to a great extent the cause of the military breakdown.

The more sans-culotte the generals were, the worse they were. Curious revelations from time to time were made as to the scandalous luxury of the generals of the Republic and of the Representatives of the people there. The volunteers who returned to Paris recounted how General Santerre lived in Asiatic luxury; that he had the most splendid carriages, the best cooks, the prettiest women. Berruyer's practices were also exposed: " Never has a general paraded such insolent luxury; one only appears before him with bended knee."

Philippeaux, a Representative, described the division at Saumur as commanded by "chiefs without morals, without talent, without mind (*âme*), moustached braggarts (*fanfarons à moustaches*) who are going to sabre every one and finish the war, but who, when the moment comes for fulfilling their promises, skulk in the rearguard or decamp at full gallop without firing a shot."

Cavaignac, another Representative, wrote of them as being "fools, drunkards, or knaves . . . men without talent and without experience; invisible in the morning, and after dinner inapproachable (*intraitable* )."

And this drinking braggart lot were as dissolute as they were stupid and incapable. Philippeaux describes as having seen with his own eyes "one of the superior officers who had sprung from the mountebank's stage to his grade of rank, affording the shameless spectacle of four courtesans (*republican Dubarrys* ) seated in a gorgeous vehicle and escorted by fifty men," going to see something of camp life, five days after the defeat at

Vihiers, " when all republicans ought to have been in a state of consternation."

Reubell, another Representative, wrote to " My dear Barère," telling him that while the generals were reporting victory upon victory they were losing their cannons and their stores.

" They only occupy themselves in inventing lies to conceal their defeats, and they console themselves for all their griefs by the pleasures of the table, and in the arms of *les sales Vénus*, with whom they concert the plans of calumny against those who do not resemble them."

Philippeaux further remarked : " The Asiatic luxury of the generals, their orgies, their examples of licentiousness presented to the soldiers, tended to make of our armies a mob of men without restraint and without courage, no less formidable to the peaceable inhabitants than to the rebels themselves."

Rossignol, the commander-in-chief and a " true sans-culotte," had a little while back set an example of shameless pillage. Mercier du Rocher—a republican—has given the details. Rossignol, accompanied by Bourbotte, a Representative, arrived at Fontenay on the night of the 21st August.

The municipality lodged him and the Representative and their suite in the house of one Beaumont. The master of this house had joined the brigands, and the official seals of the Republic were placed on the contents of it. These were broken by Rossignol and his party, and the jewels and dresses of women were confiscated, to the profit of the general and his *cortège*. " There was nothing," writes Mercier, " down even to the china ware, which did not become the prey of these pillagers, who called themselves republicans and who took about with them showy harlots. The prettiest of them were for

the highest in dignity, Bourbotte the Representative,
and Rossignol: the others were left to the inferiors.
It is thus they gave the example of republican
virtues."

When leaving Fontenay, Rossignol and his party
carried away many of the things in the house, though,
being sealed, they were national property.

If Commanders-in-Chief and Representatives could do
such things, what was to be expected of their subordi-
nates?

Two other Representatives, Bourdon de l'Oise and Gou-
pilleau de Fontenay, with stricter ideas of what was right
and wrong, suspended Rossignol for his misconduct,
and sent him to Paris. Here he appeared before the
Convention. "My heart, my soul," he said, "all is my
country's *Tout est à ma patrie*." And the Convention,
which canted itself, and gravely accepted the cant of its
officers, invited him to the honours of the sitting, and
sent him back to his position of commander-in-chief,
and recalled to its bosom the two Representatives who
had suspended him.

These then were the men who were the product of the
new régime, the upholders of the banner of the sublime
principles of "liberty, equality, and fraternity," under
which they were supposed to be fighting.

The anomaly of the thing struck Philippeaux, one of the
Representatives. "It is a strange thing," he wrote, "that
the royalist soldiers fight for despotism as veritable sans-
culottes, without gratuities, without pay, with a piece of
bad bread for food; while we, for the sublime cause of
Liberty, make a war of slaves and sybarites."

After hearing Barère's report, the Convention declared
that it "counted on the courage of the army of the west,
and of the generals who commanded it, to terminate

between that date and the 20th October the execrable war of the Vendée."

But it did more. It placed on record as its deliberate opinion and will the cruel and merciless decision that extermination was to be the fate of all the brigands in the Vendée.

It was a record appealed to in later time by Representative and officers alike as their justification for the iniquities which later they were charged with having perpetrated.

A proclamation by the Convention was issued on 1st October.

"Soldiers of Liberty—It is imperative that the brigands of the Vendée be exterminated before the end of October : the safety of the country exacts it ; the impatience of the French people commands it ; its courage ought to accomplish it."

And now great activity prevailed among the republicans.

All the generals who had any taint of *la noblesse* about them were got rid of ; even some sans-culottes were removed, Grammont and Santerre among the number ; Ronsin was given another appointment, and Rossignol was transferred to Brest : and as commander-in-chief there was appointed L'Échelle, "a man of the people, an old soldier," described by Kleber "as being the most ignorant of chiefs one has ever seen, knowing nothing of the map, and scarcely able even to write his name."

Imperative communications passed from the executive in Paris to the Representatives and generals in the Vendée. More skilful and combined plans were devised against the Vendeans. Every effort was to be made to crush, to exterminate them. The Government in Paris was in deadly earnest, and the sans-culotte generals were made to understand that no scheming or skulking would be tolerated, that they had no alternative but to fight or die on the scaffold.

The outcome of all the changes was that the actual —as apart from the nominal—command passed into the hands of a real soldier like Kleber, and a complete change came over the fortunes of the Republic.

The Vendeans themselves felt that everything was working up towards the crisis.

" In spite of such repeated successes," wrote one of their leaders, " in spite of so many brilliant victories, the clouds which had been dispersed soon began to gather again, and formed a fresh storm."

Gradually they were being hemmed in by superior forces.

They were embarrassed, too, by the vast number of non-combatants—the whole population, women, children, old people, sick and wounded, all flying before the advance of the republicans, to avoid massacre, and seeking safety behind the ranks of their own people.

" The army of the Republic," wrote the Representatives, " is preceded everywhere by terror. Steel and fire are now the only weapons we make use of."

On the 6th October the Vendeans were beaten at St. Symphorien.

On the 9th at Moulin aux Chèvres. " Six leagues in circumference are covered with dead," wrote L'Échelle, with considerable exaggeration.

On the 11th an almost lost battle was turned into a republican victory, and from the Government in Paris came fresh incitements.

On the 9th October the Committee of Public Safety

issued a savage proclamation to the troops, hounding them on to the extermination of the rebels. The triumphant example was held up to them of the republican army at Lyons, which at that moment was "cutting all the traitors there to pieces," and where it was declared that not a single one of " the vile and cruel satellites of despotism should escape."

" And you also, brave soldiers : you will obtain a victory. For long enough now has the Vendée wearied the Republic. March, strike, and make an end of it. All our enemies ought to fall at one and the same time. Each army will conquer. Will you be the last to gather the palms, to merit the glory of having exterminated the rebels and saved the country ? Hurl yourselves on the mad and ferocious hordes : crush them so that each one may say to himself, ' To-day the Vendée is being annihilated, and the Vendée will be conquered.' "

Events other than those in the Vendée were resulting in the very concentration of despotism in the hands of the Committee of Public Safety in Paris.

On the 10th October the Convention decreed that the government should be " revolutionary " until peace came ; and declared that " no other law would be followed but that of public safety." The Constitution was suspended, and the Committee of Public Safety was practically made dictator.

For the moment these changes did not affect the Vendée. There everything depended on the military campaign, the fortunes of which were hanging in the balance. The Vendeans were being gradually forced back on Cholet, fighting day after day, now winning a victory, now suffering defeat, ever coming nearer the supreme hour, the decisive struggle.

The enormities committed by the Blues, or republicans, in their advance, pillage and burning and cruelties of all sorts, had excited universal horror and indignation, and the Vendean chiefs were resolved to die or conquer in the approaching battle.

On the 17th the decisive battle was fought near Cholet. The republicans numbered about 22,000 men, including the bulk of the Mayençais troops, who bore the brunt of the day.

The Vendeans had about 40,000 under d'Elbée and Bonchamps.

The fall of these most trusted and capable leaders—both of whom were fearfully wounded—in great measure decided the fate of the day.

After a desperate fight, and heavy losses on both sides, the Vendeans were defeated; and the capture of Beaupreau, the same night, completed their discomfiture.

"Never," wrote Kleber, "have they fought so stubbornly; never in such disciplined order; but never has a day been so disastrous for them. The rebels fought like tigers—our soldiers like lions."

This disastrous defeat of the Vendeans was in great measure, if not entirely, due to the division between the various Vendean leaders. In the absence of a royal prince, or of any one of commanding position, to take supreme command, personal rivalries were great, and serious differences had most unfortunately arisen between the Vendean chiefs, differences as regards objects and as regards the means of attaining those objects.

These differences had already come to such a head that Charette with his army—a no inconsiderable force—had retired to Légé, thus weakening the Vendean fighting power, and endangering the Vendean cause in the supreme hour of its trial.

But this was not all. Among those that remained

there was confusion of counsel. Before the battle
actually took place, certain of the chiefs decided that in
case of defeat the Vendeans should cross the Loire, and
preparations for that contingency had in part been
made; but so deep was the intrigue that d'Elbée, the
commander-in-chief, was not informed of the intention.

He and Bonchamps, being disabled from further
action, and the dreaded defeat having taken place, the
decision was given effect to. The Vendean army was
to leave the Vendée, and to seek in Brittany supplies and
food and allies or recruits among the peasantry, and to
secure a port where they could obtain the help which
the leaders expected or hoped to obtain from England.

There were most serious objections to this course,
which, in reality, was adopted with a regard to royalist
aims and ambitions, rather than to the interests of the
Vendeans themselves, but it obtained plausibility from
the fact that there seemed to be no other outlet of
escape. Masses of fugitives from revolutionary fraternity,
women and children and old persons, had fled in the
direction of the river. What remained of the army had
no choice but to go after them.

And here occurred an incident which throws much
light on the character of the *vrai républicain*.

The Vendean army, in full retreat, reached St. Florent
on the bank of the Loire. Here some 4000 to 5000 republican prisoners were confined in Vendean custody. The
suggestion was made that they should be put to death.
Infuriated by defeat, and still more by the barbarous
cruelties so systematically inflicted by the Blues, the suggestion fell on willing ears. Cries were raised for their
death. But, suddenly, the order that they were to be
spared passed through the Vendean ranks.

Tradition gives the honour, and truly and unmistakably so, to Bonchamps, the Vendean leader, who, wounded to the death, was lying in a cottage near by, and heard the cries. His dying request to the men he had so often led to victory was that the prisoners might be spared. And his men respected his wish, and the prisoners were not alone spared but released.

It was a splendid display of Vendean generosity. The prisoners themselves all proclaimed that Bonchamps was their liberator. Kleber also bore witness to the fact. But it was not so regarded by the Representative Merlin (de Thionville), a shining light of the Revolution, who wrote to the Committee of Public Safety :—

" These cowardly enemies of the nation (the Vendeans) have spared more than 4000 of our men who were their prisoners. Some of those of our men allowed themselves to be touched by this trait of incredible hypocrisy. I harangued them, and they soon understood that they were under no debt of gratitude to the brigands.

" But as the nation has not yet reached the height of our patriotic sentiments, you would act wisely in not breathing a word about such an indignity. Free men accepting life from the hand of slaves! It is not revolutionary. This unfortunate action must be buried in oblivion. Do not speak of it even in the Convention. The brigands have no time to write or to start newspapers, and so it will be forgotten like many other things."

But the incident has not been forgotten—has not fallen into oblivion—nor will the light which this letter of Merlin throws upon the grotesque abortions of the revolutionary mind be forgotten either. The incident is too instructive to be so.

Three other Representatives. Hentz. Francastel, and

Prieur (de la Marne), evidently thought that a lie would
be the best way of dealing with it, for they wrote:—

"We have had the satisfaction to deliver at St.
Florent 5500 of our republicans."

One Representative, Choudieu, had the decency to
avow the truth.

"It is a pleasure to me here," he wrote, "to render
to Bonchamps full and signal justice (*une éclatante
justice*). Brave men do not assassinate their enemy when
he is disarmed."

The republicans did not follow up their great victory
quite as quickly as they might have done, and their
prey had time to escape them—across the Loire.

The passage of that river by the Vendean fugitives
was a most pathetic scene. Madame de Lescure, who
was flying with the others and tending her dying
husband, who had been wounded a few days before, has
described it.

"We arrived early at St. Florent, and then I saw
the greatest and the saddest sight which can be imagined.
The heights of St. Florent form a kind of semicircular
boundary to a vast level strand reaching to the Loire,
which is very wide at this place. Eighty thousand
people were crowded together in this valley—soldiers,
women, children, the aged, and the wounded, flying from
immediate destruction. . . . Nothing was heard but
loud sobs, groans, and cries. . . . Many of us compared
this disorder, this despair, this terrible uncertainty of
the future, this immense spectacle, this bewildered crowd,
this valley, this river which must be crossed, to the
ideas of the last judgment."

With much difficulty the Vendean army and fugitives
got over by boats and rafts.

And for a few days, on the north side of the rapid flowing river, uninterfered with by the republican troops, they obtained breathing time before beginning another act of the sad drama.

This battle of Cholet was the second great crisis in the Vendean war.

By their courage and perseverance the Vendeans had retrieved the disaster of their defeat at Nantes. Now, however, in addition to the defeat just experienced at Cholet, a decision was taken by the leaders which led the Vendeans to irretrievable disaster. Worse could not have befallen them. The fate of almost every individual in that vast crowd was sealed.

Descriptions of military movements, of the advances and retreats of great opposing forces—of their battles, their victories, and defeats—interesting as they are, leave, however, the great underneath untouched. And one must pierce through the appearance of things, and go down into the individualities so to speak, to at all comprehend or realise the real purport and meaning of it all.

Men's sympathies are moved, and their hearts thrilled, by the suffering of a single individual, when they see and realise it; their indignation is stirred by the sight of a single crime; their wrath flashes up at a single act of injustice.

But suffering, crime, and injustice on a large scale, en masse as it were, and the effect is too stunning to be at once appreciated. One does not take in what it really is.

Here, on the visible surface, was the flight or migration of a great struggling mass of some 80,000 to 100,000 people; but underneath, in each individual case, what unutterable agony and heartbreak.

Everything that each individual of that vast crowd

loved most dearly, and prized most highly, had just been
torn from their possession.

At night, the red flames which lighted up the dark
sky with a lurid glow: in day, the volumes of thick
smoke on the horizon ascending into the heavens, told
each of the destruction of their home, and with it the
destruction of all the joys of existence. To them it was
the tearing up of the roots of their life.

Underneath, too, was the agony of loss of nearest
relatives and friends never again to be seen—the anguish
of apprehension as to their own immediate fate, and that
of those who still remained to them—the despair that
peace, happiness, home, property, comfort, everything had
gone, gone irretrievably for ever.

Underneath, too, was the constant torturing sense of
undeserved wrong, and of the cruellest injustice.

And all these woes caused by the hands of their own
countrymen masquerading as the champions of liberty
and fraternity.

The republicans were wild with elation at the triumph
of their arms.

The commander-in-chief L'Échelle wrote to the Minister of War :—

" The Vendée, purged in eight days of the principal
gatherings of brigands emboldened by ephemeral successes, steaming with blood, strewn with corpses, and in
great part delivered to the flames, is a striking example
of national justice, which should intimidate countries in
which villainy wishes to create insurrection."

The Representatives wrote to the Committee of Public
Safety : " The National Convention wished the war to be
finished before the end of October. We can to-day tell
it that there is no longer a Vendée. A profound solitude
actually reigns in the country which the rebels occupied.

One can travel far in it without meeting a man, or a cottage: for, with scarce an exception, we have left behind us only cinders and heaps of corpses."

The Committee of Public Safety issued a proclamation, signed by Robespierre and others, to the army :—

"The defenders of the Republic have destroyed the haunts of the rebels; they have exterminated their sacrilegious cohorts: that guilty land has herself devoured the monsters she produced: the rest of them will fall under the axe of the people. . . . Republican soldiers: march, strike . . . so that tyrants and slaves may disappear from the earth."

And, on the 23rd October, Barère declared before the Convention that the Vendée existed no longer. And the Convention decreed that "there is no longer a Vendée," —which, of course, was conclusive.

# CHAPTER X

WHILE the republican military forces had, during the months of July to October, been making spasmodic efforts to cope with the Vendeans, at times defeating them, at times being defeated by them, the other revolutionary powers and authorities in or near the Vendée had unceasingly been pursuing their efforts for crushing, by other means than military measures, all who were not active supporters of the Revolution.

The fiat of extermination and destruction had gone forth. It had been reiterated, almost day after day, by the Revolutionary Government in Paris.

Extermination was the fixed idea of the revolutionary mind. All the advice tendered by revolutionists around or in the Vendée was "extermination." All their recommendations breathed nothing but bloodshed and destruction; all their prayers to the Convention were for more destruction, more bloodshed. Kill, destroy, exterminate, this was the burden of every letter, of every counsel: it was the refrain of the Convention itself.

Nothing but extermination or annihilation would satisfy the revolutionary craving for the punishment of those who had dared to lay sacrilegious hands on the ark of the new Republic. No composition should be made with the "brigands": no measures of conciliation should be thought of; not even submission on the part of the rebels would be accepted. On no terms would the Republic receive the Vendeans again into its fold. The only right it would accord them was the right to die.

The policy found ardent instruments in the army of the west, from the highest general down to the lowest private, so many of them profiting by it.

It had ardent instruments, too, from the Representatives down to the pettiest collection of village ruffians who erected themselves into a popular society, all of whom derived advantages therefrom.

And no single voice opposed it. The idea expressed in Biron's sad reminder that the villages which were being pillaged, and the crops which were being destroyed, and the blood which was being shed, were all French, found no echo in the revolutionary mind.

The defence made by the admirers of, or apologists for, this merciless and inhuman policy was that the safety of the Republic demanded it; and the sacred name of patriotism has been invoked as its justification. France, beset by foreign foes, had, it was argued, for very existence sake, to crush the enemies within her own border.

But crimes can be committed in the name of patriotism as well as in the name of liberty, and this policy of extermination must ever rank as one of the greatest of such crimes.

That it was a wholly unnecessary policy is manifest beyond question. For time after time, indeed during the whole war, the great bulk of the Vendeans would have gladly accepted peace, and have been glad to be

allowed to go back to their homes and resume the
ordinary course of their lives. It had only been in
sheer desperation that they had appealed to arms; it
was only in absolute despair that they continued to
fight. Death being the inevitable goal, if they might
not triumph they would at least sell their lives as
dearly as they could.

The Federalist insurrection, which occurred in parts
of France in July—one more stand by the more honest
and intelligent class of the people against the advancing
torrents of revolutionary bloodshed and violence—had
still further infuriated the Revolutionary Government
in Paris, which became wilder than ever, and more
terrible and ruthless in its measures of repression.

In this progressive increase of revolutionary energy
the office of Representative became of ever greater
importance, and his authority more all-embracing and
despotic.

More and more the Convention handed over to the
Representatives its own powers, and centred in them all
the might of the executive; and more and more it
insisted on their using those powers with a very
whirlwind of energy.

" Terror shall be the order of the day," it declared
on the 5th September, and it entrusted the sword of
sharpness into their hands, and ordered them to use it.
It reserved to itself still the legislative powers, but such
a tremendous coercive code was already in existence
that the Representatives stood in no need of any such
powers.

It reserved to itself, too, the power of recalling the
Representatives and appointing others in their places, a
power which it seldom failed to act on when it thought
there was any slackness or remissness in the energy of

the Representatives. It backed them up by declaring that those of their instruments who had perpetrated even the most appalling injustices and cruelties "deserved well of their country," and resolutely it turned a blind eye to any actions, however tyrannical or despotic on their part, their most extreme excesses, even finding in the Convention the protection of silence.

The Representatives themselves were not backward in taking their cue from the Convention.

Armed with this tremendous authority, and drunk, as it were, with the sense of their own importance and power, they flung themselves into their duties with infuriated energy.

And "liberty" vanished,—the "liberty" for which the Revolution had been made. And instead of "liberty," despotism and tyranny came, a tyranny compared with which previous tyranny had been that of a child's hand.

And, in the process, the revolutionists showed themselves to all the world, for all time, in their true character as the greatest impostors who have ever stepped this earth. Nearly every privilege won by the people, though confirmed to them by the Declaration of the Rights of Man and by other legislation, was promptly taken away from them. By force the revolutionists imposed on the people their tyrannical rule. With barefaced impudence they adopted all the vices of the *ancien régime*, and drew upon it for ideas and precedents for their own measures of persecution and repression. And to cover their iniquities, they were ceaselessly invoking the names of liberty and equality and fraternity, and posing as the saviours of the Patrie, and as the regenerators of humanity.

At the time there was none could gainsay them, the

penalty was too great; but history, at any rate, can tear
the mask from their faces, and expose their contradictions, their inconsistencies, their false pretences, and
their lying excuses for acts which were the absolute
negation of their professions.

There were frequent changes among the Representatives in the west. They were appointed, recalled,
reappointed, and shifted about from Department to
Department, as suited the convenience of the Convention; a sort of sifting process went on in which,
ultimately, the most violent and reckless came to the
top. And all the changes tended to an increase of
tyranny.

Their fierce restless energy knew no limits, had no
restraints. Some of them stooped to any infamy, any
cruelty, so long as they could compass their ends or
gratify their passion. They evoked and encouraged all
that was worst in the nature of the French people, and
stifled and trampled on whatever was good and generous.
They lied when a lie suited their purpose; they deceived
when deception redounded to their advantage. They
were merciless in their injustice. They deluged their
country with their countrymen's blood; and then, with
loathsome hypocrisy and effrontery, claimed credit to
themselves for the professed purity of their motives, and
for the patriotism of their conduct.

The first care of the Representatives was to secure
the mastery over, or complete co-operation of, the local
governing bodies. This they did by packing them with
their own nominees, or superseding them entirely, and
putting Revolutionary Committees or popular societies
in their place, thus taking away from the people their
newly-won right of electing their own local governing
bodies.

While they were engaged in the congenial task of establishing the reign of liberty, the Convention (on the 12th August), at the same moment that it decreed the *levée en masse* to repel the invasion of France by foreign powers, decreed in principle the arrest of all suspects.

The liability of all persons to be regarded as suspects facilitated very much the action of the Representatives; and the purged and renovated local authorities in and near the Vendée, without waiting for a law on the subject, began arresting all persons who could be considered as suspects; indeed, in many places, several months before the law on the subject was made, the practice of arresting suspected persons had been in full swing.

The celebrated *Loi des Suspects*, as enacted on the 17th September, decreed that all suspected persons who were in the territory of the Republic, and who were still at liberty, should be arrested, and that they should be detained until peace was made.

Those persons were "suspects" who either by their discourse or their writings had shown themselves partisans of tyranny or federalism, and enemies of liberty: former nobles, together with the husbands, wives, fathers, mothers, sons, and daughters, brothers and sisters, and agents of *émigrés*, who have not constantly manifested their attachment to the Revolution.

It has been urged in excuse of this severe law, that the definition of suspects was taken from royal edicts against persons of the "so-called reformed religion": but if it was so, the argument is a clear admission that the Republican Government was treading in the very steps of the iniquitous Royalist Government which it had supplanted.

About the same time that personal liberty was thus being invaded, commercial liberty was also suppressed. The people must be supplied with food. The scarcity, it was asserted, was the result of the grasping avarice of merchants, and speculators, and hoarders, who must be made disgorge; and so laws were passed (on 11th and 29th September) prescribing the fixing of the prices above which food and other articles might not be sold. Buyers and sellers had to conform to the tables of maximum, under penalty of being treated as "suspects"; and lest this should check business, merchants or manufacturers who suspended their commerce or manufactures were threatened with similar consequences.

Before the great republican victory at Cholet, the authority of the Representatives did not extend far into the Vendée itself,—the Vendeans were still masters there; so the Representatives were obliged to confine their activities to the towns and country around it.

Their procedure ran all on one line. The establishment of Revolutionary Tribunals and of Military Commissions to try counter-revolutionists and Vendean prisoners; and in the larger towns, such as Angers, Nantes, Saumur, and Fontenay, the creation of Revolutionary Committees to aid and advise them in their operations, and to carry out their policy and their behests.

Early in September (1793) two Representatives were sent to La Rochelle and Rochefort to secure those ports from foreign attack.

These two towns were south of the actual scene of the strife, but to a certain extent felt the effects of the war. A large number of prisoners taken in the Vendée had been sent to La Rochelle, and the prisons were crammed with some 800 of them.

K

Here an interesting incident happened which throws light on the character of these Representatives.

They created a Revolutionary Tribunal for the trial of some of the prisoners, and appointed the judges and all the officials except one, namely, " he who ought to close the procedure "—the executioner.   The nomination of this functionary the Representatives left to the popular society which existed there, as they wished "to destroy one of the most foolish and rooted of prejudices," contempt of the executioner.

At the meeting of the popular society held for the purpose of the election several volunteered for the post, which was by no means a sinecure, and finally a man named Ance was selected.  "I," exclaimed Ance, with noble enthusiasm, "it is I who ambition the honour of making the heads of the assassins of my patrie fall."

We have proclaimed Ance guillotineur," wrote the Representative Lequinio: "we invited him to come and dine with us, and take his powers from us in writing, and to libate them in honour of the Republic."  And the executioner was given the name of "Avenger of the people": and to the guillotine an inscription in large letters was attached describing it as "The people's justice" (Justice du peuple).

Here a Military Commission was also formed 'on the 28th September, by Lequinio, and a letter of his shows in what a state of dependence upon the Representative these courts were, how completely they were under his control, and what a small chance a prisoner had of fair treatment.

I ordered," wrote Lequinio, "the commissioners to sentence in accordance with the law 'that is to say, to death all the former priests, bourgeois, nobles, tax-gatherers, and deserters: and to sentence only to the galleys the workmen and labourers whose profound ignorance had enabled them to be misled."

In the larger towns the measures taken by the Representatives were on a larger and naturally bolder scale.

At Angers the revolutionists who had run away had returned, embittered by the disgrace of their flight, and keen for any atrocities which might rehabilitate their revolutionary reputation.

Here the most active of the Representatives was Choudieu, a man whose views and character can be gauged from the fact of his being president of the Society of Jacobins in Paris at the time of the September massacres there. He was extremely violent in temper, pitiless and cruel, a bitter persecutor, enforcing the tyranny of the terror with unswerving severity, sacrificing old friends in his Montagnard fervour, leaving even his mother in the clutches of revolutionary law and in peril of life for a period which he might easily have curtailed. " In revolution one is inexorable," he wrote : and inexorable he certainly was in all his proceedings in the west.

One Military Commission had been appointed in June. A fresh one was appointed by the Representatives on the 10th July, with Felix as president. But a far more important and powerful body was the Revolutionary Committee which had been appointed there, in July also, by the Representatives. It consisted of some ten or twelve members—all men of the extremest republican ideas and desperate character, true sans-culottes— with a renegade priest as president. The closeness of the connection between a Revolutionary Committee and the Representative is proved by the fact that Choudieu himself is known to have presided at it.

This Committee was to employ every means it thought proper for obtaining information about individuals suspected of rebellion, treason, incivism, or of a counter-revolutionary disposition. It was given power to arrest, examine, and imprison all who were denounced to it, as well as any persons who furthered the projects of the rebels, and it could call in the National Guard for the execution of its decrees. Practically it possessed the power of life and death over every citizen of Angers. Everything was under its rule, and nothing was done except with its good pleasure and approval. Police, military, administration, worship, justice,—in one word, everything was subject to its absolute autocratic power.

Its first act was a decree stating: "The Committee, considering that the institution of a Revolutionary Committee ought to inspire with confidence all good citizens, and with terror all bad ones," ordered that henceforth no one should go out of the town except he had a passport.

And the next thing it did was to take possession of the post-office, as two of its members went there and opened all letters to suspects, or which appeared suspicious. Having thus shut the gates of the town and barred escape, the revolutionists proceeded in their usually cowardly fashion to wreak their wrath on their helpless victims.

On 2nd September the Committee, anticipating the law of suspects, ordered domiciliary visits in the town and suburbs to arrest "*émigrés, déportés,* brigands, spies, agents of the enemies of the Republic, suspected persons, and generally all the counter-revolutionists of the two sexes who might be found in private houses."

And this same Committee, in its career of despotic

government, afforded another illustration of the frequent adoption of measures of the *ancien régime* by the revolutionists.

It might, for very manifest reasons, be thought that the people who had made a Revolution to put an end to tyranny and the host of abuses of a Royalist Government would have fought very shy of adopting any of the hated practices of its predecessors; that that would have been the very last thing they would have done.

But, so far as the French revolutionist is concerned, any such idea is completely erroneous. Whenever it served their purpose to follow royalist forms of tyranny, they did not hesitate to do so.

" Denunciation " had been one of the practices inveighed against in the most vehement language, and yet in one of its decrees the Committee wrote : " Denunciations, odious in the *ancien régime,* because they were of service to tyranny, are become legitimate because they tend to-day to the good of all. The Committee invites all good citizens to come and declare to them all that they know against the interests of the Republic."

The departmental authorities of La Mayenne went even a little further, and declared that "the first and noblest of the duties of a Republic is civic denunciation."

This theory of denunciation erected into a republican virtue was everywhere applied and set in work, and it became one of the great *moyens* or instruments of the revolutionary administrators.

This Revolutionary Committee at Angers " soon dominated all the constituted authorities in the town, carried disquietude and fright among all classes in all families, and furnished to the Military Commission an ample pasturage of human victims."

Until August 1793 the municipality of Angers had been more or less moderate and pacific. Its hand was then forced by the extremer parties, as in other places, and it was compelled to submit to the Revolutionary Committee.

In the course of October two other Representatives were sent to Angers, Hentz and Francastel, Choudieu taking other work in the neighbourhood. It was a change for the worse for all who were not sans-culottes of the *vrai*-est type, for they were men who hesitated at no injustice, no amount of cruelty or bloodshed which served their purposes.

Thus by the end of October, so far as Angers was concerned, all preparations had been completed, and all the machinery got into working order for the new régime of "liberty, equality, and fraternity."

In Saumur, which though a small town was strategically of great importance, revolutionary organisation proceeded on identically the same lines as at Angers.

The Revolutionary Committee which had been appointed here had been working diligently, crushing out the last vestiges of religious liberty: but when Hentz and Francastel came, it was not deemed to be up to the mark, and they "purified" it, appointing some new and more revolutionary members.

The most influential person on the reorganised committee was Lepetit, "a sinister gamin of eighteen" whom Bourbotte had employed for some time as his secretary, and who had come to Tours with the battalions of Paris; and he was aided by Vilnau, "a pale copy of Robespierre," and some others of the same type.

To bring revolutionary inquisitorialness down to the minutest sections of the people, the town, small though it was, was divided into four sections: and in each section there was appointed a committee of surveillance —diminutive Revolutionary Committees in fact.

And as if all this were not enough, there was a "Society of the Friends of Liberty and Equality," composed of the worst elements of the Saumur population, to aid the Revolutionary Committee in its work.

The Military Commission of Angers was within easy reach, and came over whenever its services were required.

The revolutionary organisation at Saumur was therefore complete; and at its head were Hentz and Francastel, who, according to Turreau's later dictum, were "worth more than an army to the Republic."

In Nantes the preparations were on the same lines as those in Angers and Saumur.

Carrier had been for some time one of the Representatives in the west, and at the end of September Heraut Seychelles wrote to him from Paris in the name of the Committee of Public Safety: "We implore you to go at once to Nantes. We send you a decree to purge that town. . . . We can be humane (*humains*) when we are assured of victory."

The populace at Nantes, irritated by Vendean triumphs, by Vendean reprisals for revolutionary atrocities committed in the Vendée, and by the loss of many relatives and friends, were calling for vengeance.

Moreover, there was great anxiety on account of the great scarcity of food; and there were crushings and crowds and fighting mobs at bakers' shops for the daily doles of food, and the scarcity was attributed to the wealthier merchants, to monopolists, to royalists.

The scarcity was aggravated by the working of the laws of maximum, by the increase in the number of the people in the city, and by the large number of troops constantly passing through, or who had to be fed from, Nantes.

Just previous to Carrier's arrival the council of Nantes had been "purified" by the Representatives, by the dismissal or arrest of most of its members and officers; numerous arrests, too, were made under the law of suspects; the extremer revolutionary party was rapidly possessing itself of all authority. The popular society of Vincent la Montagne, composed altogether of sans-culottes, was giving a great impetus to revolutionary ideas and acts, and the "terror" had already begun to exist before his arrival.

Before his arrival, also, a Revolutionary Committee had been appointed by the Representatives Gillet, Philippeaux, and Ruelle, as a substitute for the weaker-kneed one hitherto operating there; and to constitute it, a dozen or more of some of the choicest scoundrels in France were selected, men whom Philippeaux described as "sans-culottes, vigorous revolutionists, but at the same time sage and prudent."

Bachelier, "a man of the law," was appointed its president, but its presiding spirit of evil was Jean Jacques Goullin, a dissolute roué, a "politician of the cafés," a man of "insatiable avarice"; and among its other members were Grandmaison, an assassin; Chaux, a swindler and bankrupt; Jolly, Perrochaux, Pinard, and other "intrepid Montagnards"; all of the very shadiest antecedents, but of the loftiest and purest revolutionary principles, and all greedy for the salary of some eight francs or so a day, with the opportunities and prospects of unlimited plunder and extortion.

Their acts during the next few months showed what a hellish crew Revolution had placed in authority in the great city of Nantes.

What a disillusionment most of the inhabitants of
Nantes were to undergo is clear from Phelippes de
Tronjolly's assertion that " when the creation of a Revolutionary Committee became known, the people, always
good, but often the dupe of its goodness, believed at last
what the men greedy of place had ceaselessly vociferated,
that the reign of virtue and justice was about to begin
in Nantes."

Carrier reached Nantes on the 8th October, but went
on into the Vendée for a few days, and was at the battle
of Cholet, where he ran away, but in a couple of days he
took up his permanent residence at Nantes. By the
time of his arrival there " everything and all had received
the revolutionary impulsion, and the sans-culottes were
fully victorious."

The spirit which animated Carrier may be judged
from the speech which, soon after his arrival, he made
to the people :—

" People, people ! take your clubs, crush all these fat
merchants, all these men who have enriched themselves
by the fruit of your sweat. Go, run, burst in the ware-
houses which overflow with riches, exterminate all these
scoundrels who abuse your patience. People, you can
count on me to aid you to take vengeance on all the
vampires of the public. The guillotine will do justice
to all, and I will make their heads roll on the national
scaffold."

It was not only the Vendeans who were to be
crushed in Nantes. The so-called Federalists — the
moderates, all who had wealth or any possessions, all who
had character and respectability, all who could by any
stretch of imagination be considered as counter-revolutionists — were alike to be included in the revolutionary
anathema.

The powers of the Revolutionary Committee, as authorised by law, were most arbitrary and despotic. Its
members had the power of search, arrest, imprisonment :
and the law of suspects, "the most terrible arm which
tyranny ever had at its disposition," gave them absolute
power over all their fellow-citizens. Whatever other
powers the Committee wanted were easily obtainable
from the Representative.

The Committee lost little time in setting to work.
On the 11th October it held its first sitting.

To impose silence on its adversaries was its first task.
On the 12th October it closed the Club de la Halle, and
on the following day the various reading-rooms, assembly
rooms, gardens, and clubs were also all closed.

Thus, on the 13th October, opposition was silenced in
Nantes, and the committee had no contradiction to fear.

Some of the well-to-do citizens tried to leave the
city, but this was soon stopped. On the 24th October
the council of Nantes decreed that no inhabitant should
leave it except with a passport. All avenues of escape
were thus closed.

The Revolutionary Committee was now supreme, and
was able to dare anything; but to do everything it
required instruments, and a sort of police force was
created by decree of Carrier and Francastel, the Representatives, a "revolutionary corps" called the Marat
Company, in obedience to the wishes of its members,
who deemed that title a more splendid one. It was
composed of three corps—the Marat Corps, the Scouts of
the Mountain, and the American Hussars, these latter
being negroes or mulattoes (presumably from Domenique).

Bachelier, himself a member of the Revolutionary
Committee, has left on record the statement that the
Compagnie Marat was composed of fathers of families

known for their probity and their civism; but, in
reality, language is beggared to describe this crew.
They were selected from the refuse and dregs and off-
scourings of the populace, and were men of the most
infamous, degraded, brutal, and ferocious character.

Goullin, when he was getting this force together,
held strongly that the greatest scoundrels should be
chosen, and at each recommendation he inquired, " Is
there no bigger scoundrel ? for we want men of that
kind to bring aristocrats to their senses."

When enlisted, they took the following oath : " I
swear death to royalists, to fanatics, to coxcombs
(*muscadins*), to *feuillants*, to moderates, in whatever
colour, in whatever cloak (or mask), or in whatever form
they clothe themselves.    I swear to recognise those only
as relations, brothers, and friends who are true patriots
and ardent defenders of the Republic."

To this low and degraded crew practically unlimited
powers were given by the Representatives.    They were
given the right of surveillance over suspected persons,
over enemies of the Republic—terms elastic enough to
include everybody : they were given the authority to
make domiciliary visits as, when, and where they
wished ; and they were also given the power of arrest—
a power equivalent almost to that of life and death—
for, for any one in prison, it was but a short step to the
scaffold.    Their pay was to be ten francs a day : and, as
a whet to their zeal, Carrier decided that the spoils of
the brigands should belong to the individual making the
arrest.

In that loving republican spirit which is so beautiful a feature of the revolutionary character, Carrier
addressed these wretches as "my children"; but it is
to be remembered that he, and they, and the Revolu-

tionary Committee were all pretty much of the same sort.

The company called "the Scouts of the Mountain" was for the neighbourhood of Nantes what the others were for the city. One Lebatteux, an innkeeper, an ex-cook, and a man of desperate character, was appointed chief of it, and was given a *mandat*, with "unlimited powers," by Carrier, who described him as "*le patriote le plus pur*," "*le républicain le plus prononcé*," to make war on suspects of all classes.

Having an extended field of action, the Scouts were mounted, and their occupation was daily or nocturnal raids for murder, pillage, robbery, and every other atrocity.

There was not a horror they did not commit. Their misdeeds do not fill so large a place in history as those of their comrades in Nantes—probably there was no one to report them fully—but glimpses of their proceedings are got from time to time. Of a man working in the fields being ridden down by them and killed; of a child tending cattle and sheep being pitilessly murdered; of chapels and houses being set fire to and burned after having been pillaged; of levying unjust taxes; of stealing considerable sums of money; of a church where some people were secretly holding a service being attacked, some eight young men being seized, their graves dug, and then their being shot—in all which crimes "patriots" as well as "brigands" were the sufferers.

For the trial of prisoners in Nantes greatly increased provision was made.

A Revolutionary Tribunal was installed on the 1st November in the Palais de Justice, with power to judge revolutionarily, and without appeal, all those accused of treason or conspiracy against the Republic, all individuals who furthered the counter-revolution, or who had committed any of a whole lot of other offences.

And a Military Commission was established by Carrier and Francastel, by decree on the 31st October, which was to judge militarily all individuals suspected of having borne arms against the Republic.

This commission was completely under the influence of the Revolutionary Committee, and extreme as its powers were, it habitually exceeded them.

" Are proofs necessary," exclaimed Goullin indignantly one day, " to send a person to the *rasoir national !* "

The vigorous enforcement of the laws against counter-revolutionists resulted in the prisons in all the principal towns becoming ever more and more crammed.

It is remarkable that a large proportion of those arrested were women. The revolutionist seemed to have a special spite against them. Thus at Luçon, out of 33 persons arrested as suspects, 28 were women— sisters, cousins, aunts of *émigrés*, or deported priests.

In many of the prisons disease became epidemic, and in the prison of Rochelle some 250 persons died during the autumn. At Fontenay also a large number died. In Angers and Nantes they died by hundreds.

Extra prison accommodation had to be provided, and the Revolutionary Committee at Nantes, with a view to future contingencies, secured possession of a large building known as the " Entrepôt des cafés."

Thus then, by the time that the victory of the republican arms at the battle of Cholet, and the flight of the Vendeans across the Loire, had given more assured hopes of the ultimate triumph of the republican cause, all necessary preparations had been made for meting out, without stint or delay, revolutionary "justice" to all the unfortunate people who had already been thrown into prison, or who, by any stretch of malice or suspicion, could be construed into being counter-revolutionists.

The organisation for the reign of revolutionary government — the government of "liberty, equality, and fraternity," and of "justice".—was at last sufficiently, indeed ideally, complete: the whole paraphernalia of slaughter ready. The Representatives, armed with un-limited powers, roaming about seeking whom they might devour. The Revolutionary Committees, composed of the extremest revolutionists, the very scum of France, to aid and advise them, also with practically unlimited powers; and special or public forces to carry out their minutest directions. These for the enforcement of revolutionary authority.

For the administration of such laws as existed, or as were made by the revolutionists, exceptional tribunals, not for the liberty of the people, but for the liberty of assassination under judicial sanction, merciless instru-ments of revolutionary bloodthirstiness.

And for enforcement, a code of repressive laws enacted by the National Assemblies and by the National Con-vention, so thorough and comprehensive as to provide for every imaginable offence, or even the suspicion of offence.

Omnipotent and all-powerful, the revolutionists could now work their will: could give effect to those principles of "liberty, equality, and fraternity" of which they boasted they were the true and the only exponents; and could demonstrate to the world the splendid superiority of a Republic over every other form of human government.

They had no opposition to fear, no opponents capable of thwarting them, for the Vendean army was moving ever farther away. External public opinion there was none, for the Vendée was out of the ken of Europe. Individual resistance was impossible and hopeless.

And, finally, the guillotine was in permanence at Nantes, at Angers, at Sables, and elsewhere; and where not in permanence it was being carried about by ambulatory tribunals, and as even then it could not do the work quickly enough, Carrier was devising speedier means of execution, and was "arranging to have the greatest culprits shot."

As he grimly summed up the state of affairs at the moment, "Tout ira, mais il faut des terribles exemples" ("Everything will go all right, but there must be some terrible examples").

Every chance of escape from revolutionary justice, or, in other words, merciless tyranny, had been closed. Such protection as the law had previously given to innocence had been entirely abrogated and was utterly gone.

The victims were powerless; their throats were bared for the republican knife: their breasts for the republican bullets and bayonets,—there remained only the killing to be done. And the revolutionist began to be happy, for this was "liberty."

# CHAPTER XI

THE measures and organisation which the Representatives were thus getting into working order for the suppression of the Vendeans, and for the destruction of personal and political liberty, were equally efficacious for the destruction of religious liberty,—which object the Convention, the Committee of Public Safety, the Representatives, and the revolutionists had as deeply at heart as they had the annihilation of the Vendeans.

Practically, it was a case of killing two birds with one stone. The paraphernalia for the conviction and punishment of Vendeans and other counter-revolutionists would answer equally for the conviction and punishment of "fanatics," under which term the revolutionist included all persons who believed in the Christian faith.

In spite of the many pressing claims on their attention, the revolutionists never slackened in their assault on religion, nor in their attack on every one and everything connected with religious worship.

Though with unceasing professions of tolerance and liberty on their lips, and with the avowal of it blazoned across the republican firmament in their Declaration of the Rights of Man, and in their Constitutions, they

were unceasingly, in true revolutionary style, giving the
lie to their professions and protestations.

That is a most remarkable fact in their conduct, and
shows conclusively how through and through insincere
the revolutionists were, and what a miserable sham their
professions of liberty were.

It is one more proof of the truth which is becoming
clearer to all calm and impartial investigators of the
French Revolution under the more recent light thrown
upon it by the publication of official records, and by
different memoirs, that the revolutionist was an impostor
of the very highest rank, of the supremest order—an
arch impostor—and that all his high-sounding declarations and affirmations of liberty, equality, and fraternity
were but cloaks for the gratification of his own ambition,
the advancement of his own interests, the indulgence
of his own passions, and for every infamy which the
mind of man could conceive, or the hand of man could
perpetrate.

The Convention, taking up the policy initiated by the
Constituent and continued by the Legislative Assembly,
went on enacting law after law, each with some fresh
restriction on religious liberty, or some increased penalty
against religious worship: and it was thoroughly supported
by the authorities in the country, for there was no
humiliation which the local "patriots" could devise, no
matter how mean or petty, which they did not inflict
on the ministers of religion.

Everything they could do, too, to offend the feelings
of religious people they did.    Religion was "fanaticism," –it was therefore to be swept away with other
dark things of the earth; religious people were "fanatics,"—they were therefore to be exterminated by an
enlightened Government and State.

L

"Tolerance," wrote a Representative, "is one of the most beautiful attributes of the republican constitution, but it ought not to exist for real charlatans."

The proscription of the clergy, which had begun with those who would not take the oath, was unceasingly persevered in. Many already slept their last sleep—sent to it by the hand of the assassin or of the State executioner. Thousands had already been deported under circumstances of every possible hardship. Thousands were in prison, and those who still were at large were pursued as wild beasts.

But before long the persecution passed on to the constitutional priests also, and even those who had taken the oath were being made to feel the weight of the revolutionary hand; for they were priests, and their form of worship was the Catholic religion. A premium was offered to all who abdicated their priesthood; but other more decisive measures were adopted to secure this end.

The only conclusion at all satisfactory to those who were warring against the priests was when the priests "came to depose on the altar of philosophy and of reason the ridiculous tokens (*signes*) with which they deceive the people," when they abjured their priesthood, and "changed their doctoral hat for the bonnet of the sans-culottes."

Even then, however, they were more or less regarded as conspirators and persons to be watched by true republicans, and real contentment only came when a priest took the step from which there was no retreat—getting married.

Hounded on by the Representatives, who were as raging against religion and religious practices as they were against counter-revolutionists, the most virulent religious persecution was carried on, and a veritable war against religion was waged.

The churches were forcibly closed, and converted into places for the meetings of popular societies, or other secular purposes, and into temples for the celebration of the worship of reason.

The church ornaments, those "scandalous ornaments of gold and silver which have too long insulted the misery of the people and dishonoured the simplicity of the true religion," were carried off to be deposited on the altar of the country,—heavy toll being usually taken out of them on the way by the immaculate sans-culotte.  The bells were taken away or destroyed.

A petition from the Society of Vincent la Montagne in Nantes, in November 1793, affords an illustration of the ideas of the time.  The petition asked for measures to be taken "to destroy the remains of superstition, to overthrow entirely the edifice of errors and lies, and to warn the people against imposture and hypocrisy."

And in reply the council of Nantes decreed that all wooden or stone figures tending to encourage fana-ticism should be removed; that priests should be for-bidden to wear their clerical dress outside their houses; and that they should join the National Guard.

But what brought this persecution more effectually home to those people who believed in religion were the tremendous penalties incurred by all who had any deal-ings or communications with the ministers of religion. Attendance at a service held by an unsworn priest was a capital offence; whilst even the possession of any religious emblem was a crime also promptly punished with death.

The Convention did not leave any room for doubt as to its views, for the proceedings at its sitting on the

7th November were a demonstration of its opinion that the Catholic religion should be abolished—an opinion which was being acted on with full vigour in the Departments which were the scene of the Vendean struggle.

But in another measure it went beyond the expression of hostility to a special form of religion, and evinced its animus against all religion. On the 5th October it decreed that the Republic should have a new calendar, starting from the date of the birth of the Republic, namely, the 22nd September 1792; and on the 24th November this new calendar was inaugurated.

Like many other revolutionary crudities and absurdities, it did not long survive its creation, and it is now mainly of interest as showing the revolutionary animus against religion. It suppressed all Saints' days, but what was far more notable, it abolished the Sabbath, and substituted therefor a day of national fêtes— a revolutionary Sabbath—every tenth day, which was called a *décadi*.

"Instead of a foolish Sabbath (*un sot dimanche*)," said Mallarme, "we have the *décadi*." But the change was manifestly for the worse so far as the working man was concerned, who thus only got three days of rest in the month instead of four.

The observance of these *décadis* was made obligatory, and in that spirit of "religious liberty" which was the boast of the Republic, any recognition of the Sundays was prohibited. Any one who shut their shops or abstained from work on the Sabbath was liable to heavy penalties.

"Denounce to me," said Carrier. "the fanatics who shut their shops on a Sunday, and I will have them guillotined."

The new calendar was in effect a declaration against the State acknowledgment of the existence of any religion.

In fact, under the Revolutionary Government, which was to have been a Government of Liberty, not alone was there no vestige of religious liberty, but there was religious persecution of the most active, extreme, and bloody character. Every possible insult was heaped on religion, and every effort made to destroy all outward signs and evidence of religious worship, and to annihilate those who still dared to avow their religious belief—and extirpate it. To such a state of anti-religiousness did things come, that "Atheism became the best certificate of civism."

If anything could add to the iniquity of the persecution, it was the audacious pretence that religious liberty existed.

The Republican Government of France of this time, speaking of it as a whole, with its deputy sovereigns, the Representatives, and its other officers, has excelled beyond all Governments that ever have been in the contradictions of its professions and its acts.

Never has any Government or form of Government acted in such direct, instantaneous, and flagrant opposition to its own professions as this Government did. One would wonder that it took the trouble to make professions it so promptly violated, were it not that the professions were a part of the sham which had to be kept up.

On the 16 Frimaire (6th December 1793) the Convention had passed a decree *pour maintenir la paix et la liberté de cultes* (to maintain the peace and liberty of forms of worship).

The action of Lequinio, one of its Representatives in the west, interprets the meaning of this decree.

On the 21st December he issued a proclamation to the citizens of the Vendée :—

"All forms of worship are free (*tous les cultes sont libres*). The first of the Rights of Man is to think freely, to render homage freely to the god which his imagination depicts. But he is not free whose mind is tormented by the discourse and instigations of another. He is a tyrant who wishes to force the opinions of others into submission to his own, and to make him believe what he himself believes, and to imitate his practices. . . .

"That each of us should render his homage as he pleases, that he should exercise his worship in private, as he thinks good, here is liberty of worship. But let him beware of endeavouring to inspire others with his views—henceforward that will be a crime, and our duty will be to make the sword of the law fall on the guilty."

And it was decreed by this Representative—" With the object that liberty of worship exist in its plenitude, it is prohibited to all—be he who he may—to preach or write to bring into favour any worship or religious opinion, be it what it may. Whoever is guilty of this offence shall be at once arrested, treated as an enemy of the Republican Constitution, as a conspirator against French liberty, and handed over to the Revolutionary Tribunal established at Rochefort."

No longer was the Roman Catholic religion alone in being persecuted. All religious creeds were equally assailed.

Former or present ministers of any form of creed were expressly forbidden to preach, write or teach morals (*la morale*) under the penalty of being treated as "suspect."

And they were all prohibited from holding any public office except with the approval of the Representatives.

Laignelot, another Representative, wrote to the Committee of Public Safety his disapproval of this proclamation. "Write, I pray you, to Lequinio to be more reserved in his speeches and writings. The greater part of the deputies possess in sovereign degree the art of making themselves feared, and few that of attracting hearts. Recommend above all to those you send, as well as to Lequinio, never to forget for one single moment in their august missions that they are representatives of the people."

The Committee of Public Safety on the 7th January (18 Nivose) wrote to Lequinio that his decree was not at all in the spirit of the decree of the 6th December, and that he should take another attitude.

" You ought to have known that religious opinions cede to force less than any others.

" Your experience ought to have reminded you that in the matter of worship persecution only tends to give to fanaticism a more terrible energy. . . .

" Let the law, let the triumphant Republic crush its internal enemies by the force of reason."

This, however, was not a principle acted on by the Committee nor by the Revolutionary Government.

The censure, such as it was, was, however, purely personal, for elsewhere there was no mitigation of persecution—no condemnation expressed of the persecutors— even individual religious worship in private was dangerous, as the possession of some religious emblems was used as proof of their possessor being a counter-revolutionist, and led direct to the scaffold.

It was not, however, in the nature of the Revolutionary Government to act on its avowed principles of religious liberty, or on its avowed knowledge of the evil results of religious persecution.

# CHAPTER XII

## NANTES

THE proclamation of revolutionary government made little immediate change as regarded proceedings in the Vendée and Nantes. Despotism there had already reached such a height that no addition could well be made to it—a somewhat remarkable commentary on the Revolution whose sole justification was the abolition of tyranny and despotism, and the inauguration of a régime of liberty, equality, and fraternity.

Nantes became, unfortunately for itself, the centre of the storm of revolutionary violence in the west. Here not only were there Vendéans to be dealt with, but also priests and " fanatics," and men of means, the bourgeoisie of Nantes, the wealthier and more respectable inhabitants of the city, and merchants, and moderates, and Girondists, and the whole catalogue of persons held in abhorrence by the revolutionist.

These were the classes against which Carrier's "great coups" were to be struck, and from which his " terrible examples " were to be taken; but the great bulk of his victims were poor working men or working women,—artisans of all sorts, labourers, "the people" for whom the Revolution was supposed to have been made.

Some of the revolutionists of Nantes required working up to the true height of "patriotic principles."

The popular and republican Society of the sans-culottes of Vincent la Montagne had already done much in this direction. At its meetings, night after night, by the light of smoking lamps or flickering candles, patriotic oratory indulged in its most grandiloquent flights. And Carrier and other patriots foamed and fumed and exhausted themselves with incitements and imprecations.

"It is necessary," said Carrier, the wielder of the whole power of the State in Nantes, the sans-culotte sovereign and despot, "to strike these knaves of monopolists, these aristocrats, these moderates. Denounce them to me. No material proofs are necessary; the denunciation of two good sans-culottes will suffice me."

And Goullin, giving advice as to admission of members to the Society, said: "Take care not to admit moderates, false patriots. You must only admit revolutionists,—patriots having the courage to drink human blood."

The Society took possession of the church of St. Croix as a place "worthy of its reunions," and there was an inaugural ceremony, with republican music, attended by all the "pure Montagnards," and led by Carrier, who delivered an address from the pulpit, "so often profaned by the impure and fallacious words of sacerdotalism and of the priests.

"All could see how superior the *vrais Montagnards* are to the others by their hatred of despotism and their love of public liberties."

Carrier and the Revolutionary Committee quickly settled themselves down to govern revolutionarily, and to make the most of their opportunities.

From the moment of installation the Committee had been engaged in making or ordering arrests; personal hatred or jealousy or desire for vengeance was given free rein, and a large number of the better class of citizens, many of them late members of the various public bodies, were seized and sent to prison.

The Maratist Company were also busily employed on their own account in carrying people off to prison.

There was an ingenuity in their malevolence which was extraordinary. The device by which the Committee sifted the tares from the revolutionary wheat has been described by a Maratist.

"A conspiracy is imagined. The alarm (*générale*) is sounded. The sans-culottes, all the children of the people, rush to their posts; but the rich, the egotists, as usual, remain at home; that stamps them as suspects; and so one goes and arrests them. That is only justice. They remain at home, therefore they are accomplices in the conspiracy, since they do not come to fight against it."

On the morning of the 12th of November this device was put into operation. The town was startled by the sounding of the alarm, and the report that a plot had been discovered to murder the Representatives and all the authorities. Cannon were quickly put in conspicuous positions, and prompt measures were taken to defeat the wicked design. A whole host of arrests were then made, and in a brief time the Committee had safe under lock and key the majority of those they feared; among them many of the most respectable citizens of Nantes, well-known patriots too, but they were rich.

This was but innocent child's play compared to what was to follow.

A few days passed, and Carrier and the Committee gave to Nantes another more original and terrible demonstration of the new régime of liberty and fraternity, and of what could be done in its name.

Moored in the Loire, gently swaying from side to side as the current ran past her, lay a small sailing vessel with the somewhat proud name of *La Gloire*. For some time she had been anchored there. Now and then a boat might have been observed putting off from her, or going out to her : but these occasions were rare, and she bore an aspect of desertion, as if she had been plague-smitten.

But if her decks were almost deserted, below, stowed away in her hold, in much the same cramped way as a cargo of African slaves on an Arab dhow, were some ninety priests. Exempted from deportation on account of their age,—some were nearly eighty years of age,—or on account of their physical infirmities, they had been thrown into prison ; and as the prisons were all overcrowded, these unfortunate men had been finally transferred to a floating prison, there to endure an even harder fate.

Their crime was that they had refused to take the oath—that inexcusable crime in the eyes of the true republican—and for a period of some eighteen months they had, for their faith's sake, supported captivity, first in one prison, and then in another, and now were in their last prison, *La Gloire*.

Here, huddled together under the deck, in a habitation hermetically sealed as soon as it became dark, sick and starved, covered with filth and vermin, breathing a poisonous atmosphere, in circumstances in which it was scarcely possible for human beings to exist, it was marvellous that life remained in them : but fortifying

themselves and each other with the consolations of
their faith, which it was beyond the power even of
a Revolutionary Government to deprive them of,
they dragged out an agonising existence from day to
day.

On the 16th November they were still there. As
the day drew to its close they repeated their evening
prayers: the light faded until all was dark.

And then, in the early or middle hours of the night,
there occurred an event which Carrier described as of
"quite a new character."

Darkness veiled this event from all human ken,
except the ken of those who took part in it; but in the
calm quiet of the winter's night, for more than an hour
must it have been, fearsome cries echoed across the water,
the cries of men in their death struggle and agony, and,
after a time, all was still.

When the sun again rose, the hold of the vessel was
empty.

The next day, or possibly the day after, for the exact
date is uncertain, though the fact is beyond question,
unwonted animation was perceivable on board; the deck
was being washed down, and all sorts of preparations
were being made, and the hold was transformed
into a banqueting saloon. Where ninety priests had
for weeks undergone unceasing agony of mind and
body, a table was spread, covered with a luxurious
repast.

In the evening the guests assembled. Carrier, the
Representative of the power and dignity of the great
new Republic of France, occupied the place of honour.
On his right sat his aide-de-camp Lamberty, on his left
Laloi. Foucault, with boots on which he had taken
from one of his victims, Robin, Fouquet, and some

twelve or fourteen others were there. And as the feast
progressed, and the wine began to work, Lamberty
explained the mystery of the disappearance of the priests,
though to most of those present there was no mystery
about it. He described in glowing colours how, when
the night came, he and his trusty companions had come
on board, and had forced the priests to come on deck
two by two. There they had searched and stripped
them, and bound them, and made them descend into a
barge which had been moored alongside, whence their
next descent was into the dark flowing waters of the
river, which soon carried them beyond view, and soon
silenced their cries.

Every sentence of this horrible recital was applauded:
the "brave comrades" who had assisted Lamberty in
these foul murders (for the priests were not under
sentence of anything but detention) were pointed out to
Carrier, who became ever more and more wildly gay.
"Sing," he said to Robin, "sing the song of 'La
Gamelle'; sing the song of the 'Mountain.'" And
Robin sang :—

> Oui, sans fraternité
> Il n'est point de gaieté ;
>
> (For oh, without fraternity,
> There is in life no gaiety) ;

and Carrier and the others joined in chorus, clinking
their glasses together. And as a mark of his appreciation of the services rendered, Carrier made a present of
the vessel *La Gloire* to Lamberty.

This was the first noyade. Though the idea of
drowning, as a means of getting rid of the enemies of the
country, had been mooted before in the Jacobin Club in

Paris. Carrier and his Committee were the first to give effect to it. Doubtless he felt proud of being the first to give effect to this new method of dealing with re-calcitrant priests—a "vertical deportation" as he or Goullin facetiously called it; cheaper, too, and more rapid than deportation. Doubtless, too, the actors felt self-satisfied with their prowess.

But what an appalling scene, this drunken glorifica-tion of wholesale murder, on the very scaffold of the slaughter: what an illustration of the reality of the boasted superiority of the new gospel of Revolution as expounded by the "brave republican," by the *vrai sans-culotte!*

The industry of the revolutionists was not confined to priests.

Since the imaginary plot the Revolutionary Com-mittee and Carrier had been considering how best to deal with the prominent citizens of Nantes whom they had in their custody.

To bring them before the local tribunals at Nantes, where the patriotism of most of them was so well known, would, even at this period, have been useless; and so the Committee determined to send them to Paris for trial there by the Revolutionary Tribunal, which could be relied on to make short work of them.

And so on the 27th November, having selected about 132, they started them under escort for Paris.

There appears to have been every intention on the part of the Committee that they should be massacred *en route*, a not unknown revolutionary device for getting rid of people. "So much the better if they die," said Chaux and Goullin; "it is so much gain to the nation": and Goullin spoke of them as men no longer in existence. But the plot miscarried, and after every imaginable

hardship, from which several died, some 120 reached
Paris, and were there consigned to prison, and for a time
to oblivion.

Rid of these people, the Committee turned its attention in other directions.

Want was pressing on the city, food becoming ever
more difficult to obtain—the plague was spreading, and
exciting growing alarm.

Robin, one of Carrier's staff, pointed out the evil
which next wanted remedying. "The brigands," he said,
"eat the bread of the patriots. They had wished to
destroy the Republic. They now caused the risk of the
spread of the plague. People so notoriously culpable
had no right to live, and every one would profit by the
national vengeance being executed upon them." And
so the national vengeance was determined upon by the
Committee and the Representative—the representative
of "liberty" and "fraternity," and of the power and
authority and dignity of France.

An excuse soon arose. On the 3rd December some
half-a-dozen prisoners in the Bouffay had formed a plan
to escape by means of false keys. The Revolutionary
Committee, with the help of a spy of theirs who was
among the prisoners, magnified this into a vast conspiracy,
with ramifications throughout the prisons, for the destruction of the buildings, and the death of "patriots."

On the next afternoon the six culprits were sentenced
to death, and forthwith guillotined by torchlight. But
this was not enough. As Carrier said, "A grand measure will deliver us of the rest." The same evening the
different administrative corps in Nantes met together,
the Revolutionary Committee and Carrier himself being
present. Their proceedings are really hardly credible.
After a "tempestuous" discussion, the question was put

on Goullin's motion. "Shall the prisoners be made to
perish in a mass? Yes or no?" There was no question
of the prisoners confined in one special prison being the
victims. Their wholesale slaughter was contemplated.
There was no question of their being first tried, not even
by the rapid-acting Military Commission. The decision
of the meeting was to settle their fate without further
bother, and that decision was unanimously, "Yes."

Goullin playing the principal part, a sort of "national
jury" was appointed, which drew up lists of those who
were to be shot, and he then signed an order, together
with Grandmaison and Mainguet, to General Boivin,
commandant of Nantes, to seize the prisoners named
on the list, some 300 in number, to conduct them to
l'Eperonnière, and there shoot them.

Early on the 5th General Boivin received the order,
and protested against its illegality, none of the prisoners
having been legally tried, and some of them being only
confined on a charge of drunkenness ; and he refused to
execute it.

A fresh meeting was held, at which Phelippes
de Tronjolly, president of the Revolutionary Tribunal,
opposed the scheme, and the army having refused to
carry out the measure, the administrative bodies refused
also to associate themselves with such a measure. But
the Revolutionary Committee, though thus foiled, determined to have recourse to other means of getting
rid of the prisoners—one where obstruction was not
possible.

And one gets one or two glimpses in the next few
days of Carrier and the Revolutionary Committee, Grandmaison, Goullin, and Bachelier, sitting in solemn conclave,
with expert carpenter in attendance, organising the preparations for further drownings or noyades, designing the

most effective and commodious form of barge for the
purpose, and selecting a staff for the work.

The staff selected were sans-culottes of the *vrai*-est
type, worthy of those who employed them, and of the
rank and file of the Maratist Company, whom they
worked with, and than whom they were no better—Lamberty, previously a spy in the Vendée, and whom Carrier
had made an adjutant-general, and who was one of his
most active and trusted instruments: Robin, a dissolute
and vicious youth; Laveau, one of the prisoners saved by
Bonchamps at St. Florent, who thus showed his gratitude
to Vendean mercy; Fouquet, who, two years previously,
had been turned out of the National Guard as unworthy
of wearing its uniform; Foucault, and several others, all
men of the most cruel and infamous character, all chosen
for "their known civism, for their patriotism, and their
sans-culottic ardour."

What a light is being thrown on what French "civism"
and "patriotism" really was! Lamberty was placed in
command; and Carrier, by virtue of his unlimited powers,
gave him full authority to do practically anything, and
to go anywhere, at any time, and prohibited any one
opposing him.

While they were still at work on their preparations,
a vessel arrived (on or about the 7th December) at
Nantes from Angers, laden with some fifty-eight priests.

Carrier was asked as to whether they should be sent
to a prison. "No," he replied; "not so much mystery.
All these . . . must be put under water."

And on the night of the 9th his order was carried
out. Details are unknown: only this one, that Lamberty was not at the slaughter, and had a heated quarrel
with those who were, over the clothes and small property
of the victims, of which he wanted his share; and this

one, that the nine sailors who helped in the business each received four francs.   And on the 10th, Carrier wrote a letter to the Convention, in which he announced a republican victory which had just been gained over Charette : adding to his report, " But why was it necessary that this event should be accompanied by another which is no longer of a new kind ?  Fifty-eight individuals, described under the name of refractory priests, arrived at Nantes from Angers.  They were immediately confined in a vessel on the Loire.  Last night they were all swallowed (*engloutis*) up by the river.  What a revolutionary torrent is the Loire !—*Salut et fraternité*, CARRIER."

The reading of this letter in the Convention was, as Mercier reports, " covered by immortal plaudits."

Henceforward, no possible exculpation of the Convention as to its knowledge of the noyades.

The arrangements were at last complete.

It was night, the night of the 14th December.

The inmates of the grim and gloomy old prison. Le Bouffay, worn out with another day's misery, had sunk into fevered torpor on the vermin-infected straw, or tossed to and fro on the clammy floors in sleepless anguish.  Sickness and cold, semi-starvation and filth, and a pestiferous atmosphere, had brought most of them to the edge of the precipice which separates life from death.   They were not deep-dyed criminals, the prisoners : many were under short sentences for only petty offences, such as theft; many had not even yet been tried.

Suddenly, in the early hours of the night, an unwonted noise is heard in the prison.  Loud voices, unusual sounds, and disturbance : and presently, flickering lights, and heavy steps in the long dark corridors, and keys grating in the locks, and the doors of all the cells opened by the turnkey, and the harsh command given: "Get up at once, pack your things, especially your purses, they are essential; leave nothing behind."

And then several drunken men, wearing the national uniform, members of the infamous Maratist Company, crowd in, calling out the names on the list. "The first who does not answer," said a furious Maratist, "I will stick my sword through."

Dazed with fear, and in a panic of terror, the miserable prisoners obey the order. Those who delay are dragged out by the brutal Maratists, half-mad with drink, then all are plundered of everything they possess, are hurried to the yard, where, by the flickering light of torches, they are pinioned and bound in couples with such savage force that the ropes cut almost to the bone.

It mattered nothing what offence they were in prison for; whether they were convicted or untried; whether innocent or guilty; even whether they were patriots or aristocrats; revolutionary justice did not condescend to discriminate: they were prisoners, and all must come.

And Goullin and the big Grandmaison are there, and Mainguet, aiding in the pinioning of the prisoners; cursing and swearing and threatening—Grandmaison emphasising his oaths and threats with his drawn sword.

Some hours—the greater part of the night—are spent in this dreadful work. Horrible imprecations are hurled at the prisoners, and jocular allusions as to their fate. One asked for a glass of water, "No need," said a Maratist, "in a few minutes you will drink out of the big cup,"—so clear the allusions that one wretched prisoner exclaims, "We are lost, my friends, they are going to drown us."

And as the number on the list—155—is short by some, Goullin wishes to send to the hospital near by to complete the number: but time does not admit, and as the pinioning process is slow, he urges haste. " Dear friends, let us hurry: the tide is going out."

At last at about four in the morning all was ready, the prison gate was opened, and the miserable procession started. Resistance is impossible: escape almost hopeless; almost, for one tried it, and got away, but another who attempted it had his skull smashed in by Grandmaison. And one who, unable to walk, fell by the way, promptly had his brains blown out by a *vrai sansculotte*, the shot resounding like a volley through the empty and silent streets.

What a prolonged agony for these unfortunates, this march along the dark streets—on by the Quai de la Fosse, escorted or rather dragged or driven along by armed and infuriated demons panting for their death. Their worst fears were confirmed as they were drawn up on the edge of the river, and by a faint moonlight could see the waters rushing along. The barge which was to be their tomb was not ready for their reception, and they were kept waiting there while the finishing touches were being given to it.

At last the agony draws to its close. The barge is ready—they are made to descend into it, or are pitched in, and battened down. With several members of the Revolutionary Committee and of the Maratist Company on board, it is cast loose, and drifts for a while with the current. And now, no longer able to restrain their terror, silence is broken: fearful cries arise, cries for mercy, amongst them the reproaching cry, " Is it republicans who act thus cruelly?" But their executioners sang to drown these cries.

And then the death-struggle begins. Some had got the cords loose, and struggled to be free, pushing their arms through the gaps in the planks. Grandmaison sabred these unfortunates, and plunged his sword through the gaps in the planks, pleased doubtless by the exclamation, " Ah, the scoundrel, he pierces me !"

Opposite the island of Chaviré the barge is anchored. Goullin, Grandmaison, and their colleagues and the Maratists descend into boats, and hover around to witness the climax of their night's work. The carpenters knock away the carefully prepared planks, the water rushes in, rises, ever rises, until the barge slowly sinks with its human freight of nearly 130 souls. By some blunder of the carpenters, a few of the victims come to the surface, and endeavour to swim away. They are pursued by the men in the boats, and knocked on the head. Two, however, actually do escape, snatched from the very jaws of death ; the rest are soon wrapped in eternal sleep, victims of republican despotism which has been misnamed " liberty," and of sans-culotte savagery which masqueraded as " fraternity."

# CHAPTER XIII

## 'THE CALVARY OF THE VENDEANS'

## THE CAMPAIGN ON THE NORTH SIDE OF THE LOIRE

WHILE the extermination of counter-revolutionists was thus, in the period immediately succeeding the battle of Cholet, absorbing the attention of the revolutionists, the Vendean army and people who had crossed the Loire were moving off through Brittany, in the hopeless pursuit of better fortune, getting farther and farther away from their own country, and falling more and more a victim to the ambitions and dissensions of their leaders.

The Revolutionary Government was first startled, and then enraged, to find that the Vendeans had not been annihilated at Cholet, that the Vendean war was not yet over, that only the scene had been changed from one side of the Loire to the other.

Fear conjured up all sorts of contingencies and magnified the danger, and the Government dreaded the possibility of the Vendeans making a dash for Paris, and foresaw an alliance between them and the hated English, which should give that inveterate foe a footing in France and a basis for further operations.

Every effort must be made to prevent these dis-

asters, and imperative orders were despatched to the commanders of the republican military forces to attack, overcome, and annihilate the Vendeans as promptly as possible.

The journeyings of the Vendean army on the north
side of the Loire, with their wives and families, have
been likened unto the wanderings of the Children of
Israel after they had departed out of Egypt and crossed
the Red Sea, but the comparison is much in favour of
the latter. For the Vendeans took with them no spoils
of their enemies, only heavy burdens, in the helpless or
wounded members of their family, women, children, and
old people. For them, moreover, poor people, there was
no manna in the wilderness, there was before them no
land of promise flowing with milk and honey, not even
for their descendants.

Their time of trial was shorter—that was the only
difference in their favour. Ten weeks of strife and
battle, of restless wandering to and fro, of fatigue, cold,
hunger, and mental and physical misery in every shape;
ten weeks of despairing struggle. with the heart-wrench-
ing trial of relatives and friends dropping by the wayside,
to be destroyed by the revolutionists, as surely as the
traveller who falls from his sleigh when pursued by a
pack of hungry wolves. And then, when every avenue
of escape was closed against them, and when the human
frame could stand no more, when no asylum but death
remained for them, the final valiant, heroic effort, and
final defeat, and death.

"It was not an army," says a depicter of these scenes,
"it was more like a migration similar to those of the
ancient times, when a whole people fled before fire and
flame in search of a new land."

Having crossed the Loire, the first necessity was the
appointment of new leaders in place of those who had

fallen, and Henri de la Rochejaquelein was selected as commander-in-chief.

Strenuous efforts were at once made to evoke some order from the fearful chaos. An advance guard of some 10,000 to 12,000 men was formed. Then followed the bulk of the wanderers, anyhow, without any order, combatants mixed up with non-combatants ; "and filling up the road, artillery, baggage, women carrying their children, old men supported by their sons, the wounded who could scarce drag themselves along, and soldiers—all in confusion. . . . This sad procession occupied almost always four leagues in length."

A community of anxiety and misery welded the whole of them into one mass. "Every one experienced the wish of running common dangers and of sharing a common fate. Families and friends walked together and tried to keep united." "We are all brothers and sisters now," said a peasant ; "we must not separate."

A strong rear-guard was formed of the best troops, and in this formation the whole body started for Rennes, in the hope and belief that Brittany would rise and help them.

The republicans were quite unprepared for the sudden movement of the Vendeans across the Loire, and had no forces there which would enable them to offer any effective resistance to the Vendean advance.

The Vendeans overcame everything at first, capturing several small towns, and, on the 23rd October, capturing the large town of Laval, where they were joined by some 6000 Bretons.

By this time the republican forces had crossed the Loire, and, under the command of L'Échelle, with Generals Marceau, Kleber, Westermann, and the Mayençais troops, were following them pretty closely.

At Entrammes, near Laval, they overtook the Vendeans and attacked them (on the 27th October), and a fiercely contested battle took place.  The desperate valour of the Vendeans prevailed, and the republican soldiers, each with an "œil sur le dos," as Kleber said, were driven back with heavy loss.

"They fled like flocks of sheep," wrote a corporal present.  "Each one was afraid of being wounded, knowing well that if he were so unfortunate no one would have the humanity to help him to save himself."

The Mayençais troops, who stood their ground most valiantly, were almost annihilated.  Two republican generals and a large number of officers were killed, nineteen cannon and as many caissons were lost, also many waggons of bread and brandy, and over 4000 men were killed or wounded.

"We provided them with everything," adds the corporal.  "They were in a pitiable condition—reduced to living on apples, and carrying off the spoons from the houses they passed, to make them into bullets."

The republican defeat was so crushing that a council of war was held.  Kleber described to it the state of the troops.

"It is necessary first to settle whether we have an army or not.  Already you would have decided this question if, as I did, before daybreak, you had gone round the camp; if you had seen the soldier wet to the bone, without tents, without straw, without boots, without breeches, some without coats, knee deep in mud, shivering with cold . . . the colours surrounded by twenty or thirty, or at most fifty, men who form the different battalions; if, too, you had heard them complain, 'The cowards are at Angers, and we—we are here in the greatest misery.'"

With the army in such a state there was nothing for the republicans to do but to retire to Angers to reorganise. The Vendean army thus found itself, for a time at least, master of its movements. Once more its fate, and that of the mass of people dependent upon it, was in its own hands, or rather in the hands of its leaders.

"Here we ought to have stopped," writes Madame Lescure, "and returned in triumph to our own country, having taken ample revenge on those Mayençais who had driven us from it."

The question was decided at a council of war.

The commander-in-chief and Stofflet and some others were in favour of going back at once and in triumph to the Vendée, now that they were in a position to do so; and many of the men were clamouring for this course to be adopted. The prospect of Brittany rising to help them was proving delusive, and having no provisions and no money, the Vendean demands on the people of the country they passed through for the necessary food were awakening hostility instead of friendship. They were making more enemies than friends.

But cabals and jealousies existed among the Vendean chiefs, and considerable disunion prevailed.

Information reached the council from the *émigrés* in Jersey that an expedition to help them was being prepared in England, and they were urged to seize a seaport. Some of the new leaders of the Vendeans, such as the Prince of Talmont, a vain and incapable personage, the evil genius of the Vendeans, and Monsieur d'Autichamp, being more ambitious in their aims than those who had fallen, and dreaming of overthrowing the Revolutionary Government itself and re-establishing the monarchy, succeeded in imposing their will on the others, and the

decision was come to to move on instead of going
back.

It was a fatal decision, but the responsibility for it
rests on the leaders, and not on the rank and file.
Gradually the unfortunate Vendeans had been led away
from the objects for which they had at first risen—the
free exercise of their religion and exemption from compulsory conscription. They cared little for aught else.
And now they were powerless to give effect to their
anxiety to return to their own country; there could be
no separation from the main body; all must stand or
fall together, and so they had to bow to the decision of
their leaders.

They moved on accordingly, and attacked and captured Fougères, inflicting heavy loss on the republicans.

While there, two *émigré* emissaries arrived from
England with despatches from the English Government offering the Vendeans help, and saying that
troops were ready to bear on any port the Vendean
leaders should name, and suggesting Granville.

A reply was sent accepting aid, and asking above
all for a prince of the French royal family, or a marshal
of France, to command the army, so that an end might
be put to the conflict of private pretensions.

And they pressed onwards towards Dol and Granville. The weather was horrible, the roads frightful.
The continual marching, the wandering life in the cold
air at this late season of the year, the extreme rigour of
the climate, the privations, and the bad food were
already telling severely upon them. Dysentery broke
out, and not a place did they pass through but they
were forced to leave many sick behind—at Mayenne
some 200, at Fougères a large number.

They met with no serious opposition. A republican

army was collected as rapidly as possible at Rennes, but it was not formidable; and a force of about 1500 "requisitionists" was collected at Mayenne, but they either deserted or fled when a Vendean appeared.

"I fear to find myself alone by the end of the day," wrote their general, Lenoir.

The Committee of Public Safety had been moved to fury by the defeat at Laval. It was a rude awakening from the dream of *la Vendée n'est plus*.

The orders to destroy Vendeans and the Vendée in accordance with the decree of the 1st August were reiterated—not merely against the Vendeans on the north side of the Loire, but against the Vendée itself.

And a new decree was made on the 1st November declaring that every town which received the brigands, or gave them help, or which had not resisted them to the utmost, was to be punished as a rebel town, razed, and the property of the inhabitants confiscated to the Republic.

The Committee wrote to their colleague Prieur (de la Marne) complaining vehemently of the slackness and of the feeble measures being taken by the Representatives to crush the Vendeans. "We hope that you, with your fiery spirit (*âme de feu*), your military eloquence, and your pronounced patriotism, will repair so many blunders. We have given orders for considerable reinforcements from the army of the north."

And to Jean Bon St. André, another Representative, it wrote that it "was strongly determined to neglect no steps which would clear the territory of the Republic of this race of brigands," and that he was "to take the strongest measures that the sea or the maritime Departments should be their tomb."

On the 5th November Barère confessed from the tribune in the Convention that "the atrocious Vendée remained inexplicable."

But, he added, "the terrible day approaches when the torch of truth will illumine the depths of these dens (*repaires*) in the Vendée; the day when, with sure hand, we will tear the thick veil which still for a few moments covers all these distant intrigues (*intrigues lointaines*), all these local manœuvres, all these military treasons, and these divers ambitions of the chiefs. Victories coloured, half-successes exaggerated, fabulous tales, all will have their proper place (*tout aura sa place*), and the nation will be avenged."

Granville, the seaport, was at last reached; and the attack on it began on the 14th November; but Granville was a walled and fortified place, with a garrison of over 5000 men, and the Vendeans had no siege artillery, no scaling ladders, no military appliances for attacking such a place, and after a not too vigorous effort to capture it, they were repulsed with heavy loss.

The blow was decisive. The effect was disastrous; and the danger of the position of the Vendean army and its followers suddenly became apparent to all. The confidence of the Vendeans in their chiefs vanished; they became outspoken in their discontent with their leaders, some of whom they accused, not without apparent justification, of the intention of deserting them and escaping across the sea, and they declared their determination to return to the Vendée.

Winter was rapidly closing in upon them; the severity of the weather, the drenching rains, the penetrating winds, the bitter cold, were piercing them to their marrow. There was no sign of *émigré* help, nor of the English fleet — which by no possibility could have arrived off the French coast within the time. No course, in fact, was open but retreat, and, in consternation, they turned south again, making for Angers, in the despairing hope of there crossing the Loire and once more entering their own country.

But though in consternation they were still full of fight : and as it was said at the time by an eye-witness : " The entire army was like a wounded boar, which before perishing would crush the unskilful hunter who came in his way."

On the 20th November they had got back once more to Dol—their woes and miseries pressing ever heavier upon them—their strength failing them from hardship and privation. At nine at night the town was alarmed, and in the darkness fighting began. The next day they found themselves face to face with the army of Marceau, Kleber, and Westermann, and a desperate battle ensued. Fortune favoured now one side, now the other. " When the men were retreating great efforts were made to stop them. A number of women performed prodigies of resolution and decision of character. The priests exercised a still greater influence. It is the only time that I have seen them fanaticise the soldiers by employing all the means of religion to animate them. While the people paused to listen to the cannon, the curate of St. Marie de Rhé got upon a hillock near me, raised a large crucifix, and with a stentorian voice began to preach to the Vendeans. He was carried away by his enthusiasm ; he asked the soldiers if they would really be so infamous as to give up their wives and their children to be slaughtered by the Blues : he told them the only means of safety was to return to the battle. ' My children,' said he, ' I will march at your head, the crucifix in my hand ; let those who choose to follow me

kneel, I will give them absolution; if they die they
will go to Paradise; but the cowards who forsake God,
and abandon their families, will have their throats cut
by the Blues, and will go to hell.' More than 2000
men knelt down, and he gave them absolution with
a loud voice; and with the curate at their head they
departed, calling out 'Vive le Roi! We go to
Paradise.'"

In the midst of the fighting a thick fog came on,
and then night—and the battle was drawn.

It was resumed the next day. The Vendeans once
more fought with desperate courage, and completely
routed the republican army, inflicting very heavy loss
upon it, and Antrain was entered.

Here they learned that their wounded, which they
had left in hospital at Fougères, had been massacred
in their beds by the soldiers of the Republic. As some
republican administrators expressed it: "Our army has
given to the stragglers and the sick of the brigand army
passports to go to the devil."

Here, too, they learned some horrible details as to the
treatment of some of their women by the republicans;
and recognising among the prisoners they had captured
several soldiers who had been released at Fougères on
swearing not again to fight against the Vendeans, they
immediately shot them.

They were so exhausted by their prolonged trials,
and by their almost superhuman efforts, that they did
not avail themselves as quickly as they might have of
the advantages of their success. For them now victories
even were defeats, and everything which delayed their
march to the Vendée and augmented the number of
their wounded added to their difficulties.

A council of war was held, but the men declared that

they would only go the road to the Vendée, and their desire had to be acceded to.

With enemies on every side of them, and closing in more and more upon them, they bravely struggled on, upheld by the one hope of once more reaching their beloved Vendée.

The march from Antrain was unopposed, and on the 3rd December they presented themselves before Angers. But the town was not now abandoned as it had been in the previous June. Instead of which, the gates were closed, and inside a considerable garrison to defend it. Strong in itself, it had been made stronger by rapidly constructed defences and additional batteries. For the Vendeans to attack it with the limited resources at their disposal, and with their weakened and diminished numbers, was literally dashing their heads against the stone walls. But they were scarcely in a condition to judge what was wisdom and what was folly.

Worn out with cold and fatigue and sickness and every kind of hardship, they were in a state of appalling misery. The winter was one of exceptional and terrific severity; and grief, anxiety, hunger, and exposure had crushed the spirit of the men. Still, in their desperation to secure the means of crossing the Loire into their own land, they attacked it, but after thirty hours of valiant though hopeless effort, they had to desist. Retreat became necessary. And when, the next morning, some republican officers came out of the town to make a reconnaissance, they found in the plain the remains of the Vendean bivouacs with men and women and children lying dead there—dead from cold and misery.

Confusion among the Vendeans now was paramount. They were stunned by the disaster, and knew not whither to turn, or what to do. "They had lost every

hope of safety; the army gave itself up to the most
complete despair; it no longer saw any means of repassing
the Loire: sickness increased; on all sides were heard
the cries of the unfortunate wounded who had to be
abandoned.  Famine and bad weather added to all this
misery.  The chiefs were harassed in mind and body;
they knew not what determination to take."

Some of the men started of their own accord on the
road for Baugé—anywhither, so long as some start was
made, some action was taken; and, grateful for any lead,
the mass of the army and its unfortunate companions
followed.

At La Flèche there was a combat, and the republicans there were routed: passing through which the
Vendeans continued their journey northwards away from
home and country to Le Mans, which they reached on
the 11th.

"Everybody was overcome with fatigue . . . generals,
officers, and soldiers, everybody was cast down.  It was
evident we should be destroyed sooner or later; and that
the struggles we made were only the agonies of death.
We were surrounded with suffering; the sight of the
women, children, and wounded weakened the strongest
minds at the very time when a miraculous courage
was necessary.        Everything presaged our utter
ruin."

The following day they were again attacked, and the
battle was continued, the army of Kleber, Marceau, and
the impetuous Westermann having come up.

The combat reached the climax—the acme—of horror
of the campaign.  In parts of the fiercely, despairingly
contested field of battle the revolutionists gained the
advantage: in other parts they were worsted, but as
night fell the town had been in great part captured by

the revolutionists, and many of the Vendeans were in full flight. And all the long winter's night, in cold and snow and wet, and by the occasional gleams of a pale moon, there was desperate fighting in the narrow and irregular streets, and a fearful butchery; and when day broke the streets were piled with corpses, "many of them naked women whom the soldiers had despoiled and killed after violating them," and the houses were filled with dead and dying; and crowding and crushing out of it by the one bridge towards Laval were women and children and old people, and sick and wounded—all, in fact, who could still move.

The Representatives (Bourbotte, Prieur (de la Marne), and Turreau) in their report which was read before the Convention on 15th December gave an account of the victory.

"Chiefs, marchionesses, countesses, priests in plenty, carriages, baggage, cannon, guns, everything has fallen into our power. . . . The streets, the houses, the public places, the roads, are piled with corpses, and for fifteen hours the massacre has lasted. . . . The treasure, baggage, everything is in the hands of our soldiers, even to the silver crosses, the mitres, the croziers, the banners, the signs and instruments of fanaticism with which the priests made drunk this mad and ferocious horde. In fine, citizens, this is the most splendid day we have had during the ten months in which we have been fighting the brigands. Everything presages that those to follow it will not be less happy."

The Convention, on receiving the news, decreed that the army of the west had deserved well of its country, and called on the brave republicans of the north who were on their way to the scene of action to complete the entire destruction of the brigands.

In all some 17,000 Vendeans, women and children included, were estimated as having perished. " The Vendean army received its death-blow, and it was inevitable."

The flight to Laval was continued, the pursuit kept up. " Heaps of corpses," wrote Prieur (de la Marne), " are the only obstacles which the army opposes to the pursuit of our troops"; and Garnier (de Saintes) wrote, " In the space of fourteen leagues of the road there is not a fathom's length upon which a corpse is not stretched."

And an enthusiastic revolutionist commissioner— Maignan by name — gave his description, which also throws light on the republican character :—

"They had taken the road to Laval, and we followed them. I never saw such a carnage. The road was piled with corpses . . . women, priests, monks, men and children, all have been given over to death. I let no one off. I did my duty. There is pleasure in avenging one's country."

The republican cavalry, under Westermann, with some light artillery, vigorously kept up the pursuit, harassing and attacking the Vendeans without cessation —killing all who through fatigue or other cause fell behind; and the infantry followed by forced marches as rapidly as possible.

"One must render justice to the army," wrote Maignan. " It works well. Westermann is indefatigable ; he gives the rebels no breathing time. On the right and on the left the soldiers shoot those who have not been exterminated by his advance guard. Oh, how that goes (comme ça va) ! What a delight to see the triumphs of the Republic !"

As if the valiant republican army was not doing quite enough in the way of slaughtering, the peasants were hounded on to complete the work ordered by the

Convention.    Garnier (de Saintes), a Representative, issued
a proclamation enjoining the inhabitants of these districts
(under a penalty of death) to take guns, pitchforks, any
weapon in fact, and to pursue the brigands.

How thoroughly they obeyed this proclamation is
described by Maignan the commissioner.

" At Pouancé I saw the inhabitants of the commune
hunt the brigands as one hunts the wolves.   At Nort all
the inhabitants were hunting the scoundrels.   When I
arrived there, nearly two hundred were in the charnel-
house which they had made.   Every moment, four, five,
etc., etc., are brought in.   Immediately a shot tumbles
them over into the ditch."   And then he adds this characteristic touch of the true republican, " I am quite satisfied
with the spirit of the citizens of this part of the country."

And Benaben, a commissioner, wrote : " The peasants put the corpses in heaps alongside the roads very
much as if they were pigs for salting."

In one place, some five leagues from Le Mans, he saw
a hundred naked bodies piled in a heap.

Collected once more in a sort of way at Laval, with deci-
mated ranks, and fewer leaders, for some had fallen, some
had fled, the Vendeans attempted to make for Ancenis, in
the forlorn hope of being able to get over the Loire there.

But the Loire was no longer low, as it had been in
October : it was a great wide racing flood of brown
water.   Only a few boats could be obtained, and only a
few succeeded in crossing, their two principal leaders,
Henri de la Rochejaquelein and Stofflet, among the
number.   The rest, now leaderless, and hard pressed by
the republicans closing in on them, failed to get across,
lost some hundred men in a fight, and, turning westward, once more wandered on.

How any survived this flight is incomprehensible.

The weather was terrific—ceaseless torrents of rain: the roads in a fearful state. Their only food was such as they happened to be able to seize; for days they lived on raw turnips; their ammunition was nearly at an end. Though exhausted by fatigue and enfeebled by fever, dysentery, and disease, no opportunity for repose could be got. With ever-thinning ranks, with ever-diminishing strength, they still kept moving, pressed hard by the republicans.

On the 22nd they reached Savenay. Here, unable to move farther, the republican army overtook them. Here, on the 23rd, they made their final stand, and suffered annihilation.

The battle began at the break of day. The republicans attacked. "The *pas de charge* is heard everywhere," wrote Kleber. "Canuel overwhelms the enemy on the left, Marceau in the centre, and Kleber on the right. The cry of 'Vive la République' fills the air. The Vendeans fly, and fall under the fire of the republicans. Savenay is crossed; each column takes a different direction in pursuit of the rebels; the carnage becomes horrible; one part of them go to drown themselves in the marshes of Montoir, the remainder throw themselves into the woods and disperse there. Vehicles, cannons, everything falls into the power of the republicans, and this time the destruction of the enemy is certain."

Benaben says: "More than 1200 have been obliged to lay down their arms and to sue for life. Westermann has had about 400 [1] of them shot: the rest were shot by orders of the court-martial. . . The loss which the enemy has suffered is immense. The entire of this

[1] This number he corrected the next day, with fuller information, and stated it to be over 2000; and over and above these, he says, some 1200 were noyaded.

great army has sunk. . . . To-morrow we will all scatter ourselves as tirailleurs and make a general battue in the woods where the rebels have been able to take refuge."

Over the final horrors of the to-morrow and the days immediately following a veil may be drawn. The hunting down and ferreting out and slaughter of individuals may be left to the imagination. The one great resulting fact was that scarcely any of the vast horde of 80,000 to 100,000 Vendeans who had crossed the Loire ten weeks before lived to re-cross it. Non-combatants as well as combatants were all involved together in the common doom. Women were hunted down and slaughtered as remorselessly and triumphantly as was the most valiant soldier; children, too, of tender age were slaughtered; sick and wounded fell under the massacring steel or bullet. All, to use the expressive phrase of the Bible, were "put to the sword."

And they were valiant to the last these "fanatics," these men for whose abuse the dictionary of the French language was exhausted for terms of contumely and reproach.

The revolutionary general Beaupuy has left strong testimony as to their courage and fighting qualities. "They wanted but the uniform," he said, "to make them soldiers. . . . The troops who have conquered such Frenchmen can flatter themselves that they can conquer the allied defenders of the cause of kings."

Certainly time after time these Vendeans had, under every possible circumstance of discouragement, fought as veritable heroes: and in their dogged perseverance to the very end, they showed a sterling courage which stamps them as having possessed some of the very highest qualities of mankind.

Two incidents reported by Benaben, the above-mentioned republican commissioner, throw such a flood of light, of the grimmest kind, on the conduct of the revolutionists in the concluding scene of this bloody campaign, that they must be described, and best in his own words.

At the close of the battle of Savenay he met some republican volunteers or troops escorting some hundred Vendean prisoners to execution, and as they went they sang the " Marseillaise "—

> Allons enfants de la patrie,
> Le jour de gloire est arrivé.

And he remarks, " Here is an atrocious action."

And then he goes on to describe another. "Here is a worse," he says : " incredible, but attested by all the army."

Five hundred to six hundred brigands lay down their arms crying " Vive la nation." " Vive la République." A general (I know not which)[1] had them hemmed in by one or two battalions, and then ordered that fire should be opened on them. They all fell, some shot, some from fear. But as there were many who still moved, he cried, " Those who are not wounded, stand up." These poor people, thinking that it was intended to spare their lives, hastened to do so : but a second volley is fired into them, and those not killed are finished off with the bayonet or sabre.

" Such traits of inhumanity," he adds, " are unworthy of the most ferocious nation, are of a character to revolt every mind."

The battle over, Westermann wrote to the Committee of Public Safety :

" There is no longer a Vendée. She is dead under our

---

[1] Rumour, however, says it was Westermann.

free sword (*sabre libre*), with her women and her children. I have just buried her in the marshes and woods of Savenay, in obedience to the orders you gave me.

"I have crushed the children under the feet of the horses, and massacred the women, who, so far at least as they are concerned, will breed no more brigands. I have not to reproach myself with a prisoner. I have exterminated all. The roads are strewn with corpses. There are so many in several places that they form pyramids. The shooting of the prisoners goes on without ceasing at Savenay, because every moment brigands arrive, who pretend to surrender themselves as prisoners. We make no prisoners. It would be necessary to give them the bread of liberty, and pity is not revolutionary."

This was waging war "revolutionarily," as the revolutionary authorities in Paris wished.

Francastel, too, had written to the Convention, "No more brigands this side of the Loire": and the citizen soldier who brought the letter to Paris was invited to address the Convention.

He said, amidst applause, "We have made no prisoners, because we do not make any more": and Couthon, the President of the Convention, addressed him and said: "Soldier of the Republic, the applause of the National Convention conveys to you its lively satisfaction. Go; return to your brothers-in-arms; tell them that they have deserved well of their country."

And the Convention, wild with joy at getting the news of the annihilation of the Vendeans, forthwith decreed a vote of thanks to the army, and declared that it had deserved well of its country.

Yet over and above all the self-gratulations and votes of thanks and expressions of approval by the Convention, there rises the wailing reflection of Biron:

"Here Frenchmen fall under the blows of Frenchmen. The villages which we ravage belong to us; all the blood which we shed is ours."

And the same sentiment touched the heart of Marceau, one of the chief actors in the fearful drama; for in a letter to his sister, who had been celebrating his victories, he wrote:

"What, my dear sister, you send me felicitations on these two battles, or rather these two carnages; and you wish to have some of the leaves from my laurels. Does it not occur to you that they are stained with human blood, with French blood? I shall not return to the Vendée. It revolts me too much to fight Frenchmen. I wish to turn my arms against the foreigner. In that direction alone is glory" (or fame).

But such sentiments had no place, however, in the revolutionary mind as displayed by the Convention, and by those who were acclaiming themselves as the *vrai républicain*.

# CHAPTER XIV

## EXTERMINATION

REBELLION is rebellion, no matter how well justified it may be, and those who rebel must expect the worst if they are not successful. But after all is said in extenuation of severity, there is a limit which cannot be passed without incurring the reprobation of civilised humanity.

It is another of those extraordinary inconsistencies of the French revolutionists that the right of insurrection had been proclaimed by them in their Declaration of the Rights of Man as one of the primary and most sacred rights. Yet when the Vendeans rose in insurrection against the Republican Government, having been provoked and forced thereinto by the action of that Government, action in diametric opposition to the great principles it professed and acclaimed, no language was adequate to condemn their conduct, no measure was too severe for their repression and punishment. Perhaps those who made the Declaration thought mainly of justifying their own action in the past, and did not think of the contingency of any one exercising the right against themselves.

But even acknowledging that for self-preservation

sake the Revolutionary Government had to suppress the
Vendeans, though it itself was a Government only just
attained by rebellion and violence, and granting that,
being an *ipso facto* Government, it was justified in
repressing rebellion, though it itself had provoked and
was alone responsible for that disaster, no imaginable
reasons or excuses can justify the extreme and brutal
barbarism with which the repression was effected.

The cruelty, the mercilessness, the inhumanity, with
which the Vendeans were visited and pursued by their
own fellow-countrymen, finds no parallel in the history
of civilised races. Extermination, pure and simple, that
was the decree against them—they, and their sons and
their daughters, their man-servants and their maid-
servants, and every living thing in connection with
them—innocent or guilty—all alike. And so far as
their country was concerned, that would have been
destroyed too if the National Convention had had the
power to annihilate matter.

The exasperation of the Committee of Public Safety
has been sought to be explained, and the implacability
of the Government attempted to be justified on the
ground of the efforts of the Vendeans to get help from
the *émigrés* in the Channel Islands, and from the
English, the enemies of France. The Government, it is
said, felt that the Vendée was anti-French, and must be
extirpated to save France. "All thought the Patrie
could not exist with this 'cancer' in its side, and, with
clear conscience, gave the Vendée over to the surgery of
the Terror."

But those who use this argument ignore a fact which
completely shatters their contention, namely, that the
revolutionists entered on this process of " surgery " long
before these later incidents of exasperation. From the

very outset, when the Vendeans had dared to defy them,
they had been on bloody thoughts intent; and their
frequent defeats and humiliations in the Vendée first
exasperated and then infuriated them.

Soon after the outbreak of the Revolution, large
numbers of royalists had fled to England and the Channel
Islands, and the Revolutionary Government lived in a
constant state of alarm that they would obtain help from
England, and come back in force to attack France.  This,
too, long before the war broke out between England and
France.

Some leading royalists in Brittany had been endeavouring to organise a rising in Brittany, and a royalist
expedition, and to get help from England; but, as has
already been stated, so far as the Vendeans were concerned, the first great measure of repression, that of the
19th March, was enacted before any communication
passed from the Vendean leaders to England.  As a
matter of fact there were no Vendean leaders before the
outbreak of the civil war.

For a considerable time after the outbreak, moreover,
the English Government knew little either about the
war or the objects of the Vendeans; and it was by no
means anxious to commit itself to a landing on the
coast of France, especially on a dangerous coast with
practically no harbours.

And the Vendean leaders, conscious of the unpopularity
which an alliance with the enemies of France would
entail, desired far more the leadership of a Prince Royal,
and the help of the *émigrés*, than the actual help of
English forces.   D'Elbée himself said that they had no
want of foreign help to raise the throne again, to give
back to the clergy all their privileges, and to the noblesse
their rights.   Arms and military stores and money

they were anxious to get; but military help from the
English would certainly have damaged their cause by
exciting against them the patriotic feeling of France.

As the war went on more frequent communications
did pass between them and England, and the fact would
very naturally have intensified the fury of the Revolutionary Government against the Vendeans, had intensifica-
tion been possible; but the revolutionists were already
at white heat, breathing nothing but fire and slaughter,
destruction and annihilation against the Vendeans, and
nothing the Vendeans did or left undone could have
modified the revolutionary rage against them.

But going even further, and granting that the
Vendean leaders were culpable, and granting that communicating with the enemies of the "patrie" was in the
eyes of a Government whose sole shred of respectability
was its patriotism, an unpardonable crime, deserving the
severest punishment, it was nevertheless iniquitous in the
highest degree that the extremity of punishment should
be enforced against the Vendean rank and file, and
against the helpless and the weak, the old people and
women and children, against those whom they themselves
were always calling fanaticised and misled.

At most, only the Vendean leaders were concerned in
or cognisant of the communications with England; and
the Republican Government can never be exonerated from
the most horrible and heinous crime of ruthlessly visit-
ing the whole of the Vendean people, even to the women
and children, with a fierce and vindictive punishment for
an offence of which they are wholly innocent.

The revolutionists did not falter in their determination.
Conscience troubled them not at all, and giving people
over to "the surgery of the Terror" was quite congenial
work to them, and in complete logical accord with all

their oft-reiterated opinions.   And in so handing them over, there was no meanness, no dissimulation, no treachery, to which they would not, did not stoop, provided they compassed the end in view—the extermination of the Vendeans.

A Government is certainly expected to abide by its word.  If anything human can be binding, that is.  And the promise given by the direct representative of that Government is equally binding.   But this view was not held by the true sans-culotte.   In October, just about the time of the battle of Cholet, a terrible illustration of this fact was given.

Merlin (de Thionville), a Representative and an extreme revolutionist, himself an actor in the scene, gave an account of it some time after in the Convention:—

"Arrived at Montaigu, I issued a proclamation in the hope of winning over to us the rebels.

"'Frenchmen, for the last time the Republic opens her arms to receive you. . . . You have to-day to resist a disciplined army which has never known flight. Deliver your arms, surrender your chiefs, and this army, come to exterminate you, will become a protecting force for your persons and property.'"

In reply, the inhabitants of some twenty communes laid down their arms.   "Carrier was present when several of them arrived, and he spoke to them from the door of the headquarters.   I quitted the Vendée. Carrier, invested with full powers, remained their absolute master; and these same communes were shot.   Men were assassinated who fell on their knees and who showed my proclamation which they had kept as a safeguard."

One prominent and most discreditable feature of the revolutionary character is this, that the more the

revolutionist became masters of the position, the crueller
and more remorseless were their acts.

As quickly as possible after the Vendeans had crossed
the Loire, the military forces of the Republic were in
pursuit of them, and, as has been already stated, military
measures were taken to annihilate them. These, however, were not enough.

As the Vendean army moved on into Brittany,
encumbered by the mass of helpless non-combatants
clinging to it for protection, a miserable trail of suffering
humanity was left behind, in village and cottage, on
the roadside and in the ditches, of sick and wounded
and infirm, old men and women and children, those who
could go no farther. All these were pounced on by the
revolutionists, and fell a speedy prey to revolutionary
" Justice."

For, with the object of bringing revolutionary justice
into operation in all the places through which the
Vendeans passed, the criminal tribunals of the Departments were made ambulatory ; and, to supplement them,
the Representatives created travelling Military Commissions with their guillotines, so to speak, in their trunks,
so that all who fell out of the Vendean ranks might
be gathered by the revolutionary net, and not one
escape.

No sooner were the Vendeans at a safe distance from
a place or town through which they had passed, than a
Revolutionary Tribunal of some sort at once installed itself
there, at once seized those who had been unable to go
on, at once arrested all who were suspected of aiding
the brigands, erected its guillotine, handed over to the
executioner a number of victims, then, packing up the
bloody paraphernalia of revolutionary justice, moved on
to some other safe place to repeat the performance.

Thus, when the Vendeans left Laval, where they had stopped several days, the Felix commission came to administer revolutionary justice.

When they were repulsed at Granville, a Military Commission was promptly installed there. At Rennes, not very far off their line of march, where the prisons were crammed with Vendean stragglers or derelicts, and where typhus was raging, two military tribunals were quickly put in full function, with the usual results.

At Avranches, let the republicans tell their own tale. It helps one to realise the balder reports of others in other places. The "Administrators" of Avranches wrote to the Committee of Public Safety:—

"As soon as we had been informed that the scoundrel army had evacuated the town, we hastened to return to it, and to resume our functions. One of our first cares was to have some fifty-five or sixty of these blackguards shot whom we had arrested, or who had remained in the hospital."

And Laplanche, the Representative in those parts, wrote to the Convention:—

"We found here on our arrival many rebels who had remained behind, and to whom our inopportune arrival did not give time to fly. The hospital, equally, was full of them. The national vengeance was executed on them, and there is no further question about them."

Thus both the Committee of Public Safety and the Convention had official knowledge of these horrors, and as they did nothing to stop them, they can only be considered as accessories, and as approving of them.

Even to St. Malo Vendean prisoners had been sent, and a Military Commission appointed to try them. Women were shot, and people carried from the hospital to the field of carnage and shot. Death even should not

rob the commission of its *métier*, for it declared twenty-
five Vendeans who had died in prison as guilty, and
ordered the confiscation of their goods.

The blood of the Vendeans the revolutionists were
determined to have, and the spirit as well as the letter
of the terrible decrees against them was carried to the
extremest limit.

No fact so convincingly illustrates the extraordinary
indifference to the cost of attaining this end, or so
elucidates the almost incredible callousness of republican
authorities, as an order issued by the Representatives
Esnue Lavallée, Prieur (de la Marne), actually a member
of the Committee of Public Safety, and Turreau, to the
republican generals in Brittany who were fighting the
Vendeans there.

The generals were ordered, in case of absolute necessity,
to get rid of (*se défaire*)—in other words, to kill—their
own republican sick and wounded, should they be found
to hinder the march of the army in any important
movement.  It is true it was to be done "in the most
humane possible way."

And the reasons are given.  "The wounded or sick,"
said the Representatives, "being frank republicans as we
ourselves are, ought, as we do, to sacrifice themselves for
the public safety.  They are not able to fight and die
for the nation with arms in their hands.  It is necessary,
therefore, that they die in another manner."

If such was the state of mind as regards their own
men, what consideration could be expected from them
in dealing with their enemies?

It was not, however, only in the trail of the Vendean
army that the revolutionists at this time were active, or
indulging in ruthless severity.  Everywhere they could,
it was the same story.

Angers was crammed with prisoners. As the Vendean army might come in that direction it was felt desirable that they should be removed.

Robert, the erstwhile Paris comedian, now a general at Angers, has in a letter to the Minister of War, dated 29th November, described what became of some of them.

" I announce to you that about *two thousand Catholic prisoners* who were detained here, and whom we, acting in concert with citizen Francastel, made evacuate on different points, have perished. A part of these gentlemen *revolted against the guard, who did justice in the matter* (*qui en a fait justice*). When the rest were crossing the Ponts-de-Cé *two arches collapsed*, and they *unfortunately* fell into the Loire, where they were drowned. *Unfortunately* their feet and hands were tied. Vive la République." [1]

So soon as it was actually ascertained that the Vendeans were advancing on Angers, the members of the Military Commission there took to their heels and fled to Doué, but not wishing to be deprived of their prey in the shape of prisoners, they took a lot with them. Of these, 60 were, in the revolutionary style now becoming common, shot on the way at one place, 60 more at another place. It was, in fact, almost impossible to move prisoners from one place to another without many being shot *en route*, the republican escorts apparently being unable to keep their hands off them.

Some survived till Doué was reached. Here, on the 17th December, 69 were shot; on the 18th, 41; on the 20th, 58; and on the 22nd, 31. Statistics may be dry; these quiver with human agony.

---

[1] The words in italics are underlined in the original (O. de Chavigny).

" The fusillades took place ordinarily near a quarry
called 'Justices de Fier - Bois.' There the dead and
dying were pitched pell-mell ; the evening of an execution one could hear half-stifled groans issuing from this
tomb."

Once the fate of the Vendeans on the north side of
the Loire was sealed by their repulse at Angers, the
sphere of operations for Revolutionary Tribunals and
Military Commissions widened considerably, and there
was a tremendous glut of work for them.

The Vendean army being in process of annihilation
and unable to protect itself, much less others, those
who were dependent on it were the first victims of the
catastrophe. The thousands of non-combatants, women,
sick, wounded, old people, and children, who so far had
escaped death or massacre by the republican troops, and
who could now proceed no farther, were there to be dealt
with.

Military Commissions roved all over the place.
Wherever "great blows" were to be struck, one, or
more, was sent.

Promptly on the great republican victory at Le Mans
a Military Commission was appointed there, under the
presidency of Bignon of infamous notoriety.

Here an exceptional number of Vendean prisoners
had been made, and for long after Le Mans was the
scene of appalling horrors. At the outset many were
shot at sight—"arbitrary fusillades," as they have been
called ; but what was infinitely worse, 400 wounded,
who were unable to fly and were in hospital, were
massacred there at night.

Then followed executions after form of sentence by
Military Commissions, large numbers of women being
shot actually at the door of the house where the

Representatives Turreau and Bourbotte were stopping—
"a veritable butchery," as Benaben, an eye-witness, wrote
of it.

There were three large prisons at Le Mans, one being
the church of l'Oratoire, in which 1200 prisoners, mostly
women, were crammed. The town was without food.
The prisoners, forgotten by the inhabitants, implored in
vain for death or a morsel of food.

One who went into the church described how "a
thousand spectres rose at once and with one voice cried
'bread.'"

And in addition to hunger a pest broke out. For
days the dead were unburied, and then only half so.
Le Mans "was a vast cemetery, a centre of contagion, a
charnel-house."

Dysentery and typhus swept thousands away. The
fear of the spread of the plague, or Vendean sickness, was,
it is said, one of the causes of the expedition used in
killing them. But the sordid greed of the revolutionists
helped to their own destruction, for the clothes they
tore from their victims spread the contagion, like
Nessus' shirts, and were fatal to those who took them.

When the Vendeans, continuing their flight, had left
Laval, a Revolutionary Tribunal was established there,
also a Military Commission, and on the 16th, 17th, and
20th December 120 prisoners, from 16 to 71 years of
age, were shot. During their execution the judges, who
were installed at a window before a table covered with
glasses of wine, drank to the *sainte République* and to
the death of the *culotins*.

At Ancenis, where the flying Vendeans had also
halted for a brief while, a Military Commission was
appointed to deal with the unfortunate débris of the
Vendeans left there.

To what acts even a Representative could descend in
his consuming passion to destroy the Vendeans is shown
by a letter from the culprit himself. Merlin (de Thionville), the Representative, wrote from Ancenis in
December while pursuing the Vendeans: "The curé
Rodrigue of Basse Goulaine wished to follow the column
of brigands. I killed him with one blow of the sword.
Let Nantes be tranquil. I would go to hell to exterminate the last of the brigands."

When the final disaster occurred at Savenay the
Bignon Military Commission promptly took up its
quarters there, and in three days—25th, 27th, and 28th
December—condemned between 600 and 700 prisoners
to be shot, and acquitted none.

The mind almost refuses to take in the actuality of
these horrors, or to grasp that they had a real existence.

One sees the general picture—the retreating mass of
people, made up of sick and wounded, the aged and
feeble, struggling along, and the extemporised army still
giving what protection it could to those dependent on it,
still valiantly upholding the cause for which it had
appealed to arms, though the numbers of its fighting
men were rapidly diminishing, and the line of retreat
strewn with its dying and dead. That is easily under-
standable.

But the individual sufferings of those fallen behind,
surrounded by merciless and implacable foes, the pro-
tracted anxiety, the prolonged trials, the loss of kith and
kin, the fading of hope, the final despair and heartbreak,
who can now realise them?

A heart-wringing letter from a young wife who went
through part of the awful pilgrimage, written the moment
before going to execution, lifts a tiny section of the veil:
"I only take my pen to send you my last adieux and

those of my sister, and to beg you to give them to all those who are dear to us, and particularly to your friend Pierre.   Tell him that we lost our mother at La Flèche, my father at Le Mans, and that the guillotine ends our days at Alençon.   People consider us guilty, and try us as such.   You who knew us since infancy know what truth there is in it.   We lose our lives without regret : the miseries which we have endured for eight months are well calculated to detach us from it. . . . If you ever see my husband again, tell him I die adoring him, that death, which will soon freeze my heart, will never efface his image, that the memory of him comes with me beyond the tomb."

And she and her sister were but two out of that great mass who had crossed the Loire after the battle of Cholet.

The final destruction of this Vendean host was like the foundering in a tropical sea of a great ship, laden with people.   Disabled by a gale and rapidly sinking, she reels and plunges helplessly along, until the final plunge ; and then the sea, almost dark with ravening sharks, fighting with each other for the human victims as they struggle in the water, dashing wildly hither and thither in the reddening waves, until the last vestige of anything human has been torn to pieces and devoured.

The defeat of the Vendean arms was so overwhelming that the Republic in its hour of triumph might have shown some compassion towards those over whom it had triumphed.   Instead of this, its appetite for blood seemed only whetted, and the Representatives, "far from combating the outburst of savage passions, aided it with all their efforts ; they fanned the fanaticism of the Revolutionary Committees, they stimulated the zeal of the Military Commissions, and directed with a cold and implacable cruelty the extermination of a people conquered and taken prisoner."

In addition to the non-combatants who fell into the hands of the republicans, and in addition to the Vendeans who were taken with arms in their hands, there was a third and very large class—men who had laid down their arms on the promises given them that their lives would be spared.

There is not a vestige of doubt that promises to this effect were made to the Vendeans by the republican authorities, Representatives and generals alike, and then, most infamously, broken.

The Abbé Gruget, who resided concealed in Angers all the dreadful time of the Terror there, states in his narrative of the events there: "During the siege of Angers by the Vendeans the generals and officers had forbidden the troops to kill those they made prisoners, still less those who delivered themselves on the promise of their lives being spared on their undertaking not to bear arms again against the Republic. This was public, and every one knew of it. But Francastel refused to ratify this engagement. Those who surrendered were imprisoned, and then shot."

The Abbé Gruget further declared that Francastel set snares for the Vendeans, hypocritically causing printed notices promising amnesty to be scattered on the roads.

Many Vendeans surrendered, but they paid with their lives the penalty for their belief in republican promises.

Confirmatory of this infamous conduct on the part of the revolutionists is a declaration made about a year afterwards by General Cordellier, a revolutionary general, that he had seen at Saumur some 700 to 800 men who, he was told by General Commaire, were brigands of the Vendée, who had laid down their arms, " in virtue of the invitation which had been made them by the Representatives then on mission with the army of the west," and that Commaire had orders to shoot them, which was done. Also at Angers the same thing was done. Astonished thereat, he spoke to General Robert, and learned from him that he (Robert) had orders from Francastel to shoot or drown all the brigands who came and surrendered their arms, orders which were carried out. The practice, in fact, was general.

After the 16th December several Vendeans came to the municipality of Ingrandes declaring that they were tired of the war, and that, if promised their lives, they and many of their comrades would surrender. The magistrates of Ingrandes received those overtures favourably, as giving a symptom and hope of a near peace, encouraged the Vendeans to surrender, and about 200 were sent to Angers until their fate was settled.

General Moulin, entering into these pacific views, gave a safe-conduct to ten Vendeans to go and persuade their friends to surrender. In the course of a few days about 1200 surrendered. They were detained at St. Florent waiting for an answer from Francastel, to whom Moulin had written. Moulin, who appears to have acted in good faith, was disavowed in the promises of amnesty; and the 1200 were sent to St. Gemmes near Angers and Ponts-de-Cé, and without any trial were all shot.

For his efforts towards pardon of the Vendeans Moulin was ordered to Nantes by Carrier, where he was thrown into prison; and Carrier afterwards made him publicly state that if he had given some passports to some Vendeans it had only been with the object of getting a larger number to surrender.

Similar testimony came from other places.

At Nort, some miles north of Nantes, the republican hussars overtook the fugitive Vendeans. "Surrender, friends," they cried out, "no harm will be done you; the Republic, full of clemency, pardons you." Two hundred surrender; the infantry are massacred by the forces of that Republic; the cavalry were conducted to Nantes, and there, by Carrier's orders, shot.

This possibly is the same incident given more definitely by Mellinet, the well-known historian of Nantes. "On the faith of a proclamation," he says, "of 19th December (29 Frimaire, An ii.), promising amnesty, about 100 Vendean cavalry came to Nantes to make their submission. The next day Carrier had them shot."

That promises were made appears also from the following :—

Seven to eight hundred Vendeans came (December) to surrender their arms. Carrier ordered them to be shot. The administration asked for a delay, and invoked the promises made to the rebels who submitted themselves to the Republic. It asked for their examination, as many of them were pronounced republicans who had been made prisoners by the rebels. Carrier appeared to approve, but by the next day they had all been shot.

And one more proof is given in a later report of the popular society at Fontenay.

"The law of March 19, 1793, condemned to death all who took part in the revolt—that of 10th May limited this penalty to only the chiefs—that of 5th July defined the term 'chief.' . . . A law of October ordered all to surrender their arms under pain of being considered chiefs—and proclamations to this effect were published by Representatives and the constituted authorities. . . .

"In spite of this, the agriculturists who went and surrendered their arms — who took the oath — who returned with certificates declaring their submission to the law, these same cultivators were arrested at their own homes by patrols and put to death, just as rebels taken with arms in their hands. Where is the security of the public faith when it can be violated with impunity?"

The proofs that this system of deception on the part of the "brave, the true republican" was constantly practised are overwhelming.

If anything could have added to the agony of the last moments of these unfortunate Vendeans, it must have been the bitter sense of treachery and deceit on the part of the republicans.

With the increase in the number of persons to be tried, the procedure of the various Revolutionary Tribunals became less formal.

Letourneur, a Representative, wrote to the criminal tribunal at Alençon that "one could not put too great celerity into trying the Vendean rebels"; and Garnier (de Saintes), another Representative, wrote to the criminal tribunal at Le Mans :—

"It is here a matter of judging revolutionarily. All minute formalities should be put aside. . . . You must drop the idea that you are only judges whom the law has surrounded with forms. You assume here a different, a revolutionary character. You ought to judge revolutionarily, and promptly rid society of these monsters."

The one formula, "relations with the brigands, with arms in their hands," sufficed : whether true or not, no one could know, for no questions were asked of any one except the prisoner, and no witnesses were heard.

Soon even the Military Commission did not give
themselves the trouble to designate the offence. " They
killed, and all was said." (On tua, et tout fut dit.)

A president of one of them remarked : " Some of the
prisoners have the impertinence to ask for the proofs
the nation has against them. The nation has suppressed
this abuse of the *ancien régime*. They are guilty
because we wish it."

As Babeuf asked : " What did the slaughterer risk ?
His judgments and their execution were subject neither
to scrutiny nor revision."

The revolutionists were far from confining their efforts
to the wake of the Vendean army.

Saumur had not been in the line of retreat of the
Vendean host, but nevertheless revolutionary activity in
it had been great. All through the autumn the Revolutionary Committee, with its subordinate committees, had
been hard at work there. The municipality and the
Revolutionary Tribunal had been brought under the complete control of the Committee. Incessant requisitions were
made for all sort of things—suspects, real or imaginary,
had been arrested and crammed into prison ; the Military
Commission from Angers came thither on *une tournée
patriotique* (a patriotic tour), *pour dégorger les prisons*,
and the guillotine had been erected *en permanence*.

The " terror " in a small place like this was awful.

" Those who had the right, or arrogated to themselves
the right, of ordering arrests, were infinite in number.
Generals, Representatives, members of the Revolutionary
Committee, commandants, even the doorkeepers of the
prisons, rivalled each other in zeal."

As the result of this facility of arrest, the prisons
were crammed. There were three of them, and a church
used as such : in one there were once 400 prisoners ; in

another nearly 250, including women, and children of four and even two years of age.

Too much reliance must not be placed on these figures, for the prison registers were most imperfectly kept; how imperfectly. appeared in evidence. On one occasion some prisoners escaped. The gaoleress was arrested. With difficulty she escaped death; all the more so, as she was asked to account for forty prisoners inscribed on the register. about whose fate nothing could ever be ascertained.

And the mortality was frightful. In six months 1699 deaths were declared at the Mairie.

The Military Commission aided disease to the best of its capacity in emptying the prisons, having recourse, as time went on, to executions *en masse*.

On 24th December the church of Nantilly was full of prisoners. The Military Commission sent one of its members, Roussel, "to empty it."

He went, took down their names, interrogated them; and apparently, with compunction as to the youth of some, separated all under eighteen years, and had them confined in the choir.

That evening 79 were shot at Asnières; and, two days later, 75 more.

On the 26th December the Military Commission went to the prison, interrogated, convicted all, except those under eighteen: and the same evening 235 were, on the pretence of a walk, taken by a detachment of 300 men to a field near Munet, where they were shot—all except two. who actually escaped in the falling shades of night.

The youths and children had been spared. Were the *vrais sans-culottes* relenting: losing some iota of their savagery? About a month after. in the beginning of

February, 112 prisoners were taken from the prison of Nantilly in carts to Parnay, and there shot.

"Among the number," deposed the gaoler Poitou, "were 50 children and youths from twelve to eighteen years of age, the greater number from twelve to fifteen, who had been excepted from the first fusillade at Bournan."

These children cried *comme des malheureux*, and asked to be allowed to serve the Republic, but, just the same as the others, they were shot; the members of the Military Commission being present, as they usually, if not invariably, were, to see their sentences carried out. One wonders of what stuff these men were made, to go on witnessing day after day the wholesale slaughter of men, women, and children, whose deaths they had themselves decreed without the semblance of evidence.

Saumur, in fact, presented on a small scale one more illustration of the ways of the *vrai sans-culotte*—of the methods and principles of revolutionary "justice"—of the freedom and justice guaranteed to men under the new régime of "liberty, equality, and fraternity."

Revolutionary atrocities were not confined to the east and north-east of the Vendée.

Away in the south-west, at Fontenay, another Representative, Lequinio, was ruling revolutionarily. On the first night of his arrival at Fontenay, 9th December 1793, he appeared before the popular society there, and read it some chapters of his book against the existence of a Supreme Being, of a Divine Providence, and of a life to come. The next day an incident occurred which presented him in a less harmless light than reading out his own absurdities.

Some of the prisoners abused the wife of the gaoler on account of their ill-treatment. One of them caught her by the throat. She shrieked. The guard rushed in

and killed the prisoner.  Lequinio was banqueting with
the popular society. in the "Temple of Reunion," formerly
the church of Notre Dame.  He was informed of the
revolt in the prison.  Furious at being disturbed in the
middle of his repast, he ordered the alarm to be sounded ;
had the prison surrounded : and, having sent in a guard
and made all safe, went in himself, blew out the brains
of the first man he saw, made his officer kill another, and
then returned to the society to glorify his firmness, and
to receive its applause.  The next day he established a
Military Commission, which promptly set to work, condemning women as well as men.

On the 15th December Fontenay got a fright, that
the Vendeans were advancing to attack it.

Lequinio, who was at Rochefort at the moment, was
at once informed.  He sent a reinforcement of troops,
and at the same time an order to shoot all the prisoners
at Fontenay, several hundreds in number, without form
of trial. if the enemy appeared before the walls.

His letter, informing the Committee of Public Safety
of his action, was read before the Convention on the
19th December :—

"I must tell you that. without such measures, you
will never finish the Vendean war.  It is the abominable
moderation of the administrators which has created the
Vendée.  It is the moderation of the administrators and
generals which continued it.  I have said everywhere
that no prisoners should be made ; and. if I say it, I wish
that similar measures were adopted in all our armies. . . .
As to the Vendée, that is indispensable if you wish to
be done with it."

The local authorities, not so bloody-minded as the
Representatives, sent the prisoners off to Niort, and so
evaded the fulfilment of this horrible order.

The Military Commission he ordered to dispense with ordinary formalities, and prohibited them paying any regard to representations made to them in favour of any prisoner. Within a few months it sentenced about 200 persons to death, mostly simple peasants.

Here, as in other places, it was the people (in whose favour the Revolution was made) who furnished to the scaffolds the great mass of victims.

Not content with the ordinary methods of slaughtering the Vendeans, the republicans were devising new ones.

A somewhat common one was to shoot their prisoners while escorting them from one prison to another.

The massacre at Ponts-de-Cé has already been described.

On the 2nd December some 400 prisoners—mostly Vendeans—who were being transferred from Saumur to Orleans by order of the Representative of the people, Levasseur (de la Sarthe), arrived at Chinon. They had as escort a company of infantry and some dragoons under the command of " Le Petit," aged eighteen, the president of the Revolutionary Committee at Saumur.

The next morning, at five o'clock, they were conducted out of the town, as if to continue their journey. On a signal from Le Petit, a general volley carried death into their ranks. More than 200, among whom were women and children, were stretched on the earth, dead, or writhing in the last convulsions of agony.

The wounded were then finished off. The remainder were collected, and marched on; many of them only to suffer death in a similar manner farther on.

The prisoners had never even been tried, and Le Petit's excuse was that he had orders from Levasseur to shoot them all.

Convoys of prisoners melted away, being shot on the road.

"Woe to those who couldn't walk," writes Benaben. "On the pretext of there being no vehicles to convey them, they were shot."

A convoy of seventy-two prisoners was sent to Nantes from Ancenis, of whom only four arrived at their destination. One of the escort said : "They were shot in parties every now and then," and the excuse given was that they had attempted revolt. The removal of prisoners was, in fact, a sort of human paper - chase, the course being tracked by bleeding corpses.

It really did not matter very much. It was only a question of a very little sooner, or a very little later, for if they reached their destination their fate was equally certain.

In addition to the unfortunates who thus were being done to death by one means or the other, north, west, south, and east, there were those who died in the prisons. Anything approaching complete records are not available, but from isolated records one can get an idea of what the general state of things must have been. The number who died in Saumur prisons has already been mentioned.

At Doué, in one month (December 1793), 134 persons died in the prison.

At Montreuil in Anjou, where a lot of women were confined in the Chateau, typhus broke out, and over 200 died—died at the rate of 20 to 30 a day.

And these were but two prisons of the great number which existed.

And so, over the whole scene of the Vendean struggle during these winter months, Representatives and Revolu-

tionary Committees and popular societies were filling the
prisons, Revolutionary Tribunals and Military Commissions were hard at work emptying them—meting out
death to the unfortunate persons brought before them,—
innocent and guilty alike.

And from the sandhill top at Sables to the Place du
Ralliement at Angers; and from Granville and Rennes
in the north to Fontenay and La Rochelle in the south :
the blade of the guillotine was rising and falling with
awful frequency ; and day after day musket-volleys were
ringing out their messages of death : and all men were
being shown what " fraternity," according to the idea
of the brave republican, really was,—not fraternity, as
he with lying lips asseverated, but the very antithesis of
it—" fratricide."

# CHAPTER XV

## THE TERROR AT ANGERS

IN the history of the iniquities and tyrannies of the great French Revolution, Nantes has occupied a most conspicuous place.

But there was another town also involved in the Vendean revolt which was the scene of revolutionary brutalities rivalling those of Nantes, a town where, during this awful period, demonstration was also given of how the Revolution worked out in actual practice, and where the real character of the true republican and *vrai sans-culotte*, from the highest State official downwards, was revealed in all its hideousness and repulsiveness.

This was Angers, the capital of the old province of Anjou, one of the oldest fortresses of France, still surrounded by high walls, with gateways and towers, and commanded by the ancient, grim-looking, and formidable Chateau. "Black Angers" was it called, from its narrow and gloomy labyrinthine streets, and from the dark hue of the high and centuries-old houses, with their overshadowing style of architecture: a town crowded with churches, and convents, and public buildings, and cemeteries; a veritable relic of the dark ages.

And now, in the guise of liberty and fraternity, the dark ages had come back to it again, with all their horrors of tyranny, and intolerance, and religious persecution multiplied a hundredfold.

It was an important town, situate on a river, doing a good trade, and many of the inhabitants were wealthy, which was a temptation to revolutionary cupidity.

Here, as has been already described, by the end of October, all the preparations had been made for the free working of revolutionary ideas, for the full play of revolutionary government.

The epoch of "liberty, equality, and fraternity" had some little while back dawned on the town; now its inhabitants were about to revel in the full noon-tide splendour of those glorious principles as interpreted by the *vrai républicain*, the true sans-culotte.

Here, with nobody to gainsay them, no public opinion to check them, the revolutionists had it all their own way, and were to give another illustration to the world of their true character, another realistic portrait of those most repulsive individuals.

No heed whatever had been paid by the Government in Paris to the protest of the electors against the demoralising rule of the Representatives, except that two of the Representatives then ruling despotically there had been recalled, in October, and two worse despots sent— Hentz and Francastel.

Bad and tyrannical as Choudieu had been, Francastel was worse—was in fact one of the very worst of those tyrants which the era of "liberty" had given to the people of France—a cold-blooded, cautious scoundrel of the cruellest type—a merciless despot.

Nature does not always associate a brutal exterior with an infamous character. Francastel "was a gentleman.   His exquisite elegance and the beauty of his face formed a singular contrast with the cynicism of his acts and words." He dressed the part of a revolutionist very accurately, as he wore constantly the three-cornered hat, embroidered coat, the tricolour sash, and short breeches, with varnished top-boots. But neither features nor dress could cover the depths of wickedness that filled his whole nature. He was cooler-headed than most of the conspicuous figures on the revolutionary stage, and was ever careful to avoid giving any written orders, or leaving any written proof of his actions as regarded the brigands. "He ordered us to burn all these monuments (or records) of death," said one of his instruments. Enough, however, remains to enable us to realise his real character.

"As for me," he wrote in one of his letters, "penetrated with the sense of duties imposed by true justice and the welfare of the people. I will always fulfil my mission with the same inflexibility. The Vendée shall be depopulated, but the Republic shall be avenged and tranquil. Let Terror not cease to be the order of the day, and all will go well."

And on the 26th of November he wrote to the Committee of Public Safety : " Fire and steel have not yet been sufficiently employed in this cursed country, in spite of reiterated orders. Continually prisoners are sent us and more prisoners." (*On nous envoie continuellement des prisonniers et toujours des prisonniers.*)

Mercilessness and ruthless severity were prominent features in his character.

" Not even a child in the cradle should be spared," he is reported to have said.

And so, with an irresponsible bloodthirsty despot of this type in supreme authority in the town ; with the

gates closed to all except those who could obtain a
revolutionary passport; with a Revolutionary Committee
and two Military Commissions in keen working order;
and with a guillotine erected in permanence in the Place
du Ralliement, the preparations were all complete for
the administration of revolutionary justice, and the
population was given full assurances for their enjoyment
of the blessings of liberty, equality, and fraternity which
the Revolution was supposed to have brought.

Just as at Nantes the Revolutionary Committee was
made up of a gang of infamous wretches, so here was
the Committee composed of men of the most infamous
character.

With the sacred names of liberty, equality, and
fraternity on their lips, they gave themselves over to
every form of atrocity. Though professing to do everything for the Republic, they did everything for themselves. They stole, they plundered the public funds,
they levied money illegally, they appropriated everything
they wanted, they lived on the proceeds of pillage.
They abused their power to debauch girls and women
in prison. They revelled in drunken orgies. And to
do this they waded through rivers of blood, the blood
of their own countrymen and countrywomen, even the
blood of children, setting every principle of justice and
humanity at naught, and perpetrating such crimes that
posterity could not credit the facts were they not
vouched for by ample evidence.

The Revolutionary Committee had throughout the
summer been in a state of feverish energy, filling their
days with ordering or superintending domiciliary visits,
and arrests, and imprisonments, and sending victims to
the Military Commissions to be formally sentenced to
death—and executed; and spending their nights in

drunken orgies and debauches. They were, so to speak, let loose on society, and were making the most of their opportunity. "A single suspicion, a single verbal denunciation was sufficiently powerful motive for our arrests," they themselves wrote.

The religious persecution in Angers had been unceasing in its activity and virulence. Under the active instigation, first of Choudieu, and then of Francastel, who was a revolutionary inquisitor, the anti-religious mania was given full swing.

The proceedings in the Convention on the 7th November 1793 added fresh impetus to the persecution, and religious persecution ran riot. In this enlightened era, with its boasted "liberty of opinion" and "freedom of worship," there was neither one nor the other, only very much the reverse. Priest-hunting had been carried on unintermittently, and still afforded good results. To have been at the celebration of the mass by an unsworn priest was a crime punished by death; to have taken part in a religious procession, even a year before, was a crime punished by death; to be found in possession of any religious emblem was a crime punished by death.

The anti-religious fury vented itself even on inanimate objects. The monuments in the churches, the sepulchres, inscriptions, marbles, the altars, everything destroyable was destroyed, and everything portable was carried away; even members of the Committee helped in the destruction, and one of the members of one of the Military Commissions cut some of the pictures to pieces with his sabre. The buildings themselves were turned into prisons, or stables, or to any sort of secular purpose, all except the cathedral, which was converted into a Temple of Reason that new and enlightened

worship which was to succeed the low and degrading
superstitions of Christianity.

It might be thought that the revolutionist would
have had enough of the real thing to prevent him
hungering after the counterfeit presentment. But this
would be a misappreciation of the revolutionary character, for at the theatre at Angers a piece was acted
called " The capture of Cholet, or the destruction of the
brigands of the Vendée." The Revolutionary Committee
—whose permission for its performance had of course to
be obtained—blessed it as " a piece which breathed the
purest patriotism."

The hero—a *vrai sans-culotte*—declaimed sentiments
in accord with the revolutionary feelings of the moment.
" I fear not death," he said, " but I pray I may be
spared till I have exterminated the last of the tyrants,
and their odious satellites. Kings I detest. Priests—
the mere name infuriates me — I abhor. Nobles I
despise"; and then he burst into song: " Let us strike,
till their vile blood streams under our blows." And
then, as if there were not enough death and destruction
going on outside, there was a stage fight between the
republicans and the Vendeans, the hero with his sword
hewing daylight through the latter, capturing cardboard
castles, and finally planting the tricolour on the highest
tower. And the Jacobins, and soldiers, and public
functionaries loudly applauded, and betook themselves
to their homes with fresh zest to participate the next
day in the real business, the fusillades or guillotinings
of their unfortunate fellow-countrymen.

The repulse of the Vendeans in their attack on the
town on the 3rd and 4th December, and their crushing
defeats at Le Mans, Laval, and Ancenis, brought thousands
of them within the reach of the arm of revolutionary

justice, and quickly the prisons of Angers, and several
churches and other large buildings converted into prisons,
were filled to suffocation with them. Here they underwent all the miseries, all the cruelties which imprisonment at this time entailed.

But it was not merely the Vendeans who were seized
on by the revolutionists; all those who had, or were
suspected of having, given the Vendeans any help, or
food, or shelter during their wanderings on the north
side of the Loire, were also treated as enemies of the
Republic. And prisoners were brought in "in batches
of 50 or 100 without any *procès-verbaux*—without any
denunciations, without even a list of their names."

Francastel rose to the occasion. He wrote to Felix,
the president of the Military Commission :—

"Your presence here becomes very necessary. Every
place is crammed. A sort of policy (*une sorte de police*)
sends this herd to our prisons. The time will come to
judge them all. Indulgence, forgiveness for the past,
compassion, tenderness, all these beautiful names only
cover weakness, moderation, and perfidy. You know
that a herd of several hundred women were taken at
Mans. They are amazons, royalist paladines, concubines
of priests, *des dames en pelisse*, etc. Well, all that
inspires interest. To whom ? To the revolutionists ;
to the members of a Military Commission. Come here
—I count on you—I know your principles ; your
republican inflexibility, your unshakable intention to
purge the Vendean generation, to bleed it till it is white "
(*saigner à blanc*).

And Felix came, and hundreds were promptly haled
before his Military Commission—the proceedings of
which were like all the other Military Commissions in
that part of the country, "a profanation of justice."

Legally, the majority of the prisoners should have been tried before the criminal tribunal, but it was the privilege of the Representatives to ignore all laws.

Even Felix and his commission could not keep pace with the work expected from it, and so another was appointed, with Proust as president, and Vacheron and Morin, two awful scoundrels, among the members.

So great was the press of work that the judgments were noted in the registries of the court with a single letter—"F" to fusillade or shoot, "G" to guillotine, and an "X" to detain. And so keen were the judges to slaughter, that against many names the fatal letters "G" and "F" were doubled—as if they wished to have the unfortunate people guillotined or shot twice over.

One of the members of the Revolutionary Committee declared that if it was necessary to note the particulars of those who deserved death one would never be done. "Let us rather than lengthen our work by writing, shorten it by beheading."

Even yet, however, the procedure did not meet the necessities of the case, and Francastel ordered that the members of the Commission should go to the prisons and there interrogate and deal with the prisoners.

This was done; and the prisoners were interrogated in batches, and condemned in batches, Vacheron and Morin being conspicuous, and Hodoux and Lepetit also aiding. And report says that the members of the Military Commission outraged some of the women before their execution.

What an exhibition of "justice"—a justice claiming to be superior to all the world had yet seen or imagined, revealed now to an ignorant humanity by the gospel of Revolution.

Glance at it as depicted by those who saw it. A

large chamber or corridor in one of the temporary
prisons, crowded with prisoners steeped in misery and
physical suffering—men, women, and even children,
many scarcely alive.

"Your name," says a judge to one. "Your name,
and yours, and yours—"

Possibly in a few cases a question or two in addition
was asked, but there was no attempt at taking evidence,
for there was no one to give it. There was no attempt
at identification even. They were there in prison: that
was evidence enough; they were guilty.

And then turning to the lot of them, he says: "You
have been interrogated. You are all convicted of having
conspired against the sovereignty of the French people.
The Commission, in the name of the law, condemns you
to the penalty of death. The sentence will be immediately carried out."

In a way worse even than this, a large number were
never interrogated at all—being sick—their names were
simply put on the list at the caprice of one man, sometimes of a drunken man, and in many cases mistakes
were made, and persons were executed for others.

Even this very cursory procedure was sometimes
waived.

Hundreds of those taken prisoners were sent to execution on the mere direction of Francastel, without any
interrogatory or form of trial. There is no vestige of
evidence anywhere that they were brought before a
military court-martial first, as directed by the law of
19th March. On the contrary, at Vial's trial it was
stated in evidence that "prisoners were sometimes taken
to Francastel, and on coming out of his house were led
away 100 yards or so and shot." They were conveniently regarded as *hors la loi*—outlaws—and batches

of them were put to death on the edge of the river in the centre of the town, within half a gunshot of the street where Francastel resided; even women and children were there butchered, whose cries in the silence of the night struck terror into the hearts of the inhabitants.

Daily the guillotine ended the lives of numerous priests or royalists or other victims of the better class — men and women alike. And every ingenuity was exercised to add insult and ignominy to the sufferings of the victims.

Death by decapitation was reserved for persons of a higher position, as being more humiliating than death by shooting. A letter, dated 1st January 1794, from the Mayor and municipality of Angers to the Mayor of Paris ran thus: " Our holy mother guillotine works. Within three days she has shaved eleven priests, one former nun, a general, and a superb Englishman, six feet high, whose head was *de trop*. It is in the sack to-day."

Victim after victim of revolutionary intolerance —— of revolutionary tyranny—ascended the fatal steps, 105, it is said, on one day, the 12th January 1794 ; the drums rolled to prevent their final words or cries being heard, and the blade fell. And the Abbé Gruget, who was in concealment in a house which commanded a partial view of the scaffold, has recorded how he heard the cries, or rather the howls, which burst forth as each head fell, and how he saw hats waved in the air to the cherished cry of "Vive la République!" in sign of approbation.

The members of the Military Commission, not content with sentencing hundreds to death, seldom deprived themselves of the pleasure of witnessing the execution of their sentences. They had a room in a house near where the guillotine was    so near that the victims could hear their jokes and buffooneries—with a window whence between the mid-day dinner and the coffee and liqueur which followed it they could lick their lips (*lécher du regard*, at the sight of the blood of their victims.

Report has it that noyading, or execution by drowning, was also had recourse to.

Carrier said, later, there had been noyades at Angers, and a letter from the Revolutionary Committee at Angers —who would have known for a certainty—supports his statement. Writing to Francastel as to the disposal of sixty priests, the Committee asked, "Shall we send them to Nantes? Shall we give them over to the Military Commission? Shall we have them shot at a corner of a wood? or shall we embark them on the Mayenne (the river which runs through Angers) to make them fish for coral opposite la Baumette? Speak, citizen, and whatever may be your decision, you may be sure it will be punctually carried out."

The reasons given, or rather the excuses made, by the Military Commission for sentencing to death were remarkable. Some persons were sentenced for being "enraged fanatics," others for being "real pests," for being "gossips," for having "dangerous tongues," one for being "an old scoundrel who would not take the oath," one, an old woman, "an aristocrat, not liking any one, accustomed to live alone," one for being "a fanatical beast," one a *fanatique en diable*. Property was of course a crime. One, Leclerc by name, possessed 40,000 francs; "*égoïste par conséquent*"— and therefore must die.

A priest, J. Moreau, was asked if he "had seen the famous miracle of the resurrection of the brigands." He replied, "No. Those who have been killed have no wish to come to life again for fear that the same fate might again befall them,"—and he was sentenced to death; but he would have been any way, so it was not his answer which doomed him.

The criminal tribunal was but little better, for it sentenced to death a man who, by his position, had obtained the release (from the Vendeans) of several prisoners—"patriots" presumably—on a charge of having communicated with the rebels.

Neither age nor sex was considered by the revolutionary judges. One old man of eighty-four was guillotined, and, on 19th January 1794, among the list of persons sentenced to death by the Military Commission, are recorded the names "Femme Meunier and her six little children."

And whilst on the side of the judges and the Revolutionary Committee and of the Republican Government of France there were thus these appalling cases of brutal injustice and cruelty, on the side of the unfortunate and wronged victims there was a display of magnificent heroism.

People of the very humblest class, as well as those of the higher classes—men, women, and children—all, in this dark hour of trial, acquitted themselves with splendid fortitude, with an heroic courage. Some members of religious societies, by their answers, condemned themselves. With the fearless spirit of true martyrdom, they scorned equivocation or lies; "would rather die than take the oath, being convinced that their conscience would be compromised"; and they died.

Their conduct drew admiration from even the Revolutionary Committee of Angers. In March 1794 it testified, "Our nobles go to death with firmness (caractère), and our charlatans of priests piously and in sacerdotal dress."

But the number of those guillotined was small as compared with those who were shot.

The narratives of the butchery and slaughterings of these unfortunates are somewhat confused. But it is absolutely clear that thousands perished at Angers and at the Ponts-de-Cé by fusillades. Of that there is no shadow of doubt.

This latter place was some two and a half miles from Angers, and was a village composed of the houses on and on both sides of the series of bridges which here, from island to island, crossed the Loire.

Here on the 27th, 28th, and 29th December about 800 prisoners were fusilladed on the Prairie de Saint Gemmes, a great open space near the river, the majority being men who, trusting to the lying promises of the *vrais républicains* that no harm would be done to them if they surrendered and laid down their arms, had surrendered, but who now were murdered, by order of Francastel, the Representative, without trial or legal process of any kind.

On the following days further fusillades took place, bringing the number up to about 1500; and, on the 12th January, another lot of 300 were put to death here. They were made to kneel with their faces towards the Loire, and were shot in the back. Two members of the Revolutionary Committee (of whom Vacheron, a Parisian volunteer, was one) were present, and even actors, killing with sabre or bayonet; and Vacheron, the secretary to the Representatives, and their house manager or butler, used to make himself conspicuous by a ferocious joy and by his barbarous songs. The dead or dying were not even buried, but flung naked into the Loire, a process described by one of the republican generals as "sending them to Nantes by

water," their clothes being torn from their bodies and
taken back to Angers and sold.

It was not, however, alone at the Prairie de Saint
Gemmes that the fusillades took place. A larger number
of victims of revolutionary injustice and fury were
slaughtered in the park of the priory of La Haie, a wild
and secluded spot some little distance out of Angers,
stretches of rough grass land surrounded by trees and
tangled undergrowth of wood.

The actual fusillades or shootings are almost too
horrible for description, but the unpleasant task must
be gone through, as the proceeding throws a flood of
light on the French revolutionist as he really was.

The victims who had been sentenced in such unjust,
off-hand, and callous manner by the members of the
Military Commission were bound together in couples in
the respective prisons, and then led to a central meeting-
place in the town.

Here they were formed into one long procession;
and then, through the dark and gloomy streets of
Angers, they took their final way.

What a sight for humanity to gaze at, humanity to
shudder at.

Watch them as they pass.

The military band playing patriotic airs leads the
way. And then, proud with the importance of office,
the commandant of Angers and the members of the
Military Commission, gorgeous in uniform and with
tricolour cockade.

And then the long chain of prisoners—sometimes
100, sometimes over 400 in number—bound together in
twos and twos, with soldiers on their right and on their
left to prevent their escape, and presently to do them to
death.

And the prisoners —infamous criminals, according to *la justice révolutionnaire*, but, in reality, unfortunate, miserable, wronged, mostly innocent victims of revolutionary tyranny and injustice. They, in twos and twos, worn and haggard from privation and suffering, heartbroken in appearance and fact, half-starved, and many smitten with mortal disease, walk with staggering, faltering steps to their unjust, their iniquitous doom: some in dazed and silent agony, some in prayer, some in the triumph of martyrdom singing a hymn.

Usually the majority were women, the greater part of them poor Vendeans whose greatest crime had been that rather than face the brutalities of the republican troops and *vrais sans-culottes* in the Vendée, they had bravely followed their fighting relatives, and shared their sufferings in the disastrous Vendean campaign on the north side of the Loire ; or women whose unpardonable crime had been that, unable to stifle the feelings of humanity, they had given food or help to their starving and perishing fellow-countrymen and women, or who were suspected of having done this thing.

Immediately behind the prisoners were some carts carrying those of the condemned whose age, weakness, or infirmities prevented walking ; or those who fainted by the way, and who were picked up and pitched into them any way. And then more soldiers closed the procession.

Down the steep street they come, past the Chateau, across the bridge, then up the rough ascent to the old gateway, out through it along the " Chemin de Silence," on to the Parc de la Haie, where the last scene was to be enacted.

No spectator dare show the slightest sign of sympathy as the sad procession passed along. One woman, one

day, unable to repress a cry of indignation at the sight
of the unfortunates piled anyhow in heaps in the carts,
was seized on the spot, was fastened on to the "chain,"
and led off with the others to share their fate.

The procession entered the park; an immense ditch
was there yawning to receive them. Placed in a row on
the edge of the ditch, they awaited death with that
fortitude which their faith gave them. The dread
signal was given, the drums rolled, but loud above the
drums rang out the death-dealing shots. The bullets
missed some. Then the soldiers hurled themselves
sword in hand on the survivors, and finished them off
with sabrings, and bayonetings, and blows from the
butt-ends of their guns, trampling with fury upon their
miserable victims, wallowing, as it were, in blood and
slaughter.

And then, when the last has been done to death, and
the butchery was over, the blood-stained clothes were
torn from the bodies and carried ostentatiously back by
the uniformed executioners to town, where they were
sold. Sometimes, like the *tricoteuses* in Paris, the
dealers, allured by the prospects of gain, waited actually
on the scene of the slaughter for the sale of the clothes
of the victims whose end they witnessed.

And while these appalling scenes were going on—
the sounds of the shots reaching the ears of those still
left in prison—republican fêtes were being constantly
held to inspire the people with the beauties of republican
principles, to lead them into the paths of liberty and
enlightenment, and to prove to them that the new
Republic was an arcadia of peace, innocence, pure enjoyment, and freedom.

A fête of childhood, with its procession of children;
a fête of old age, with its procession of aged people;

fêtes of agriculture ; fêtes of industry. On one day, the *décadi*, the revolutionary Sabbath, a republican procession to the Temple of Reason, where patriotic discourses were delivered, followed by a civic banquet and public games. And on the other days of the revolutionists' week processions of helpless and innocent women and children and old people along the Chemin de Silence to the revolutionary shambles in the park, and to eternal silence.

During one fearful month there were nine fusillades on a large scale at the Parc de la Haie, and some two thousand persons were butchered.

One special feature of horror attaches to these fusillades at Angers, placing them in atrocity alongside, if not above, even the crimes at Nantes, and that was the dreadful fact that an enormous proportion of the victims were women, though at Nantes, too, women were massacred wholesale.

Of the 300 persons shot on the 15th January, about one-half were women.

Of the 408 shot or hacked to death on the 20th, 300 were women.

On the 22nd, when 88 were shot, all were women.

On the 1st February, of the 400 shot, about half were women.

What a scene must have been presented that 20th January in the Park, when 300 women were brutally massacred. A long row of 300 helpless and feeble women, bound hand in hand, trembling and half-dead with fear, standing on the edge of a great ditch so soon to be their grave, and opposite them a number of soldiers, the representatives of the authority of the Republic of France, clad in the full panoply of war, with muskets loaded and bayonets fixed, waiting for the signal to slaughter these weak and defenceless victims. And then the signal given, and then the bloody work.

A scene which should burn itself into the brain of humanity by its inapproachable horror.

The infinite cruelty of it—these masses of armed men who might have been serving their country to some purpose on the frontiers instead of massacring helpless French women at home. The infinite pathos of it—many of these poor people absolute heroines and martyrs dying for their faith as much as the martyrs in a Roman arena, others whose only crime was that they followed their husbands or brothers across the Loire to avoid the brutalities of the revolutionary troops — their own countrymen. And now, after the long sufferings and privations, the agonies of weeks, this was their cruel doom.

How can such a stain ever be wiped from the escutcheon of a nation?

Immeasurable in cowardice, unfathomable in wickedness, were these wholesale holocausts of women. The first laws of humanity should have made the judges and the executioners, and all concerned, recoil from this dastardly inhuman work. But they did not.

Was the newly-founded Republic in such a critical state or position that it was endangered by the existence of these women? Were they all slaughtered out of patriotic exasperation because some few of the Vendean chiefs had asked England for help? Justification there can be none, but what explanation is there possible?

Whatever explanation may be attempted, the fact remains, and is beyond question. It was not even a sudden outburst of passion by people uncontrolled by the Government. It was quite the contrary, for week after week, with cold deliberation and with carefully organised arrangement, the revolutionists, from the Representative

Francastel down to the lowest sans-culotte official, proceeded in the perpetration of atrocities which would have been a disgrace even to barbarism.

That they should have been persevered in so long displays the innate brutality and cruelty of the French revolutionist, of the *vrai sans-culotte*. That they should have been uninterfered with by the Government in Paris —with whom the Representatives were in direct and constant communication—incriminates the authorities there also, the National Convention and the Committee of Public Safety.

There is but one consolation to be derived from these appalling iniquities.

Their occurrence gave to the world, for its information and guidance, one more invaluable illustration, one more example, of revolutionary "justice"—in all its stages of cruelty and unfairness, arrest, imprisonment, trial, sentence, execution—revolutionary justice, not as theorised about by philosophers, or idealised by enthusiastic republicans, but the actual thing as it worked out in practice.

# CHAPTER XVI

## NOIRMOUTIER

IN the far west of the Vendée lay Noirmoutier, an island when the tide was in, a promontory when the tide was out, a wild and melancholy storm-swept, storm-beaten place, lonesome even when basking in the summer sun, but desolate beyond description in the gloomy, stormy days of winter.

A sort of idea existed among the Vendeans that as there was a port there, although it was but a small one, it might be of use to them to obtain supplies from England or Spain, and among the republicans there was a constant dread that it might be used as a base for a landing by the English. And so it had been fought for on more than one occasion.

Early in the year it had been taken by the Vendeans, then captured from them by the republicans. In October it had again been taken by the Vendeans under Charette, and nearly 200 republicans shot, as reprisals for some of the barbarities inflicted by the republicans on the Vendeans; some republican soldiers in the hospital even, it is said, being massacred, so embittered were the Vendeans. But after the fearful atrocities already committed by the republicans reprisals were only to be expected.

It had remained in the hands of the Vendeans until the end of the year, although the Committee of Public Safety had given the order on October 21 that it was "to be captured or sunk in the sea." Hither for safety sake had come many refugees, priests, and other victims of revolutionary fury; hither had been brought the Vendean commander-in-chief, d'Elbée, with chest ripped to pieces by the fourteen wounds received at the battle of Cholet.

After the annihilation of the Vendeans on the north side of the Loire, the republicans, anxious to complete their triumph, determined to wrest this place from the Vendeans. Plans were made accordingly, and Turreau, the commander-in-chief, had come to be present at the assault. Generals Haxo, Dutruy, and Jordy were in charge of the actual operations, and three Representatives, L. Turreau, Prieur (de la Marne), and Bourbotte, were there to supervise.

On the 3rd January a combined attack by sea and land was made, and after a somewhat feeble defence the Vendean garrison surrendered. Far better if they had fought it out to the bitter end, for they could not have fared worse.

A German hussar brought to the Representatives a formal capitulation. The Representatives accepted it on condition that the Vendeans piled their arms and submitted to being made prisoners. The Vendeans, who ought by this time to have known their opponents better, expressed their willingness to do so. There were about 1100.

On the approach of the republican troops, the royalist officers presented themselves before the Representatives, and declared that the garrison submitted to the Republic, and undertook not to serve against it if their lives were spared. Not until the white flag was hauled down would the Representatives listen. When that was done, they said, " We ought not, and we do not wish to come to any terms with brigands. Let them all be put to the sword."

The action of the Representatives in accepting the surrender implied acceptance of the terms on which it was made; but truth, honour, every moral obligation, were as naught when the revolutionary cause was thought to be served by setting them aside.

It was known that the Representatives were very much disposed towards massacre. Carrier, speaking at Nantes, at the Society of Vincent la Montagne, with reference to the coming attack on the island, had said: "Every one there must be exterminated—everything burned. Soldiers who are truly republican ought never to allow themselves to be moved by a false pity. Nothing more beautiful than to be willing to sacrifice all human sentiments to national vengeance."

His opinions were fully shared by his colleagues at Noirmoutier. Their ideas of the beautiful coincided.

The Vendeans were made prisoners, and promptly marched off to the church, and there imprisoned.

Those of the inhabitants of Noirmoutier who had not to reproach themselves with having helped the royalists, thought that they could present themselves to the republican army as peaceable people, but they were quickly disillusioned, and were the first to become the victims of the fury of the soldiery. In vain they begged for mercy. To such appeal the republicans were ever deaf. Without caring to distinguish the innocent from the guilty, and as if they had entered a town taken by assault, they indiscriminately put to death all the men they found.

This portrait of one of the republican troopers who took a prominent part in this slaughter—a brute named Félix—is drawn by F. Piet, an eye-witness :—

" A sombre and *farouche* air, eyes of fire almost hidden beneath heavy eyelashes, a swarthy complexion, hard features, long red moustaches, a forehead furrowed by debauch, which usually gave to his face a ferocious aspect. Stained by the grossest of vices, keen for pillage, he knew how, without emotion, to face dangers. A butcher does not drive the knife into the throat of the animal he kills with greater calm than Félix massacred his fellow-creatures. This monster alone killed more than twenty heads of families."

Once captured, the island was ransacked to find any persons who might be concealed on it.

" After having encircled the island by the vessels of our little fleet," wrote the Representatives to the Committee of Public Safety, " we searched it from one end to the other, as one would do at a rabbit-hunt ; and this battue forced from the woods, even from caves and underground places, a deluge of priests and wives of *émigrés*."

Among the captured, and to the intense joy of the Representatives, was d'Elbée, the commander-in-chief of the Vendeans, still hanging between life and death.

All of them, as well as the prisoners who had surrendered, were doomed to death.

The decision is specially noteworthy as having been shared in, if not actually imposed, by the Representative Prieur (de la Marne), who was himself a member of the Committee of Public Safety. It was decisive proof and demonstration of the determination of the Revolutionary Government to accept no surrender from the Vendeans at large, and no stronger affirmation of the policy of extermination could possibly be given than that a member of the Committee of Public Safety should himself in person give such an order.

A Military Commission of " men of the right temper " was appointed on the spot by him and the two other Representatives " to administer prompt justice to all the traitors."

It was purely a form, and the prisoners, some 1200 in number, were all promptly sentenced to death.

General Haxo, a general of the Mayençais, made a valiant stand against this wholesale execution. " Representatives," he said, " we are soldiers, not executioners, we do not know how to massacre our enemy when he is unarmed." In vain he pleaded that the lives of men who surrender at discretion ought to be as sacred as that of the unfortunate who has been hurled on the shore by the tempest.

His efforts were useless. The necessity was pointed out to him of conforming to the decrees of the Convention, and of giving a great example to the enemies of the Republic. The prisoners therefore must die.

" We had a two days' job of it " (*Nous en eûmes pour deux jours*), wrote a republican soldier, who was evidently a participator in the slaughter. And a republican officer has left a gruesome description of the horrible proceedings : " In the space of two days all the under officers and soldiers succumbed to the murderous lead. They were taken from the church in batches of sixty at a time. They were conducted to the quartier of Banzeaux, on the border of the sea. There, pushed along and often wounded before receiving the mortal blow, they made useless efforts to escape it. Amidst the smoke of the musketry they appeared as bloody shades—fallen to the ground they were stripped and buried."

Before this horrid work was begun General Haxo

had left with the greater part of his army to attack
an assembly of Vendeans somewhere on the mainland.
General Turreau also, for different motives, started by
sea for Nantes.

Specially instructive is the light thrown upon the
real character of these three Representatives by a revolutionist. F. Piet, who, as aide-de-camp to General Dutruy,
was brought much in contact with them, and was an
eye-witness of the scenes he described.

Describing the Montagnards he says: " It is easy to
see that their *délire* is that of a political fanaticism, of
which all the excesses are the same as those of religious
fanaticism.  Their hearts were hardened, they struck
without remorse, knew no law but their own frenzy, and
looked on as a crime the defence of those whom they
named as enemies of the Republic; they were furious
with their own fury, and it seemed to them that death
was too light a punishment for their victims.

" Such were the three Representatives—Bourbotte,
Prieur (de la Marne), and L. Turreau.  Bourbotte possessed in an eminent degree the 'revolutionary energy.'
Prieur and Turreau were not so sanguinary as Bourbotte,
especially when not excited by drink, which they took
immoderately.  Unceasingly they had on their lips the
words patrie, liberty, fraternity, which they used as talis-
mans to dazzle and inflame credulous minds. . . . Up to
this time they had no occasion to unveil (or betray) to
me their real character.  I was far from thinking that
they only preached certain social virtues the better to
command crime.  Their title of *mandataires* of the
nation gave them great importance in my eyes."

He evidently, like many others then and since, had
at last to suffer disillusionment.

D'Elbée was too important a person to be treated as

summarily as the ordinarily soldier. For two days,
whilst lying on his bed of suffering, he was interrogated
by the Representatives, and the commander-in-chief
Turreau, who were anxious to get from him all the
information they could before they closed his mouth for
ever.

How easily the whole trouble in the Vendée could
have been assuaged had the Revolutionary Government
been capable of taking a statesmanlike view of the position,
and of subduing within themselves their savage and
vindictive "possession" against the Vendeans, is apparent
from d'Elbée's statement.

Asked as to what means he could suggest for the
pacification of the Vendée, he is reported to have replied : "A general amnesty—the refractory priests not
included; but leaving the toleration of them to the
discretion of agents who should be employed to effect the
pacification. . . . In each district there should be an
agent known and trusted by the rebels to work in concert
with the local authorities."

He swore upon his honour that although he desired
a monarchical government reduced to its proper degree
of authority, he would have lived as a peaceable citizen
under any form of government, provided it assured his
tranquillity and the free exercise, or, at least, the tolerance
of the religious faith he had always professed.

And then he said : " I am so little an enemy to the
republican system, that, if my execution is delayed until
this system is well on foot, and I am no longer required,
I offer to work under any surveillance."

And he named several districts which he could pacify.

But a conciliatory policy was not revolutionary, indeed
one may say that common sense was not revolutionary,
and his offer was declined.

His fate was inevitable, and he was sentenced to be shot. And, doubtless, with the deliberate design of adding to his grief,—for these revolutionary Representatives were refined in their schemes for inflicting suffering, —his friend de Boissy, and his brother-in-law Duhoux, were to be shot with him.

The closing scenes are pathetic and dramatic to a degree, but horrible in their exposure of the brutality and reckless injustice of persons of such exalted positions as the Representatives.

"The evening before, at a supper at which I was present," wrote Piet, " the Representatives were discussing the military arrangements for the execution, when one of them pretended to be annoyed that it was not a *partie carrée*, a party of four. " Eh, *sacre Dieu*," said Bourbotte, " haven't we got the traitor Wieland ?" (Wieland was an officer of the Republic who had unsuccessfully defended Noirmoutier against the Vendeans in October—since which time he had been residing there, a prisoner of the Vendeans, on parole.)

No sooner suggested than agreed to. Wieland should make the fourth ; his death was decided on.

What an illustration of the secret ways of revolutionary justice.

The court of justice—a supper-table. The tribunal —three drunken or semi-drunken Representatives. The trial - no prisoner, no witnesses, no proof, no evidence, no opportunity given for explanation or exculpation, only a sentence— death.

The Vehmgericht or the Inquisition could not have improved on this, could not even have equalled it.

A more shameful murder can scarcely ever have been perpetrated in the name of authority. Even " revolutionary justice " could scarcely go further than this.

The next day Wieland was sent for, and for form's sake was brought before the Military Commission. He asked for a delay of twenty-four hours, but the Representatives " ordered the Commission to send him to execution without listening to anything."

Forthwith is he led to execution with the others. In vain he claimed the right, sacred in all nations, except France, the right of being heard before his life was taken from him; but it was denied him. And in vain the Vendean leaders his companions in doom—exonerated him from the charge of communicating with them. He had been their enemy and not their friend, they said. But the will of the Representatives must take its course.

And so, that wild winter's afternoon, the last scene of their lives was enacted.

D'Elbée, too ill to walk, was carried to the place of execution in a chair. And then, just as the signal for the fatal volley was about to be given, Madame d'Elbée, the loving wife and faithful companion of all his dangers and trials, in a transport of agony, rushed shrieking on to the scene, " precisely under the windows where the Representatives were feasting their eyes on the frightful spectacle of their victims waiting to receive the death-shot."

And the drums roll, and the volley rings out, and there is a *partie carrée* of bleeding corpses; d'Elbée still in his chair, the others lying on the sand.

And the troops march off the ground as usual with flying colours, and bands playing lively republican airs; and the Representatives retire to refresh themselves after their labours, and to contrive some new display of revolutionary justice which shall equally redound to their credit.

For was it not a great work satisfactorily ac-

complished?   Noirmoutier captured: the Vendean
commander-in-chief finally got rid of; the "national
vengeance" executed on "the traitor Wieland"; and
down there in the sands, some little distance off, the
bodies of 1200 or more who would never again trouble
the Republic.

Once more, "Ça va!" "Ça ira!" "Vive la République!" "Vive la justice révolutionnaire!"

# CHAPTER XVII

IF events at Angers were giving an illustration of how the principles of " liberty, equality, and fraternity " really worked out in actual practice under the newly-formed Republic, Nantes was giving exactly a similar illustration, only on a larger, and, in some ways, an accentuated scale.

Carrier had been ruling it with a fierce and cruel despotism which was becoming ever more violent and extreme as time went on.

He expressed himself to the Committee of Public Safety as quite pleased with the progress made.

" You cannot form an idea," he wrote (about 12th December), " of the rapid progress which the public spirit has made here in the last three weeks. You would have difficulty in believing that it is at the full height of the Revolution—everywhere one only hears cries of the most ardent civism—the tricolour floats from every window— everywhere are patriotic inscriptions—the old churches become public establishments—everything announces the death of fanaticism and of superstition, and the assured triumph of patriotism."

A few days after this, however, even so extreme a body as the Society of Vincent incurred his censure—

that popular club which contained the *élite* of Nantes
sans-culottism, which had done so much to further the
Revolution in that city, and where he and his friends
were in the habit of ventilating, amidst echoing applause,
their wildest and most atrocious ideas, their crudest
theories. He fell foul of it about the case of one
Garnier, and on the 15th December came down to the
society, abused its members all round, there and then
dissolved it, and had the key of its meeting-place brought
to himself. For three days the society remained non-
existent: then with his permission it was reopened: but
the incident left a scar on the society—"Liberty," they
said, "had been invaded."

Other more serious matters, however, engaged his
attention and that of the Revolutionary Committee.

So worried (*désolé*) was the Committee by the
perpetual appeals made to it by the relatives of the
prisoners for their release, that it issued a notice on
14th December (24 Frimaire) announcing that it would
be deaf to any such appeal, and furthermore that it
would regard as a suspect any individual who solicited on
behalf of a prisoner.

Nantes being a great city, with an estimated population of 100,000 persons, would in itself have afforded
ample material for the display of revolutionary energy.
There were enough people in it to keep the guillotine at
work, and even fusillades and noyades, in full swing.

But the gradual dissolution of the Vendean army on
the north side of the Loire, and its miserable followers,
from the time of the repulse at Angers to the final
catastrophe at Savenay, had resulted in constant arrivals
at Nantes of large numbers of Vendeans who had been
taken prisoners, or who had surrendered on revolutionary
promises of amnesty.

"The defeat of the brigands," wrote Carrier to the Convention on the 20th December, "is so complete that our posts kill them or capture and bring them to Nantes by hundreds. The guillotine is not equal to the task. I have taken the line of having them shot. They surrender themselves here and at Angers by hundreds. I assure to these the same fate as those. I invite my colleague Francastel not to put aside this salutary and expeditious method. It is on principles of humanity that I purge the soil of Liberty of these monsters."

This letter was read before the Convention on 26th December.

But it was not only by shooting that the revolutionists at Nantes were purging the soil of Liberty.

After the first successful demonstrations of the feasibility of drowning, it also was used as an expeditious and effective method; the guillotine, too, was kept steadily at work; and supplementing them all was the unceasing death-roll of the prisons,—hundreds upon hundreds being let die, rapidly or slowly, through deliberate neglect and indifference.

Nantes, in fact, presented at this period the appearance of a great slaughter-house or *abattoir*, only instead of cattle and sheep, human beings were being slaughtered, —men, women, and even children,—and the butchers were the *bons* and *braves républicains*, and the *vrais sans-culottes*, animated by "patriotism," and imbued with "pure principles" of the highest Montagnard standard.

The unfortunate Vendeans who came or were brought to Nantes were mostly sent at once to the "Entrepôt."

Rossignol, the commander-in-chief, had once absurdly remarked, "Since I assisted to overthrow the

Bastille, no prison ought to exist," and the saying is interesting as being typical of the absurdity of many of the views of the revolutionists; but prisons not alone went on existing, but, as revolutionary liberty developed. they rapidly increased in number, and for the one prisoner in custody under the ancient régime, hundreds were in custody under the new revolutionary régime.

The old Bouffay, which for centuries of tyranny had answered all the requirements of the times. held, when densely packed, some 200 prisoners. The Chateau of Nantes also held a considerable number. For the new era of liberty, however, they were quite inadequate, and so the Convent of St. Claire, emptied of its previous inhabitants, was pressed into service, and packed with prisoners. Then, with the object of separating the women from the men, all having hitherto been stowed indiscriminately together anyhow, a building called "the Good Shepherd" was taken. Here, where 200 persons might have been lodged, 700 women were put, as many as 30 to 40 being crammed into a small chamber, sick and dying, all together.

And there were several other prisons, the favourite one of the Revolutionary Committee being the Entrepôt, a great barrack of a place, where several thousand prisoners could be kept. It was the favourite on account of the facilities it afforded for the free play of revolutionary "fraternity."

It was situated at the extremity of one of the least inhabited parts of Nantes; close to the Loire, which simplified the noyades; and close to the great quarries of Gigant, which were a safe and convenient place for the fusillades. The prisoners had not to be conveyed far to meet their fate.

Here were sent pell-mell in December some of the

débris of the Vendean army; on three days, the 24th, 26th, and 28th December, 1500 arrived, having surrendered on the faith of the amnesty promised by the republicans.   Hither, too, were drafted from the other prisons in Nantes the suspects and counter-revolutionists whom the Revolutionary Committee had determined to get rid of.

It was the last stepping-stone to death.   No sooner was it nearly emptied by noyades and fusillades than it was promptly filled again; and of the 8000 to 10,000 persons imprisoned here, only a very few escaped the destruction decreed by Carrier and his accomplices.

Its condition was appalling—"a veritable slaughterhouse, a tomb where the prisoners perished of misery, and were practically buried alive."   Epidemic disease raged in it: and so fearful was its state that even the soldiers mounting guard on it died of illnesses contracted there.   Fever and dysentery were specially virulent, and the prisoners attacked by illness were left to die in their misery.   Medical attendance there was none; food in sufficient quantities to maintain life was scarcely forthcoming, and the only drinking-water was contaminated by sewage and every filth.

The cold, moreover, during that fearful winter was dreadful, and the prisoners died by scores, sparing the various Revolutionary Tribunals the trouble of trying them, and the revolutionists the trouble of deciding whether to drown or shoot them.

Pest-houses were all these prisons, and a committal to any of them was almost tantamount to a sentence of death.

Life in them was literally hell upon earth.

From the dawn of one day, when the cold gray rays of morning light slowly illumined the festering mass of human misery within the walls, until the dawn of the next day when the sun rose on the same spectacle of republican "fraternity," what human agony was endured!

The misery of cold, the gnawing pains of semi-starvation, the brutalities of the gaolers, the endless sight of suffering, the grief and woe, and mental and physical torture, the awful heartbreak from destruction of home and loss of family; and then at night, the fevered sleep on sewage-soddened earth or vermin-laden straw, the ceaseless moaning of the sick or dying, all crowded, crushed, and crammed together. How life remained under such circumstances is almost incomprehensible.

And over and above the hopeless misery of it all was the infuriating sense of cruel, infamous, and irremediable wrong.

Nor was there any sign of mercy or shadow of turning on the part of those in authority in the new Republic. Mercy and pity and justice all had vanished under the new régime, which was to have introduced "liberty and equality and fraternity" into the countries of the earth, and to have been the prelude to, if not absolutely itself, the millennium of humanity.

As if there were not enough tribunals at Nantes for the form of sentencing the inmates of the prisons, the Representatives Prieur (de la Marne) and L. Turreau ordered the Military Commission of Le Mans, presided over by the infamous Bignon, which had done such expeditions work at Savenay, to proceed at once to Nantes, and there administer revolutionary justice.

Arrived in Nantes on the 28th December, it set to work on the following day, and as a beginning sent 100 persons to be shot. In thirteen days it sentenced 1669

persons to death, and did not acquit a single one, as
many as 289 being condemned in one single day.   It
devoted two days to women and girls, sentencing to
death 62 one day, and 45 the next.   By the 19th it
had brought up its total of capital sentences to over
1900.   And then, *relâche au théâtre rouge* ("vaca-
tion at the red theatre").   And this was the work of
but one of the Commissions there sitting—the worst, it
is true.

It is impossible now to present anything approaching
a complete account of the victims sentenced by the Military Commissions or Revolutionary Tribunals, or of the
infamies perpetrated by the Revolutionary Committee, by
Carrier, and by the Marat Company, complete records of
persons imprisoned, tried, and punished not being available.   Records were but very incompletely kept, if at all,
and the time came when every effort was made to hush
up these revolutionary abominations, and to destroy the
proofs and traces of them.

These 1900 unfortunates, and thousands of others,
many without any form of trial, were mostly noyaded or
fusilladed, only a comparatively small proportion being
guillotined.

As regarded fusillades, the services of the members of
the Revolutionary Committee were scarcely required, and
so the members devoted themselves mainly to carrying
out noyades.   Fusillading was quite a simple process.
A chain of prisoners, a military escort, a short march to
the quarries of Gigant, a volley, some bayoneting, and
the thing was done.   But noyading required much
greater preparation, and the Committee, together with
Carrier's aides, Lamberty and Robin, gave a great part
of their time to this congenial work.   With the facility
begotten of experience, they embarked on larger opera-

tions, and on or about the 23rd December a great coup
was made. Some 800 persons were noyaded. It was
night. "Two barges," said an eye-witness, "laden with
people, stopped at a place called Prairie-au-Duc. There
I and my comrades witnessed the most horrible carnage
that could possibly be seen. More than 800 persons of
all ages and both sexes were inhumanly drowned and
cut to pieces. I heard Fouquet and his satellites reproach some among their own people that they did not
know how to use their sabres, and he showed them by
his example how they ought to use them. The barges
did not sink to the bottom quickly enough, so they fired
with their guns at those who were still above water.
The cries of these unfortunate victims only seemed to increase the energy of their executioners.

"I wish to observe that all the individuals who were
drowned this night were previously stripped naked as
one's hand. In vain the women besought that they
might be left their chemises: but the drowners laughed
at their tears, and joked about the figures of their
victims, with horrid comments according as they were
old or young. Their rags, their jewels, their assignats
were the prey of these anthropophagi, and what one can
scarcely believe is, that those who thus despoiled them
sold these spoils the next day to the highest bidder."

Humanity itself is stained by such an appalling
atrocity. Eight hundred men and women, old and
young, helplessly bound, driven along at the sabre's
point, stripped naked in this bitter mid-winter night,
and hurled into two great barges: for hours exposed in
their nakedness to the frigid blasts of the night wind,
while the preparations for their doom were being completed; battened down to prevent their escape; and
then, as the barges sink, the gradual rising and final

inrush of glacial water, and a hail of bullets to make all
sure; and then, at long last, release for ever from revolutionary " fraternity."

Such a scene is almost above what the wildest
imagination of the human mind has pictured to itself in
its attempts to realise the horrors of a hell. What must
their sufferings of mind and body have been? What
must have been the physical and mental torture they
underwent? Horror upon horror piled upon them, all
the surroundings serving to heighten their terror—the
cold, the darkness, their nakedness. And the vast
majority of them as innocent of offence against their
country or the State as the child unborn.

And while scenes such as these were being enacted,
Carrier, the Representative of the great new Republic
which was to be the shining light to all nations of the
world, Carrier, whose mere word could have stopped
them, was usually spending his night in feasts and
drunken revels at the home of luxury he had made for
himself at Richebourg, and in the arms of one of his
numerous mistresses, or of some unfortunate victim of
the Revolution who had taken his fancy.

The noyades continued. On Christmas Eve there
was one: on Christmas night another: and well on into
the second half of January.

All through these fearful human sacrifices to the
Fetish of Sans-culottism one does not come across one
single trace of feeling or generosity on the part of those
concerned in them. Nothing but brutality of the lowest
sort, from Carrier down to the meanest wretch of the
Marat Company: no mercy: none snatched from doom,
except now and then some women, more well favoured
than the rest, who were smuggled off to the harems of
these sans-culotte butchers.

Foucault having said one day that two vessels were to be despatched that night, Bachelier threw his arms round his neck (*lui sauta au col*) saying, "You are a brave man, and I don't know a better revolutionist."

One day in Nivose—the exact date is unknown—Lamberty was chatting with several generals, and, pointing to the Loire, he said, "Well, some 2800 have already gone that way." One of the generals asked what he meant. "Oh yes," said Carrier, who was one of the party, "2800 brigands are in the national bath."

One thing is absolutely certain, and that is that from the middle of November 1793 to well on into the following January noyades constantly took place. The exact number may be in doubt: the precise number of victims at each of them may be in doubt; but that thousands of persons thus perished at the hands of the revolutionists of Nantes is beyond all shadow of doubt.

The process of noyading was somewhat changed as time went on. Prisoners, instead of being taken *en bloc* from the Entrepôt, were drafted out in small numbers at a time to floating prisons, to vessels moored in the river, from which, on convenient occasions, the noyades were made. Nor were the noyades confined to night. They took place sometimes in broad daylight, and so carelessly was the system worked, that on one occasion the existence of a lot of prisoners in a vessel was absolutely forgotten for forty-eight hours. When the hold was opened to receive some fresh arrivals, they were discovered, but some sixty of them were dead; and Robin had the bodies thrown overboard by the new batch of victims arriving on board.

And there appear to have been noyades of women exclusively—one of 144 women, and another, it is said, somewhat dubiously, of about 80 women of improper

character, which latter incident is seized on by some
admirers of the Revolution as proof of Carrier's high
morality, and of his desire to improve the moral condition
of Nantes.

The noyades were not confined to grown-up people.
Children were included in the roll of victims. There is
no room for doubt in the matter.

Bignon, the president of the notorious Military
Commission, declared, some time after, that "Carrier had
pronounced sentence of death against certain children,
and had the barbarity to have it carried out." Goullin,
the leading member of the Revolutionary Committee—
also some time later — declared that it was by order
of Lamberty and Fouquet, Carrier's executioners, that
children were drowned. Fourier, the director of the
revolutionary hospital, said, "To my knowledge they
noyaded fifty to sixty children at a time." And Phelippes
de Tronjolly said, " In these noyades have been included
the children of persons who have been guillotined—
children of the age of ten to twelve and thirteen years."

As many as 600 children are said to have perished
in the noyades, and, according to some reports, children
of four to six years were among the victims.

And there was one " sabrade " or execution by
sabring.

Seven or eight persons one night came out from the
presence of the Revolutionary Committee to be taken
to the Entrepôt. It being late, and the distance to go
considerable, their escort massacred them under the
windows of the meeting-place of the Committee. The
next morning, blood, bits of clothing, and other traces
of the massacre were found.

The Revolutionary Government in Paris cannot be
exonerated by any plea of ignorance from the crime of

allowing those horrors to be perpetrated, for knowledge of the fact that noyades were taking place at Nantes was not confined to Nantes.

The news was published in Paris as conspicuously as any news could be.

At the sitting of the Commune of Paris on the 11th Nivose (31st December 1793) a letter from Nantes, dated 26th December, was read containing this passage:—

"The number of brigands which have been brought here within the last ten days is incalculable. They arrive at every moment. The guillotine being too slow, and as shooting them means the expenditure of powder and ball, one has adopted the plan (*on a pris le parti*) of putting a certain number in big boats, conducting them to the middle of the river about half a league away from the town, and there sending the boat to the bottom. This operation is continually taking place." This letter was published in Paris on the 2nd January in the *Gazette Nationale* and other papers.

While the noyades, these nocturnal executions, were proceeding, fusillades were turning daylight to account in getting rid of Vendeans and counter-revolutionists, real or alleged.

The exact numbers so done to death are unknown. Carrier admitted that about 100 to 200 a day were shot. But the fusillades were nearly, if not quite, of daily occurrence, and so great was the slaughter that the burial of the victims could not keep pace with the executions, and repeated complaints were made to the council of Nantes of the negligence in interring the dead.

The Society of Vincent la Montagne on the 12th January stated that the bodies were scarcely covered by a few inches of earth. "Often one sees the limbs of the corpses appearing above ground"; and on the 18th January the council decreed that all capable citizens should be employed in burying the dead; and two days later it made another urgent decree on the subject, "owing to the public health being endangered by an epidemic caused by the corpses of men and animals."

The fusillades mostly took place at the quarries of Gigant at the western end of the town, some also at the extremity of Richebourg.

The procedure here was the usual one. " The unfortunate prisoners were conducted between two rows of soldiers, 30 to 60 or more at a time. They were led to the border of a ditch where they were to be buried, so as the sooner to be done with the job. A roll of drums gave the signal for the fusillade, which did not cease until all had fallen. Unfortunate he whom the balls had spared, for he was finished off with the bayonet. The bodies were then stripped and thrown into pits. For several months 300 to 400 men were engaged burying them."

Here too, as at Angers, there were special fusillades of women.

"One day I commanded," deposed Debourges, a commandant of a battalion of the National Guard, "a detachment of National Guards who escorted some women of 16 to 18 years of age who were being taken to be shot at Gigant. On arriving at this place of horror, I saw a sort of gorge, where was a quarry in the form of a semicircle. There I perceived the dead bodies of 75 women. They were naked, and by a refinement of barbarism they had been turned over on their backs. . . .

" When these unfortunates had arrived at this quarry, already strewn with the corpses of those of their own sex, they were ranged in a row and shot, and those who escaped the bullets could watch the guns being loaded which were to finish them off; others were assassinated by blows of the butt-ends of the muskets. After these massacres the Germans searched them, and other barbarians stripped them naked and turned them over on their backs."

"The Germans searched them"—the phrase requires explanation.

In palliation of the infamy thrown on the Republic by these atrocities, it is said that the executioners were not Frenchmen, but Germans, who had deserted and found their way to Paris. But the defence is worthless; for even if some of the butchers were foreign members of the Parisian volunteers, the circumstance does not extenuate the Government, for they were in the service of the Republican Government, and they acted under the orders of republican officers.

Nor does even this flimsy excuse apply to the noyades, where all the executioners were real sans-culottes and republicans, and many of them members of that exalted body, the Revolutionary Committee of Nantes.

This treatment of women and children, of innocent girls, and wives, and mothers, and of tiny and utterly irresponsible children, is the finishing touch to the infamy of the French revolutionist ; for there is a special brutality about it which exceeds even the brutality of their other crimes. There is an extra degree of cowardice about it, as women were incapable of defending themselves, and there was the very climax of injustice about it, as their ignorance and dependence on others were the strongest claim to considerate treatment. But any such claims on their behalf were ignored.

Carrier's views on the subject are on record. Time

after time he inveighed against women and children in
the most vehement and vindictive terms, accusing them
of every crime so as the better to justify his own severities
towards them.   "The women of the Vendée are all
monsters," he said.   " . . . The women of the Vendée!
It is by them that a hostile race grows again.   The
children — they are vipers to be crushed"; and it
was in this spirit that he and his aides persistently
acted.

But he only voiced the general revolutionary ideas
on the subject.   Even in the Convention itself anathemas
were hurled against both women and children.   They
were spies, and they fought, they murdered, they tortured
the "patriots."

And so to women the *vrais sans-culottes* were pitiless.
They shot them by hundreds at a time, they drowned
them by hundreds, they imprisoned them by thousands,
they guillotined them, they sabred them.

In and around the Vendée, where Revolution had
free room for the display of its true characteristics, unchecked by any external influences, a Vendean girl or
woman was, in the eyes of the sans-culottes, too often
but a creature to satisfy their lust, and, from the highest
to the lowest, power and position were abused to secure
the gratifications of their passions.

In ways the revolutionists aggravated their atrocious
conduct.   In the noyades at Nantes women were stripped
naked by members of the Revolutionary Committee and
Maratist Corps before they were drowned.   In the fusillades they were stripped after being shot.

Other brutalities are also narrated, but over them
the veil of silence must be drawn.

Even had the women been the most infamous
wretches, the conduct of the sans-culottes would not

have been justified. But thousands of the victims were absolutely innocent of offences, except that they were inhabitants of the accursed Vendée, or fanatics of superstition: whilst hundreds of them were "patriots" and republicans, though even that did not secure them against outrage, for they were women.

The treatment of children by the revolutionist was on a par with his treatment of women. The laws of all civilised and modern races treat children with indulgence. But so it was not under the glorious régime of liberty and the French revolutionist. The same callous brutality was displayed to them as towards women, the same unreasoning and vindictive cruelty. "They are vipers to be crushed."

Hundreds, indeed thousands of them, from years of discretion down to the babe at its mother's breast, were cast into prison to rot and die in those pest-houses, and hundreds and thousands of them died.

But even worse was the deliberate way of doing them to death by formal legal procedure.

"Many of these little scoundrels have been tried and condemned by the Military Commission," said Carrier afterwards in the Convention.

They were condemned as "brigands" — as counter-revolutionists — for having borne arms against the Republic.

And as the result of such condemnations every form of death which was meted out to the most formidable counter-revolutionists was meted out to them too.

They were guillotined. Thus at Nantes, on the 17th December, four were put to death : one of whom as it was being bound to the fatal plank of the guillotine addressed this question, agonising in the innocence of it, to the executioner. "Will you hurt me much ?"

They were noyaded—they were fusilladed.

What atom of excuse can be offered for such inhumanity ?   Were children of tender years such dangerous enemies of the Republic that they must be slaughtered? Did the " safety of the country " demand the sacrifice of these innocents ?   Did "patriotism," that cloak for the iniquities of the revolutionist,—that first and last plea and excuse for all his crimes, — exact the death of beings of such tender age that they were incapable of knowing the difference between one form of political government and another ?

Manifestly the *vrai sans-culotte* thought, or chose to think so.   Manifestly their destruction was part of the creed of the " brave republican," for from the Representatives downward, little mercy was shown towards children : and by the acts of its servants the French Republic of that time has been stamped indelibly with a crime than which a more heinous one can scarcely be conceived.

An alternative policy was once suggested to Carrier, some time early in January.   Savary went to him to speak to him of the horrors of which the details were being spoken about in the town.

" I arrived at Carrier's, who received me well.   We spoke about the Vendée.   ' You desire, no doubt,' said I, ' the end of this frightful war.'   ' Yes, certainly,' he replied.   ' Well, a first-rate opportunity presents itself at this moment to attain that object.'   ' What is it ?' ' This is it.   You know the present disposition of the people in the Vendée; you know that they only sigh for repose and tranquillity : they only ask for indulgence and protection : these are the best arms to employ now.' At these words Carrier assumed a somewhat more reserved air.   ' It is said,' I added, ' that there exists in the depôt a large number of Vendeans, old men, women, and children piled on top of each other, in want of everything, dying of cold and misery; it is said even that a frightful epidemic prevails among them. You can put an end to this scourge; you can even draw from this circumstance the means of assuring the peace of the Vendée.' 'And what are the means?' he asked. 'This.' I replied. 'These prisoners belong to all the families in the country; the old men, the women, the children, are not to be feared; give them back their liberty; let them return to their hearths and homes; they will narrate to their families and to their neighbours what they have undergone; the disasters to their army; and these living witnesses of misfortune will be for the others a terrible lesson which they will never forget.' Carrier reflected a few moments, and then said to me, 'Go to the depôt; bring me a list of those who are there.' I went to the depôt. It would be impossible for me to retrace in all its hideous colours the frightful picture which presented itself to me in this pestiferous *empesté*) place. . . . The next day I went to Carrier, who appeared to compassionate the fate of this crowd of miserables. 'I consent.' he said, 'to give them their liberty, and to send them back to their homes.' 'Well.' I replied, 'give me the order or authority in writing; I will take care of the rest.' 'An order in writing.' he replied; 'I do not wish to get myself guillotined.' Such was the sad result I obtained."

While these atrocities were in full swing, and all the revolutionary authorities were working at fullest power, there emanated from the Committee of Public Safety the most urgent commands to vigour.

Though the suspension of the Constitution and the establishment of revolutionary government "until peace came," had been decreed on the 10th October 1793 (19 Vendémiaire, An ii.), it was not until the 4th December (14 Frimaire, An ii.) that the Convention adopted a law setting out in detail the organisation of the Revolutionary Government, which was in reality a new — a revolutionary—Constitution. And it was not until the 29th December that, by circulars to different bodies, the Committee of Public Safety interpreted the decree of 4th December, and set forth clearly and precisely the revolutionary system of government in its entirety. Circulars to the Representatives, to the generals commanding, to the Revolutionary Committees, to the popular societies, to the Departments, to the districts, to the communes, to the national agents with the districts, and to those with the communes, to the Revolutionary Tribunals, the criminal tribunals, the Military Commissions, and the public accusers of same, and, as regarded military offences, to the citizens composing the military tribunals.

Unrolled before us, in the fustian grandiloquence of revolutionary rant, is the whole plan of revolutionary government, the whole machinery of revolutionary despotism.

The Representatives were told that they had been sent to cleanse the air of liberty, to open a large passage to the Revolution which found the scattered fragments of monarchy and the débris of federalism.

The generals were told that the time of disobedience was past; and they were reminded how Rome sent to execution those of her children who had not paid heed to her commands.

The Revolutionary Committees were invoked as "sentinels of liberty," and they were told that they were the hands of the political body of which the

Convention was the head. " You are the levers it uses
to crush resistance. You are like the redoubtable and
warlike implements which, placed by the general, wait
but the electric communication of flame to hurl forth
terror and death.

" Approach this terrible *ministère* with an upright
heart and pure hands. . . . Be so great (*grands*) that
even the eyes of your enemies can never discover in your
conduct a single stain."

The popular societies (which, under the control of the
Society of Jacobins in Paris, had become almost official
bodies of the State) were called on " to place the pinnacle
on the edifice of the Revolution of which, vigilant
sentinels at the advance posts of opinion, they had
already created the indestructible foundation—they were
to unveil the intriguer . . . to tear the mask from the
Tartufes of patriotism, to denounce the faithless agent,
the cowardly deserter, and the egoist who had no
country ": they were to be the torch to the Representatives in their task of purifying the constituted
authorities.

The Revolutionary Tribunals—Military Commissions
included — who were charged with " the national
vengeance," were told that there was no treaty between
virtue and crime : they were to purge their souls of all
weakness ; they were to have no family but *la patrie*,
and were to sacrifice (like Brutus) brothers, friends,
children, if they were culpable. " Such is the high
level of your duties."

And the district authorities were told that the law
ought to take the flight and the talons of the eagle :
they were the sentinels of the Revolution : that it was
by their eyes the Government saw : that, so to speak,
they were the electrical conductors of its thunderbolts :

and they were charged with supervising the execution
of revolutionary laws and of the measures of the
Government.

These incitements to energy were not wanted at
Nantes, or Angers, or elsewhere in the Vendée, for
every section of the republicans there was acting up to
the fullest height of Montagnard fanaticism.

To make the system uniform throughout France, a
new decree as to Representatives was made, also on the
29th December. As to measures of " public safety,"
their powers remained unlimited, but were confined to
the Departments in their charge. Francastel was reappointed to Angers; and Carrier, "as a new mark of
its confidence " (*confiance*), with Prieur (de la Marne) as
associate, was confirmed in his appointment, which is as
conclusive proof as can well be given that the Committee
of Public Safety approved of their actions.

# CHAPTER XVIII

CARRIER has figured largely in the pictures of the
French Revolution, and he has been made more or less
the scapegoat for the worst of the revolutionary horrors.

He has been depicted as a being so towering over
others in wickedness, so entirely abnormal in tempera-
ment, and exceptional in ferocity, that other malefactors,
and other crimes, by contrast, were made to look not
really so bad; and it is argued that it is not fair to
judge the Revolution by the standard of his atrocities.

This view, though consoling to the apologists and
admirers of the French Revolution, is, however, fundamentally false.

Had he been the sole product of his kind, such an
argument might have had some little plausibility; but
there was such a host of malefactors, both military and
civilians,—some who aided him in his atrocities, others
who perpetrated atrocities quite as bad in their own
spheres,—that he was very far from having possessed a
monopoly of cruelty and tyranny, as is usually implied,
and is very far indeed from standing on that pinnacle of
wrong which would isolate him from his fellow-workers.

By no means does he stand alone. A stronger light falls upon him. That is all. And in the shadows and background was not merely a crowd, but a great horde of wretches as bad as he was, only not so conspicuous or notorious, because not so well seen.

As a matter of fact, in Nantes alone there was little difference in all the vicious elements of character between him and the members of the Revolutionary Committee, between him and his own staff, or between him and the members of the Marat Company.

Nor was there much difference between him and several of his Representative colleagues. Francastel, for instance, at Angers, was quite as eminent in cruelty, tyranny, and injustice of all sorts, though not so notorious, being endowed with a greater amount of prudence, doing his work more secretly, not talking or ranting so much about it and liberty; being careful not to leave so many proofs of his iniquities behind, and never having been dragged into the publicity of a court of law as Carrier was.

Nor is there sufficient to confirm the theory of Carrier having been insane, which is also put forward in mitigation of his misdeeds.

He was of an extremely violent and unrestrained temper; but he cannot escape the execration of posterity on the plea of insanity. Conspicuous through all his acts were the very common and matter-of-fact motives of vanity and self-indulgence; and his furious violence was often but the result of his ease and self-indulgence being interrupted and interfered with.

An arch-impostor he was, as all his colleagues, aides, and underlings were; spinning grandiloquent phrases about "liberty," but practising a brutal tyranny; canting about "equality," and only pulling down everything to raise themselves into the places of those they pulled down, and to enable themselves to perpetrate on a more extended scale, and with intensified energy, the very misdeeds and crimes and self-indulgence for which they slaughtered their predecessors.

Disinterested not one of them was. No fact stands out clearer in all this horrible business.

Here in the Vendée and its surroundings, where one sees the revolutionists in their unchecked, unrestrained, and, therefore, natural character, able to do as they liked, and undeterred by any outside opinion or comment, one sees that revolutionary principles were only the cloak for the gratification of their passions; and the expression and parade of those principles were only the means for attaining their own selfish ends. To obtain the means of gratifying all their passions, be the cost to other people what it might, and then to gratify them to the utmost possible extent, that was the creed; those were the consistently worked for objects, of the men who claimed for themselves the title, and acclaimed their comrades with the title of "true patriot" and "brave republican."

A Revolution which placed such men in authority was a calamity, a curse of the direst sort, and not a blessing.

Unfortunate indeed was it for all classes at Nantes that he and his picked crew of ruffians ever came into authority in the place.

That a great city should fall under such government and such tyranny must have been indeed a surprise to those who had helped to destroy the old régime because it was tyrannical, and who expected liberty and freedom under the new régime.

Carrier, when he came to Nantes, was deeply imbued with very thorough sans-culotte revolutionary ideas.

"In the Vendée," he said, "every one is a brigand, all are counter-revolutionists."

There may not have been much justice in the idea, but it simplified things very much.

And as to Nantes, he said, "The people of Nantes act only from motives of coterie. . . . Steel, water, and fire shall nationalise their town. . . . All the Nantais are scoundrels. One must play ball with their heads."

Against every one possessing any property, too, he held equally thorough views.

In a speech which he made before the popular society at Ancenis, a small town on the Loire, he said, "I see everywhere beggars in rags. You are as stupid as they are at Nantes. Plenty is close to you, and you want everything. Don't you know that fortune, the riches of these fat merchants, belongs to you? And is not the river there?"

And at Nantes, speech after speech which he made contained fierce indictments against "the fat merchants," agents, tradesmen of every rank and sort and kind, whom he charged with being monopolists, who only sought to deprive the citizens of the necessaries of life; and incitements to the lowest of the populace to exterminate them, and to appropriate their property.

His ideas soared even higher than this: for once, at a dinner, he declared that the population of France was too large for the food produced—that it ought to be reduced—by the nobles, magistrates, priests, businessmen—then working himself up into a fury he cried out, "Kill, kill!"

Extermination and destruction, these were his ideas, these his passions.

As to the methods of carrying out his views he had no scruples.

Death—that was the one penalty. "All the brigands and all the conspirators ought to be shot."

Noyades, fusillades, sabrades, guillotine, death by disease and hardship in prison, all served his purposes, and served them thoroughly.

The guillotine by itself not being sufficiently rapid, he had recourse to noyades; and even wholesale noyades not getting through the work of destruction quickly enough, he had recourse to fusillades.

The Military Commissions and other tribunals even did not work rapidly enough to suit him; for on one occasion he gave an order to Citizen Phelippes de Tronjolly, president of the criminal tribunal, to have immediately executed, without trial, twenty-four "brigands" who had just been arrested with arms in their hands—although there were four children among them aged thirteen and fourteen years.

A couple of days after he similarly sent twenty-seven to execution without trial—of whom seven were women, four of them sisters—the youngest seventeen, stated to be "brigands taken with arms in their hands." " But we have not been tried or heard," cried these unfortunate girls. "It is an order of Carrier's," was the reply; "at nine o'clock it will be carried out "—and carried out it was.

And on another occasion he sent for the president of one of the Military Commissions and told him that if all the prisoners in the Entrepôt were not condemned within two hours, he would have all the members of the Commission shot.

There were in fact no limits to his sanguinary ideas.

"We will make a cemetery of France," he said, "rather than not regenerate it in the manner we want"; but that too was the policy of the Convention as to the Vendée, as expressed in its decrees.

He lived in an incessant impulse of slaughter. Speaking to some of the municipal authorities as to the treatment of Vendean prisoners who laid down their arms, he exclaimed :

" You set of imbeciles. You are poor ———s, I must tell you that. The fusillade and the guillotine must be kept going ; that is the only way to get any repose. It is better to kill the devil than to let the devil kill one-self."

One day he fell foul even of the Revolutionary Committee.

"What is this Committee about ?" he exclaimed. " Five hundred heads ought to have fallen by this time. I don't see one. Your heads will have to answer for the execution of my orders."

He had but one regret, and he expressed it strongly, that he had not the power himself to butcher all his victims.

But he did the next thing to it. Reports give us a glimpse of him driving up to close proximity of the guillotine on the day of the execution of the twenty brigands and four children, sent to death by himself without trial, and looking on at it at its deadly work. He must have been at it on other occasions too, for speaking much later to a merchant of Nantes of the measures against the priests, he recalled the pleasure he enjoyed in seeing the grimaces which these       s of priests made when dying.

Again, he was present while some unfortunates were being put into a barge to be noyaded, and was seen speaking to Goullin. And he is said to have been seen one night, in a cloak, accompanying the procession of victims on their way to a noyade, and to have been heard saying, " Hurry up ; walk in line."

When shown one of the barges which was to be used for a noyade, he remarked, " Comme c'est commode."

This was one side of his life—this "cleansing of the air of liberty," as the Committee of Public Safety called it—this "opening a large passage to the Revolution"; and if one part of his time was given up to these horrors and iniquities, the rest was given up to the other side of his life—an almost unceasing debauch.

While all around him death was reaping a tremendous harvest ; while thousands were suffering from sickness and disease which a wise governor might have checked and alleviated; and while almost the whole of the people of Nantes, some 100,000 in number, patriots and republicans constituting the vast majority, were half starving, this ruler of the new régime, far from sharing with them their miserable diet of a small ration of *pain d'égalité*, or bread of equality, as it was called, was showing the new spirit of equality and fraternity by revelling with some chosen friends in every procurable luxury.

His cook used to go out early, before the usual market hour, to get poultry for him.

Had he been a royalist, his house would have been burned down by an "enlightened" mob of sans-culottes, and his head would have been paraded through the streets stuck on a pike.  But he was a sans-culotte, a Montagnard, a member of the Convention, a Representative of the people, with unlimited powers, and no one could say aught against him.

He had a villa at Richebourg, one of the suburbs of Nantes, and here his nights, and sometimes his days, were spent in the wildest debauch.

His favourite sultana was "la Caron," a daughter of one of the directors of the vessels used in his *noyades*.  She figured in the fêtes of the Montagne as the goddess of liberty, where she showed herself half naked, adorned with a red cap, and with a pike in her hand.

After thus displaying herself to the people, she went to preside over the scandalous orgies at the Palais du Bœuf, the name of the house which Carrier had given her: "where he realised with his friends and their mistresses everything that the imagination could invent in the way of luxury and orgy."

In the bacchanals at this villa, one saw these women showing themselves off, covered with magnificent sets of diamonds torn from the victims of the Revolution before their heads fell beneath the knife of the executioner. And Goullin—"a charming man"—when Carrier was not present, amused himself lingering the beautiful jewels, and saying, "Ah, this belonged to the beautiful Countess of X——. It is Venus who has the heritage of Madame de Pompadour. It is the *parure* of royalty on the breast of liberty."

One night, in the midst of one of these orgies, three of the Maratist Corps came to tell him that some 500 prisoners were arriving, men, women, and children, and asked what was to be done with them. "Pretty sort of question," he replied, furious at being interrupted: "send them to drink in the glass of the *calotins.*" An answer which excited the ferocious laughter of the guests. But as the stupid executioners of the Compagnie Marat did not always understand the symbolical answers of their master, one of them said, "What orderest thou, Citizen Representative?" "*Parbleu*, let them be pitched into the water," replied Carrier. "And the children?" added one of the Maratists, with hesitation. "*Sacra mille dieux*, in what country am I?" he cried in a ferocious voice: "all of them just alike." A slight remonstrance from one of them. "Am I Representative of the people or not?" he cried furiously, taking his sword in his hand, "do you want to go in their place?" Then taking his glass, he proposed the health of those who were going to drink *à la grande tasse*, and the guests drank the toast, repeating the words of the Representative.

And on one such evening O'Sullivan, who had distinguished himself at one of the noyades by massacring some of the victims with a small knife, imitated the grimaces of his victims as the knife pierced their throat, a performance which made Carrier roar with laughter.

Carrier did not always take his pleasures at home.

He had made Lamberty a present of the ship *La Gloire*, and here Lamberty, following the footsteps of his master, had established his own seraglio. Thither Carrier often went, doubtless as a change from the distractions of his own residence.

Thus Carrier's hundred and ten and odd days and nights passed at Nantes—an uninterrupted spell of injustices, crime, cruelty, and debauch—illustrating for the information and advantage of posterity what the true revolutionist was when he was free from all restraint, and when he was in a position to act according to his own ideas.

The proceedings of the Revolutionary Committee at Nantes also afford deep instruction as to the real character of the new régime, as it came home to the people. Instead of the city gaining an enlightened, intelligent, and honest governing body as presumably it should have under the régime of "liberty," its control passed into the hands of a gang of reckless, ignorant, and criminal men well described as "a committee of assassins."

A more unmitigated lot of scoundrels than they were cannot be imagined. There was not a crime which

they did not commit; not a vice in which they did not
indulge. They perpetrated every iniquity for which
they accused the *ancien régime*, adding some new ones
to the répertoire of their predecessors, and multiplying
the number a thousandfold. Assassination, robbery,
rape, lying, and every form of deceit—these were their
daily acts, their nightly occupations. They murdered
justice, and made their own depraved wills the standard
of law. As one of them said, when told that even
under a Revolutionary Government some laws existed
which ought to be followed, "A republican makes laws
for the occasion" (*lois de circonstance*).

Of their cruelties something has been already said;
but those narrated were only examples of their general
conduct. Their callous cruelty, their indifference to
suffering and bloodshed, were appalling. Murder and
assassination on the largest scale scared them not.
They did not stop at ordering slaughter, nor even at its
supervision, but many of them degraded themselves into
being actually the executioners, many of them perpetrating with their own hands the deed of blood.

They killed as they liked; they stole as they wanted,
silver, food, wine, tobacco; and there was no defence
against them, no protection from them.

Cruelty and bloodthirstiness were, however, but one
side of their character. And just as they excelled in
these things, so they excelled in cupidity and rapacity,
and turned their position to account. The extenuation
of patriotism even cannot be allowed them; for, under
the mask of patriotism, they only thought of themselves,
and how to gain wealth, how to obtain the means and
opportunity for gratifying their vanity and indulging
their passions.

The most devouring cupidity possessed them. Peculiarly sans-culottish was their conduct as to articles of food. Vehement denouncers of monopolies of food, and declaimers as to the enormity of the crime of making money out of this necessity of life, they themselves made money by their transactions in it; forcing the owners of food to sell it at the price fixed under the law of maximum, and to take payment in assignats or worthless paper money; and then reselling it for two or three times the price by exacting payment in hard coin.

"A good republican," it had been said, "ought to despise gold or silver—the vile metal of the slave." This view was not, however, shared by them.

They robbed people right and left. Domiciliary visits and arrests gave them complete facilities for doing this. An unfortunate sent to prison on any charge they chose to make, his property (which strictly should have been under the protection of the law) was at their mercy; and they quickly took all of it that was of value.

One case may be cited as an example of their rapacity — that of two brothers, Thoinnet by name—two of the richest merchants of Nantes, and devoted to the Republic, as proved by their gift of 300,000 francs to the city for the purchase of corn. While they were fighting as volunteers against the Vendeans, the Marat Company came one night to their house, opened everything, carried away money and everything of value they could lay their hands on, then put the official seals on; and then other Maratists came and broke the seals, and took more things, and re-sealed. Seven times this happened; and Chaux and Goullin carried away 227 barrels of wine, and a lot of grain, and other things.

And when the brothers Thoinnet returned from fighting they were arrested as "suspects." Their only

crime being that they were rich), were sent to prison
and let die there, leaving twelve children who would
have died except for some kind attendants. Chaux
said they were aristocrats, had communications with
rebels, and that their spoils (*dépouilles*) belonged therefore
to the Republic—in other words, to himself.

If capable of such a coup as this, it may be easily
inferred how other people were treated.

And then also they sold pardons, secretly of course.

Posing as immaculate patriots, they compromised
with counter-revolutionists for cash down, and gave
liberty to men who but for such payment would have
been included in the next list of prisoners for execution.
They knew well how to inspire fear, and thus made the
rich pay heavy ransoms.

One, Geslin, paid 80,000 francs (or over £3000)
not to be arrested. In another case 70,000 livres, or
nearly £3000, was paid them for the release of a
prisoner. One, Job, gave 50,000 francs to secure his
acquittal and release.

Individually or collectively mattered not. Chaux
took 5000 livres ostensibly for the "salubrity" of the
air," but gave no receipt : and on another occasion with
threats demanded "an offering to the Committee."

Goullin extracted 24,000 livres from a lieutenant-
general of the ex-admiralty, Lieutand by name, " for
the poor, and the salubrity of the air."

Adjutant-General Richard and four of his satellites
took widow Mallet to prison and carried off her money
and 70,000 lbs. of tobacco—pretending that it was in
requisition. She was let out, but as she asked for her
property back, she was again imprisoned.

Pinard robbed " an honest family " of 4000 livres of
jewellery and other things.

And not content with robbing those they put in prison as suspects, they robbed their own friends the republican citizens of Nantes by arbitrary impositions, and exactions, and taxes.

And not content with this, they robbed the State too—the *patrie*, the beloved France, the *République* one and indivisible—to which they professed such devotion, and which was in sorest need.

The property of convicted rebels was confiscate to the Republic, but, very conveniently, the Committee made no lists of the money or property seized, and they quietly carried off to their own houses wine, wood, and other articles from the houses of *émigrés* or prisoners, without having bought them, or giving account of same to the nation—a process by which the goods " reached their patriotic destination."

In some at least of their proceedings there was a stroke of humour, however reprehensible the act may have been. Bachelier, the president, a notary, imprisoned six of his rival notaries, so as to get their practice, three of whom died in prison. Goullin, who succeeded Bachelier as president, got rid of a debt by letting the man he owed it to die in prison; and he quietly settled himself down in a furnished house from which the owner had been sent to prison, and on which the seals of the Republic had been placed. And on one occasion, where some very valuable jewels and other property were being sold by auction, they arranged that bidders should be kept away, and that things should fetch nothing. Lace worth 100,000 francs was sold for 18 francs.

Chaux also used his power to imprison his creditors; a receipt for his debt to them released them, a refusal doomed them to the scaffold. He also bought some national property for 60,000 francs, but never paid for it.

As Phelippes said, *Le Comité recevait de toutes mains* (" It received from every quarter "). And Goullin, with that loathsome hypocrisy and cant which were so prominent and remarkable features of the revolutionary character, wrote to some district authorities :—

" Brave comrades, let us work in concert to establish (*asseoir*) and enrich the Republic. She claims the vigorous arms and the disinterested hearts. So many traitors disturb her, so many knaves pillage her. Constancy and incorruptibility and her throne will become immovable."

All the pictures we get of the lives and habits of these men show them as doing everything which the *ancien régime* had been so execrated for doing, and which it was wiped out for doing.

They revelled in sumptuous repasts, whilst the " patriot " poor of Nantes were suffering from want or dying of starvation. They indulged themselves in every obtainable luxury, whilst many of those from whom they had wrung the means for such indulgence were steeped in poverty and misery. And to win and keep their power so to do they stopped at no crime.

No record exists of all their crimes—only a part, a small part, are known. One can only form an idea of the full measure of their iniquities by those which are known.

With women they were merciless ; sensual brutes, availing themselves of their power and opportunities to appropriate any on whom they cast their eyes. Carrier had given them the lead and example, but they needed little encouragement.

Phelippes, who knew them probably better than any one else did, and who had better means than any one of forming an opinion, wrote :—

T

"There is no crime of which the Revolutionary Committee has not made itself guilty.  It has played with
the laws and violated them, even those of the Revolutionary Government.  It has covered with mourning
and desolation the Department of Loire Inférieure.
The extortions are frightful.  The revelations are terrible; . . . they would be more horrible if the dead
could speak.  But terror, night, the Loire, and death
have shrouded under impenetrable veil more than half
the crimes committed by these men."

The tale of revolutionary scoundrels at Nantes is not
yet complete.

Carrier did not rely solely on this Committee to do
his work.  He had several aides-de-camp, persons more
directly receiving their orders from him.

There was Lebatteux, who commanded the "Scouts
of the Mountain," and levied contributions wherever he
went, and gave no account of them; there was Fouquet,
whom he had raised to the rank of adjutant-general of
artillery; and there was Robin, a dissolute and cruel
youth of nineteen or thereabouts; and there was Lamberty, who appears to have been his right hand in carrying out the noyades, whom also he raised to the rank of
adjutant-general of the artillery.

Between them and the Revolutionary Committee there
was little to choose, for some members of that Committee
took part in all their iniquities.

To have any communication or dealing with brigands
was a capital offence; but where women were concerned,
these *vrais sans-culottes* made "laws of circumstances"
for themselves.

Lamberty, to stock his seraglio in the ship which
Carrier had given him, had made it up of women who
were in prison as counter-revolutionists, and whom he

secretly abstracted from the clutches of the Republic;
unhappy women, who could not hope to save their lives
except by yielding themselves to his passions. Among
the women he took was a certain Giroust de Marcilly,
"an ex-noble"—"the most inveterate enemy of the
Republic; a woman who in her hatred of the Revolution
could only be compared to Marie Antoinette."

He and his friend Fouquet had succeeded in carrying
her and her maid off while she was on her way from trial
by the Military Commission, where they had been
sentenced to death. He appropriated her, while Fouquet
took her maid. She was only one of a number. There
was Gingreau, the maid of Madame de Lescure ; also two
sisters Dubois, taken out of the prison of the Entrepôt.
A whole lot of women were thus taken, and the whole
gang of Carrier's henchmen were mixed up in this business, O'Sullivan, Lavaux, Robin. So common had
become such procedure that the Revolutionary Committee
at last made a decree ordering all who had withdrawn
brigands (*retiré des brigands*) to remit them to the
established authorities for judgment.

It was this Lamberty who, in one short but luminous
phrase, quite unconsciously described the Revolution as it
had in effect worked out.

Foiled one day in an attempt to abstract some female
prisoners from one of the prisons at Nantes, he turned
on the officer of the prison who was thwarting him, and,
drawing his sword, with menace of death declared that it
was the *la glaive de la loi* (the sword of the law), and
that the officer should suffer.

He spoke truly. It was so. The sword of the law
—or, in other words, the authority of the State—had
passed into the hands of depraved and degraded and
cruel ruffians like himself.

It had come into the hands of men who were every-thing that was lowest and basest in humanity—tyrants, murderers, slaughterers of the innocent, liars, thieves, debauchees, and drunkards, uneducated, ignorant, and degraded wretches; men utterly devoid of any sense of right, or justice, or humanity; men who, mouthing about "liberty," "equality," and "fraternity," were the incarnation of the opposite ideas—tyranny, inequality, and fratricide—and the accentuated embodiment of all the vices they condemned in others.

This was the great reality of the Revolution; this is how it worked in practice; very different indeed from all those high-flown theories of justice and humanity and all the virtues with which people dressed up the Republic. And it is exactly because *la glaive de la loi* (the sword of the law) had come into such infamous hands that the revolutionary Republic stands, and must for ever stand, condemned in the judgment of rational men.

The régime which had gone before them may have been all that its enemies said—may indeed have been deserving of the fate which befell it; but in everything for which they condemned it, this revolutionary régime is more strongly to be reprobated.

Instead of liberty succeeding tyranny, only a greater tyranny followed; instead of equality succeeding in-equality, only another form of inequality was substituted; and instead of all men rushing together in fraternal embrace, a bloody and prolonged civil war broke out, and whole hecatombs of Frenchmen were slain by their own countrymen and brothers.

It may give a shock to those persons who associate "liberty" with the Revolution to find that the nearest precedent in civilised history to the methods and actions of the Revolutionary Committees of Nantes and Angers, and indeed of the Revolutionary Committees and Government generally, was that afforded by that fearful engine of religious tyranny, the Spanish Inquisition. And it even, in the height of its might and power, fell short of its revolutionary imitator.

It would seem indeed as if the revolutionists had had the precedent of the Inquisition in their minds when devising and organising the Revolutionary Tribunals and Revolutionary Committees, improving on it as an instrument of tyranny where improvement was possible, and making the procedure more stringent and severe, and the escape of innocence more impossible.

The Inquisition has been graphically described by Motley.

" It was a bench of monks, without appeal, having its familiars in every house, diving into the secrets of every fireside, judging and executing its horrible decrees without responsibility. . . . It arrested on suspicion, tortured till confession, and then punished by fire. Two witnesses, and those to separate facts, were sufficient to consign the offender to a loathsome dungeon. Here he was sparingly supplied with food. . . . He was informed of the testimony against him, but never confronted with the witness. . . . The torture took place in a gloomy dungeon. The victim, whether man, matron, or tender virgin, was stripped naked and stretched on the wooden bench. . . . The executioner, enveloped in a black robe from head to foot, glared at his victim through holes cut in the hood which covered his face, and practised successively all the forms of torture which the devilish ingenuity of the monks had invented."

Almost verbatim might the description be applied to the Revolutionary Committees and Tribunals, only it would but inadequately describe the persecuting and iniquitous system of the revolutionists.

The Revolutionary Tribunals were benches of civilian or lay judges, or military commissioners, from whom there was no appeal, and the mockery of legal forms employed was certainly greater.

The Revolutionary Committee had, like the Inquisition, its familiars in almost every house, diving into the secrets of every fireside, and executing its horrible decrees without responsibility.

It arrested on suspicion, but, worse than its prototype, took guilt for granted, without asking for confession; it did not even inform the prisoner of any testimony against him; it confronted him with no witness—indeed usually had no witness to confront him with; it punished with the mental and physical torture of an awful imprisonment in dens of disease and filth and semi-starvation, and then with death, by water, steel, or lead.

One slight difference there was. Instead of the executioner being clad in a black robe from head to foot, and with face concealed, the revolutionary executioners, Grandmaison, Lamberty, or Vacheron, for example, were undisguised, and swaggered in the national uniform of the new Republic, displaying conspicuously what delusively was regarded as the emblem and insignia of "liberty," the tricolour cockade.

Even in the final scene of all, the similarity of procedure was remarkable.

With the Inquisition, "the *auto-da-fé* or execution of the victims was a solemn spectacle. . . . The procession was formed with great pomp. . . . The monarch, the high functionaries of the land, the reverend clergy, the populace regarded it as an inspiring and delightful recreation."

With the French revolutionists, on gala days of great fusillades, the authorities usually attended in full uniform, and military bands played; even he who was actually the sovereign, the Representative, the despot with unlimited powers, has been present at executions. At other times the judges looked on at the executions from the windows of their dining-room, "between their coffee and liqueur"; and at the guillotinings the populace exhibited their appreciation of the delights of the recreation by attending in considerable numbers and by shouting "Vive la République!" as each head fell under the blade of the guillotine.

A comparison between the Inquisition and the revolutionary system of government as exhibited in the Vendée is to the advantage of the Inquisition.

For one thing, the Inquisition was more merciful. An avowal of error, or recantation and submission to the tenets of the Church, often secured a pardon or a mitigated punishment.

With the Military Commission there was no such leniency. An avowal of error, no matter how genuine or submissive, was answered instantly by a sentence of death. For another thing, too, the Inquisition confined itself mostly to religious practices and opinions, whilst the Revolution covered the whole field of political, civil, religious, and social life.

And if one finishing touch to the repulsiveness of revolutionary tyranny were required to make it wholly execrable, it was that its crimes were perpetrated under the false name, and under the cloak, of "liberty."

# CHAPTER XIX

## TERROR

When ... Revolution became an accomplished fact, and the Rep... was declared as a great existent reality. Liberty was placed first and foremost of the three great ... the new order of things introduced by the Revolution. To Liberty, ecstatic apostrophes were daily ad... ... impassioned invocations were unceasingly made ... ... of thought, expression, or action. Liberty was ... the be-all and end-all, the climax, the apotheosis ... but may exist ... only under a Revolutionary Government could true liberty exist.

It might naturally be concluded, therefore, that tyranny ... would vanish at least from France. ... that under the new order of things liberty would exist.

... it might logically be expected that the more ... the revolutionary ideas were realised, the ... would ... all ... and that the ... ... ... ... the ... ... ... ...

... ... ...

... ... difference between theory ... ... is this that ... ... in this

the French Revolution, that not merely have grave
doubts arisen whether the Revolution was all even its
apologists claimed for it, but it becomes ever plainer that
it was, in fact, a greater and more transparent "sham"
than the unrealities which it was lauded for having
swept away.

For, if one finds that a system of government, however theoretically admirable, when put into actual operation and practice, works out diametrically opposite to
the theories on which it is based, it is only natural
that the soundness of the system should be vitally
impugned.

Certainly it is a fact that, as revolutionary opinions
gained greater ascendency, liberty became less and less;
until, at last, as revolutionary government was really
perfected, and one public authority after another was
reduced into obedient implements in its hands, liberty
ceased to exist.

Nantes affords a remarkable illustration of this great
truth. Of most cities in France it ought to have shown
the beauteous effects of revolutionary principles. There
liberty should have flourished, for whatever anti-revolu-
tionary leaven there had been in it had been eliminated.
Republican and revolutionary clubs and societies, by dint
of a process of purgation, had attained the height of
principles beloved by ardent revolutionists; the local
authorities were strongly republican; a Revolutionary
Committee was in full and undisputed authority over
everybody and everything; and over all, in supreme
power and with unlimited authority, was the delegate
of the Convention, the "Representative of the people,"
selected by Robespierre himself. Here, then, there should
have been the fullest enjoyment of liberty, the most complete absence of any vestige of tyranny.

But so it was not. In defiance of all avowed principles of the Republic, liberty did not exist.

Of personal liberty there was none. On every house a list had to be posted up on the door of the people inside. From where one was, there was no departure. Movement to any part of the country was impossible without a passport, which was only obtainable if one were a professed sans-culotte, or, through intermediaries, got access to some sans-culotte in authority, who for a sufficient consideration would grant it.

Within one's house, too, one was liable at any moment to domiciliary invasion, and search and arrest.

Liberty of trade—liberty to earn an honest livelihood—was there none. The law of 26th July 1793, directed against monopolists, declared all to be guilty of monopoly who kept any articles of first necessity from sale, in which articles were included almost every article of daily food or use, even to clothes and metals; and the law of maximum, which fixed the prices above which the articles might not be sold, fixed them at such ruinously low prices that there was a heavy loss on their sale. Moreover, every merchant or tradesman was ordered to write up the list of supplies he had in his stores, and disobedience to these injunctions entailed dangerous, even the extremest penalties. To enforce these laws a system was devised, so ruinous to all concerned (except the revolutionary officials), that all trade was destroyed.

And in addition to these laws, there were constant requisitions on the part of the Government, or of the local authorities and Revolutionary Committees, not merely of food, but of all sorts of things, at prices which were quite unremunerative to makers or to producers, and no one could refuse to obey under pain of confiscation or worse. Production was thus discouraged, was practically stopped, whilst the whole system of distribution was first disorganised, and then ceased to be.

In fact, tyranny in trade and commerce was extreme ; and if the law was in any respect not quite despotic enough to secure its object, the Representatives gave more extensive interpretation to it. Thus "the private industry and personal initiative of citizens were struck by complete paralysis," and the commerce of Nantes—the life of the great city—was destroyed.

And as for religious liberty, not alone did it not exist, but it had been perverted into the most vehement and violent religious persecution. The original Declaration of the Rights of Man on 25th August 1789, and the new edition of those Rights made on 8th December 1793, had solemnly declared that no one was to be interfered with (*inquiété*) on account of his opinions, even of his religious opinions. But, despite this solemn declaration, religious freedom had been deliberately annihilated. From the very outset, as has been seen, a violent religious persecution was one of the features of the new régime of liberty. The ministers of religion had been swept away ; churches closed and turned into meeting-places for Revolutionary Committees, or other secular purposes. Fêtes of reason were substituted for religious fêtes or worship ; and, finally, the revolutionary calendar, abolishing the religious Sabbath, and substituting a secular Sabbath for it, was designed to be an obliterating blow against religion.

Public religious worship was thus non-existent. Even private worship was almost impossible ; for the possession of a prayer-book, of a string of beads, or of any religious emblem or token, was held to be proof of correspondence with refractory priests, an offence visited with arrest, and sentence, and death.

Nor was it any different as regards liberty of expression or thought.

Political opinions, not in full accordance with the latest phase of sans-culotte ravings, were ruthlessly suppressed. Hundreds had been sent to the scaffold for some expression which was twisted into some disrespect to the Republic.

Not step by step, but stride by stride, had republican opinions become extremer, and the more extreme they became, the more violent became the true republican against those who did not keep pace with him, or who showed any signs of hanging back. Moderates, Federalists, Girondists, were all accursed, and regarded as dangerous enemies of the Republic, as were the royalists and clericals.

Revolutionary Government could not abide even the suspicion of a rival. It could not brook the slightest imputation against itself. Criticism of its acts was an offence punished with death. It lashed itself into fury at the faintest sign of opposition or even disapprobation, and its fury was terrible in its unreasonableness, appalling in its injustice, and remorseless in its operation. Before its wrath every vestige of liberty was annihilated, and nothing remained but a despotism so complete, so evil, so unjust, so merciless, and cruel, that the world's history must be ransacked to find a parallel to it, and then the parallel could not be found.

And there was the special and peculiar aggravation of this despotism, that revolutionary ingenuity had drawn the net so tightly round all men that they were defenceless against any blow that might be aimed against them.

Law after law had been passed against every form of depreciation of or opposition to the Revolutionary

Government; but lest any possible loophole should still remain, suspicion was made tantamount to guilt. Suspicion covered everything. And the courts of justice, the last safeguard of the innocent, were perverted into obedient instruments of tyranny, and afforded no protection to even the most manifest innocence.

The executive machinery of the Revolutionary Government was perfect in its malignant despotism. In Nantes as in Angers it was in the hands of a horde of "apostles of carnage," responsible to no one, keen for blood, covetous of other men's goods, and eager to raise themselves to revolutionary power and fame, though the steps by which they ascended should be the heaped corpses of innocent men and women and children.

And the result was that not " liberty " but " terror " reigned ; an appalling terror ; terror racking unceasingly the minds of all : for at last it came to such an extreme that none, not even the republicans and revolutionists themselves, had any security against being the victim of the next blow.

Mutual trust was completely destroyed, for the friend might, for self-preservation's sake, become an enemy. No one dared to communicate his thoughts to another, through fear of being overheard, or that an evil interpretation might be put on his words.

" It was a time to have ears that would not hear, and eyes that did not see."

" If one met one's brother, one dare not address him,—one dare not speak to him, through fear of being suspected of evil intentions." Men became afraid even to look at each other, lest a plot might be read in a look of grief or disdain. Spies surrounded them :

their conversations were listened to, their correspondence
was opened and read. The slightest sign of humanity,
or of sympathy with the victims of the revolutionists,
or of giving help to any one was dangerous, for pity
was regarded by the revolutionists as a crime and not
as a virtue.

And the terror grew as during the dark winter
months the saturnalia of carnage grew wilder, as the
*vrais sans-culottes* plunged ever deeper into the abysses
of infamy : and as men realised that they could not even
show that they knew anything of the horrors being
daily perpetrated in their midst without imperilling
their individual safety.

And the feelings of all were weighed down by the
sense that nothing they could do, or abstain from doing,
could secure them against disaster. There was no refuge
possible, no safety anywhere. Even a cringing submissive obedience to the laws did not secure immunity :
for in one sense there was no law, and every one's life
was at the mercy of any malicious individual who chose
to fabricate a charge against one.

And there was no appeal for mercy, or even for
justice to any one : for he to whom the appeal would
come, if it ever reached him, was the person charged
by the Revolutionary Government to perpetrate the
very acts complained of : whilst in Paris, the Committee of Public Safety and the National Convention
turned a deaf ear and a blind eye to the acts of their
deputy.

On the people of Nantes the perpetual guillotinings,
the noyades, the fusillades had, as they were intended
to have, a tremendous effect. To the victims of those
inhumanities the end at any rate had come of their
miseries and sufferings. But those who survived

cowered under the tempest of revolutionary violence,
and were struck with absolute terror. Complaint meant
death; and so they had to suffer in silence, and groan
in secret, and they sank into a dumb stupor. The
agony begotten of the unceasing dread that they, or
the beloved members of their family, might at any
moment be torn from hearth and home, and sent to
death, weighed them down to the lowermost depths
of mental anxiety and torture. No man left his house
but with the fear that he might never come back to
it again, or if he did come back to it, might find it in
the possession of the Maratist Company, sealed with
their appropriating seal, and his wife and children
swept away to prison. Once there, they were beyond
help, for merely to ask for mercy for a prisoner had
been made a crime by the Revolutionary Committee,
and once in prison, they were on the outer sweep of
the whirlpool, certain a little sooner or a little later
to be drawn into the vortex, and to disappear for ever
in the devouring abyss.

And daily they had visible or other proof of the
possible fate awaiting themselves,—in the processions of
victims through the streets on the way to death; in the
sound of the volleys of musketry borne to the ear as the
victims met their fate; or, if they passed the Place du
Bouffay, in the dull thuds of the blood-besmeared guillotine, and the cheers of "Vive la République," as one
head after another fell into the fatal basket, and the
blood, despite three feet of sand to absorb it, trickled in
little streams across the Place until it reached and fell
into the river.

Daily their nostrils were assailed by the pestilential
smells arising from the unburied or half-buried bodies of
the thousands of victims of revolutionary cruelty, or the

festering masses of a still living humanity in the numerous revolutionary prisons.

Their eyes, too, were shocked by the dead bodies of the noyaded or fusilladed lying on the banks of the river, left there by the current. Or, most horrible of all, by the sight of half-starved dogs slinking along with bloody jaws, and in their mouths bones or lumps of flesh torn from the half-buried corpses of the Vendeans or other victims done to death in the name of liberty.

Even night brought no relaxation of the mental strain nor offered any repose; for darkness afforded no protection against violence and arrest. Rather did darkness add to their fears, were that possible. Every sound almost, the roll of distant wheels, the heavy footstep of the chance passer-by, the gusts of wind which shook their doors, was felt as the herald of danger and death. Frequently, too, the cries of their neighbours being haled to prison made them realise how very real and near the danger was, whilst the shrieks of the victims of the noyades chilled their hearts and souls with dread that such might soon be their end.

And then, thanks also to this most desirable of forms of government, their material circumstances caused them the deepest anxiety. The necessities of life were scarcely obtainable.

With many families actual famine prevailed; whilst want was universal, except among the sans-culotte officials who monopolised for themselves all the luxuries they could lay hands on. The needs of the Government entailed a ruinous taxation, and the grasping avarice of its corrupt administrators consummated the ruin of those who had any property.

And as if all these ills were not enough, disease came, and a dangerous epidemic raged throughout the

town. The overcrowded and pestilential condition of
the prisons had resulted in a fearful prevalence of fever,
and dysentery, and other sicknesses, which not alone
thinned the number of prisoners, but clutched those outside the prison walls as well.

Thus everything, in this era of Liberty, combined to
make both the mental and physical condition of the
people miserable beyond description.

It is impossible to even imagine the terror, the misery,
the suffering which existed.

For months, all through the weary winter months of
gloom and wet and cold, this terror grew and grew, and
became ever more and more accentuated as crime after
crime was committed, and as the victims, from being
numbered by tens and hundreds, passed into thousands
and thousands.

It was like the terror of the nightmare in which the
agonised cry for relief can find no utterance.

Gradually, too, the terror involved all classes in its
fearsome grip.

" Scarce a house in Nantes but was wet with the
tears of the wronged or the suffering. Scarce a stone
but was stained with blood."

" Nantes was frozen with terror."

# CHAPTER XX

IF man remained silent under these appalling violations of all the principles of humanity—if no human hand or voice were raised to check them—Nature, at least, would not remain an assenting witness of the diabolical infamies of the "good republicans" of Nantes, of the "true sans-culottes" of the Revolution.

And so, far out over the Atlantic the storm begins to move—to gather force. The clouds of heaven become darker—the wind increases in energy—the sea labouring ever more and more, in deep agitation. A western gale sweeps in on the coast of France; higher and higher mount the waves; and the great masses of water are driven before its fury.

No common gale is this, but such a one as in the memory of man had not been witnessed before, lasting on and on, in furious wrath and grandeur, banking up the waters of the vast deep, and hurling them at last right up the estuary of the Loire.

And as the great mass of waters swirled and foamed up the tidal way to Nantes, under the leaden sky of the cold winter's day, they gathered in their embrace the countless bodies of those whom a demoniacal cruelty had sent to death in the frigid bosom of the river.

The great Ocean would repudiate participation in the crimes of the murderers who sought to bury in the secrecy of its depths the evidence of their infamies, and now, with indignant might, it forced the river to bear back the accumulated proofs of their guilt, to affright the gaze of the great city with the magnitude of the crimes committed within its precincts.

And so, borne on the rising, rushing tide, come these ghastly remains of the victims of French revolutionary "justice." Somehow there was in it a resemblance to a school of porpoises, as one sees them disporting themselves in the waves, suddenly appearing and disappearing, just long enough on the surface to catch the eye of the beholder; but these tenants of the waters, appearing and disappearing, were of a different hue and kind, and instead of being full of life and volition, they were helpless and inert.

In all stages of decay—in all the horrors of decomposition—in the fixed and ghastly attitudes of an agonising end—in all the rigidity of death—naked as when they were born into this world of woe and misery —many displaying the gaping wounds inflicted by the *vrais sans-culottes* who had done them to death, or by those Maratist "friends of the people" who were the trusted henchmen of the Revolutionary Government— come these bodies, borne on the dark and angry tide.

On they come, in horrid ghastly procession, jostling each other as they roll inertly, impassively along. Here and there a hand or arm appears above the water, as if to demand the attention of living men—here and there a pallid face appears for a moment above the waves, then disappears; then whole figures are seen rolling and swaying in the waters of the river, and every now and then a body is pushed up on the bank, and left there, so that all men may indubitably know what those moving, white, shadowy figures beneath the water are.

In hundreds upon hundreds they come. Old and young—men, women, and children—a great final gathering of the dead—to make one final, united protest against the hellish fiends who had done them to death, and against the system in whose name they had been destroyed.

It was a silent protest, for those mute lips could never open in speech again; but it was a protest which will last through all time.

Nor did it at the moment pass quite unheeded. The municipal authorities of Nantes made a decree ordering the inhabitants of the city to abstain from drinking the water of the Loire, and from eating any fish caught in the river; and an extra number of grave-diggers were employed to bury the bodies thrown up on the banks.

And so, once more, "En avant!" "Vive la République!" "Vive la justice révolutionnaire!"

# CHAPTER XXI

## 'THE INFERNAL COLUMNS'

### PART I

JUST as Carrier's régime at Nantes, Francastel's at Angers, and that of other Representatives in other places presented to the world startling and appalling illustrations of tyranny under a Republican Government, and of the negation of liberty and justice which had to be endured under it, so the régime of Turreau, the commander-in-chief in the Vendée, disclosed another illustration of the limitless powers for evil in the form of government which was being heralded to mankind as the acme of liberty, the ideal of justice, and the embodiment of brotherly love.

In Nantes, in Angers, and in many other places, one saw under the banner of " liberty, fraternity, and equality " a despotism of the civil power—every natural right of man set aside and contemned, every form of liberty crushed, every protection of justice ignored.

In the Vendée under Turreau's régime one sees a fierce military despotism, where the musket and the bayonet and the torch were the instruments of a tyranny rivalling in injustice and atrocity even that of the civil power.

The general idea of Turreau's procedure had been set out a little while previously by Carrier.

It might be thought that, what with noyades, fusillades, and guillotinings, nocturnal debauches, and all the other pleasures of the *vrai sans-culotte*, Carrier would have had enough to occupy him. His soul appears, however, to have hungered for further fields of energy, for on the 11th December he wrote to the Committee of Public Safety :—

"I am as interested as you are in the prompt extermination of the brigands. You can, you ought to rely on me. I understand, yes I understand to-day, the business of war. I am on the spot. Remain at ease, and let me act. So soon as the news of the capture of Noirmoutier shall have reached me, I will send an immediate order to Generals Dutruy and Haxo to put to death, in all the revolted country, all the individuals of both sexes who are found there, indiscriminately, and to accomplish the burning of everything.

"For it is well that you should know that it is the women who, with the priests, have fomented and sustained the war in the Vendée : that it is they who have had our unhappy prisoners shot ; who have butchered many : who fight with the brigands : and who pitilessly kill our volunteers when they meet any detached ones in the villages. They are an *engéance proscrite* (a cursed breed), like all the peasants, for there is not a single one of them who has not borne arms against the Republic. They must be absolutely and totally purged from the soil."

The Committee of Public Safety took no steps to prevent such a horrible programme being carried into effect, made no protest even against the extreme character of those views and intentions, and so must be held as approving, at any rate as not discountenancing, the idea.

The day after writing this epistle, he wrote to General Haxo, who was in the western part of the Vendée:—

"It forms part of my plans, and these are the orders of the National Convention, to carry off all the means of subsistence, every commodity, all the forage, in one word, everything belonging to this accursed country, and to give every building in it to the flames, and to exterminate all the inhabitants." And he added this order: "You are ordered to burn all the houses of the rebels, to massacre all the inhabitants, and to carry away all the food."

But the atrocious credit of converting these brutal and merciless ideas into actual facts must be given to another than he, namely to Louis Marie Turreau, who had been appointed commander-in-chief in the Vendée (as successor to L'Echelle); and if Carrier is for ever infamous on account of the noyades, so may General Turreau take his place beside him in the temple of infamy as the organiser and director of the "infernal columns" which massacred thousands upon thousands of unarmed and innocent citizens, "patriots" as well as brigands.

The idea of reducing the whole of the Vendée to a blackened mass of desolation by fire, and to a desert, by the massacre of all the inhabitants, was certainly quite in accordance with the reckless brutality of revolutionary procedure, and was as a matter of fact in accordance with the opinions of the Committee of Public Safety and of the Convention in Paris.

It did not appear to matter that by the end of 1793 the triumph of the republicans in the Vendée was practically complete. Once the great mass of the Vendeans had migrated from their own lands across the Loire, and once the fight had shifted to the north side of the river, the Upper Vendée had quieted down; there were no assemblies of brigands; "not ten men were assembled in arms; one could go through it with an escort of four orderlies," wrote a general; the administrations and various local authorities had resumed their functions, and confidence was being re-established. And in the Lower Vendée, though Charette was still spasmodically carrying on the strife, the peasants, wearied of the frightful war, were imploring the protection and clemency of the republicans; and Haxo was able to report that all the roads were safe and that the country was free.

The annihilation of the Vendean host on the north side of the Loire, and the complete triumph of the republicans there, made the Vendean cause more hopeless than ever. The few remaining chiefs were leading a wandering and hunted life of hardship and hourly danger. "There existed no longer a Vendée." "Everything was tranquil in the insurgent country."

The war, in fact, might have been considered at an end,—would soon have been completely so, if wise or moderate counsels had any existence.

The general cry was for peace. But peace was not to be—indeed, one might say, peace was not revolutionary.

Turreau had come, a *bon sans-culotte*, with a "great idea" in his head, the realisation of which would make him for ever famous—"a promenade" in the Vendée, as he lightly called it. The attempted realisation of his idea lighted up a second war in the Vendée.

On the 15th January he was at Saumur, and there he wrote to the Representatives announcing his great idea, which, he said, he had formed before his appointment.

"My intention is to burn everything, reserving only some few places as cantonments for the troops most suited for the destruction of the rebels : but this great measure should be prescribed by you. I am only a passive agent. . . . You must also pronounce in advance as to the fate of the women and children I come across in the revolted country. If they are all to be put to the sword, I cannot carry out such a proceeding without an order which will relieve me from the responsibility."

The Representatives, L. Turreau, who was his cousin, and Bourbotte, left the letter unanswered, and wrote to the Committee of Public Safety asking for their own recall on the ground of ill-health.

Nevertheless, two days later, he issued a general order, organising six divisions of troops, each in charge of a general.

The six divisions were commanded by the generals Bonnaire, Boucret, Cordellier, Duval, Grignon, and Moulin.[1] Each of the divisions was to be divided into two columns. These twelve columns, amounting to about 12,000 men in all, placed on a line embracing practically " the diameter of the country," were to sweep the Vendée from east to west. All the corn and forage and provisions found were to be seized and put in carts, and sent to safe centres for the benefit of the Republic. The most scrupulous search was to be made for the rebels, all of whom were to be bayoneted, whilst the villages, farm-houses, woods — in fact, everything that would burn — were to be given over to the flames.

---

[1] Savary, jealous of the reputation of the Mayençais troops, says : "No general, no officer, nor any portion even of the troops of Mayence were employed" (Savary, iii. 45).

Thirteen communes out of the whole country were exempted from this decree of destruction as being proper places for the necessary garrisons.

This barbarous plan surpassed in atrocity even the decree of the Convention of the previous August, which, though ordering the destruction of the Vendée, did not condemn the population *en masse*, but directed that the old men, women, and children should be removed before the villages were destroyed. No such exception was made by Turreau.

On the 19th January he wrote to the Minister of War announcing his plans for the extermination of the rest of the rebels, and informing him that the columns were to make "a general battue," and so definitely purge the country of the brigands. And on the same day he wrote to the Committee of Public Safety informing it in full detail of his intended "military promenade," which, he expected, would be finished about the 3rd or 4th of February, and sending it a copy of his letter to the Representatives.

"I have reason to hope you will approve. Please send me an answer by return courier. . . . I am abandoned by the Representatives."

Doué, from which he wrote, was little more than a couple of days' post from Paris, but he would not wait for a reply. As a matter of fact, some three weeks passed before one was sent.

He had established his headquarters at Doué, and there he held a council of war, informing the generals of his great plan. Some of them remonstrated as to the impolicy of the scheme, but he crushed remonstrance by saying that his plan was approved by the Committee of Public Safety.

The generals were given their detailed instructions.

What they were may be gathered from Cordellier's orders to his column :—

"All the brigands who are found with arms in their hands, or convicted of having taken them to revolt, shall be bayoneted to death. Girls, women, and children in similar circumstances shall be treated in the same way. Suspected persons shall not be spared either; but in their cases the general must have given an order for their execution. Persons of whose civism the general shall be satisfied, would be at liberty to go to the rear of the army."

And so, on the 21st January, all preparations being made, the " infernal columns " are let go, and the Vendée is delivered to fire and sword, Turreau himself taking command of the centre column to see how his plan worked out.

In the previous year the fight had been more or less of a fair stand-up character—that much could be said for it—now, there is no fight; it is a horrid and unprovoked massacre of defenceless and surprised men, women, and children, for none are spared. No inkling had reached the unfortunate people of the fate in store for them; no warning had been given them; they were not in arms fighting—had made no sign of taking to arms—nor had they done anything to draw down such violence upon themselves. The thunderbolt fell before the lightning flashed. To them the first tidings of the fate in store for them are the furious invading horde of armed men, the rough capture of their fellow-villagers, the loud reverberations of the death-shots from the muskets, the shrieks of the falling victims, the prodding and hewing and hacking of bloody bayonets or sabres, the blazing torches.

Like a cyclone of destruction these " infernal columns" swept down upon their hellish mission.

Stretched out in échelon, searching right and left, on they come: the cavalry sometimes with their horses' hoofs muffled so that no alarm might be given and the surprise be complete.   Here, in the recesses of a valley, a farm-house is found, the farmer is seized, "suspect" of course: his servants, male and female, are captured, brigands also: lucky if his wife and daughters are not violated before his eyes before they are killed; a few minutes and all are lying mangled, mutilated corpses, or writhing in their death agonies: and then, whatever property or valuables there are in the house are swept into the soldiers' sacks, or hoisted into the carts or waggons, to be divided later between the plunderers— generals, officers, and soldiers: fiends with lighted brands rush hither and thither, setting fire to the house, to the sheds, to the woods, to everything that will burn: and then, with shouts of "Vive la République!" "Ça-ira!" push on to further conquests.

In the villages the procedure is a little slower; the slaughter and destruction being on a larger scale, the amount of pillage greater, the search for it more pro- longed.   There, sometimes, the victims were kept over- night—and what a night.

Here is one night, in one place—a scene multiplied by many in the earlier period of the "infernal columns."

"Everything was quiet in the bourg until about six o'clock in the evening—near the time of pillage.   But as the citizens knew that their houses were to be burned the next day, they attached little value to their property, knowing that they could not save it from the flames. At this hour the aspect of affairs changed.   The soldiers, possessed with the idea that they were to burn and kill everything in this unfortunate country, gave themselves up to all sort of excesses,—the women were violated,

pillaged, mutilated: the men were struck down; and
soon the greater number of officers, worse a thousand
times than the soldiers, allowed themselves the greatest
violence against the unhappy women who had prepared
their supper for them, flourishing their naked swords
and threatening to cut their heads off if they did not
consent to the officers gratifying their brutal passion.
They breathed only blood and carnage, and threatened to
kill every one."

The fearful night slowly drags its length along, every
moment an agony to the unfortunate and innocent
villagers surrounded by these drunken fiends; dawn at
last breaks — the cold, gloomy, clammy dawn of a
winter's day; and then the final scene—the collecting of
the terror-stricken women and children; the shootings
and sabrings and bayonetings, till the last villager
has been done to death, and a heap of slain lies
there, jocularly called a "patriotic mountain" (*des
montagnes patriotiques*).    And the column passes on
with its plunder, leaving behind it blazing roofs and
rafters, and charring corpses, and a village—wiped out.
Once more " En avant!" " Vive la République!"

Think of it.    Eleven[1] "infernal columns" under
republican generals and officers, scattered in one great
line across the Vendée, most of them hard at work at
this hellish employment, most of them revelling in it,
getting up in the morning to it; killing the women and
girls they had violated and outraged in the night, and
the children, to get their hand in for the day: seizing
anything valuable that they could get, appropriating all
the food and drink they could find, setting ablaze the

---

[1] Those historians who have vaguely noticed these horrors say there
were twelve columns, but Moulin could only form one column, not
having enough troops for a second, and being himself ill, had to appoint
a substitute to take the command (Savary, iii. 82).

roof that had sheltered them, and then, moving on to
new slaughtering grounds, adopting the devices of a
hunter to secure their prey : shooting, stabbing, hacking
all through the day all they unearth ; burning everything that will burn, until the evening comes ; a fresh
village is captured, and the night's debauch of drink and
violation once more comes round.

" What did I find there ?" wrote a republican officer who
had seen some of these places in the wake of the
republican troops.  " Fathers, mothers, children of every
age and both sexes, bathed in their blood, naked, and in
attitudes which the most ferocious person could not look
at without shuddering."

And so, under the presidency and immediate supervision of Louis Marie Turreau, commander-in-chief of
the republican army in the Vendée, the merciless
slaughter and destruction by the republican troops and
generals go on, day after day.  Villages and bourgs, or
small towns, right and left, are burned ; farm-houses
destroyed ; everything that will burn is burned, every
human being killed, every living thing slaughtered or
driven away.

Horrible and incredible in brutality as their proceedings were, the generals wrote jocular reports to Turreau :

" To-morrow," wrote Grignon, " I shall begin the *feux
de joie*, burning and bayoneting everything that comes
in the power of my column."

And Cordellier wrote : " I will arrange so as not to
be cold to-morrow morning before starting" : and on
another day : " The municipal authorities declare to me
that the only anti-revolutionists in the commune are
some women whose husbands are away with the brigands.
As they appear to me to be suspects, I will take care
that they get their breakfast to-morrow morning."

Playful terms also were used. "All those we find go
to the headquarters," a phrase which with "to go to the
hospital" or "behind the hedge" were equivalent expressions to their being sent to death.

Several of the generals were keen in their work.
"I arrived here this evening," wrote Grignon, "after
burning and smashing heads à l'ordinaire. . . . We
kill about 100 a day. Perhaps 300 were killed
yesterday."

And Boucret wrote: "There are about 1500 houses
in these communes, not counting farm-houses. I do not
wish that there remain a trace of them; the country
shall be purged with fire and sword. Not a brigand
shall escape me."

Now and then an even ghastlier note is struck.

"I have to inform you," wrote Grignon to Turreau,
"that the soldiers break their guns in killing with the
bayonets the brigands whom they find in the broom and
in the woods, and the brigands resist (se révoltent).
Would it not be better to kill them by shooting them;
that would be quicker?"

The columns are tracked by "cinders and corpses.
. . . The eyes met nothing but bloody objects in every
direction; the fields near the road were covered with
butchered victims."

It is a carnival of butchery, pillage, rape, and confla-
gration; everywhere burnings—"at this moment forty
farmsteads light up the country"—and everywhere
slaughterings, mostly of women. "This morning," wrote
Boucret, "I had fourteen women and girls shot"— a
truly valiant deed to record, one of which a French
general of the régime of liberty and fraternity was
apparently proud.

On the 25th January, Turreau, the arch-organiser

and superintendent of it all—the nominee of the Committee of Public Safety—wrote to the Committee :—

"I have begun the execution of the plan I conceived of crossing the Vendée in twelve columns. Haxo has divided his army into eight parties, who come to meet us. My columns on the right and left have already done wonders. Not a rebel has escaped their search. . . . If my intentions are well supported, there will not exist in the Vendée in another fortnight houses, food, nor army, nor inhabitants, except those who, hidden in the depths of the woods, have escaped the most scrupulous search. . . . It is important that this country be entirely cleared out, even of those who are believed to be revolutionists, and who perhaps wear but the mask of patriotism. . . .

"Behold, citizens, this is the third letter I write to you without a reply. I beg you to be so good as to tell me if you approve of my dispositions, and to inform me by special courier of the new measures you adopt, so that I may conform to them."

Only two loopholes for escape from death and destruction had been left to the unfortunate inhabitants of the Vendée.

One was that persons only "suspected" were not to be killed without the order of the general, and no harm was to be done to those in whom the general recognised civic or revolutionary sentiments, and who were accordingly to be free to go to the rear of the army.

And for escaping destruction by fire, houses or farms were not to be burned until the stores of food in them had been removed.

But both these exceptions were entirely illusory, for in most cases the soldiery took the decision into their own hands, not waiting to inquire whether persons were suspects or not, and when they found they could not carry away the stores, they usually set fire to them.

At the very outset of the movement of the " infernal columns " it was found that many districts inhabited by " patriots," and men who had actually been fighting the Vendeans, came within the sphere marked out for the action of the columns. Some communes escaped, because a few of the generals were less bloodthirsty than the others. Some houses, too, escaped being burned, because the corn and supplies of food could not be moved from them, there being no vehicles.

General Duval wrote : " All the places I have passed through are inhabited by patriots," and he braved responsibility and spared them. Moulin wrote : " The conduct of the communes of Rochefort and Chalonne has not been such as to justify their being involved in the general proscription." Grignon found one place so " patriotic " that he did not burn it : whilst even Turreau himself could find nothing against one place he passed through, and had to spare it.

But usually this was a matter of no consequence : no discrimination was exercised : as a matter of fact, the orders left no room for discrimination, and patriot communes were devastated : the success of the plan depended on a clean sweep being made, and the patriot inhabitants were massacred, their property being as good as that of the brigands.

Plunder was what was wanted by the columns, and it was quite immaterial whence it came, or who was the victim.

It was not alone, therefore, the brigands who were butchered : the blows of the revolutionists fell remorselessly upon their own allies, friends, and comrades, " patriots " and republicans.

The sans-culotte generals, with their impatient sweep of revolutionary mind, considered all in the Vendée as rebels, and only fit to be exterminated.

"There are only brigands in the Vendée," wrote Grignon. "I wish to exterminate them all."

Even National Guards, although republicans, and men who had actually been fighting against the brigands, were shot. Even the local and municipal authorities in their scarfs of office, and "patriots" with certificates of civism, were not exempt from slaughter by these valiant generals, by these heroic officers and soldiers.

All, in fact, within the sphere of these "infernal bands," were involved in one huge system of indiscriminate slaughter and destruction, one vast scheme of pillage and plunder. The columns were "armies of exterminators."

And so the columns continued their daily, their nightly, career.

"For the good of the Republic, Les Echaubrognes exists no longer. Not a single house remains there."

"Meslevrier—all the houses burnt; not one left."

And so on, and so on.

"Continue, my comrade," wrote Turreau to Grignon, "to burn this country and to exterminate the rebels."

And Francastel wrote to Grignon on 29th January: "I find you ever before your posts, acting with the same activity and the same revolutionary inflexibility." Having in a previous letter to him, written before the start of the "infernal columns," censured him for making too many prisoners. "You make too many prisoners ... our prisons are bursting ... with them. Prisoners in the Vendée!"

The conduct of the republican columns was appalling

"The delinquencies" (*délits*), wrote Lequinio, one of the Representatives at the time, "are not confined to pillage; violation and barbarism of the most outrageous description are to be seen in every corner. Republican soldiers have been seen violating women on the stone-heaps at the side of the roads, and the next moment shooting or stabbing them. Others have been seen carrying babies on the point of the bayonets or pikes which had pierced at the same blow mother and child. Nor have the rebels been the sole victims of the brutality of the soldiers and officers; the daughters and wives of the patriots even have often been *mises en réquisition*, as the phrase is."

Doubts have been thrown by republican writers upon these statements of Lequinio. Jullien, about whose revolutionary republicanism there can be no question, amply confirms even his strongest, most startling assertions: "Entire communes destroyed, burned, communes which had opposed the rebels. Would you believe it," he says in a letter to the Committee of Public Safety, "that under pretence of following your orders they butcher children, women, municipal authorities in their scarfs of office after a civic banquet given by them to a division of the army? Would you believe it, that at a moment when famine appears to threaten the country, they set fire to the supplies of food, and those not burned are left to the enemy? Would you believe that your generals give the example of pillage, and wish to degrade to the vile trade of thief the sublime employment of defender of the *patrie*?

"The inhabitants of a commune which had helped to arrest some of Charette's scoundrels, fearing to be the victims of the devastation ordered by the commander-in-chief, went to General Bard, who gave them a certificate in these terms : ' I declare that the commune of . . . has always shown itself well disposed, that the inhabitants have daily brought me brigands to shoot, and that they ought to be treated as friends of the Republic.'

"The municipality presents this certificate to the general charged with the execution of 'great measures,' as they are called. He answers that he has contrary orders ; he has these unfortunates disarmed ; he allows their wives and daughters to be violated in their presence, and ends this scene of horror by massacring all, even to the children at the breast. Everything is given over to pillage and fire."

Jullien adds :

" I have read not one but twenty letters from different soldiers or officers of different corps. I have heard generals, citizens, inhabitants of the localities, strangers who were witnesses of the facts, all unite to unveil the same crimes.

" I send herewith a proclamation of General Turreau, which alone is, in my eyes, an offence, because it presents a tissue of lies, because it depicts as victories the massacre of children and women, or of unarmed peasants, and that he conceals all the reverses : and it is thus that one deceives a free people."

The Vendeans who " had gone asleep, so to speak, in the hope of peace," and been awakened from their slumber by flames and death-shots all around them, and by the tales of fugitives, recovering from the first shock of incredulous surprise, fled in advance of the troops, concealing their property as best they could, and driving their cattle away.

" Even to the domestic animals," it was said, " every living thing fled at the sight of the national uniform without waiting to be pursued."

As many as could rushed once more to arms to defend or avenge themselves.

And the "patriots" in the Vendée, affrighted by the rumours and reports reaching them as to the treatment of their friends, began soon to take alarm, and to fear that they themselves would be carried away by the devouring flood of military revolutionary violence; and remonstrances and petitions began to flow in to the generals and Representatives and governing authorities; petitions from communes, and towns, and villages, and patriot municipalities, and republican local authorities—all for exemption from the decree of proscription and destruction.

"This commune has always been faithful to the law." . . . "These communes have always shown themselves supporters of the Revolution." . . . "If there is one commune which should remain intact it is this one."

Some went so far as to protest to Turreau about the conduct of his troops.

"General," wrote the president of the district authorities at Cholet, where Turreau himself was, "your soldiers, calling themselves republicans, deliver themselves over to debauch, to all the horrors of which cannibals even would not be guilty,"—a protest for which Cholet had later to pay dearly.

But the petitions were ignored. Such trivialities as the destruction of some "patriots" could not interfere with the carrying out of the great idea of a sans-culotte general. And so the massacres and burnings went on, and drove all those who could escape from them, and who were threatened by them, into revolt :—forced even those who had not taken part in the first war to take part in this new one, fabricated once again by the republicans themselves.

Elsewhere than in revolt there was no chance of safety: for there was no opening left for conciliation, nothing was gained even by submission, for submission meant a prompt and cruel death.

The immediate result of all the hellish work of these "infernal columns" therefore was that the whole of the inhabitants, patriots as well as brigands, were flung into the arms of the remaining Vendean leaders, Charette and Stofflet. Once more war broke out, and "all the Upper Vendée, which a fortnight before could have been regarded as pacified, was again in insurrection."

In other ways, too, all did not go as smoothly as the military despots in the Vendée desired. Difficulties began to crop up. The woods would not burn: they were too wet. The roads, too, are execrable,—prevent the fulfilment of projects: the weather wet,—not suited for burnings. And then, to the annoyance and indignation of the generals and troops, come rumours of assemblages of brigands, a circumstance which necessitates care, and suggests danger: and then resistance begins: and then worse, sudden attacks out of the mysterious depths of the unburnable woods as of yore: and then republican defeats.

Once the "infernal columns" and their chiefs were faced, once the element of danger to themselves came in, they quailed.

Once more the battle-cries of the Vendeans struck terror into the republicans. Sometimes not even battle-cries were required. "At the first sight of the scoundrels our brigade, without firing a shot, fled as far as Nantes and wished to enter it."

"Ducasse is here more dead than alive: not one of his soldiers had wished to fight, and forthwith were in

utter rout." Moulin wrote of his soldiers " all trembling " ;
and Dubois - Crancé, a Representative at Nantes on
special duty, wrote to the Minister of War :—

" As this war is cruel and no prisoners are made one
side or the other, our soldiers fear the brigands as
children fear mad dogs."

And so there are defeats—defeat at Gesté on the 1st
February, where one of Cordellier's columns was routed ,
defeat near St. Fulgent, where Grignon was routed—the
" commandant " of the battalion of Paris being the first
to fly. The soldiers, too, of the columns begin to be
worn out :—the debauch of murder and rape and arson
being somewhat fatiguing ; — bread fails them. " My
soldiers have passed a detestable night (in bivouac) " :
that is, a night when there was no drinking, violating,
or murdering. Numbers become sick and invalided, or
want to get back with their plunder to the towns to
spend it in riotous living ; their boots melt off their
feet ; their clothes are torn off their backs ; fever breaks
out ; gradually, in fact, the columns come to a stand-
still.

Turreau complained that he had been deceived as
to the true state of the country ; and, with unconscious
self-inculpation, declared that he was " far from imagin-
ing that the brigands were in a condition to oppose
the least resistance to the imposing march of his
columns."

And throwing the blame on his generals, he got
himself back on the 4th February to Nantes.

# CHAPTER XXII

## 'THE INFERNAL COLUMNS'

### PART II

### MILITARY DESPOTISM

THE second Vendean war, thus so wantonly created and set aflame, differed essentially from that which ended at Savenay.

In the earlier campaign, the idea of the restoration of royalty had been kept constantly before the people by the leaders; and had been believed in by them as the best means of recovering their religious liberty; but now most of the leaders had fallen, and almost the whole of their followers with them, and the idea had ceased to have much influence.

Now the war was purely one of self-preservation. Great ulterior motive there was none.

The few remaining leaders —Charette, Stofflet, and Sapinaud—still fought under the white flag of royalty, and still proclaimed that they wished to restore the monarchy; and so the strife still bore the aspect of a royalist war. But the people who now were appealing to arms did so, not for the purpose of re-establishing royalty, but for things affecting them more closely and immediately — for self-preservation and protection, for the means of defence against destruction, and for the opportunity of retaliation on their merciless foes.

Royalty, indeed, had little claim upon them.    It had done nothing to arouse their enthusiasm or even to earn their affections.    For almost a year they had continued the desperate and fearful fight against the tyranny of the revolutionists.    But though the seaport of Noirmoutier was for months in their possession, no royal prince had come to lead them, not a single royalist *émigré* of distinction or commanding position had come to their aid; no financial or other help had been given them, not even the cheap encouragement of words, beyond a few insincere and ridiculous letters.    They had been left entirely to their own resources, and whatever regard for royalty they may have once felt, had very considerably, if not entirely, cooled off.

This, however, is now a matter of minor consequence, for it is the conduct of the revolutionists, and not that of the Vendeans, which is of surviving interest.

Turreau's action which caused the outbreak of the war was a demonstration how short, under the republican form of government, was the step to actual military despotism; and how slender the protection possessed by the people against military domination and violence, even though those people were republicans and " patriots."

The government in the Vendée was, as a matter of fact, seized by Turreau.    He may have thought that his position as commander-in-chief authorised him to do anything, but undoubtedly, viewing his proceedings as a whole, he usurped an authority which no recorded decree of the Convention, nor even an order of the Representatives, authorised him to assume or possess.

He formed his own plans, even to the provoking of a second war; and he went his own way regardless of any one or of any laws.

And the Committee of Public Safety made no move. It seemed, indeed, as if the Committee had chucked the reins, and was willing to let any one do its vile work for it; to let any enormity be perpetrated provided "the cancer" of the Vendée was effectually extirpated.

And, certainly, enormities were perpetrated scarcely credible in their merciless cruelty, their low barbarism.

The "terror" in Nantes under Carrier and the Revolutionary Committee, fearful though it was, was rivalled in injustice and severity and destructive fury by the "terror" under Turreau and his "infernal columns."

The one was a despotism of the civil power; the other was a military despotism; the former kept up the pretence of acting under the sanction of revolutionary law, such as it was; the latter acted under no law except that which the generals and soldiers made for themselves.

Turreau did not wait for the approval of the Committee of Public Safety, nor even for that of the Representatives. He did not wait for Representatives to be attached to his troops. He wished to do it all himself, and to be independent.

Differing from the ordinary practice of Military Commissions following the troops for the trial of prisoners and other suspects by orders of the Representatives, and according to such laws as existed, on this occasion no such commissions and no criminal tribunals accompanied or followed the columns.

He made his own provision for such contingencies. Military authority was to be supreme, none other to be recognised.

And so the existence and the property of the inhabitants of the Vendée, "brigands" and "patriots" alike, were completely at the mercy of the military power.

Primarily, the fate of all the people the military came across, as they proceeded on their "promenade," was in the hands of the soldiers, who, acting on instructions, usually, when they saw any one, killed him or her straight off without asking questions.

But a certain number of cases were reserved for decision by the generals, who thus became the arbiters of the fate of those not immediately done to death by the soldiery.

Here the generals sometimes appear to have improvised courts-martial, though whether in the form prescribed by the law of March does not appear.

Benaben has rescued from oblivion the records of the proceedings of two or three of such courts-martial—records which throw a lurid gleam of horror around their actions. And as, presumably, the acts described in these records are but examples of the proceedings of all the other "infernal columns," one can understand somewhat of the enormity of the cruelties and abominations of which these columns, with Turreau at their head, were guilty.

For cold-blooded, deliberate, cowardly cruelty, where can a parallel be found?

On the 25th January such a court-martial sat at Les Gardes in the Canton of Chemillé—which was in the sphere of action of one of Cordellier's columns; and on that one day, or more probably in the evening, after the day's marching of the column was over, it condemned to death one man, thirty women, and twenty-four children—among those fifty-five, two mothers, each with her four children; one mother with her three children; and three mothers, each with her two children. And, the climax—a little mite, a girl of four, "Jeanne Gourdon, *quatre ans*"—an orphan, probably, as her name stands by itself.

Imagine what one can of the scene—a little girl of four being formally tried by drum-head court-martial, with fierce-looking armed and blood-besmeared men round her waiting impatiently for the business to be got through: the merciless sentence on this tiny innocent incapable of understanding aught, scarcely able yet to do more than speak, and that not well; and then the dragging her away to a distance, and the doing of her to death by bullet and bayonet by some *braves sansculottes* in the national uniform of the new Republic.

"*Jeanne Gourdon, quatre ans, exécutée par le moyen de la fusillade.*"

("Jeanne Gourdon, four years, executed by means of the fusillade.")

In the majority of cases the generals appear to have acted quite alone in the sentences to death, for their reports are full of their own doings.

"I ordered him to be shot." . . . . "I had them shot." . . . . "I have sent behind the hedge about 600 persons of both sexes." . . . . "They have just brought me two brigands who would declare nothing, so I pronounced death."

That "I" so dear to revolutionary sans-culotte vanity; no mention of court-martial, or any kind of tribunal. That would have been derogatory to the dignity of a sans-culotte general.

Even Turreau himself transgressed this way. That is proven. Writing from Cholet on the 25th January to the Committee of Public Safety, he said :—

" Another capture in our nets, one Dutrehan, captain of cavalry of a corps of rebels, and M. Meloux, royal notary, will be shot to-morrow by my orders."

Evidently there was to be no form of trial, even by court-martial, for the committee of surveillance (or Revolutionary Committee) at Cholet wrote to Turreau that it was important that as Dutrehan was well known as a chief of the brigands, he ought to be sent before a Military Commission to be tried in accordance with the law. " However, in case you decide to have him shot, we ask you to send us a ' discharge ' for this individual." The Committee, in fact, felt responsible for him, and was anxious to be able to account for him should any questions be asked.

At the headquarters where Turreau himself was, the proceedings were of the most summary kind. Any Vendeans who arrived, or were brought in, men and women alike, were interrogated by the staff, Turreau being himself sometimes, if not usually, present. The sittings were generally held after the mid-day dinner, and afforded evidently a sort of digestive occupation or distraction. A few questions were asked. The only compassion shown the prisoners was silence as to their fate. A sign to their guard, and they were led out and shot.

" Thus each day," wrote Beaudesson, who was present in Cholet on duty, " one saw new crimes of this sort. I had not the slightest idea whence could come these sanguinary orders which were executed on only the verbal directions of the staff."

Turreau—when later he was himself in the toils of the law, his own infamous acts being called in question—laid down the proposition with emphasis : " Nothing—no, nothing can legitimatise the arbitrary act which deprives an accused person of the means of exculpating himself.   It is thus that despotism acts—thus the despot does not try (*ne juge pas*), he assassinates."

But when sitting in judgment on the unfortunate Vendeans, he acted to the full the part of the despot he describes.   He never gave to the accused persons the means of exculpating themselves—thus, tried by his own dictum, he did not "try" but he "assassinated."

One of the crimes for which Carrier subsequently was convicted was, that he ordered people to be executed without trial by existing tribunals.

In this respect Turreau and his crew of generals were worse criminals even than Carrier.   Moreover, against him and them the damning fact is, that no decree of the Convention had exempted them from the revolutionary laws which prescribed tribunals for the trial and sentence of counter-revolutionists, and that he and they acted without regard to such laws.

Not even a decree of the Representatives had authorised him to act as he did.

Turreau, disregarding all law, was determined to make himself absolute military dictator in the Vendée. Even to the overriding of the local civil revolutionary authorities existing there, he meant to be dictator.

He avowed it clearly in a letter which he wrote to the Challans administrative body :—

" Each of the generals whom I have the honour to command has received from me positive orders to execute these rigorous measures without permitting themselves to listen to any reclamations : even those of the constituted bodies.   They have orders not only to act militarily against the administrative bodies, but even against you if you dare henceforth to oppose the least obstacle to the execution of my orders."

And in a letter to General Carpentier, he wrote:

"Consider above everything that the pretended constituted authorities are nothing in this infamous country,
that everything should be done militarily."

Thus, just as Nantes and Angers afforded the illustration of the Revolution resulting in a fearful despotism of
the civil power, supporting and keeping itself in power
by the perpetration of every injustice, cruelty, and
brutality imaginable, so the Vendée afforded the illustration of another abomination, a military despotism of the
most cruel and brutal character, enforced by men of the
same kind and category as Carrier and his crew.

Together we get a real view of the great, the glorious
French Revolution as it worked out in practice, and as
it affected not the king and royalists, not the noblesse and
aristocracy of France, but a large mass of the actual
people of the humbler classes—the labourers and artisans, and the working women as well as working men.

And so under this precious Republican Government,
whatever way one looks, one is confronted with despotism
of the most extreme, violent, and horrible character; the
"liberty," "equality," "fraternity," which the Revolution
was supposed to bring having vanished as the mirage
of the desert.

And as for the new man, the product of the Revolution,
the enfranchised, enlightened individual, freed from the
fetters of tyrants and the shackles of superstition—of
him too we have a view at which humanity must ever
shudder.

To massacre in cold blood men of his own country
and race, even his own political friends and comrades;
to outrage, violate, and slaughter Frenchwomen; to kill
the children of his own countrymen, even to the babe at
its mother's breast; to hack to pieces the helpless sick
and wounded lying in any hovel or even ditch that gave

Carrier two months previously had told the Committee what he intended ordering; and Turreau had informed it fully and in plain language of his intentions, and in part of his performances.

But the clearest demonstration of the real views of the Committee and of the Convention was the fact that, while the devastation and severities were mildly blamed, nothing was done to stop them.

"Why did not the Committee," asks Savary in reviewing its conduct, "at least compel respect for the part of the decree of 1st August which ordered that the old people, women and children should be conducted into the interior of France, and their food and safety provided for, with all the regard due to humanity?

"And why did they not recall Turreau?"

The answer is to be found in a letter from the Minister of War to Turreau, written somewhat later—early in March 1794—but referring to this very point: "You have not taken in its right sense the letter of the Committee of Public Safety, which was only written with the intention of giving a great impulse, and which in no way announced a diminution of confidence. You ought to know that if this diminution of confidence had any existence the Committee would not have left you in your place.

"So you should continue to serve with the generous devotion which belongs only to the *crai sans-culotte.*"

All that the Committee and the Convention did was to appoint two Representatives, with whom Turreau was to confer as to more effectual means of exterminating the Vendeans. Garrau and Hentz, "men whom Hell has vomited forth for the misery of these countries," —as they are described by Lofficial, a revolutionary Representative.

Avowedly the Government was influenced by the consideration that the great campaign against France's foreign enemies was approaching; and policy exacted that it should be believed that the war was over in " this shameful part of the Republic "—this *partie honteuse*, as Barère, speaking in the name of the Committee of Public Safety, described it.

And so, with full knowledge of all that was going on there, the Vendée was deliberately abandoned to the caprices and fury of the infamous Turreau, and of the Representatives newly attached to his army; and the approbation of the Committee of Public Safety, and of the Convention, was given to those appalling inhumanities which have indelibly stained the French Republican Government of that period, and which have exposed to mankind the true character of the much vaunted régime of " liberty, equality, and fraternity."

# CHAPTER XXIII

In Nantes the excess of evil at long last began to awaken some faint degree of energy among the citizens who had not been struck down by the revolutionists in power. Murmurs of anxiety and discontent began to be breathed from one to the other, then to find a little stronger expression. Then complaints began to be made, until at last the hottest patriots, with the exception of some of the Revolutionary Committee and Carrier's more immediate *entourage*, all desired Carrier's removal. They were realising the unpleasant fact that Carrier was making " terror " the order of the day against themselves. Fear, however, dominated all to such an extent that they did not dare to act—dared not write either to the Committee of Public Safety or to the Convention : and the real crisis was not provoked until Carrier laid hands on one of the republican anointed, one Champenois, a member of the municipality of Nantes, a sans-culotte, and an ardent and zealous republican.

A " patriot " who had come into possession of information which he believed would lead to the arrest of the redoubtable Vendean leader Charette had for three days tried to see Carrier, but had been refused audience. He confided his information to Champenois, who, being a personage, went himself to see Carrier, but, being also refused audience, went to the Society of Vincent la Montagne, to which he imparted his knowledge. The Society, impressed with its importance, sent a deputation to see Carrier on this and other matters. Carrier's secretary received them, and declared that if they were enraged citizens come from the devil or hell they should not see him.

One would think France was still under the old régime and under a royal sovereign, when one reads that on the 31st January 1794 a *lettre de cachet*,[1] that weapon of royal tyranny which was so furiously inveighed against by all revolutionists, was issued by Carrier, the great Representative of the new reign of liberty, against Champenois, and that he was arrested upon it, marched through the streets by a force with fixed bayonets, and brought before the "supreme tribunal," in other words, before Carrier himself, "an event recalling the old régime," as a member of the popular society said of it.

The municipality plucked up its courage sufficiently to ask Carrier for an explanation of his treatment of one of its members. Carrier replied by removing Champenois from his official functions.

Altogether, a serious row was brewing.

Carrier, furious, went to a meeting of the society, mounted the tribune, raged against its members, and threatened them.

And the now alarmed Society wrote surreptitiously to Paris to inform the Committee of Public Safety and the Society of Jacobins of the way Carrier had been conducting himself.

---

[1] This designation of *lettre de cachet* is given to it by the popular society of Nantes in their register.

"We reproach him for his severity . . . we reproach him for being almost inaccessible to good patriots . . . whilst he accords his preferences to his women and to the coxcombs who surround him . . . we reproach him for having threatened with the bayonet the first magistrate of the people who went to see him to ask him to procure some bread for more than 80,000 mouths in want of it, saying to him when he referred to the difficulties of getting audience with him, that 'if the functionary had done his duty he would have stuck his bayonet through his belly.'"

Other reproaches there were too.

"A deputation of the three administrative bodies of this town was badly received by him; taken by the throat (*pris à la gorge*), and one of his phrases was this, 'Last year I rode an ass which spoke better than you.'

". . . All which proves how much liberty we have. . . . The Society is really not free, since one cannot express one's opinion without running the risk of being arrested." In addition to these communications the Society sent off a deputation of two persons to Paris to see the Committee of Public Safety.

How the strife would have ended is quite uncertain, but the scale was suddenly turned by the arrival on the scene of Marc Antoine Jullien, a young man of eighteen, son of Jullien the friend and confidant of Robespierre. He was in the Departments in the west on a special mission, a secret agent of the Committee of Public Safety.

In the course of his mission he had already felt obliged to urge the Committee to recall Carrier, on account of a quarrel with another Representative; but the letter had fallen into Carrier's hands, who was therefore furious with him.

Jullien's arrival at Nantes and his proceedings at a meeting in the church of Saint Croix, where the Society of Vincent sat, were duly reported to Carrier, and also his attendance at some secret conclaves held immediately after.

On returning to his hotel Jullien was met by General Vimieux with a large body of soldiers, and was immediately arrested. Although the night was far advanced, he was taken off in a carriage to Carrier, who received him in bed.

"It is you, you d—d . . . who has denounced me to the Committee of Public Safety as an ultra-revolutionist. But I have you now, and you shan't escape me. Know that in one instant I can cut the thread of your life, and as it is sometimes of moment to the general good to get rid secretly of certain people, I will not take the trouble of sending you to the guillotine, I will be your executioner myself." Then, turning to Vimieux, he said, "Let him be despatched to-night" (*expedié*), "you shall answer me for it."

What a lightning flash this on the methods of revolutionary "justice," baring to the world's vision the dark places of sans-culotte tyranny, illuminating in one second the very acme of despotism—sentence of death without trial—verbal command by one of the highest officers in the State to a general officer to murder.

Jullien let him talk. Then he faced him. "Listen," he said. "You may make me perish in the darkness of to-night; but don't forget that I hold a mission from the Committee of Public Safety. My death will not remain unpunished, as those of your other victims. My father is a Representative. He and I are friends of Robespierre. In ten days or so you will be called to render account for my blood, and you will yourself perish as a vile assassin." Upon which Carrier subsided, pretending that there was a mistake in the warrant of arrest, that it was another Jullien who was to have been arrested. And so Jullien got back safely to his hotel.

Then, without losing a moment of time, and with all possible speed, he fled to Angers, out of Carrier's jurisdiction, having been "obliged to leave with precautions, which an agent of the Committee ought not to be obliged to take" (as the Committee of Public Safety itself wrote soon after).

Thence he indited several letters, and sent two Nantais to Paris with them. To his father :—

" On receipt of my letter fly, I pray you, to Robespierre. It is imperative to stille the Vendée, which comes to life again. It is imperative to recall Carrier, who kills liberty."

To Barère he wrote :—

" It is imperative to save Nantes and the Republic. I have found there the *ancien régime*. . . . I have seen in Carrier a satrap, a despot, an assassin of public spirit and liberty. I do not exaggerate."

To Robespierre he wrote :—

" The public spirit is stilled : liberty no longer exists. Recall Carrier."

And to Robespierre again, a day or two later, he wrote, giving fuller details. He informed him of the fusillades : he informed him of the noyades : " I am assured that he had all those who filled the prisons of Nantes taken indiscriminately, put into boats, and submerged in the Loire." He informed him of Carrier saying to him that one could only effect a revolution by such measures. " No one dares to speak, to write, nor even to think. . . . Public spirit is dead : liberty no longer exists. The energies of the sans-culottes are

stifled; the true republicans weep with despair to have
seen despotism reborn. . . . I have seen in Nantes the
*ancien régime.*"

And so it had come to this, after all the strivings,
and strugglings, and slaughterings, and bloodshed, and
horrors of the Revolution, after the holocaust of hundreds
of thousands of French men, women, and children, that
the Revolution had reproduced, and in an intensified
manner, the very thing which it had intended to destroy.

Instead of a royal despot in the seat of authority,
there sat a sans-culotte republican despot. That was
the sole difference; with this variation, that the new
despotism was infinitely worse than the old—more coarse,
more brutal, more ignorant, more depraved, more merciless, more bloody; that every vice which disgraced the
old régime disgraced also the new—disgraced it with vices
more accentuated in character, and of a deeper and more
horrible dye; and, over and above all these things, the
new despotism knew not what justice was, or meant—
had not the crudest or most elementary ideas on the
subject.

Proved up to the hilt was it, and never again unprov-
able, that a republican form of government, as then
organised in France, afforded no safeguards against the
extremest abuse of tyrannical power; that it gave no
shadow of a guarantee for liberty, equality, or fraternity;
or for the enjoyment of any of those rights of man which
had been so loudly proclaimed; that it gave no prospect
even of justice; that it had, in fact, no greater claim to
be regarded as God's truth than any other form of government which humanity has tried.

While Jullien's letters were speeding to Paris, the
reaction against Carrier was making way.

Utterly unexpectedly, Carrier was braved by the

members of the Revolutionary Committee, which had done most of his cruel work for him; not out of any regard for "liberty," but out of regard for their own skins and perquisites. The Committee appeared to have got an inkling that sundry of his aides and instruments, such as Lamberty, Fouquet, Robin, and others, were plotting to oust them; Carrier, too, they believed, had formed the project of purging the Committee, as he did not find it docile enough; so they took the initiative and struck.

On the 10th February (22 Pluviose), Fouquet, adjutant-general of artillery, one of his most active henchmen, and manager of noyades, was arrested by order of the Revolutionary Committee, and shut up in the Bouffay, in one of those dark cells to which he had doomed hundreds of human beings, and from which he had dragged them to drown them in the waters of the Loire.

Before Carrier could strike a return blow, Jullien's letters had been considered by the Committee of Public Safety; where, in spite of opposition from some of the members, it was decided that Carrier should be recalled; and, on the 8th February, the Committee had written to him :—

" You have desired to be recalled.[1] Your heavy labours in a city so little patriot, and so near the Vendée, deserve that you repose yourself for a little; and all your colleagues will see you again with pleasure in the bosom of the National Convention. Your health has been impaired by your constant occupations. The intention of the Committee is to give you another mission, and it is necessary that you come and confer with it."

And on the same day they appointed one of their own body, Prieur (de la Marne), as his successor.

_____

So far, no trace of the expression of any such desire on his part has been discovered.

In their letter to Prieur they wrote: "Carrier has been perhaps badly surrounded. Intriguers are the curse of Representatives of the people. Carrier has been harsh (*dur*) in his methods. He employed means which do not make the national authority beloved."

Prieur had himself employed means which did not make the national authority beloved, and the change was by no means as great for the better as could have been desired; but still it was a change, and that was something.

On the evening of the 14th Carrier made his adieux to the municipality of Nantes, and the next day left, so quietly, that people scarcely knew whether he had gone or not. And so Nantes was rid of Carrier.

He had had his day, his full swing, unchecked, unthwarted. Never had revolutionary principles such an opportunity for showing their merit; never had a sansculotte revolutionist a better field for convincing men of the beauties of republican government. He had given the "terrible examples" which he said he would; heads had rolled on the scaffold as he said they should roll: he had carried out all his threats; thousands had drunk from "the great bowl" (*la grande tasse*); thousands had been shot: the air of liberty had been cleansed (*déblayé*); religion had been annihilated; the teachers of superstition destroyed; the country had been purified by fire, purged and purged, and bled till it was white.

And yet the effect was totally different from what those who carried out these drastic measures had anticipated.

The result was, not the glorification of Revolution and of the new system of government, but the condemnation of it.

To great masses of the people the reign of terror

was a revelation of suffering and misery, of insecurity, of evils, compared with which those which had gone before were indeed light, and a disclosure of dangers hitherto unthought of, and they recoiled from it. Not suddenly, for that they could not do, but slowly, and with fear and trembling. lest any rashness should provoke a repetition of the disaster.

The one abiding effect of this reign of revolutionary authority had been to discredit irreparably the system of government under which such things had happened. For what greater evil could be imagined by a people than having to live under a form of government where such things are possible ?

# CHAPTER XXIV

## PART III

HAPPY would it have been for the unfortunate inhabitants of the Vendée if their hard lot had received any mitigation at the same time that Nantes was being relieved of Carrier; but Turreau and his "infernal columns" were still roaming about seeking whom they might devour, and the Representatives Hentz, Francastel, and Garrau were attached to his army to advise and help him: and military despotism continued to reign there, rampant and omnipotent.

Harrowing and heartrending indeed is the history of the events of the next few months there, and there is a monotony of horrors and injustice about it which absolutely repels the historian; but fresh incidents were constantly occurring which disclosed fresh traits of the revolutionary character, and presented fresh aspects of the new régime of liberty, equality, and fraternity.

One never seems to come to the end of the blackguardisms of this crew of revolutionists, Representatives, generals, or men. Always below the apparently lowest depth of cruelty and blackguardism another deeper discloses itself; and were one to throw a veil completely

over the events of the next few months it would be
difficult to believe or to realise that the horrors which
accompanied the march of the " infernal columns" were,
to the utmost capabilities of the republicans, persevered
in for month after month, through the spring and into
the summer, until at last repression exhausted itself, and
it began to be forced in on the mind of the Revolutionary
Government that the course hitherto pursued in the
Vendée was not leading to a consolidation of the power
of the Republic, but, if anything, was endangering it.

Lequinio, phrasing the feelings of the Vendeans, wrote :
" Pardon was promised to those who laid down
their arms. The promise was broken. By the law of
July only the chiefs were to be punished. We are
punished according to the laws of March. The revolutionary columns confounded the innocent with the guilty.
They burned and pillaged everything and bayoneted
women, children, and old people. I have lost everything.
I have nothing left. I shall fight to live."

And they fought—and considerable numbers of the
" patriots" had now been driven to fight too. And so
they made common cause.

Jullien had let in light on Carrier's proceedings at
Nantes : his letters confirm the statements of other
republican writers who let light in on the proceedings
of republican officers placed in power by the Revolution.

All through the history of the strife between the
Republic and the Vendée appears the fact damning to the
revolutionists, that there was on the part of the republican *sans-culotte* generals a deliberate intention to prolong
the war.

Their salaries and perquisites and plunder were too
valuable, their mode of life too enjoyable to be ended one
moment sooner than avoidable.

"I have seen among the generals," wrote Jullien, "a well-formed design of prolonging the war. . . 'We will finish it when we want to,' they said."

He accused them, too, of actually corresponding with the Vendean chiefs: "It is proved," he said, "that they often let a comrade be defeated through motives of jealousy of his success; it is proved that time after time they allowed themselves to be defeated, so that they could say that the stores had been taken by the enemy, and thus conceal and cover their own robberies; it is proved that they had sent a 'patriot' colleague to certain defeat and death because he knew too much of the abuses going on."

All those things, he said, were proved.

Those who were not traitors were intriguers, who occupied themselves with satisfying their own personal ambition, and not the public interest.

"Egotism, vanity, avarice, and perfidy have eternalised the Vendée.

"The Vendée is at the gates of Nantes, and the generals are inside the walls steeped in pleasure and indolence.

"An army is in Nantes without discipline, without order; and small corps are sent out to butchery. On one side people pillage, on the other they kill, the Republic. A crowd of generals (un peuple de généraux), proud of their epaulettes and the gold embroidery on their collars, rich with the salaries they steal, bespattering with their carriages the pedestrian sans-culottes, are always with women at the plays and spectacles, or at the sumptuous fêtes and repasts which insult the public misery."

The description reads like an echo of the indictment of the old régime; for these were precisely some of the causes for offence which were cited as justifying the Revolution. The monstrous contrasts of wealth and poverty, of self-indulgence and privation, so passionately inveighed against by revolutionists, and which were to be abolished by them, had been quickly revived by them, and again flourished, only this time it was under the revolutionary order of things, and it was the revolutionists who had possessed themselves of the wealth and were the self-indulgent.

Jullien's judgment was not tinged by impetuosity, for a fortnight later he wrote :—

"Each day brings me fresh proof of the villainy of our generals."

This picture of the French military authorities in the Vendée was not overdrawn, for even Prieur (de la Marne) and his colleagues issued a rigorous decree against "the military of all ranks who, in considerable number at Nantes, wallow in idleness and debauch, while their brave brothers-in-arms are in incessant pursuit of the brigands."

And again, somewhat later, their successors, Bo and Bourbotte, whose revolutionary characters were above reproach, also issued a decree against military abuses, in which they give a description precisely parallel to that given by Jullien, and announced penalties against—

"The military, officers as well as soldiers, who had left their corps and abandoned their posts to come to Nantes, where, unblushingly, they spent voluptuously in the theatre, in the cafés, and other places of pleasure, the time which they have sworn to consecrate entirely to the defence of the country."

Drunkenness was too universal a habit in those times to be considered as a vice, but it was prevalent in all ranks. "Our sans-culotte generals know nothing of the business of war," wrote a national agent, "but very well that of drinking from morning to evening." Commanders-in-chief even set the example. Rossignol was always drinking. Turreau was also addicted to the practice. "I have seen Turreau twice, and drunk both times. Many people informed me it was his custom." His generals spoke of him as one *qui ne se désoûlait pas*, who never got sober.

And once Grignon—himself not immaculate in this respect—had to complain of Huché: "General Huché appeared at the head of my column drunk, and addressed me in a manner not becoming for a general to be addressed in presence of his troops. I knew for some time past that his head did not belong to himself after midday, and that the service of the Republic might suffer." A report supplemented by Adjutant-General Liebaut, who said: "He must have drunk a lot."

As to other comparatively minor delinquencies on the part of the sans-culotte revolutionary generals, such as lying, duplicity, untrustworthiness, they were so habitual as to excite no notice. But now and then some illustrative incidents are incidentally recorded.

Thus Huché, appealed to by the local authorities of a commune not to devastate it, told them that he would write to Turreau for his decision; but simultaneously with his letter to Turreau, who was several days' post away, he gave orders to his troops to destroy the commune the very next day.

A precisely similar act is reported of Grignon.

Not the slightest reliance could be placed on the words or promises of these men. Lying was, according to their standards, a justifiable finesse. For truth they had no regard. Of honour they had not the slightest conception.

One general, with evident self-satisfaction as to his cleverness, has recorded how, tired with pursuing the brigands, he announced an amnesty for all those who surrendered voluntarily. " My ruse succeeded. Twenty-one were sent yesterday to Nantes, with the request that they should be made accept the constitution behind the hedge. What matters it what means one employs ? "

These, then, were the new military " patriots " which the Revolution had hoisted into authority, and in whose hands were the lives and property of every inhabitant of the Vendée and its neighbourhood, " patriots " and " brigands " alike—men who prolonged the internecine war for the sake of their own profits and emoluments : paying in the life's-blood of their own countrymen and women the cost of their pleasures and the gratification of their passions ; and plundering their country and fellow-citizens so that they themselves might live in self-indulgence and vice. And presiding over them all, and over this saturnalia of crime and bloodshed, Turreau.

Theoretically the Revolution aimed at abolishing iniquity in high places—aimed at installing in power a better class of men than were there. Practically, however, as it worked out, it installed a far worse lot, and initiated a severer and bloodier despotism.

Turreau having got a new lease of power, and being bound therefore to do something energetic, he and the Representatives held a council at Nantes to devise further plans for bringing the Vendean war to an end.

There was not much room for further great ideas.

Unable, therefore, to devise any fresh atrocity upon the Vendeans, the new measures were devised with the intention of crippling them through the " patriots " re-siding in the Vendée, and accordingly were directed against those loyal to the Republic.

The decree of February, ordering the disarming of the people in all the communes in or near the revolted country, patriots as well as suspects, was already being acted on, but was exciting great hostility.

Its object was to prevent the brigands obtaining arms or ammunition.

With the object of preventing them obtaining men, it was determined to remove from the revolted country all the inhabitants who had not taken arms—in other words, the "patriots," because some, under the appearances of neutrality, secretly favoured the rebels, and because others, although republicans, gave them help under compulsion.

And a circular was addressed to the administrators of the Department by Hentz and Francastel setting forth with innocent simplicity the advantages of such a proceeding.

"You surely are penetrated with the importance of this measure, which will have the effect of leaving only rebels in the revolted country, whom one will be able more easily to destroy without confounding with them innocent and good citizens."

The impracticability of such a plan was quickly pointed out to them by the inhabitants of Nueil, who declared that it was impossible to obey this rigorous order to quit their homes and to leave their property at the mercy of the enemy.

"The distance of some six leagues from the nearest town, the impracticable state of the roads, their wives, children, furniture, animals to be transported to heaven knows where, are insurmountable obstacles. Moreover, the cultivation of the land and the culture of the vines, without which they would be reduced to starvation, are considerations which merit your attention."

And then, even the unfortunate "refugees" from the revolted Departments were not yet far enough away from the Vendée. Among them also traitors might lurk: " they were evil-disposed persons, aristocrats, scoundrels," so all were to be moved farther on—only not nearer to Paris than fifteen miles. " If they are patriots," it was sententiously remarked, " they will endure this removal."

Thus, " covered with opprobrium and infamy, condemned in public opinion by the decree of the Representatives, ruined, without help and without support, they were obliged to move away, and to beg the protection of some distant administrations where they were exposed to insult and outrage."

These measures taken, it was hoped that a sufficient display of energy had been made.

And all the while the ghastly work of killing and burning and destroying went on. February, March, April, May—no longer by definite " infernal columns" working on a definite plan, but as, when, and where possible, whenever sufficient troops could be got to move, any detachment of troops under any general, in the Upper Vendée and in the Lower Vendée, in the Bocage and in the Plain— not a day passing without tens or hundreds being massacred under every conceivable circumstance of cruelty. General Duquesnoy (February 16, took credit to himself for having killed 3000 of them—" to wit, 2000 taken without arms, and 1000 killed at Pont-James." Other generals also sent in large death-rolls.

Turreau, on the 2nd March, told the Committee of Public Safety that 15,000 brigands had been destroyed by the columns.

Making ample allowance for gross exaggerations, it is evident that fearful cruelties were being inflicted on the people in the Vendée " patriots " and " brigands " alike

Huché, one of the worst of the whole revolutionary lot—an actual assassin, a drunken monster, this "tiger," this "enemy of humanity," as Lequinio called him, sent Turreau an account of the sortie he had made from Cholet against the Vendeans :—

"I stirred them up pretty lively (*Je les ai égayés de bonne manière*). More than 500, as many men as women, were killed. This *canaille* had the audacity to provoke us by defiances, and shouts, and reproaches. I had the copses, the ditches, the hedges, and the woods searched, and it is there we found them cowering. All were bayoneted or sabred, because I had prohibited the waste of ammunition."

And Turreau wrote in reply : "Courage, comrade, and soon the neighbourhood of Cholet will be cleansed of rebels. If each general or superior officer would only kill them as you do, by the hundred, one would soon be at the end of the business."

The end was by no means so near as Turreau wished, although several generals were little if at all behind Huché in the killing way.

Charette and Stofflet held head against the republicans, appearing and disappearing here and there and everywhere, in the most unexpected way, pouncing on convoys, sweeping out of the woods on to weakly-held posts ; now and then braving the larger columns of the republicans ; ever being destroyed (according to republican accounts), yet appearing again ; their followers scattered and killed, yet coming to life and collecting themselves together again ; taking terrible toll every now and then for the republican barbarities ; paying the republicans back in their own coin ; and receiving constantly fresh recruits to their ranks from the "patriots" driven to desperation by revolutionary or "patriotic" atrocities.

The Representatives were every bit as bloodthirsty as Turreau.

"We are convinced," wrote Hentz and Francastel on the 14th March, "that the Vendean war will not be finished until there remains no single inhabitant in this miserable country."

And Garrau, the third Representative, thus expressed his views :—

"It has been long enough and too long that this infernal Vendée occupies us. If one could get a burning glass large enough to burn and consume it entirely, one would be doing well."

Thus from top to bottom of the revolutionary hier- archy, all were bent on destruction ; and the burnings of villages and farms and wholesale destruction of grain and forage went on in spite of protests from "patriot" sufferers. The demon of destruction had possession of the revolutionists, and military tyranny and injustice stalked throughout the land—a land which under the new régime of "liberty, equality, and fraternity" that the Revolution was to introduce should have been the peaceful and happy home of an emancipated people ; but which, thanks to the Revolution and the way revolutionary theories and principles worked out, had become a veritable "inferno."

The short-sighted folly of this destructive policy was remarkable.

It mattered not that Nantes was suffering from almost a famine ; it mattered not that the troops them- selves were often half-starved ; it mattered not that the Republic itself was in urgent want of food for its million of soldiers. Revolutionary generals and Representatives could not descend to such considerations—and so the burnings went on.

Other forms of destruction, which also would by and by tell against themselves, were recklessly indulged in; mills—wind-mills and water-mills—were destroyed; wind-mills especially, as it was believed that they were used as means of signalling between the Vendeans.

"To-day I burned a dozen wind-mills," wrote Cordellier.

Ovens and bakehouses, these too were destroyed. And so, when the need came, the troops could not grind the corn they captured into flour, or bake the flour which they found into bread.

One butchery on a large scale took place at Bouguenaix, on the river some little distance below Nantes.

Some republican cavalry who had been attacked near there early in April, surrounded the place, and captured 210 men (if boys of 15 to 17 can be included in that category) and 22 women.

Hither came, in hot haste, from Nantes, the Military Commission under Bignon, and in two days it sentenced 209 men to death, and acquitted one aged 13.

They were promptly shot.

"I have seen a great deal of war," wrote General Hugo (father of the poet), in later years. "I have gone over vast fields of battle. Never has anything struck me so much as the massacre of these victims of opinion and fanaticism."

The trial of the 22 women was postponed a little and left to another tribunal, and they were acquitted.

Gradually the "patriot" opposition gathered volume, and remonstrances from the popular societies in different towns in the Vendée, which were republican, and not counter-revolutionary, presaged the commencement of a storm of opposition against the severity of the Turreau military régime.

Once more, as in the case of the sans-culottes at Nantes and Angers, no sooner were revolutionary principles applied to themselves than there were mutterings and resistance.

Astonishment and wrath flare forth in a letter which the Committee of Surveillance at Fontenay wrote to Turreau, March 29 :—

"Do you wish to know what the thousands of men have done whom you wish to tear from their hearths in delivering those hearths to the flames ?

"They have detested tyrants and fanaticism. . . . Never did they take part in the crimes of the enemies of the patrie—they have fought them—they have beaten them . . . they have devoted life and fortune to the Republic.

". . . Hasten, general, to convince us that you protect virtue and liberty."

But it was not in the nature of a sans-culotte general to protect either virtue or liberty, nor did the Revolutionary Government do so either.

The gradual disillusionment of some of these "patriots" as to what revolution meant, and as to how revolutionary government practically worked out, is most interesting.

"We think," wrote the popular society at Luçon to the Representatives, "it cannot enter the minds of any of our legislators to confound the innocent with the guilty—the patriot with the enemy of the State."

But the recent history of revolutionary government had very clearly shown that this was one of the chief things that the revolutionist did do. And they themselves were quickly to have it proven to them.

General Huché, the drunkard and murderer, at the head of a body of troops, arrived there, and literally ran *amok.* Forthwith he sentenced two men to be shot. The tribunal was the dinner-table; the judge, himself; the prosecutor, himself; the evidence, the answers he extracted from the prisoner.

This was revolutionary "justice."

The next day he had two more shot; one, Bardou by name, whose innocence had just been recognised by a Revolutionary Tribunal which had acquitted him. There was no trial, nor other formality; nothing but Huché's mere order.

"I had them shot," wrote Huché, "as is customary and right."

But Turreau by letter mildly reproved him for this.

"One ought not," wrote Turreau, "to employ those measures when one has a Military Commission or Revolutionary Tribunal close to one. Leave that to your chiefs of columns to do when they are on the march."

And then he ordered the destruction and burning of commune after commune in the neighbourhood — patriot communes — perpetrating every imaginable enormity.

Furious at opposition from the administrators of the district, he wrote: "In the Vendée, no constituted authority, according to my mind and that of all good republicans, ought to hinder, contradict, or oppose itself to military operations."

On receiving a remonstrance from the president of the Committee of Surveillance as to his proceedings, he said:

"What, Mr. President, you dare to criticise my conduct. Do you know what are my orders? I have the right to order you to be shot, and this very moment you shall be." And on his being told that the president was an excellent patriot, and one of the best on the

Committee, he threatened to have the whole Committee shot.

The revolutionists and patriots at Luçon at last recognised what the new government really was.

"We are bursting with horror," they wrote, "at seeing the abominable despotism which surrounds us."

Just as Jullien had truly seen what revolutionary government at Nantes was—namely, the *ancien régime*—so now these "patriots" of Luçon under the enlightening process of experience had come to see what revolutionary government really was—"an abominable despotism."

That is just what it was. No "liberty" about it,—no "fraternity," no "equality," and no justice. Only despotism, an "abominable despotism."

It was a despotism, too, which with cold-blooded indifference victimised its own republican supporters—if even by that means it could get at those it considered its foes. On the highly moral principle enunciated by Collot d'Herbois, "If one spared the innocent. too many of the guilty would escape."

While Huché was at Luçon, one of his most trusted officers, his lieutenant, Goy Martinière by name, had been given an illustration of sans-culotte proceedings. He was in charge of a detachment of troops, and had been pillaging and burning and murdering in "patriot" communes—communes so indisputably "patriot" that in one of them the tree of liberty was growing. At Mareuil he had had a woman shot and her three children—one child of six months was in its mother's arms. At Bellenoue he collected a lot of women and little children one day, and had them all shot the next. He violated innocent girls, and then had the barbarity to have them assassinated. He promised a man his life for money, took the money and had the man shot.

The Revolutionary Committee, with full proofs of these atrocities, for which he probably would not have been punished, and of some very definite offences against the Republic—a more serious matter than these atrocities—called on Huché to order his arrest,—a request which Huché dared not refuse.

He was tried before the Military Commission, was sentenced to death, and guillotined on the 11th April.

Ten days later the Representatives Garrau, Hentz, and Francastel wrote to the Committee of Public Safety as to this brutal murderer, violater, and pillager :—

" The Republic should be in mourning the day when la Martinière was guillotined for having done his duty as a republican. . . . We groaned over it, and still groan."

Strange idea of duty this,—stranger epitaph has never been written by high State officials on a criminal so infamous.

In endeavouring to form an idea of the extent of revolutionary barbarities and crimes, one must always recollect that those which have been recorded are but an infinitesimal portion of those which were committed, a few isolated instances or illustrations of widespread practices. A corner of the veil only is lifted just for a moment as we peruse the description of one scene of crime ; that is all.

We get a glimpse of an " infernal column " at its hellish work on two or three occasions. The details of the horrors perpetrated day after day and night after night, by it and the eighteen others, are concealed from us. We only know from chance statements here and there that one day was as another—one night was as another — during those awful weeks — those fearful months.

We get glimpses of soldiers, officers, generals, and even Representatives, plunged in drunkenness and debauchery and crime, and know that that was the chronic condition of most of them.

For a moment one gets a glimpse of a Revolutionary Committee at work—of a Military Commission administering revolutionary " justice "—of Representatives exercising their despotic powers in the secrecy of their chambers, and we know that day after day these engines of revolutionary tyranny and terror were in similar manner dealing out injustice and death to innocent and guilty alike.

Occasionally one gets from some of the actual victims of tyranny and injustice the narrative of their maddening wrongs and sufferings ; but even so, these are but a few of the voices of the tens upon tens of thousands who went down in silence to their graves ; or if they voiced their agonies and their wrongs, could not make their voices reach the outer world or the tribunal of posterity.

As it is, one stands appalled at the horror of that much of it which is known, and at the depths of human depravity presented to one's gaze even by the momentary raising of one corner of the veil ; one is overwhelmed if one tries to realise what the fearful drama must have been in its entirety, as enacted behind the now impenetrable curtain.

Some republican writers contend that it was all necessary for " the safety of the fatherland "—others that it was justified because some Vendean leaders had made appeals to England for help, and that these people were allies with the enemies of France.

Such contentions only show the straits to which they have been put in their efforts to defend those who committed these enormities, and they bear their refutation on their face. For how can it be contended that the violation and murder of women was essential for the *salut de la patrie?* Or that tiny children, down to the babe at its mother's breast, were allies of the English, and that so their destruction was justified?

The quarrel between Huché and the Revolutionary Committee at Luçon continued briskly.

"Who has clad this man who seeks to overwhelm us by terror, with absolute power?" it asked of the Representatives.

The true answer to such a question was "the new régime of liberty—the Republic," but the Representatives would be little likely to give it.

The Committee—boldly persevering—issued a warrant of arrest against Huché for various crimes, among them that of having had Bardou shot; and for burning corn and forage, instead of having them carried away; and for the great crime of dispersing by the bayonet the republican society, "which abuse of authority was the most terrible blow against the liberty and against the sovereignty of the people."

The warrant was executed—Huché's troops sympathising with the people instead of with their general. He was arrested and sent to Paris.

Hentz and Francastel were furious at this audacious proceeding. At the popular society at Niort, Hentz eulogised Huché, Grignon, and their agents. "Huché was a good and frank sans-culotte the very man for the Vendée. He had been reproached for having dissolved the popular society. He had a right to do so. In a counter-revolutionary town, such as it was, the military are everything. I recognise no civil authority there. A general is sovereign. Generals were above being denounced or complained against. It would be absurd to imagine that a Revolutionary Committee could arrest a general. A general ought to exercise supreme authority. There should be no civil authority in the Vendée."

Then on to Fontenay, where Hentz harangued the popular society for two hours on its audacity in making protests against the incendiarism of patriot communes, dissolved it, and formed a new one of their own creatures.

That done, they hurried to Luçon, the " execrable Luçon " as they called it. Martinière they could not bring to life again, but they suppressed the Military Commission which had dared to convict him, " without giving him time or the means of defending himself," and declared Luçon in a state of siege ; they dissolved the popular society, and soon after had the members of the Committee arrested and sent off to Paris.

It was a perilous undertaking to protest against the proceedings of the *vrai sans-culotte.*

Four members of the popular society at Niort were sent by the people of Niort to Paris in April to depict to the Government the horrors they were suffering under the hands of Huché and Grignon and their agents, the devastation and incendiarism of communes faithful to the Republic, and the butchery of old people, and women, and children, and carrying with them the proofs thereof. They were treated as counter-revolutionists ; accused of having advanced false facts ; and were told that Hentz and Francastel were on the spot, and had not reported anything about it. And they very nearly paid for their zeal with their heads.

Even the troops at last showed signs of wavering. Discontent was spreading among them, and began to show itself. The men were sickening of the life they were leading. They had pretty well had their fill of plunder, and many were anxious to secure its enjoyment. Many were undergoing desperate hardships, having been shamefully neglected by their generals. Bread failed them, and clothes, and boots. Torrential rains poured down upon them, illnesses of every kind swept the ranks, and every now and then the Vendeans fell upon them.

"I am in a terrible position," wrote Adjutant-General Dusirat. "My column, on which you rely to make up the 3600 men which you wish to confide to me, cannot furnish me with more than 500 to 600. . . . You have no idea of the spirit which reigns in our troops, and especially among the officers. They murmur loudly against your dispositions." And in a letter to Turreau he wrote, April 12th: "There is one great fact: that it is impossible to end the Vendean war quickly with the troops which compose the army of the west. . . . Nothing decisive will ever be done with the troops which we command at the present moment."

This view is passed on to the Minister of War, and endorsed by Turreau. The cowardice of the soldiers, which Turreau emphasised, was, he said, due "to the riches of the soldier who had pillaged much." And as to their state of health, he said that more than 20,000 filled the different hospitals in different places around the Vendée.

One finishing touch to the picture is given by General Dusirat :—

I begin to perceive that the greater part of the soldiers I command prefer defeat to victory. That is not surprising. After defeat one goes to Doué (a small town, but still a town), and after a victory one pursues the brigands."

And one more touch : " I tell you the truth, citizen general. The cry. 'Here are the brigands,' inspires terror among our soldiers ; and I can assure you that if there is any place in the world where terror is the order of the day. it is at St. Florent, and in some battalions of my column."

One graphic expression of the time summed it all up : " The army. sleeping in crime, succumbed under the weight of pillage and debauch."

As month succeeded month, and no definite result was secured, the Committee of Public Safety had been becoming more and more discontented with the conduct of the war, their disapproval not merely being confined to Turreau, but to the Representatives Hentz and Francastel, who were with him.

Was it the first turn in the tide which induced the Committee on the 9th April to order the Representatives to issue a decree preserving factories (*usines*) from destruction ? The inculcation to preserve anything in the Vendée was a remarkable portent.

Hentz and Francastel endeavoured to back up Turreau and the miscreant sans-culotte generals, and to fan the flame of hostility against the Vendeans.

" Every breathing thing in the Vendée is brigand . ." they wrote. " There is wanted in these parts a man like Carrier. who saved Nantes by the vigour of his measures, or some one like him." They denounced the conduct of those who wished to lead the Committee to grant an amnesty to the brigands. " To-day all the brigands whom we take say nothing else to us but 'Only leave us alone, and we won't trouble any one'"; but they (Hentz and Francastel) scouted such an idea. They were too confirmed in ways of bloodshed and brutality during their despotic rule in the Vendée to take any new or sensible view of the position.

At the end of the month the Committee of Public Safety recalled them.

Their departure was a happy riddance for the unfortunate inhabitants of the Vendée, brigand and patriot alike.

Cruel, bloodthirsty despots—men dead to every sense of justice or honour; associated in iniquities innumerable, in cruelties untold, friends of Carrier, admirers of and applauders of Huché and Martinière—they were two of the most infamous wretches which the Revolution in the name of "liberty" produced.

Turreau remained a little longer.

For nearly another month the war dragged on; now Vendean victories, now Vendean defeats; all on an ever-diminishing scale. But success did not come to the Revolutionary Government. The Vendée was not anni-hilated, and the limit of forbearance towards even such a true sans-culotte was at last reached. The Committee of Public Safety could no longer ignore the increasing volume of complaint and reprobation, and on the 13th May it removed him from his command. But being a *vrai sans-culotte* he was let down easy. He was given another appointment—the Governorship of Belle-isle-en-Mer—by Robespierre, it was said; and the Vendée was rid of one whose presence and career in it had been altogether evil.

Personally Turreau was a despicable creature—one of the vainest and meanest of those who strutted for a short time on the revolutionary stage. Militarily he was a bungler of the highest order; and, as a leader, what can be thought of the man who, in an address to his "brothers in arms" urging them to action, says, "I will follow you; do not doubt it"?

To humanity now he is only interesting as another specimen of the *vrai républicain* in authority, and as a demonstration of how the Revolution worked out in practice.

The military despotism exercised by him under and in the name of the Republic was as absolute a despotism as any which had been exercised by any previous royal despots in France; it was, too, a despotism exercised against, not the noblesse or wealthy classes, of whom there were not many left, but against the people of the humblest class, the rank and file of the agricultural and industrial population—the people who had helped to make the Revolution, and who were to have been bene-fited by it.   Nor was it exercised alone against the Vendeans—who were considered as rebels; but also against the "patriots," staunch supporters of the new régime.

Turreau's military despotism in the Vendée was the complement to Carrier's civil despotism in Nantes.

In one way it was unquestionably more iniquitous, inasmuch as his severities were unprovoked, and wholly gratuitous.   Carrier was given his authority publicly by the Convention itself.   Turreau usurped his.   Carrier found the prisons full; found also at Nantes a number of opponents to the extremer ideas of revolution, and he had been sent to deal with them.

Turreau found the Vendée peaceable and anxious for peace—upon that point there is an almost unanimous opinion of the republican officials most qualified to speak about it—and he deliberately created the occasion for his inhumanities.   He had no mission such as Carrier.   He himself has avowed it in a letter to the Minister of War dated 14th February 1794: "You know that, without any authorisation, I have taken, and put into execution, the most rigorous measures to end this frightful war." He made an absolutely wanton attack on masses of peaceful people, great numbers of them being "patriots" and republicans, and not "brigands," and he remorselessly proceeded to apply to them a military despotism in its cruellest and bloodiest form. He created a fresh civil war, causing a vast loss of innocent life, and the destruction of an enormous amount of property—a war lasting not alone for the time he was in command, but for months and months after he had been superseded.

But there is little profit in discussing his and Carrier's relative positions in infamy.

The real, salient, emergent fact is, that each, in his own sphere, and in different ways, proved the same conclusion—that a Republic could be as tyrannical, cruel, and unjust a Government as any other form of government which humanity had ever tried and suffered under.

And as their combined spheres of authority covered the whole field of government, the general conclusion possesses irresistible force.

Together these two high officials of the Republic afforded awful proof of the abominations of cruelty and inhumanity which could be committed by, and in the name of, a Republic, which posed as being a revelation to mankind of the liberty and fraternity and justice which should prevail upon the earth : and their actions, aided, abetted, and in most part approved, by the Executive Government in Paris, exploded once for all the colossal pretensions of the new Republic to be regard as the realised ideal, the faultless paragon of Governments.

Indeed, not only was it demonstrated to be, not a Government of law, justice, liberty, and order, or even of any one of those things, but it was demonstrated by the incontrovertible evidence of actual experience and visible fact to be a Government excelling in lawlessness, injustice, tyranny, and disorder—a Government which afforded no guarantee, no safeguard, no shelter even, against the invasion and destruction of all the most cherished, the most elementary, rights of man.

# CHAPTER XXV

It is a relief to turn one's eyes for a moment from these unceasing horrors to a phase of the life of a Representative which, while instructive, is in lighter vein,—to a little bit of autobiography which, being apologetic or deprecatory, is refreshingly free from the vanity and brag and revolutionary cant of their usual reports, which takes one, as it were, behind the scenes of a part of their life when they were not actually occupied in devising or carrying out deeds of bloodshed and tyranny and injustice.

The Representatives were, of course, paid by the Convention for their labours, and some of them managed, one way or the other, to get through good round sums.

They travelled about with a regular retinue—one or two secretaries and copyists, with military officers, couriers, and others, vaguely called *personnes*; and then they required house or lodging, and such things cost no small amount of money.

The Convention made a decree ordering them to send in an account of the money they had received from the Republic, and of their expenditure.

Among the accounts sent in was one from Bourbotte,

—he who at Noirmoutier proposed and decreed Wieland's death, and who also was guilty of many other atrocities.

Justifying his expenditure, he described "the necessity the Representative was under of having several people with him, secretaries, copyists, also of having to entertain generals, officials, and other public functionaries" (Lequinio once entertained the executioner, it will be remembered). His wine bill he was evidently anxious about, which confirms Piet's statement that he took wine immoderately.

"The excessive scarcity and dearness of wine decided me to requisition the administrators of the district to furnish me with that coming from (*prévenant des*) the *émigrés*, or those condemned to death, for my consumption and that of the persons with me.

"On different occasions I received from the people proofs of affection which became for me the cause of some indispensable expense, notably at Nantes, Troyes, etc.

"After having made several civic promenades, and sung hymns in honour of 'liberty,' the crowd was so large, the heat so excessive, our *courses* and our dances so fatiguing, that I felt it my duty to provide some refreshment for several of the citizens who reconducted me to my lodgings.

"I only enter into these details to give you an idea of the nature of the expenses to which a Representative on mission can be forced."

There was also an item of 250 livres for "refreshments furnished occasionally to mounted orderlies who accompanied me and the general-in-chief when we went to make some reconnaissances."

And there were items for new outfits. At the

capture of Saumur by the Vendeans, he says, "the Representatives lost everything, saving only what they had on." He himself got some of his things back, but he had to replace many. Worse befell him, however, at the republican defeat and rout at Vihiers, where he lost his horse, arms, and equipage, and where all his things were pillaged. " To escape from the fury of the rebels, who pursued me even in the night," he continued, " I had to disembarrass myself of all my clothes which impeded my march. I took off my boots. I threw away my coat, without thinking an instant (for it was difficult to do so in such circumstances) of what was in my pocket."

The " what " was a pocket-book with 2100 livres in it.

He winds up his report : " Here is my account. I should have very much desired to have been able to import more economy into my expenditure ; but, whilst putting ostentation and luxury away from me, I also thought that if a Representative on mission pushed the simplicity of republican manners, of which he should give the first example, beyond reasonable bounds, he would, in the eyes of those over whom the power of modest and reserved appearances has a useful effect, diminish the consideration with which he is in need of being always surrounded."

# CHAPTER XXVI

WHILE Turreau had been devastating the Vendée with
his " infernal columns," the revolutionists in Nantes and
Angers, and elsewhere in the surrounding districts, had
been continuing their campaign in their usual way ; but
so many tens of thousands of Vendeans, counter-revolutionists, and " patriots " had been wiped out of existence,
that the revolutionary battues could no longer be on the
splendid scale they had been.

Proceedings, moreover, were becoming somewhat
tempered by the slowly awakening opinion among larger
numbers of the people that the action of the revolutionists in power was being carried to too great lengths ;
by misgivings on the part of some who hitherto had
aided or abetted in the atrocities, that they themselves
might be marked down as the next victims, and on the
part of others by the desire to rest under their laurels,
and to enjoy at leisure the fruits of their plunder and
triumphs.

With Carrier's recall, the climax of tyranny, so far
as Nantes was concerned, was passed ; but only the
climax, for, for some time after his departure, tyranny
there remained rampant ; the prisons being full of

prisoners, the Revolutionary Committee still making arrests, perpetrating fresh iniquities, and expressing its intention "to prevent as far as possible aristocrats from fouling the streets with their mephitic presence." All the machinery of revolutionary government remained in operation, and Nantes and its inhabitants had still to go through a great deal before the peace necessary for happiness, and the security necessary for material prosperity, once more prevailed.

And away from down the Loire. from Bourgneuf, there came, like a distant peal of the thunderstorm which has passed, the news of a noyade ordered by Foucault of noyade fame, promoted to the Governorship of Paimboeuf.

There, on the 24th February, a noyade, not with sinking of barge as at Nantes, but simply throwing, or chucking. overboard into the rapid running river, 41 bodies and souls, as "rebels to the law"—2 men, one of them aged 78 and blind, a dangerous rebel, 12 women, 12 girls, and 15 children, of whom 10 were between 5 and 10 years of age, the remainder in arms. The fact is not contested, was avowed by Foucault himself.

After a little while the energy of the Revolutionary Committee was somewhat cramped by the enforced absence of Goullin and Chaux ; these two "true patriots," as Carrier called them, having been summoned to Paris to explain a somewhat discreditable transaction on their part.

Prieur, moreover, merciless and cruel as he was, did not lend himself in Nantes, as Carrier had done, to measures of wholesale and extreme violence.

That things had improved by the latter part of March is evident from the fact that seventy-two priests who were in prison on board a ship in the Loire were there alive, and not noyaded.

The proceedings against Lamberty and Fouquet, although kept as secret as possible, helped somewhat towards the change of feeling.

These two criminals had been sent before the Military Commission, of which Bignon was president, by the Revolutionary Committee on a charge, not of the countless murders and noyades and other crimes they had committed, but of abstracting from the Republic and defrauding the sword of justice of several women who were counter-revolutionists.

To murder counter-revolutionists, and even innocent people, was evidently, according to the revolutionary standard of morality, not an indictable offence. To prevent them being noyaded, or, in other words, to deprive the Republic of its prey, was a capital offence.

When the lives of only " brigands " or counter-revolutionists were at stake, a few minutes, if even that, usually sufficed to dispose of a case once it came before a Military Commission : but now where sans-culottes were concerned, revolutionary justice proceeded more hesitatingly. Bignon considered it " a very delicate affair," and unusual delay took place between the commencement of their trial and the decision. Communications with Carrier were deemed necessary, the culprits having defended themselves by pleading the necessity of obeying Carrier's orders.

But Carrier refused to intervene in any way ; he would throw no light on the matter, being probably glad to secure the destruction of two accomplices who knew too much, and who would be dangerous witnesses should he himself by any chance be put on trial. He protested that they were " the two best patriots of Nantes," but none the less he took no step to clear them, or to help them to avoid their fate.

They were convicted on the 14th April—that one act of justice the Bignon Military Commission performed—and they were sentenced to death and guillotined, and with their deaths eternal silence fell over countless of the most heinous crimes of the revolutionists at Nantes.[1]

While Goullin and Chaux were away in Paris, Phelippes de Tronjolly had been looking into things. From being president of the Revolutionary Tribunal, he had been reduced to being public accuser before it, and he had become a bitter enemy of the Revolutionary Committee owing to a well-founded belief of its intention to *débarrasser* itself of him by the guillotine or other equally efficacious means. No one was better qualified to unveil the iniquities of the Committee, and, carefully choosing his ground, he, in virtue of his office, formally called on the Committee for explanations as to certain, for them, very awkward matters—for instance, for the production of two men who had been prisoners in the Bouffay, of whom he could get no account; and also for an account of moneys received by the Committee, which, according even to revolutionary law, they were bound to supply, but which obligation they had hitherto ignored or evaded.

Just at this time, too, the power of the Committee was also crippled in another very material respect. Hitherto it had had the various tribunals of revolutionary justice in Nantes almost absolutely under its control. It only had to signify a wish as to the fate of a prisoner, and the wish was obeyed. On the 8th May an order of the Committee of Public Safety suspended the operations of all the Military Commissions established in the Depart-

---

[1] The records of this case are not in existence (Berriat St. Prix, p. 4).

ments, and all persons accused of "conspiracy" were to
be sent before the Revolutionary Tribunal in Paris.

Thus the power of dictating to the tribunals which
were to try their victims was taken from them, and they
were deprived of the means of murdering their victims
under the forms of law.

How effective these Military Commissions, which
clad murder with the mantle of the law," had been can
be realised from the fact that the celebrated Bignon
Commission, the worst of all of them, it is true, in a little
less than five months, namely, from the 14th December
1793 to the 8th May 1794, sentenced 2919 people to
death, 8 to deportation, 9 to irons, 1 to prison, and
acquitted 40. Of these, some 800 or so had been
sentenced before the Commission came to Nantes.

A change of Representatives also made things less
favourable for them.

Prieur (de la Marne) was sent to Brest, and Bo and
Bourbotte succeeded him. Bo's arrival towards the end
of May marked, it is said, the end of the actual "reign
of terror" there, though not the end of much injustice
and cruelty.

Phelippes all the while was hard at work ferreting
out some of the misdemeanours of the Revolutionary Committee, and on the 31st May he reported to the Representatives that the members of the Committee had on
different occasions ordered the removal to their own
dwellings of wine, wood, and other articles taken from
the houses of *émigrés* or suspects, and had rendered no
account thereof, as by revolutionary law they were bound
to do, and he demanded an account of same, and also particulars as to certain instances in which the official seals
had been broken.

The Revolutionary Committee, said Phelippes, had

received more than a million livres. It contented itself with surrendering 73,000 livres, but could give no account of the balance.

The matter was so serious, it was reported to the Committee of Public Safety, and on the 6th June Bo and Bourbotte, acting under the direct instructions of the Committee, called for a reply within twenty-four hours.

The replies not being forthcoming, the Representatives on the 12th June ordered the arrest of the members of the Committee, and the same day these *bons et braves républicains* found themselves experiencing some of the miseries to which they had unjustly doomed thousands of their countrymen.

Gradually the trend of affairs continued towards moderation. The Revolutionary Government in Paris, although Robespierre was still supreme, and also the Convention, was becoming more impressed with the conviction that moderation would have better effects with the Vendeans than extreme measures, and the Representatives Bo and Bourbotte, taking their cue from Paris, persevered in a milder régime.

The Revolutionary Committee being under lock and key, the people slowly gathered courage to speak. Light, too, was thrown on the state of the prisons of Nantes, which still were crowded, the prisoners venturing on appeals for mercy.

On 17th June some 500 women, imprisoned in the old Convent of the Good Shepherd, sent a petition to the Representatives :

"Our misery is at its climax. Shut up more than eight months ago in an unhealthy building, contagious diseases carry off every day some of our companions. You would be touched, Representatives, to see 500 women heaped together—some infirm, some even blind, some of over seventy years of age, pregnant women, nurses, mothers of families, poor and indigent——the greater number victims of private hatred. We have not been able before this to make known our innocence, as our relatives were prohibited asking for our release."

And in the next month, being still in prison, they again complained: "The devouring heat of the sun consumes our bodies, weakened by grief. The want of water, increasing our thirst, becomes a new torture."

What an awful picture of revolutionary "fraternity."

A commission of inquiry reported that in all there were about 4000 prisoners in Nantes, of whom more than 1000 were women. And their report was the old story: "The afflicting picture of masses of men breathing a mephitic atmosphere, lying on the ground or paving-stones, without straw or covering, without linen or clothing, without sufficient nourishment"- a story which, though it may weary one by repetition, has to be borne in mind, for it was a constant factor in the system of revolutionary tyranny, the sufferings of the imprisoned thousands never ceasing. For now considerably over two years, under the régime of "liberty and fraternity," thousands of prisoners were each day and night weltering in misery and physical agony in the revolutionary torture-houses.

But enough has been said on this painful subject to convey some faint idea of what revolutionary prisons were. They played a great part in the tyranny of the "good republican" and crai sans-culotte. They were the means of inflicting untold suffering and infamous injustice upon all, whether guilty or innocent, whom the revolutionists marked down as their prey.

Various have been the estimates of the number of persons who actually died in the prisons of Nantes during

the régime of the revolutionists. Dr. Laennec said
10,000, Lallié 9000, Guépin 5000, Goullin 2000. The
truth probably is much nearer 10,000 than 5000.

But Nantes was only one place where these evils
existed. All around the Vendée, or wherever in it
revolutionary authority existed, in Angers, Doué,
Saumur, Fontenay, Noirmoutier, there were prisons
crammed with prisoners, and the same evils, the same
misery existed. The roll of victims of revolutionary
"justice" who died in prison in the Vendée and its surroundings, could it by any possibility be obtained, would
be appalling, and the infamy of it is increased by the
fact that the vast bulk of the prisoners were "untried,"
and, according to the theory of even revolutionary law,
innocent.

The plain matter of fact truth is that the revolutionists—utterly reckless of human life, utterly regardless of human suffering—let the unfortunate prisoners
die *en masse*. It mattered not whether the prisoners
were innocent; whether age, infirmity, or physical incapacity absolutely prevented them taking any action
against the revolutionary *régime*; they were in prison,
let them die; their death saved further trouble.

As it was in Nantes this spring and summer of
1794, so was it in Angers, only there the tyrannical
rule of the Revolutionary Committee and of the Representatives died more slowly. The Committee kept up
its character. Perturbed at a change of opinion which
it noticed, it wrote a long letter to Francastel defending
its actions and its principles.

In their "revolutionary infancy" they said they had
been too considerate or lenient, and had done things
which they had since rectified.

"As long as you leave us our powers we will go our

way, proud, full of confidence in the justice of our past and future operations: we will revolutionise, we will electrify, we will 'Maratise' our fellow-citizens, and our last cry will be 'Vive la Montagne! Vive la République! one and indivisible ; war against traitors and anarchists!'"

A fusillade on the 10th February resulted in a quarrel between the Military Commission and the Revolutionary Committee. The previous day some twenty persons had been arrested in their own houses for no other offence than being aristocrats, and were included in the fusillade, though they had not even been tried.

The Revolutionary Committee, which aspired to holding exclusive power, thought that the Commission was taking too much upon itself. "You stop our march, and we will not suffer it any longer. It is more than can be put up with (C'en est trop)." "Do not accuse us of ambition," the Committee sanctimoniously remarked : "the sole ambition we have is to administer justice"; and it prohibited the members of the Commission from going any more into the prisons to draw up there the death-lists. The quarrel resulted in a cessation of the fusillades for a time, but they were resumed, though on a smaller scale, and terror continued to reign.

The state of affairs in Angers at this precise time is graphically set forth in the following highly descriptive and characteristic letter from the Revolutionary Committee to the Committee of Public Safety :—

"Our prisons empty themselves ; then they are filled up again ; then they are emptied again. One would believe that the country was purged. Eh, well, not at all. It is a hydra. One may cut away (on a beau couper), there always remains a head."

The ferocity and injustice of the Military Commission had become such that some of the best "patriots" of

Angers, and at last even many of the Jacobins, did not feel themselves safe.

When the patriots became possessed of the idea that their own heads might be the next to be cut away, they began to think that the existing state of things was not quite so desirable as it had hitherto seemed, and they leagued themselves with the Moderates against the extreme Montagnards actually in power.

In March the Revolutionary Committee was dissolved, and a new one appointed, somewhat less violent, and with somewhat curtailed powers.

But executions on a considerable scale did not even then end, for on the 8th April 441 women were interrogated, of whom 84 were ordered to be shot—a proportion of acquittals which shows a great change; and on the 15th April 99 persons, of whom over 40 were women, were condemned, and shot the following day at La Haie, in presence of Félix and the other members of the Commission.

The movement against the proceedings of the Military Commission gained strength, and at last complaints began to voice themselves against even the Representatives.

Early in May, all the Military Commissions came to an end: but a special exception was made as to the Commission under Félix. He and it were sent to Noirmoutier, there to continue the brutalities which had distinguished them at Angers, and which had earned for them a certificate of character from Hentz and Francastel. "The Representatives announce their satisfaction with the energetic manner, revolutionary and full of dignity, with which the Military Commission of Angers has exercised its functions."

Revolutionary vindictiveness against women did not terminate with the extinction of the Military Commissions and Revolutionary Tribunals in the provinces. Several batches of prisoners were sent up from the Vendée for trial in Paris.

One list is on record showing that a batch of 22 Vendeans were removed to Paris for trial. Of these, 21 were women.

The act of accusation against them expressed the views of the revolutionists in authority in Paris as regarded Vendean women.

"They were all the instruments and the accomplices of the priests and the nobles who, in the name of Heaven, inundated French territory with the blood of its citizens. In the Departments of the Vendée, Deux-Sèvres, and others, all have contributed, either personally or by their husbands or their children, and by the help they have given, to this disastrous and sanguinary war, which has cost the country so many citizens, and which has delivered entire Departments to devastation and fire, in fact to all the excesses of an expiring fanaticism."

They appeared before the Revolutionary Tribunal on the 25th June 1794, and out of them all only two were acquitted, one of them being a girl of fourteen years of age.

Noirmoutier, probably on account of its remoteness, to the last retained its notoriety as the scene of revolutionary horrors of the most atrocious type. Thither had been sent prisoners from Fontenay, from Challans, from Sables, where "the prisons were infected with a pestiferous and mortiferous air," until at last the island became "one vast prison."

One day the Revolutionary Committee at Sables d'Olonne sent over a small ship with about 200 prisoners. Tyroco, a captain, and a member of the Military Commission, went down with soldiers to receive them. When disembarked, some 50 or 60 were too ill or weak to walk, and lay there helpless on the ground. Said Tyroco, "Their condemnation is certain. They have only been sent here to be shot. Help can only prolong their sufferings, and defer their death by a few days. Comrades, let us end their ills, let them be shot."

And so some 50 persons perished there and then on the sands, done to death—people innocent according even to revolutionary law and the Declaration of the Rights of Man.

"Posterity," wrote Piet, "will have difficulty in believing in such crimes": but posterity, having at last learned what infamous wretches the revolutionists were, and what crimes they committed, has no difficulty whatever in believing his narrative.

Félix and his Military Commission must, however, have slackened in their energies as time went on, for a few days before the 9th Thermidor—the date of the downfall of Robespierre—Carnot had written on behalf of the Committee of Public Safety to the Representatives at Niort a letter with quite the old ring about it. He told them instanter to order that revolutionary justice at Noirmoutier should resume its course, and that vigorous measures should be taken against the promoters, chiefs, and abettors of the cruel war.

"Whence has been taken the idea that the Government wish to pardon the authors and abettors and instigators of the outrages committed in the Vendée against the sovereignty of the people?

"Hasten, on the contrary, dear colleagues, to deliver to the avenging sword all the promoters and chiefs of this cruel war, that the scoundrels who for so long have torn the bowels of the patrie receive at last the deserts for their crimes."

After the 9th Thermidor, when more moderate Representatives came there, they found over 400 prisoners "groaning in irons for a long time, and in the most frightful misery."

How many had died there before these were tardily released? How many had been done to death by revolutionary "justice" in that remote place, that secret prison-house, away from the vision of men, and out of the ken of the world, who can tell?

# CHAPTER XXVII

THERE is no clearer proof of the iniquity of the system of government which had been carried on in the Vendée than the admission by the National Convention and the Committee of Public Safety that they had been wrong. Not an open and avowed confession—that would have been too much to expect—not even a complete and generous reversal of policy, but, at first, a hesitating and grudging reversal, forced on them by the inherent strength of the Vendean cause, the inherent rottenness of the revolutionary cause, and by the failure of their policy of extermination.

The Committee of Public Safety, sensible at last of the disadvantages following Turreau's method of finishing the Vendean war, determined on a new procedure, and on the 13th May gave precise instructions to General Vimeux, his successor.

Though a mitigation of the previous system, the new one was still very severe, but, within little more than a week, the Committee again toned down its views.

The fact was that the curses of the revolutionists were coming home to roost.

The insensate destruction of the great stores of grain

and other food found in the Vendée, which had been one of the keynotes of the policy of the Revolutionary Government, was telling now against themselves.

Starving the Vendeans into submission was found to entail starvation of themselves first. Nantes, with its 100,000 inhabitants, mostly republicans, was nearly famished, the people being reduced to live on less than a pound of bread a day. The republican troops there and elsewhere in the west were also on starvation rations : Paris itself was daily bordering on insurrection on account of the want of food. The great armies on the frontiers, amounting to almost 1,000,000 of men, had also to be fed. Every grain of corn, therefore, was wanted.

And so a change of policy was imperative. The Convention, forced to see the danger of a continuance of the scarcity, became deeply concerned as to the prospects of the next harvest; and the Committee of Public Safety, Robespierre included, made an elaborate decree with the object of getting into cultivation again the land which it itself had ordered to be laid waste.

A Commission of Agriculture was appointed to undertake the task. A census was to be made in each commune : seed was to be supplied to those who had none ; workmen were even to be paid to do the work which the agricultural classes had previously done in their own interests, preparing the land, sowing the grain, reaping the harvest.

And to put a stop to the pillaging practices of the troops, the strictest military discipline was ordered to be maintained, and, what was most important, only those were to be treated as rebels who carried arms, who had no domicile, and who did not come to the assemblies of the commune and inscribe their names there.

The military necessities of the Republican Government had also considerable influence in the change of policy. The French had lost the important position of Kaiserslautern, which covered the Lower Rhine, and it was a matter of the greatest urgency to send help to that part of the frontier. Troops accordingly must be taken from the army of the west.

But the Committee of Public Safety was mistaken in thinking that the Vendean war was almost finished, and was over-sanguine as to what troops could be sent, for a great part were absolutely without arms, and more than one-third of the army was in hospital.

Moreover, the situation in the Vendée still was more serious than the Committee thought. Charette and Stofflet were still able to show a bold front and to strike heavy blows.

" The affair of the 1st June," wrote General Dusirat, " cost us 243 men, 1 colour, and 19 carts."

The new commander-in-chief (Vimeux) made no concealment of the real state of affairs. " The end of the war," he informed the Committee on the 14th June, " depends absolutely on the means which you fix, and the combined and persevering measures you order. There are still battles to be fought, and many brigands to be killed. Not alone do we find them in force, but they even attack us. . . . To tell you this war will end in so many decades—only an ignoramus or a charlatan could hold such language."

The change of policy on the part of the Government quickly found imitation on the part of the generals. Their acts became more moderate, and their reports also. Women and children and old people were brought in as prisoners instead of being murdered : sometimes even men who were not found actually in arms. But still the generals report attacks on the brigands, and their defeat with heavy losses—some real, some more or less exaggerated.

Boussard, on the 14th June, made an attack on le Marais, capturing with it old people, sick, and 300 to 400 women, also an enormous quantity of grain—"at least 30,000 sacks," he said.

"Thirty men without arms surrendered."

"Two hundred men have parleyed with Reboul. The gentler means (les moyens de douceur) of the Committee of Public Safety assure the return of a large number of the others. Happy presage for the harvest."

As June went on the tendency towards clemency continued.

The agents of the Agricultural Commission continued their work to the best of their capacity, and (on the 21st) the Commissioners issued a proclamation to the Vendeans :—

"Men, misled or intimidated by certain measures which the Government never authorised, the Patrie opens its arms to you. Return to your hearths, continue to cultivate your fields, prepare to secure your abundant harvest, and be confident that the Government will shut its eyes on the past. One will think no more of the evil than to seek the means to cure it. . . . Return to your hearths with confidence, surrender to us your arms, and we give you the most positive assurance that you will not be disturbed.

"When the Republic promises safety and protection, she always keeps her word. Those who tell you to the contrary are 'calumniators.'"

And Vimeux issued an address to the army on the 26th June :—

"Soldiers of the Patrie, you are called to take

part in the execution of the beneficent measures decreed
by the Commission of Agriculture.

" Frenchmen and republicans, you will fight the rebels
who oppose in arms the national wish.   But you will
open your arms to the men seduced or carried away by
violence, who have ceded to the perfidious suggestions of
the priests and of the nobles; and who, recognising
their error, return to their hearths with the olive-branch
of peace in their hand, with repentance in their heart,
and with the firm desire to obey the laws of the
Republic.   You will respect property.   It is the base of
society; it is the riches of the nation.   You will
protect individuals.   Humanity commands it, your
glory exacts it."

The style of these proclamations was very different
from those of the previous year.

The results of the new policy might have been more
effective and rapid were it not for what had gone
before.

The base deceptions practised by the republican
generals had very naturally destroyed any possibility of
now believing in the promises held out.

" The brigands declare," wrote Grignon (July 8th),
" that the amnesty now offered them will no more
avail them than that of last year, that one is only
treating with them to deceive them, and that after
surrendering their arms one would put them in prison
and shoot them, as had been done to their comrades the
previous year."

Thus was another curse coming home to roost.   The
shameful breaches of promises given by republican
Representatives, generals, and officers had produced the
natural result of a complete distrust of any pledge or
promise or proclamation now tendered by them.

And the Vendean chiefs issued proclamations warning the Vendeans against these overtures.

"You invite us to return to our hearths," said some of them to the republicans. "Where shall we find them? You have burned our houses and massacred our wives and children. You wish now to get our crops and our arms."

Though the Republic had entered on a more moderate course of action, there was still a hankering after severe measures, especially when the proposed healing measures were so badly received. Even Bo wrote to the Committee of Public Safety :—

"I think it will be necessary to put all the columns in march, and fall vigorously and promptly on the brigands, who only take the sheep's skin to conceal the rage of the wolf."

The Committee of Public Safety, after considering generally the state of affairs in the west, gave orders that the troops should be kept in constant activity. The generals were to report to the Representatives what they had done "for the extermination of the brigands." Each day of inaction would be regarded as a crime. "They will be responsible for indiscipline among the troops, as well as for any acts of inhumanity, which can only aggravate the evil instead of putting an end to it."

Another incident occurred which showed that the Committee of Public Safety were still rather sitting upon the rail between coercion and conciliation.

A report got about at Nantes that the Committee had decreed amnesty to the brigands of the Vendée. The Committee wrote (July 7) indignantly denying the truth of the report, and saying: "Any one who knows the principles of the Committee cannot give the slightest credence to such calumnies."

The upshot of it all appeared to be that the Committee had gone back to the policy of the neglected decree of the 10th May of the previous year, to spare the rank and file, " the duped and fanaticised," as the republicans always talked of them, but to be merciless towards the chiefs who had misled them.

The conduct of the Vendean chiefs should have facilitated the task of the Republican Government, for bitter dissensions broke out between them, and unity of action on their side need no longer be feared.    The chiefs went their own ways and fought independently ; and there were combats here, there, and every place, sometimes important, sometimes unimportant, but less formidable than previously, the forces being smaller.    Fighting, however, was, on the part of the Vendeans, manifestly necessary, for not yet was revolutionary cruelty over.

Huché, who, inconceivable as it may appear, was, in spite of all his infamies, still entrusted by the Revolutionary Government with a command, broke out into a week's debauch of massacre and incendiarism and pillage in July.

" Four columns have been set in motion.    Castles, mills, bakehouses burned and destroyed, more than 300 persons of both sexes found here and there, bearing convincing proofs of their brigandage. killed . . .", he himself reported.

It was quite in his old form ; a repetition of brutal horrors, a revival of the promenades of one of Turreau's " infernal columns," ruthless massacre of peaceable and innocent men, women and children, reckless destruction of grain and provisions urgently wanted by starving people, and this too in face of the proclamation of the 21st June of the Agricultural Commissioners.

Complaint now more quickly reached the Government

in Paris, and once more Huché was removed from his appointment and ordered to appear before the Committee of Public Safety; and the Representatives on the 30th July, on the same day that the news of Robespierre's downfall reached Nantes, issued a decree condemning acts such as had been perpetrated.

But they also, harking back to the severer methods of revolutionary government, decreed that all rebels captured with arms in their hands would be treated as rebels and brigands, and those taken without arms, who were recognised as having taken active part in the rebellion, should be tried by the Military Commission still existing at Noirmoutier.

The decree produced a very bad impression, as it was very naturally interpreted as contrary to the generous and loyal application of the promises given by the Commissioners of Agriculture.

On the 27th July—the 9th Thermidor—Robespierre fell, and the policy of comparative moderation which, with much vacillation, had been entered on, received a fresh and strong impulse.

Not until the latter half of August, however, did the remodelled Committee of Public Safety get time to take up Vendean affairs.

It then decreed (on the 18th, that "justice and disinterestedness should be made the order of the day"; good manners. the way of persuasion, good faith, should be put in force (*mises en vigueur*). Representatives should exact that the chiefs of the army should set the example of energy and austere principles; the military staff was to be purified—in a good. and not the revolutionary, sense of the word; and no headquarters were to be fixed in a town.

And as regarded the Vendeans. the order was reiterated that all the chiefs and officers should be punished

with death, but those who had only been misled, or
carried away by violence, should be pardoned.

A new set of Representatives was sent to the Vendée
to give effect to the policy of the new Government in
Paris, and they at once proceeded to remove from the
public bodies those who were most notorious as "terror-
ists," and suspended a lot of generals——among them
Huché and Carpentier (who had already been suspended),
Dutruy and Grignon, all of " infernal column " fame; and
Guillaume, a hairdresser who under revolutionary régime
had developed into a brigade general, and now was sent
to prison "on account of the extraordinary and dangerous
measures he had employed."

So long as harvesting operations lasted there was
comparative quiet, but those over, it was easy for the
Vendean chiefs to collect assemblies to attack the republicans.

It was still only the autumn of the year that Turreau
and his "infernal columns" had been devastating their
homes and fields with fire and sword, and had inflicted
on them or their kith or kin the greatest cruelties and
sufferings that one class of humanity can inflict on
another.   The feelings of infamous wrong and injury
still rankled so deep that numbers were panting for
revenge.   The offers of pardon were very naturally dis-
trusted; and so, once more, the Vendeans assembled
together in small armies, and on the 18th September
they captured even the fortified camps of the republicans
at Roullière and at Freligné, inflicting a loss on their
enemies of 300 men.

Beyond that, however, they did little.

And the republican army was incapable of making
any great efforts, for it was going from bad to worse,
growing weaker from day to day.

Nor were the efforts to strengthen it of much avail. The new levies arrived destitute of everything, and the military authorities had nothing wherewith to supply their necessities.

Except by spasmodic efforts every now and then, the republican forces were unable to undertake any important movements.

A report from the Representatives sums up the state of affairs at this time.

" You told us," they wrote to the Committee of Public Safety, " that this army was at least 70,000 strong.

" Since the 30th August we informed you it was only 45,000, from which had to be deducted at least 15,000 (at present 17,000 to 18,000) sick. Of the remaining 30,000, 14,000 are scattered in all sorts of places, and scarcely 20,000 are well armed. . . .

" The brigands are more numerous than is thought. They are in possession of 400 square leagues of country. . . . We require greater forces. . . . These countries, in spite of the devastations to which they have been subjected, still have a population of 250,000 persons, an immense quantity of cattle, and the fields are covered with grain and forage sufficient to feed the army of the west for a year."

A new commander-in-chief, Dumas, a mulatto, who had succeeded Vimeux, added his quota of testimony to the information already in possession of the Committee of Public Safety.

" The Vendée has been treated as a city taken by assault. Everything has been sacked, pillaged, and burned. *Il existe peu de généreux capables de faire de bien.* There reigns in all the army a deplorable confusion (*abandon*) and a spirit of insubordination and pillage. How convince the inhabitants of these

countries of your justice while the troops violate justice?
—of your respect for persons and property, while they
pillage?" and soon after he resigned.

The well-informed Savary has summarised the condition of things on both sides.

Of the republicans he wrote: " The army, disorganised,
scattered around the Vendée in small posts, with no
power of resistance, awaited the arrival of a commander-
in-chief and of generals to replace those who had been
suspended. It was reduced to inaction."

And of the Vendeans: " Lassitude has succeeded to
the prolonged efforts of the peasants of the Vendée.
They sighed only for repose. The chiefs and the strangers
surrounding them were alone interested in continuing
the war—to preserve their authority and their existence.
. . . One heard no further talk of hostilities."

Thus, as the end of the year approached, both sides
were nearly exhausted.

# CHAPTER XXVIII

EVENTS elsewhere than in the Vendée were accentuating
the change in general policy of those in authority in
Paris.

To Paris in July had been conveyed the members of
the Revolutionary Committee of Nantes, about twenty in
all, realising in mild fashion some of the sufferings they
had inflicted on others ; for Guépin, the historian of Nantes,
recounts that they were treated " with the greatest inhumanity," being in chains, and each with an iron collar
round his neck.    But they were driven while others had
walked ; they were fed while the others had starved—
altogether there was no comparison between their journey
and that of the Nantais they had sent to Paris in the
previous November.

While on their way they received tidings of the
downfall and death of Robespierre.    Dismay fell upon
them.    Goullin exclaimed, " Good heavens, is it possible ?"
Grandmaison said, " If it is true, we are lost."    Chaux
wept and tore out his hair.

It is quite possible that they might have escaped trial
for their crimes had it not been for the fact that the
survivors of the 132 Nantais whom they had arrested

and sent to Paris were still lingering in confinement there, and were pressing their request to be brought to trial.

These Nantais appear to have been forgotten, there having been a long delay in furnishing even the modicum of evidence required by the notorious Fouquier Tinville. Nearly forty had died either on the forty days' journey to Paris or in prison there; and inasmuch as the remaining ninety-two were acquitted, the practical outcome was that nearly forty innocent men were wrongfully sent to death by the Revolutionary Committee—were, in plain words, murdered.

Some revenge the survivors had. In September, six weeks after Robespierre's downfall, they were put on their trial before the Revolutionary Tribunal in Paris, together with Phelippes de Tronjolly, who had been also accused by the Committee. The trial, with its fearful disclosures, almost instantaneously seized and absorbed the attention of Paris, and it soon took an unexpected turn. The principal witnesses were the members of the Revolutionary Committee. Brought from prison to give evidence before the tribunal, they soon had to answer for themselves, the tables were turned, and the accused Nantais, by their replies and questions to the witnesses, took up the role of accusers.

Phelippes de Tronjolly, answering the charges against himself of being a federalist and not a republican, turned on his accusers and said:

" It is *de toute évidence* that the Revolutionary Committee has been the origin and motive power of all the miseries which the best republicans have suffered. . . . This Committee is stained with every crime ; and particularly so is Goullin. I accuse him to his face. I undertake to establish beyond denial all the crimes (*délits*), to show his turpitude, all the chain of misdeeds and atrocities which deserve for him general execration, which call down upon him the vengeance of the law."

The president, evidently impressed by this language, turned on the witnesses with searching questions.

Then, as Goullin shielded himself by the plea of only executing Carrier's orders, Carrier was called upon to give evidence. He came, and swore that he "knew nothing either of the noyades or fusillades. Had I had the least notion of these horrors," he said, "of these barbarities, they would not have been committed."

And the other witnesses, Joly, Pérochot, Durassier, Mainguet, sank themselves and each other deeper into the mire, and exonerated the accused still more.

"One needs but a glance at the faces of the accusers," said Tronson Ducoudray, the avocat, "to be fully convinced that crime is accusing innocence." The public prosecutor abandoned the charges against the greater number of the accused.

The remainder of the ninety-two Nantais and Phelippes were declared to have conspired against the Republic, but were acquitted of having done so with wicked or counter-revolutionary intent, and all were set at liberty.

This was on the 13th September 1794.

Hot upon the disclosures made at this trial came the charges made in the Convention against certain of the republican generals who had served in the Vendée.

There, on the 29th September, Maignen brought into full publicity details of the infamous conduct of the generals.

"One has only kept in the Vendée generals who have committed the greatest number of crimes. . . ."

After enumerating some of the crimes committed, he continued: "It is time to tell the truth—the war in the Vendée has only been rekindled by the horrors which have been committed in this country.

"The state of the Vendée is not alarming for the Republic—but men covered with blood, men whose crimes have remained unpunished, have organised the war. The principal of these men is Turreau, the commander-in-chief."

After describing some of the horrors, he said: "Under the eyes of what Representatives do you think all that passed? One blames Hentz and Francastel. Soldiers were allowed to put on the points of their bayonets children of one or two months old."

"Turreau," he said, "ordered several communes to unite at one spot, and when they were assembled he had them all shot regardless of age or sex."

(The Convention manifested the greatest indignation.)

"I told the Committee of Public Safety, but it would not listen to me" (*il ne m'a pas écouté*).

And he read a letter from Saumur in praise of the new Representatives there, contrasting them with former ones—"those great shearers of heads (*ces grands coupeurs de tête*) who shouted like lunatics and pretended to see in every direction crowds of aristocrats."

The Convention ordered the arrest of Turreau, Huché, and Grignon.

The disclosures at the trial of the Nantais so deeply implicated the members of the Revolutionary Committee of Nantes that the authorities were compelled to put them on their trial.

And so, about a month later, Goullin, Chaux, Bachelier, and the rest of them, appeared in the dock, not a little indignant at being called to account.

Goullin and Chaux declaring: " It is not enough to bring charges against us in a body (*de nous inculper en général*), to throw odious suspicions upon the members of the Committee collectively : it is necessary to articulate precise facts, and to bring authentic proofs in support of the wrongs (*griefs*)."

And they had their wish. Precise facts were articulated, authentic proofs were piled one on the top of another, till a great part of their iniquities was driven home. Witness after witness, whose mouth had been sealed by terror, now came forward, each proving the horrors already described, and day after day the flood flowed, and the horror grew.

And as the trial went on, and the prisoners' position became more desperate owing to the accumulation of proofs against them, Carrier's presence was demanded by them, Goullin declaring that all the crimes which had been committed were by Carrier's orders, and that the Committee was but a passive instrument of his orders and his fury.

But it was not as a witness that Carrier had to appear. The evidence which had been given was such that the *gradin* (or dock), and not the witness-box, was his destination.

Not, however, until after a long debate in the Convention as to whether a member of the Convention, and a Representative, should be subjected to legal proceedings, and after a commission of twenty-one members had considered and reported on his case, and then further debates upon their report.

And then this man, who, at Nantes and in the Vendée, had set aside all forms of law, who was so impatient of them that he condemned people without any form of trial even, did his very utmost to avail himself of all the forms of legal procedure, to throw difficulties in the way of his trial, and claiming among other things "an unbiassed jury." He even urged sickness as a plea for procrastination.

When at last compelled to defend himself before the tribunal, he denied some of his crimes, pleaded ignorance of some of the others; or, when the proof was too clear and overwhelming, he admitted them, but threw the responsibility of his acts on the Convention.

" I informed the Convention that brigands were being shot by the hundred. It applauded the letter, and ordered its insertion in the Bulletin,"—a statement which was true.

His main justification, however, was the decree of the 1st August 1793, and that bloodthirsty and merciless proclamation of the Convention of the 1st October, which had declared that "it is necessary that the brigands of the Vendée be exterminated before the end of the month of October."

" For himself, he had only executed the decrees of the National Convention, which put *hors la loi* all the enemies of the people."

There was no symptom of madness in his defence, nor in his conduct during the trial; nothing more than the fury to be expected from any scoundrel who finds the tables at last turned, and he himself in imminent danger of unexpected punishment.

This defence did not serve him, nor did the plea of " purity of intentions," which so often afforded the means of escape to criminals of his sort. The jury gave its verdict. He was convicted of having given unlimited powers to members of the Marat Company, of having sent to death certain prisoners without trial, and of several other of the charges brought against him; and

on the 16th December was sentenced to death—he
and Grandmaison and Pinard — who had massacred
men, women, and children, and who based his ferocity
on an order he said he had received "to spare
nothing."

These three were convicted, and no more; and a few
hours afterwards—so far as the death of each could be
a penalty for countless murders each had committed—
they each paid it.

The other members of the Committee—even Goullin,
Chaux, Bachelier, and Jolly, the *garrotteur par excellence
des prisonniers*—escaped the guillotine. They were found
guilty of most of the crimes charged against them: but,
" not having done these things with criminal or counter-
revolutionary intentions," they were acquitted, and forthwith released.

How preposterous this result of the trial was, is
evidenced by the fact that so much indignation was expressed in Paris, and in the Convention, that they were
re-arrested. But there it ended: for though in the
following April their trial at Angers was ordered, it
never came off, and so they all escaped practically scot-
free.

Revolutionary justice seemed, in fact, to consider that
it had fulfilled all its duties in making Carrier and two
of his accomplices scapegoats for the crimes of the herd of
sans-culotte brutes who had participated in their crimes,
or had perpetrated other similar ones.

And French historians have followed very much the
lead thus given. By making Carrier notorious, and by
thrusting him into as conspicuous a position as possible,
the inference has been suggested that he was an exceptional product of the Revolution.

And the Convention, in putting him on his trial, is

supposed to have cleared itself from any reproach of
sanctioning such atrocities.

The theory, though plausible, is absolutely untenable.
Infamous as he was, there was practically nothing to distinguish him from the regular sans-culotte type, which
was as infamous and cruel as himself when it got the
chance.

But though Carrier's plea of obedience to superior
orders is an extenuation of some of his acts, it can never
be an exculpation.

It is true to a great extent that he acted under the
general, if not precise, instructions of the Committee of
Public Safety, and of the Convention, and that they were
fully aware of most of his proceedings at Nantes, and did
not stop them till the work they had sent him to do had
practically been accomplished.

" *Il a fallu cela à Nantes* " (" That had to be done at
Nantes "), Robespierre is reported to have remarked
when complaint was once made to him of Carrier's
iniquities.

As Carrier himself said in the Convention, when
addressing it for the last time, " *Tout ici est coupable,
jusqu'à la sonnette du Président.*"

Nor was any effort to punish him made during the
many months he was in Paris after his recall, where he
lived, as he himself said, " in the sweet satisfaction of
having rendered the greatest services to the patrie."
On the contrary, he was well received by the Convention,
and was appointed first secretary to it, and performed the
functions of that office under the presidency of Robespierre.

And though it is impossible to exonerate or acquit
him on such a plea, the main blame for such infamies as
he perpetrated must fall on the system of government
which used the services of men such as he was, which

connived at their abominations, and which profited by their iniquities.

It is, in fact, the Republican Government, as then constituted in France, which primarily was stained by the acts of its chosen servant, and which ultimately must bear the responsibility for his crimes, and for the crimes of other of its servants, military and civilian, who fell little if at all short of him in every quality that can disgrace humanity.

But, at the same time, his career in the Vendée was another illustration of how the Revolution worked out in actual practice, and another proof of the true nature of the *brave républicain*, the *vrai sans-culotte*, when left free, of his true character, when, unchecked and uncontrolled, he was able to give effect to his theories and his ideas, and able to go his own way.

While the trial of the Revolutionary Committee was proceeding, the popular society of Angers denounced Hentz and Francastel, and Choudieu's name was added to the denunciation — "to the end that the National Convention may be informed of all the evils which the country has suffered, and know those who caused them."

Thus murder was coming out, not only as to Nantes but also as to Angers.

The public disclosure in Paris of the horrors committed in Nantes and in the Vendée gave a great impulse towards a milder treatment of the Vendeans. "People in the Convention only spoke of humanity and justice"; and the Representatives in the west, sensible of this change of feeling, were active in inaugurating and even pressing on the Convention a policy of conciliation.

And as they moved about their districts they released a large number of unfortunate prisoners.

Their reports show the classes of people who were

victimised and tyrannised over by the patriots and sans-
culottes—show therefore the classes who were dealt with
by the Military Commissions and Revolutionary Tribunals,
and who afforded the material for the guillotinings and
noyades and fusillades by the revolutionists.

At Angers more than 500 were released — small
farmers, day labourers, and artisans.  At Saumur 83
citizens and citizenesses, all artisans, labourers, and workmen, " who are detained for no reason " (*détenu sans aucun
motif*).

At Fontenay " more than 400 prisoners groaning
this long time past in irons have been released.  We
have given liberty to all those who appeared to be
victims of intrigue or passion, and whose infirmities or
old age could justify, on the ground of humanity, the
mitigation of the severity of measures of safety, to all
labourers, artisans, workmen, tradesmen, and fathers of
the defenders of the patrie."

And on the 5th December Bezard wrote : " I have
released from the prisons at Nantes all the unfortunates
who were there detained *sans motifs*, the greater part
workmen and agriculturists, also about sixty ex-nobles
whose only crime was their birth."

This was nearly ten months after Carrier's recall
from Nantes.  Truly revolutionary mercy worked but
slowly.

Still slower was it in reaching Rochefort.  Here it
was on the 12th January 1795 that Blutel, the Representative, wrote : " I have just ordered the release of 300
Vendeans who were in irons, who claim the benefit of
the amnesty."

In the latter part of November the idea of an amnesty
to the Vendeans gained ground.

On the 1st December certain deputies of the Vendée

and Deux-Sèvres presented to the Committee of Public Safety an *exposé* of the situation, and of the measures which they considered best calculated for terminating the war.

" There are two lines to take," they wrote. " One is to exterminate the last inhabitant of the country. . . . The Convention has never wished that." (It would have been truer to state that it had tried it and failed.) " The other is to listen to the voice of humanity, to show indulgence, and to conquer these Departments by persuasion rather than by arms. But this course must be accompanied by real and imposing forces. Military order and discipline must be enforced, because the conduct of the generals and Military Commissions has made more partisans to royalism than fanaticism has done."

On the 2nd December the Convention approved the conclusions of this *exposé*, and made a decree that all persons known under the name of rebels who surrendered their arms within the period of a month would be neither disturbed nor called to account for the fact of their having taken part in the revolt.

It was, in fact, an amnesty ; and as it drew no distinction between the chiefs and the soldiers, it was an amnesty to all.

Simultaneously with making the decree the Convention issued a proclamation to those who had taken part in the revolts in the west. " There remains for you an asylum in the national generosity. Yes, your brothers, the entire French people, wish to believe you as more misled than culpable. Its arms are extended towards you, and the National Convention pardons you in its name if you deposit your arms, and if repentance and sincere friendship lead you back to it. Its word is sacred, and if faithless delegates have abused its confidence and yours, justice shall be done."

It is indeed strange how extraordinarily blind the Convention was to the truth of their proclamation in a different sense from that which they meant.

" For two years," the Convention said, " your countries have been the prey of the horrors of war. These fertile climes, which nature seemed to have destined to be the abode of happiness, have become places of proscription and carnage. . . . Fire has devoured the habitations, and the earth, covered with ruins and cypress, refuses to those who remain the livelihood of which it was so prodigal. Such, O Frenchmen! are the grievous wounds which pride and imposture have inflicted on the country."

It was true — every word of it; but the evils described were the handiwork of the republicans themselves; the pride was the pride of the sans-culotte, who professed to believe that his own gospel was the only true one; and the imposture was the imposture of the revolutionist, who was the absolute antithesis of all his professions of liberty, equality, and fraternity.

# CHAPTER XXIX

## VENDEAN VICTORY

THE amnesty decreed on the 2nd December 1794, though helping towards a settlement of the difficulties in the Vendée, was not sufficient to induce the Vendean chiefs to end their opposition to the Republic, or to give their consent to their troops doing so. Thus to have ended the strife would have been to sacrifice the objects for which the appeal to arms had been made.

But both the republicans and the Vendean chiefs were feeling the pressure of circumstances which made them anxious to come to some satisfactory settlement; and, first, overtures were made, and then negotiations entered into between them.

Nantes was almost at starvation point; at times having scarcely a day's food in the city for the people, and scarcely any forage for the horses, which were dying of starvation; and not only Nantes, but several of the smaller towns in and around the Vendée, and even some of the larger communes were almost without food, and supplies were almost impossible to obtain. And the Vendeans, though they had food enough, had scarcely any gunpowder or other material of war left    not

30 lbs., it was said, over and above the few cartridges which some of the men had.

The impulse towards a settlement came from the Government in Paris; and a Commission of Representatives, under the presidency of Ruelle, took up its abode at Nantes with the object of arranging matters.

And then began the revolutionary *débâcle*. Decision after decision, proclamation after proclamation, decree after decree followed each other: all made, endorsed, or approved by the National Convention, which, with its predecessors the Constituent and the Legislative Assemblies, had caused the evils which it was now sought to remedy : all acknowledging out of the mouths of the revolutionists and republicans themselves in the clearest and most precise terms the outrageous despotism—the infamous cruelties--the shameful persecution which under the name of "liberty, equality, and fraternity" they had subjected their countrymen to.

The negotiations began with Charette--Stofflet, who had quarrelled with him, taking no part in them.

On the 2nd January (1795) the Representatives issued a proclamation informing the Vendeans of the amnesty, and of the conditions on which the past would be forgotten, and their re-entrance into the great French family would be allowed.

" For too long has blood flowed in your unhappy countries. Let the carnage cease--let your country re-take in the Republic the position it never should have quitted. . . . Let us stop the effusion of blood—let brothers no longer massacre each other. Your chiefs are included in the amnesty.

" What motives except pride and imposture can any one give you to check the execution of this beneficial law ?

"Your cottages are burned. We will aid you to rebuild them. Our own hands shall construct them with you.

"Your lands are uncultivated. We will give you help; animals, harness, ploughs.

"The arms are wanting to make your fields valuable. . . . We will leave you for the purpose the young men of the requisition; and if your children who for the love of the patrie flew to the frontiers are necessary to enable you to repair your misfortunes, they will be restored to you.

"Your manufactures are destroyed. We will procure you the means of restarting them."

It was, in a way, an abject appeal, and its contrition would have made it pathetic, but contrition could not obliterate the awful past.

For there were some things beyond the power of the Representatives, or even of the Convention.

They could not give back to the Vendée the unnumbered thousands who had been deliberately butchered by the republicans. They could not call back to life again the victims of republican tyranny and persecution, whose blood still stained the land, and whose graves still formed high mounds of newly-turned soil. They could not re-create the happy homes which had been broken up and destroyed with every form of atrocity which revolutionary passion could devise. They could not give back to heart-broken men and women their wives, husbands, and children, nor restore the countless families swept from the face of the earth. These were things beyond remedy or alleviation, irrevocable, which could never be undone, however full an *amende* the Government was now willing to make.

The Representatives in their negotiations and efforts

to win over the Vendeans had to reiterate over and over
again their sincerity ; for previous violations of republican
promises were too vivid in Vendean minds and too base
to have been forgotten.   It was humiliating, but necessary,
and those very protestations are proof and admission of
their previous deceptions.

"This law is no make-believe amnesty. . . . Do not
distrust it.    Ah, do not doubt French loyalty and
generosity. . . . No.    Frenchmen do not doubt the
sincerity of the amnesty which is offered them."

And to give greater effect and emphasis, the proclamation was posted up in public places to the sound of
drum and trumpet.

In Nantes a great function gave weight to the
declaration.    The Representatives, at the head of the
constituted authorities, and in presence of the garrison
and a great crowd of people, solemnly proclaimed the
amnesty, after a salvo of twenty-one guns, and amidst
enthusiastic cheering.

By mutual agreement between the Vendeans and
republicans hostilities were suspended for a month, and
the time was turned to account in making arrangements
for a conference.   There was not over much time to
spare.    "In the country the leaves will come," wrote
Lofficial, the Representative, "and you know how very
difficult then the war is in this country."

The preliminaries were at last settled, and on the 12th
February the conference took place in a large tent, at a
place called la Jaunaye, near Nantes on the road to
Clisson.

The ten Representatives came, accompanied by the
principal military officers of Nantes and an escort of
cavalry and infantry.   Charette also, with a large cavalry
escort and many officers.

Lofficial has left a description of these redoubtable warriors :—

" All his officers had large white belts, and plumes of the same colour. Charette, in a flesh-coloured coat *(veste)* trimmed with red and facings *à fleurs-de-lys*. At the end of his belt a large piece of black lace : on the left side of his coat an embroidered medallion enclosing an embroidered crucifix with this motto, *Vous qui plaignez, considérez Mes souffrances*—' You who complain, consider My sufferings.' In his hat a plume of green, black, and white feathers, with two rows of gold braid. The other chiefs each wore a small gold cross on their left side."

The Representatives sat at one side of the table, Charette and his chief officers at the other, and the conference began.

And, as in one's mind's eye one views this scene, what a descent it was from those lofty heights of republicanism which the true revolutionist had paraded before the people as the true revolutionary ideal : what a departure from those standards of revolutionary morality which the *vrai sans-culotte* had set up, the great Republic no longer dictating to its rebellious children, but through its Representatives humbly treating with their chiefs, entertaining the demands of "fanatics" who were championing an "abominable and accursed superstition," holding converse with the upholders of a vile and detested royalty, tolerating "their mephitic presence," and making concessions to those for whose iniquities a short time before no punishment was deemed adequate.

For six days the conference continued, the republicans meanwhile entertaining the Vendean chiefs with princely hospitality.

Finally, on the 17th an agreement was arrived at, the terms of peace were settled.

On the Vendean side the concession made was their submission to and recognition of the Republic—not a very great concession considering how little during the long and costly strife the royalist party had done to aid them; considering too that they had lived under the Republic for some time before the outbreak took place, and that in reality the free exercise of their religion was the first object of their appeal to arms.

On the republican side short of this one thing—everything for which the Vendeans had fought was conceded. The young men of the first requisition were left in their homes. For a certain number of years the Vendeans were to be exempted from compulsory military service; but what was even of greater importance was the decision that the churches were to be reopened, and even the refractory priests were to be allowed to officiate in all parishes where the patriots were not in a majority.

The settlement was embodied in a set of five decrees made by the Representatives at Nantes on the 17th February. But in a way more important even than the settlement arrived at was the avowal made by the revolutionary Representatives as to the responsibility for the war, and for all its attendant horrors. In the preamble of the decrees it was written :—

"Considering that the Departments of the west have been devastated for two years by a disastrous war, that the troubles which agitate them have their origin in the closing of the temples and the interruption of the peaceable exercise of all worship whatever:

"That the men, the authors of these evils and these disorders, are those who wished to plunge France into anarchy, and who, by persecution, sought to establish a special worship (*un culte particulier*) of which they wished themselves to be the pontiffs: that these anarchists, after having audaciously violated the rights of man, have been reached by the sword of the law ;

"Considering that the National Convention never intended to prohibit any form of worship (*n'a jamais entendu interdire*) : that by Article 7 of the Declaration of the Rights of Man and the Act of the Constitution it, on the contrary, authorised the peaceable exercise of worship; the Representatives decree :

"I. That every individual, every section whatever of citizens, may exercise freely and peaceably their worship.

"II. The individuals and ministers of all forms of worship are not to be troubled, disturbed, or proceeded against on account of the free, peaceful, and indoor exercise of their worship."

And, by another decree, they directed that the insurgent chiefs and inhabitants of the Vendée, by virtue of their submission to the Republic, should be free from all *recherches* for the past, and should enter once more into their property. Indemnity was to be given to the people for their losses, and help to enable them to rebuild their houses, re-establish agriculture, and restart trade.

The young men of the requisition were to remain in the Vendée to re-establish agriculture, and make commerce flourish.

On the same day that the Representatives made their decree, a declaration was made by Charette and his principal officers :

"We have felt that we were Frenchmen, that the general good of our country should alone animate us: and it is under the influence of these sentiments that we declare solemnly to the National Convention, and to the whole of France, that we submit ourselves to the Republic one and indivisible, that we acknowledge its laws, and that we undertake the formal engagement not to make any attack against it. . . .

"We make the solemn engagement never to bear arms against the Republic."

And a short time later, as some of Charette's officers, discontented with the peace, were endeavouring to excite fresh troubles, he and three others issued an address to the inhabitants of the Vendée explaining to them fully what had been done and won.

"The peaceable exercise of your religion is accorded to you: you can use this imprescriptible right with security. . . . You are free from this moment to offer to the Supreme Being, in accordance with your ancient usages, your homage and your gratitude. . . .

"The National Convention contracts to-day to indemnify you for your losses, and to repair, if it is possible, all the evils caused by a régime of proscription and injustice."

To duly, formally, and publicly mark the fact of peace having been established, a great military and official function was again held at Nantes. The Representatives, the generals of the army of the west, Charette, and the Vendean chiefs, in one great procession, entered Nantes, to the music of military bands, the salvos of artillery, and the cheers of the crowds. The city was filled with joy and resounded to the cries of "Vive la République!" "Vive la Convention Nationale!" "Vive l'union!" and there was a state dinner given by the Representatives to the Vendean chiefs, and a gala spectacle; and the next day the city was *en fête*, and a ball was given, and Charette was greeted with cries of "Vive le héros et le pacificateur de la Vendée!"

He and the Vendean chiefs paid a visit also to the

popular society, where they were received with "fraternal acclamations."

At the same time the Representatives issued a proclamation to the inhabitants of the Departments—beginning it with familiar words which excited such joy in the Convention in previous years, when that august body thought that the Vendée had been destroyed. Now, however, they bore a different sense.

"There is no longer a Vendée, the Departments of the west re-enter the bosom of the Republic. Its unity and indivisibility have just been recognised by the chiefs of the Vendean army."

It was a great triumph for the Vendeans to have extracted from the Representatives the admissions as to where the responsibility for the war lay, but it was as nothing to that gained by extracting a similar declaration from the National Convention itself.

About a fortnight later (on the 14th March) the National Convention itself, the walls of whose chamber had time after time resounded with awful imprecations and maledictions against the Vendeans and all their works—with cruel and bloodthirsty decrees against these enemies of the country—the National Convention decreed unanimously that it approved these decrees of its Representatives—approved them with their account of the causes of the war, namely, the closing of the temples, and the interruption of the peaceable exercise of worship.

Not many weeks later Stofflet, together with his principal officers, gave their adhesion to the terms of the pacification accepted by Charette, and on the 2nd May they signed at St. Florent their formal assent.

And the decrees consequent thereon were in identically the same terms as those at la Jaunaye, and once more the Convention converted into law the decrees of its Representatives, and in so doing once more reiterated its condemnation of its own previous action.

Thus all sections of the Vendeans had come to terms with the Republic, and the war for a time was over.

Republicans have claimed the peace of la Jaunaye as a triumph, and from one point of view it was so, for the Vendeans made their submission to the Republic.

But the triumph was an empty one, for the Vendeans had been republicans till they had been driven out of the Republic by republican tyranny, and to get them back in diminished numbers into the republican fold afforded little ground for boasting.

The real victory lay with the Vendeans; for they won back the essentials of religious liberty. That they should pay their own ministers, and that service should be indoors, and that no emblems should be publicly displayed, were small matters, so long as they could worship and were allowed to have their own ministers.

Over and above this, however, there was another triumph, and it is this which is of abiding importance.

They wrung from the Republican Government, through the acts of its Representatives and the decrees of the Convention, the confession, that revolutionary and republican legislation and administration were the first cause of the Vendean war.

In adopting, approving, and giving the force of law to the decrees of the Representatives, it placed on record in the clearest terms a positive refutation of the contentions of the revolutionary writers who, both before and since, have lauded the Revolution and all its works in the Vendée, and have cursed the counter-revolutionists and all their works.

It acknowledged that "the troubles which had

agitated the Departments of the west had their origin
in the closing of the temples and the interruption of the
peaceable exercise of all worship whatever."

It acknowledged that the rights of man had been
" audaciously violated."

It acknowledged that there had been " persecution."

Manifestly, therefore, the contention of revolutionary
writers from the time of the Revolution down to the
present day, namely, that those troubles had their origin
in the machinations of the noblesse and the intrigues of
a fanatical priesthood, is wholly false and untrue.

Manifestly, too, as the closing of the temples and
other acts of persecution were the acts of the Revolutionary Government, the whole onus of responsibility for
the Vendean war, with its ruin and bloodshed, and the
whole shame and infamy of the revolutionary proceedings and actions in the Vendee, lie on the Republic.

And precluding any argument as to this acknowledgment being only words, there is the decree of the
Convention that indemnity was to be given to the
people for their losses, and help to enable them to start
afresh.

It was a tremendous avowal for the Convention to
make, for it was an absolute exculpation of the Vendeans,
and an inculpation of the Revolutionary Government, not
merely of Robespierre and his colleagues, but of the
National Assembly, of the National Legislative Assembly,
and of the National Convention itself.

And coming from the body which had directed and
enacted the vast portion of the measures of revolutionary
tyranny, there is no going behind it.

To have, out of the mouth of the Convention itself,
the verdict " guilty " in the charges brought against the
revolutionary Republic is decisive.

Here then we may stop, as the peace made between the Vendeans and the republicans is practically the end of the period in which the true character and unfettered nature of the revolutionist are best studied. Subsequent events throw little or no further light thereon, nor do they alter the ineradicable records of accomplished facts.

In connection with the Vendeans, however, there are just a few incidents more which are of interest, and bring their history also to the end of a definite period.

Not long after the peace of la Jaunaye and the peace of St. Florent, differences once more arose between the Vendean leaders and the Government. Indeed, actual peace and quiet had not been realised even for a brief period, for the country had remained in a disturbed and restless state. The excitement entailed by the war could not quickly be allayed, nor could fierce passions quickly cool; there were many desperate men left who were so habituated to a life of violence, and so dependent on war for their livelihood, that they could not settle down to peaceful ways.

And there were robberies, and assassinations, and violence, and small armed bodies of wandering pillagers, and disturbance in many parts of the country: and it soon became apparent that the peace was little more than a mock peace.

And then some of the Vendean leaders—Charette himself included—either impelled by royalist pressure, or unable to restrain their more violent followers, violating the oath they had taken not to bear arms again against the Republic, again took to arms: and, on the 25th June, once more raised the standard of revolt, and without giving any notice attacked and captured the republican camp of "des Essarts," and inflicted a loss of some 50 to 100 men on the republicans.

Once more there was months of fighting, now, however, on a very much smaller scale.

And while the fighting was going on there occurred one episode which has added deep pathos to this final stage of the struggle. He for whose leadership the Vendeans had been beseeching, he in whose cause they had been so valiantly warring, came, saw, and made the great refusal.

The Count d'Artois, the brother of the titular King of France, embarked on an English frigate, the *Jason*, and reached the Ile d'Yeu on the 2nd October.

Four leagues off was the continent where Charette awaited him—Charette who some months previously had received a letter from the Regent (now the titular King), dated 1st February, which had taken nearly five months reaching him—an effusive letter:

"At last I can communicate direct with you. I can tell you of my admiration, of my gratitude, of the ardent desire I have to join you, to partake your perils and your glory. I shall fulfil my desire, even if it should cost me all my blood."

He had not come, could not come, but his brother had, and was there, within sight and reach of France. But "this magnanimous prince," as Charette in his illusionment had called him, unable to gather courage, to risk one drop of his blood, after weeks of hesitation, gave up the idea, and sailed away for England, well deserving the scornful, scathing, contemptuous, condemnation which Charette wrote of him to Louis XVIII.:—

"Sire, the cowardice of your brother has lost everything. His return to England has decided our fate. In a little while nothing will remain for us but to perish uselessly for your service."

And perish he soon did. The struggle was disastrous

for those of the Vendeans who still were in arms; disastrous for Stofflet, who was captured and shot; disastrous, too, for Charette, the leader of a hundred fights, for he, too, was captured and condemned, and one afternoon in March 1796, on the small Place at Nantes now known as the Place Viarme, he, with unbound eyes, bravely faced the firing party, and gave the signal for the shots which ended his stormy and courageous career.

But the new campaign did not last long. The skilful hand of Hoche quelled any further resistance; the essential had, moreover, been already conceded by the Republic—religious liberty—and once more comparative peace resigned.

It is but right that tribute should be paid to the Vendean people for the splendid struggle they had made, and for their victory.

Hundreds of the Vendeans during the war performed feats as valorous as any ever recorded in other wars; thousands of them faced and met death in the battlefield as courageously as the most disciplined soldier, or as the most valiant knight ever did; and thousands, women as well as men, were as genuine martyrs for their faith as were those early Christians who fought the wild beasts in the Roman arena. Nor were their trials, their sufferings, their deaths in vain. They were victorious in the cause for which they really fought, that of religious liberty; and against them all the power and tyranny of the Revolutionary Government did not prevail.

# CHAPTER XXX

THE picture which has been presented in the previous
pages of the French revolutionist, he who was acclaimed
by himself and his associates as " the good," " the pure,"
" the brave republican," and " the true sans-culotte," is
the picture of him in the plenitude of his powers, in the
full flower of his existence, in the days of his uncontrolled liberty, when his instincts and his passions had
full, free, and unchecked play, and when he showed his
real self. And painted as it is by himself and his
comrades, the picture is there for a wondering world
to contemplate, a sign and portent to the end of time.

So wrapt up was he in his own glory, so proud was
he of all his sayings and doings, so confident that men
would take him at his own valuation, that tyranny could
be passed off as liberty, and fratricide as fraternity, that
he was reckless in displaying qualities, and performing
acts which the world and posterity might not judge in
quite the way he expected.

A few touches are still required to complete the
picture, for one phase of his character has not yet been
touched on, the phase of his adversity.

In the Vendée he showed himself as what is

familiarly known as "a poor creature," always blaming other people for his own ignorance, blunders, and misdeeds. "Nous sommes trahis" (we are betrayed), shouted the soldier as he bolted from the field of battle, the only betrayal or treason being his own in running away. "We are starved," said the sans-culotte, the starvation being the result of the reck-less destruction of corn and food by himself and his comrades, or his absurd interference with the great laws of supply and demand. "We are stricken with plague," he said, and the infection which laid him low was the result of his own inhumanities, the overcrowding of his prisoners in the republican pest-houses, or the imperfect burial of his victims.

Some men, however atrocious their lives and acts, succeed in winning a certain measure of admiration by presenting a bold front in their adversity, and by their faithful adherence to their principles when circumstances change and go against them. But not many of the revolutionists were of this metal. The moment the measure they had meted out to thousands was meted out to themselves they whined.

Chaux, for instance, a prominent member of the Revolutionary Committee of Nantes who had actively helped and participated in the perpetration of many of the horrors which have been described, when arrested, howled over his ill-treatment, his imprisonment, his being torn from his family, his being put in irons, his being put in a carriage already full, reduced to beg some clothes, having been only allowed five minutes to change his shirt, proscribed, dragged before the tribunal of blood, his being thrown on a handful of straw, devoured by insects, living in a place intended for the enemies of his country, groaning under false accusations which confounded him with assassins, which presented him as a cannibal, as a false patriot gorged with gold and crimes, covered with the blood of his fellow-citizens.

He is so overcome by his reflections that he says:

"At this thought the pen falls, at the recollections of my sufferings my ideas become troubled and confused." But it was only his own sufferings which he thought of, those of the thousands he had made endure a crueller lot, a worse fate, were ignored.

Goullin, who, while in power, had violated every form of law, and jeered at the sufferings of his victims, complained indignantly of what he considered the violation of the forms of law in his treatment, and of his being confined in a prison intended for the greatest scoundrels, as if it were not an appropriate place for him.

The gentle Carrier was so aggrieved by being called a tyrant, that he exclaimed, "How harassing it is to me to be called a tyrant!"

History has rather generally attributed the responsibilities of the horrors of the French Revolution to one individual—Robespierre—but gradually it has been recognised that he was by no means the sole culprit; that the disease was far more widespread, more deep-seated in the French constitution; and that there were countless willing hands in all this horrible work.

And history, too, has attributed all the horrors at Nantes and in the west to Carrier, and pinned him down as the culprit.

It would naturally be consolatory to a great and high-spirited nation thus to limit the number of its infamous sons; but facts do not fit in with the theory.

In Nantes, Carrier was by no means the only culprit; nor at Angers was Francastel the only culprit; nor were these two Representatives the only culprits among the Representatives who ruled in the Vendée. Bourbotte, Choudieu, Hentz, Esnau Lavallée, Prieur (de la Marne), in many ways ran them close. Nantes, Angers, and Saumur, and all the towns in or around the Vendée, were inundated with "apostles of carnage." Revolutionary Committees, Revolutionary Tribunals, Military Commissions, popular societies, sans-culotte generals and revolutionary tyrants were everywhere; all of these throwing themselves heart and soul into the most horrible measures of oppression, cruelty, and bloodshed: civilians and military vying with each other in revolutionary energy, in deeds of atrocity, scrambling for plunder, regardless whether it was taken from friend or foe, and revelling in the proceeds.

And then, when brought to book for their infamies, they all tried to throw the blame and responsibility on some one else than themselves, instead of boldly avowing their handiwork, as really sincere and conscientious men engaged in a great and good cause would have done.

The military despots defended themselves by the plea of the necessity of military obedience. Turreau, the commander-in-chief, the chief of them, pleaded the decrees of the Committee of Public Safety and the Convention. The Revolutionary Committees pleaded the necessity of obedience to the orders of the Representatives, and the Representatives sheltered themselves under the necessity of carrying out the policy imposed upon them by the Committee of Public Safety and the Convention.

This left the responsibility altogether on the shoulders of the Convention; but it evaded most of it by asserting that things had been done without its orders or approval, or even its knowledge.

And so, as it worked out, no one was to blame.

As to some of the most notorious cases, the Convention loudly announcing that "Justice was to be the order of the day," made a show of energetically pursuing some of those who committed the atrocities, but its energy did not carry it very far.

Its conscience was appeased by a few small concessions. It delivered Carrier up to justice. It ordered the arrest of a few Representatives who had been denounced to it, Hentz and Francastel among the number; and so that there might be material for the proper consideration of the matter, it decreed that the correspondence of the Representatives with the Committee of Public Safety and their reports should be printed. The reports never were printed, however.

It ordered the arrest of Turreau and a very few of the most notorious of his generals of "infernal column" fame; and as the basis of an indictment against them it ordered that a report should be made to it by the Committee of Public Safety as to the conduct of the generals and the acts of the Military Commissions.

A prolonged inquiry was made as to the horrors which had been committed, the testimony of numerous witnesses was taken in different localities, a great mass of evidence collected, but the result never saw the light of day, and the report never appeared either.

Evidently, the reputation of the *vrai républicain*, such as it was, could not have stood the weight of such an *exposé*. A full disclosure would have been too terrible, the iniquities narrated too appalling for ears to hear or eyes to read, the injury to republican government too overwhelming; and so the 1200 documents which were collected, describing some of the infamies and cruelties which had been committed, were buried in the secrecy of the vaults of the Republic. They would be thrilling and instructive reading were they now published.

And with the exception of Carrier and his gang, the few culprits who had been singled out were not even put on their trial. They were kept in custody—that was all. And then, as the existence of the Convention drew to an end, that august body, frightened at the number of culprits who, if there was any justice under a Republic, ought to be tried, and possibly with misgivings as to its own share in the nefarious business, wishing, in ending its labours, to throw a veil over all its own transgressions and iniquities, decided on a dying deed of dazzling generosity and forgiveness, and forgave itself.

On the 26th October 1795 (4 Brumaire, An iv.), the last day of its existence, it passed a law giving amnesty to all those who in their acts relating to the Revolution had overstepped the limits of their duties (*étaient sortis des bornes des devoirs*)—a form of condemnation—so mild as to amount to approval, and all proceedings against such persons were extinguished and destroyed.

And so Hentz, and Francastel, and Huché, and Grignon, and the rest of them, men steeped in every iniquity, and saturated with the blood of innocent men, women, and children, were released from prison, and the authoritative revelation of their crimes, which would have brought disgrace and infamy on the Convention itself, was obviated.

And the sponge of revolutionary oblivion was passed across the slate on which were written in blood the records of the atrocities, the injustices, the crimes of the whole revolutionary crew of Military Commissioners, Revolutionary Committees, Maratist Companies, soldiers, generals, and Representatives.

!Turreau, with diplomatic effrontery, refused to avail himself of the amnesty, and insisted on being put on his trial. On the 19th December 1795 he was tried by the

Military Council sitting at Paris, and whitewashed; the Council unanimously declaring that "all the charges *inculpations*' against him were unfounded and calumnious, and that he had worthily performed his duties *rempli ses fonctions*' in the said command as a soldier and citizen"—a decision which in downright moral obliquity has only a parallel in that passed by Hentz and Francastel upon Guy Martinière.

And in later years this *vrai sans-culotte*, the organiser and commander-in-chief of the " infernal columns," passed on into employment under the Emperor, and then under the erstwhile detested Bourbon royalty, against which he had fought, accepting honours and decorations from both; and in the train of royalty, as Lieutenant-General of the army of the King, and Chevalier of St. Louis, once more revisiting the Vendée, the scene of his infamies.

And so, out of the vast numbers of evildoers but an infinitesimal few were brought to account for their iniquities.

One can almost count on one's fingers the number of those who suffered the extreme penalty of the law for their crimes.

Carrier, Grandmaison, Pinard, Lamberty, Fouquet, Martinière, and a few others. But what are they among so many who deserved the same fate?

Some few suffered a short imprisonment, awaiting a trial which never took place, but the great bulk of them escaped all punishment whatever.

It has been the fashion to account for and palliate the crimes of the revolutionists by saying that they were mad.

Some excuse would, in charity, be devised to remove from the French character the stain of such fearful cruelties.

But there is little to confirm such a theory, whilst there is much to refute it. ·

Violent and extreme they were, but even if they were all mad, that does not exonerate the Republic as a form of Government which permitted madmen seizing possession of it, and governing.

There is, however, little sign of that motiveless irresponsibility of wickedness which is the mark of insanity.

For, when one examines the lives of the revolutionists as seen on the Vendean stage, one finds one object consistently running through all their evil deeds—the object of self; one finds their actions prompted by very common and base passions—greed, covetousness, lust; and by a very common ambition—the love of power, of fame, of position, of wealth: the desire for the means—*coûte que coûte*—of gratifying their appetites. These were their motives, these their incentives. Even patriotism, with which it has been sought to cover the multitude of their sins, had no share in their acts and objects,—nothing but self. Their high-flown professions of adoration of the great principles whose names they prostituted were nothing but cant.

No sooner did the opportunity offer than they did the very things themselves which they decried in others.

Carrier, Goullin, the whole of the Revolutionary Committees at Nantes and Angers and elsewhere, having pulled down all authorities, placed, or got themselves placed, in authority.

Having decried wealth as a crime, they appropriated as much as they could lay their hands on—wading through blood to get it.

Having decried luxury, they revelled in orgies of food and drink and lasciviousness.

2 E

Not one crime or sin committed by those whom they destroyed, but they themselves committed when they got the opportunity.

It was as if Lazarus had assassinated Dives on account of his self-indulgence and inhumanity, had seized on his wealth, had clothed himself in his fine robes, fared sumptuously every day, and then spurned the unfortunates who had taken his place at the gate, and posed to them as a redresser of evils, as a regenerator of mankind, as a true patriot.

But they did not content themselves with pulling down the aristocracy, the noblesse, the clergy, the wealthier section of the bourgeoisie; they fell upon the people, for plunder was to be got out of them too. Of the 200,000 persons destroyed in the Vendée, but an infinitesimal portion belonged to the upper and governing classes against whom the Revolution was made. Of the hundreds and thousands they robbed and plundered, only a small proportion belonged to the wealthier classes of society.

The people were the victims, the people in whose favour the Revolution was declared to be made.

The administrators of Roche-sur-Yon wrote once to Huché protesting against the actions of his soldiers, and urging in support of their protest the statement that "republicans do not pillage their friends and their brothers." This prevalent superstition could not have been put more tersely. The whole treatment of the Vendée, from the very inception of trouble downwards, proved that this was the one consistent thing the republicans did do—that that was in fact and effect the Revolution. The revolutionists could not stop, after appropriating the property of the noblesse and the Church, but they went on to pillage their friends and their brothers. And what is worse, they did not content themselves therewith, but went on to put them to death with every form of fiendish injustice and brutality they could devise or carry out. Mouthing incessantly about justice, they were the incarnation of the most outrageous injustice. Indeed from the highest executive authority in France, the Committee of Public Safety, backed by the Convention, down to the lowest private soldier in the ranks, the same spirit of injustice was rampant.

Here and there there were exceptions. A few of the Representatives had some sense of right and justice, had some feeling. Among the generals of the army also were several against whom no dishonourable charge can be brought—Biron, Marceau, Kleber, Savary, for instance. And here and there both officers and men, at the risk of their own lives even, showed that they were human, that they were made of better stuff than the regular revolutionist, but they were the exceptions.

The bulk, the vast bulk of the revolutionists as seen in the Vendée, were such as have been described.

A chance phrase often sums up a whole policy. N'y en a-t-il pas un plus scélérat ?" ("Isn't there a bigger scoundrel ?") Goullin is reported to have asked when enlisting the most debased, depraved, and blood-thirsty wretches who could be found for the Maratist corps of revolutionary fiends at Nantes.

That this was the guiding principle of revolutionists in authority is evidenced throughout the Vendean war. Carrier and Francastel and Hentz could only have been appointed to their important posts of Representative after a " No " to the question of the Committee of Public Safety, " Is there no bigger scoundrel ?" Rossignol, " the cherished child of the Revolution," " the eldest son of the Committee of Public Safety," and Turreau could only have

been appointed as commanders-in-chief after the same
question and the same answer; whilst as for them, and
the generals of divisions or of brigades such as Huché,
Grignon, Cordellier, and a host of others, members of
Revolutionary Committees such as Goullin, Vacheron, or
of Military Commissions such as Bignon, Félix,—" No, no:
humanity has reached its lowest, basest, most infamous
type; there are no greater scoundrels."

It is marvellous that the French Revolution should
have imposed on the world so long, but the explanation
is that its praises have been so vociferated and dinned into
the public ear by those whose work it was, or who had or
have an interest in keeping up the delusion, or by those
who have seen in it great "realities" and "verities"
which had no existence, that men have accepted what
the revolutionists told them as true—have taken the
revolutionists, in fact, at their own valuation. They
have taken those fellows at their word: they have
accepted their professions as genuine: they have accorded
to them all the honours of their being apostles of liberty
and equality and fraternity, as if they had been really so.

Whereas, in reality, the *vrai républicain* was the most
transparent impostor.

He filched from the Christianity which he derided
and persecuted and did his very utmost to destroy the
great principles of liberty and equality and fraternity,
and proceeded then to give to each his own selfish and
degraded interpretation.

And in and around the Vendée that interpretation is
seen actually at work.

The revolutionist is seen there through no disturbing,
distorting medium. He is seen as he really was—the
living lie to each of the three great cardinal principles

of the political creed which he professed, "Liberty,
equality, fraternity."

His idea of "liberty" was unrestrained licence for
himself to pillage, rape, rob, and murder with impunity,
and he acted on it. His idea of "equality" was to pull
down all authority, and to put himself in the places of
those he pulled down, and he acted on it. Whilst his
idea of "fraternity" is graven for ever in letters of blood
and fire throughout the Vendée.

"Justice" had no place in the new political motto,
for the French revolutionist had not the remotest idea of
what the word meant, or what the thing was.

The conclusion which emerges with the most absolute
clearness from the history of the Revolutionary Government in the west in those years is that the republican
form of government as then organised in France had the
very widest capacities for tyranny.

Every evil in the monarchical form of government
which the Revolution aimed at destroying was reproduced
in an intensified form under the Revolutionary Government.

Personal liberty was invaded in a more wholesale
manner and on a far larger scale than under the
monarchy. The right of anything even approaching fair
trial was completely ignored.

Freedom of expression could not have been more
rigorously suppressed.

Religious liberty was annihilated, and a republican
form of government showed that it was as capable of a
religious persecution as infamous as that which directed
the Massacre of St. Bartholomew, or as that of the Spanish
Inquisition.

The rights of property were systematically invaded
and set at naught.

All the rights of production, of manufactures, of commerce, of business dealing between man and man —everything, in fact, on which the industrial prosperity of a country depends—were broken in on and destroyed.

And over and above all there was no justice, only rampant and brutal injustice.

Everything that the freedom-loving, intelligent man struggles for, would give his life for—free thought, free speech, free worship, justice, security for life, security for property, these great blessings which are the highest object of true statesmanship to give to a people - were conspicuous by their absence under the revolutionary régime.

The fact, so plain and evident, so incontrovertible, is a crushing refutation of the laudation which has been so lavishly bestowed on the revolutionary cataclysm in France.

No rational people would risk a repetition of such sufferings or the occasion for such wrongdoing; no rational nation would wish to lay itself open to a repetition in its own body of the appalling horrors of the Revolution.

To attain ever nearer the Christian ideals of real liberty, equality, and fraternity will doubtless be the very high desire and ambition of many existing and future nations and races, but for those who wish to attain those ideals the French Revolution is a warning signal of the clearest, most portentous, character.

And just as ships sailing across the waters of the great deep see the light which tells them of danger and shipwreck, so in future ages will the great nations of the world in their voyage towards their unknown destinies see in the history of the crimes, and cruelties, and horror.

and terror of the French Revolution the warning light that there lie injustice, and tyranny, and inhumanity, and fratricide, and all those dangers and miseries which are the negation of the aims and desires of a civilised and intelligent people.

# APPENDIX

## LIST OF THE PRINCIPAL WORKS USED IN THIS BOOK

Anon.—La Loire vengée (Paris).

Babeuf, F. N.—Du système de dépopulation, etc. (Paris, 1795).
Bachelier, J. M.—Mémoire pour les acquittés (Angers, An iii.)
Baguenier-Desormeaux—Documents sur Noirmoutier (Vannes).
Baralère- Acte d'accusation contre Carrier (Paris, 1794).
Barruel, A.—Histoire du clergé pendant la révolution française (London, 1801).
Benaben, L. G.—Rapport (Angers, 1795).
Blordier-Langlois—Angers et le département de Maine-et-Loire de 1787-1830 (Angers, 1837).
Bonchamps, Madame de—Mémoires sur la Vendée de (London, 1823).
Boureier, Camille—Essai sur la terreur en Anjou (Angers, 1870).
Buchez, P.-J.-B., et P.-C. Roux—Histoire parlementaire de la révolution française (Paris, 1834-38).
Busserolle, Carré de—Les Vendéens à Thouars (Montsoreau, 1890).
   Massacre de 200 prisonniers (Tours, 1884).
   Souvenirs de la révolution, etc.

Carrier, J. B.—Rapport de la Commission des Vingt-un, etc. (Paris, An iii.)
Cavoleau, J. A.—Description du département de la Vendée (Nantes, 1818).
C***, Comte de—Séjour de dix mois en France (Londres, 1795).
Chardon, E. H.—Les Vendéens dans la Sarthe (Le Mans, 1869-72).
Charette—Correspondance secrète, etc. (Paris, 1799).
Chassin, Ch.-L.—La préparation de la guerre de Vendée (Paris, 1892).
   La Vendée patriote (Paris, 1893-95).
   Les pacifications de l'ouest (Paris, 1896-99).
Chondieu, Pierre, et C. J. Richard—Les représentants du peuple (Saumur, 1793).
Courtois, E. B.—Rapport de la commission ; papiers de Robespierre (Paris, 1795).
Cretineau-Joly—Histoire de la Vendée militaire (Paris, 1840-42).
Croix, Blocquel de—Une page de la terreur à Nantes (Vannes, 1894).

2 E 2

Deniau, F. Abbé—Histoire de la Vendée, etc. (Angers, 1878-79).
Dugast-Matifeux.—Carrier à Nantes (Nantes, 1885).

Fillon, Benjamin—Recherches historiques sur Fontenay-Vendée (Fontenay, 1847).
    Poitou et Vendée (Niort, 1862-87).

Gensonné, J. A., et A. G. Gallois—Rapport sur la Vendée (Paris, 1791).
Godard-Faultrier, V.—Le champ des martyrs (Angers, 1855).
Guépin, A.—Histoire de Nantes (Nantes, 1839).

Lallié, Alfred—Le district de Machecoul (Nantes, 1869).
    Les noyades de Nantes (Nantes, 1879).
    L'église constitutionnelle dans la Loire Inférieure (Nantes, 1883).
    Les fusillades de Nantes (Nantes, 1882).
    Les prisons de Nantes (Nantes, 1883).
    Le sans-culotte J.-J. Goullin (Nantes, 1880).
Lemarchand, Albert—Album Vendéen (Angers, 1856-60).
Lequinio—Guerre de la Vendée et des Chouans (Paris, An iii.)
Leroux-Cesbron, C.—Lofficial, représentant du peuple (Paris, 1896).
Lockroy, Edouard—Une mission en Vendée (Paris, 1893).

Mellinet, Camille—La commune et la milice de Nantes (Nantes, 1840-44).
Mortimer, Ternaux—Histoire de la terreur (Paris, 1862-81).

Philippeaux, Pierre—Compte rendu à la convention.
Piet, F.—Recherches sur l'île de Noirmoutier.
Port, C.—Dictionnaire historique de Maine-et-Loire (Angers, 1871-78).
    La Vendée angevine (Paris, Angers, 1888).
    La légende de Cathelineau (Paris, 1893).
Portais, Chanoine—L'Abbé Gruget : sa paroisse, etc. (Angers, Paris, 1896).
Pressensé, E. de—L'église et la révolution française.
Prix, Berriat St.—La justice révolutionnaire (Paris, 1870).
    Des tribuneaux et de la procédure, etc. (Paris, 1859).
Proust, A.—La justice révolutionnaire à Niort (Niort, 1869).
Prudhomme, L. M.—Histoire générale des erreurs commis, etc. (Paris, 1797).

Quernan-Lamerie—Les conventionnels du département de la Mayenne (Laval, 1885).
    Notice sur le théâtre d'Angers (Angers, 1889).

Rochejaquelein, Madame de la—Mémoires de (Paris, 1816).
Rossignol, J.—La vie véritable du citoyen (Paris, 1896).
Rousset, C.—Les volontaires 1791-1794 (Paris, 1870).

Savary, J. J. M., Adjt.-Gen.—Guerres des Vendéens et des Chouans contre la république française (Paris, 1824).

Tronjolly, Phelippes C.—Noyades, fusillades, etc. (Paris, 1794).
Turreau, L. M., General—Mémoires, etc. (London, 1796).

Vial, J. A.—Causes de la guerre de la Vendée (Angers, 1795).
    Ligue de l'amnistien Delannay (Angers, 1795).

Verger, F. J. -Archives curieuses de la ville de Nantes (Nantes, 1837-11).
Valette, R.—La commission militaire de Fontenay (Fontenay, 1894).

Wallon, Henri A.—Histoire du tribunal révolutionnaire de Paris (Paris, 1880).
    La terreur (Paris, 1881).
    Les représentants du peuple en mission et la justice révolutionnaire (Paris, 1889).
Westermann, F. J., General—Campagne de la Vendée (Paris, An ii.)

---

Procès verbal de l'Assemblée Nationale.
    Do.    de l'Assemblée Nationale Législative.
    Do.    de la Convention Nationale.

---

## REVIEWS

Revue de l'Anjou, 1852, etc. (Angers).
  Do.  de Bretagne et de Vendée, 1857, etc. (Nantes).
  Do.  historique de l'ouest, 1885, etc. (Paris).
  Do.  du Bas-Poitou, 1888, etc. (Fontenay).
  Do.  de la révolution, 1883, etc. (Paris).
La révolution française, 1881, etc. (Paris).

*(The articles in these magazines on subjects connected with the Revolution are too numerous to mention separately.)*

---

## PAMPHLETS

To enumerate separately the pamphlets would require much space. Those utilised are mostly contained in the following list of volumes described in the special catalogue recently compiled by Mr. G. K. Fortescue of works relating to the Revolution which are in the library of the British Museum.

F.R.—61 (3) | 85-88 | 221-222 | 226 | 229-230 | 267 |
R. 105 | 147-148 | 235-237 | 238-239 | 568-569 | 578
F.—858 (1) | 959-961 | 968-970 | 1046-1048 | 1049-1051 | 1082 |
1550-1552 | 1568-1570 | F. 31*5* | F. 67*

# INDEX

THE END

Printed by R. & R. CLARK, LIMITED, Edinburgh.